"Aren't you afraid I'll get used to this?"

With her arms around his neck, and her face so close she could breathe him in, Kirby forced herself to relax in his arms, though it seemed an impossible task. The nearness of this man did strange things to her, speeding up her heart rate along with her breathing.

Outside her door he turned his face so that his mouth was almost brushing hers. She felt the soft whisper of his breath on her face as his gaze traveled down to her lips and was almost afraid her heart would burst out of her chest.

For what felt like an eternity, they shared a heated look before Casey broke the moment, saying, "Maybe you ought to be the one to worry that I'll get used to this."

"This talented writer...invites you to join a little journey that has you biting at the bit for more."
—Fresh Fiction

REED

"4 stars! Ryan's latest book in her Malloys of Montana series contains a heartwarming plot filled with down-to-earth cowboys and warm, memorable characters. Reed and Ally are engaging and endearing, and their sweet, fiery chemistry heats up the pages, which will leave readers' hearts melting...A delightful read."
—RT Book Reviews

LUKE

"Ryan creates vivid characters against the lovingly rendered backdrop of sweeping Montana ranchlands. The passion between Ryan's protagonists, which they keep discreet, is tender and heartwarming. The plot is drawn in broad strokes, but Ryan expertly brings it to a satisfying conclusion."
—Publishers Weekly

MATT

"Ryan has created a gripping love story fraught with danger and lust, pain and sweet, sweet triumph."
—Library Journal, **starred review**

THIS COWBOY OF MINE

R.C. RYAN

FOREVER
New York Boston

Copyright © 2020 by Ruth Ryan Langan
Cover design by Daniela Medina. Cover photography © Rob Lang.
Cover copyright © 2020 by Hachette Book Group, Inc.

Forever
Hachette Book Group
1290 Avenue of the Americas, New York, NY 10104
read-forever.com
twitter.com/readforeverpub

First Edition: December 2020

Forever is an imprint of Grand Central Publishing. The Forever name and logo are trademarks of Hachette Book Group, Inc.

The publisher is not responsible for websites (or their content) that are not owned by the publisher.

The Hachette Speakers Bureau provides a wide range of authors for speaking events. To find out more, go to www.hachettespeakersbureau.com or call (866) 376-6591.

ISBNs: 978-1-5387-1688-5 (mass market), 978-1-5387-1687-8 (ebook)

Printed in the United States of America

OPM

10 9 8 7 6 5 4 3 2 1

*To the dreamers, searching for their
happily ever after.*

*And to Tom, who taught me to believe in
happy endings.*

THIS
COWBOY OF
MINE

PROLOGUE

Merrick Ranch—Devil's Door, Wyoming
Fifteen Years Ago

The Merrick family was running on pure energy. They'd spent days up in the hills during one of the busiest calving seasons ever, and extra wranglers had been hired to assist with their chores. And though it was early May, a fierce snowstorm had blown in across the Tetons, turning the already difficult time into chaos.

Now, as they gathered around a campfire outside one of their range shacks, Bo Merrick looked around. "Where's Casey?"

The adults looked to eleven-year-old Brand. As the oldest of Bo's three sons, he was expected to keep an eye on his brothers, ten-year-old Casey and eight-year-old Jonah.

Brand shrugged. "Last time I looked, he was helping Ham."

Everyone turned to the patriarch of the family.

Hammond Merrick frowned. "I haven't seen the boy in more'n an hour."

Ham's son Egan wrapped his hands around a steaming mug of coffee. "That's about the time I saw him take off on Thunder."

Bo looked at his father incredulously. "He took off on my horse? In this storm?" Bo swore. "What the hell am I going to do with that crazy kid? He breaks all the rules we set. Argues with his grandmother while she's trying to teach him some schooling. Fights with his brothers. And now he's off to who-knows-where in a damned snowstorm." He tossed the last of his coffee on the fire, setting up a cloud of steam as he turned toward the corral. "When I find him this time, he won't be able to sit a horse for a week."

"Hold on." Old Hammond caught his grandson's arm. "You stay here with the others. I have an idea where he might be."

Before Bo could argue, Hammond strode away and minutes later was swallowed up by a curtain of snow as he rode his horse up the mountain.

Ever since Bo lost his wife, Leigh, in a tragic house fire and had returned to the old family ranch, his middle son, Casey, had become a wild child, regularly flouting the rules set up by his elders. He resented his Gram Meg, who had appointed herself their home-school teacher, since they lived too far from town to attend a regular school. To escape his brothers, Casey had taken to riding across the hills, spending hours in the wilderness. The only place he seemed to feel at home was high in the Tetons, surrounded by mustangs, wolves and coyotes.

Hammond urged his mount faster as the snow continued to pile up. He hoped and prayed he was right about where Casey might be. Otherwise, it could prove to be a long, cold night for the boy alone on the mountain.

Up ahead he spotted something on the ground in a stand of trees. He felt his heart give a quick jolt.

"Casey! You all right, boy?"

A head came up, and Hammond took in a quiet breath. Alive. At least the boy was alive.

"What do you think you're doing, boy?" When he drew close enough, he was out of the saddle and racing toward the boy, who was down on his knees in the snow, cradling the head of a newborn foal.

Tears coursed down Casey's cheeks. "I heard wolves. I think they got his mama."

Hammond's eyes narrowed. "It's a wonder you heard them, boy, over the bawling of the herd."

Casey swiped at his eyes, embarrassed to be caught crying. "Without his mama to feed him and keep him warm, he'll die up here in the hills."

The old man's mouth tightened into a grim line. It was natural for a boy who'd lost his mother at such a young age to identify with the foal's loss. Still, this was a ranch, and someone had to teach him the cold, hard facts of life. "That's nature's way, boy. Only the strong can survive."

The boy struggled to his feet, holding the wriggling foal to his chest. "He can grow strong enough to run free with the herd."

"Where do you think you're going with him?"

"To the barn."

"In the dark?"

"He can't stay here. The wolves will be back."

"And then what? You going to go without sleep to bottle-feed a scrawny critter that probably won't survive more'n a day or two at most?"

"If I have to." Without waiting for an argument,

Casey turned away and grabbed the reins of Bo's big roan gelding. The horse began walking beside the boy and his burden.

The old man watched as he mulled how to handle this. Then, in a moment of inspiration, he began walking beside Casey.

"Why don't you let me carry the foal on my horse? That way, we can both ride back to the barn."

Casey turned with a look of surprise. "You'll help me? Even though you're needed with the herd?"

"I will. But I'll want something from you in return, boy."

"What?" With a look of suspicion, Casey paused.

"You had your pa worried sick. You had all of us worried. I want your word that from now on, when you get the urge to disappear, you'll tell someone where you're going and when you'll be back."

Casey thought about his great-grandfather's words before giving a nod. "Okay. Promise."

Hammond released a long breath before pulling himself into the saddle. "Hand him over, boy."

Casey did as he asked before mounting Thunder.

As the two began their descent, Hammond nodded toward the campfire in the distance. "On the way down, we'll stop and assure the others that you're safe. Your pa's suffered enough. I won't have him worrying a minute more than necessary."

"Do we have to?"

"We do. And you'll apologize for leaving without telling anybody where you were headed."

Casey lowered his head, avoiding the old man's eyes. "Yes, sir."

Hammond's stern voice turned as frigid as the

weather. "Say it like you mean it, boy. And mean it when you say it."

Casey's head came up. He met Hammond's direct stare with one of his own. "Yes, sir."

Hammond Merrick was bone weary. His clothes were caked with mud and ice as he trudged into the barn and unsaddled his horse, rubbing it down before leading it into a stall with fresh feed and water. He'd been in the hills for more than a week, and all he wanted was a hot meal, the longest shower in history, and his own bed.

He was just about to leave when he heard a soft voice cooing in the adjacent stall. Looking over the rail he saw his great-grandson kneeling in the straw, stroking the head of the mustang foal.

"You've been here all week, boy?"

Casey looked over. "Pa said it was all right if I slept out here and looked after little Storm until he was stronger."

"You gave him a name? I suppose next you'll want him to be a pet."

"No, sir." Casey stroked the foal's head. "As soon as he's strong enough I want him to join his herd. But I thought I'd stick around and make sure the cow Pa brought me would take to him."

That was when the old man noticed the cow dozing contentedly in a corner of the stall.

At his arched brow Casey smiled. "Pa brought her down from the herd this morning. He said she'd just lost her calf, and he figured she might be willing to accept this little orphan, just until he was big enough to eat on his own."

Hammond removed his wide-brimmed hat and

slapped it against his leg to hide his surprise. "What was your father thinking? A cow's not the same as a wild horse, boy. How's he supposed to learn how to run and jump and live free with a slowpoke cow for a mama?"

"When he's strong enough, he'll figure it out. Isn't that what those ducklings did when you put those duck eggs under one of our laying hens?" Casey's eyes lit up with the memory. "That poor old hen nearly went crazy racing along the edge of the river when her babies jumped in and started swimming away."

Hammond threw back his head and roared. "You're right, boy. I guess I forgot about that." He scratched his head. "This poor old cow. I'd hate to see what she'll do when her calf starts jumping over her back and racing around like those mustangs do."

Casey stood and the little foal scrambled up to stand beneath the cow. In no time the foal was feeding, while the cow reached around to lick its soft hide.

The boy stepped out of the stall before leaning his arms along the rail to watch. "Maybe next year she can have herself another calf. Then she won't have time to worry about this little guy."

The old man put an arm around the boy, and the two of them stood, savoring the moment.

Hammond's voice was gruff. "That foal looks healthy. You did good, boy."

"Thanks, Ham." The boy looked up at him with a smile of pure delight. "When I grow up I'm going to know all there is about animals, just like old Doc Mercer."

"So." Hammond cleared the unexpected lump from his throat. A tough old bird, he insisted on being called

Ham rather than any of the warm and fuzzy names usually associated with elderly relatives. He'd been ranching all his life, and he rarely got emotional about something as simple as the spectacle of a newborn animal. But this was so much more than that. This was an opportunity of a lifetime.

"It takes a heap of schooling to become a veterinarian, boy."

"I don't care. It's what I want."

"That means you'll have to stop fighting your grandmother about your schooling. And you need to stop fighting your brothers while you're at it. You'll have to take your lessons seriously and pour all your energy into learning all you can."

"I will, Ham. I'll do whatever I have to."

His great-grandfather turned away. "You coming inside, boy?"

Casey shook his head. "Gram Meg said she'd bring me some supper later. I think I'll sleep out here for another night or two. You know, just in case I'm needed."

"Well then, good night, boy."

"'Night, Ham."

Hammond Merrick turned away, his eyes narrowed in thought. It was plain to see that Casey had a deep and abiding love for all animals. But only time would tell if the boy had the brains and the discipline, not to mention the determination, to reach such a lofty goal as becoming a doctor of veterinary science.

CHAPTER ONE

Merrick Ranch—Present Time

'M̲orning, Billy." Casey Merrick helped himself to a tall glass of freshly squeezed orange juice before joining his family, seated around the big fireplace.

At the stove, Billy Caldwell, the ranch cook for more than twenty years, nodded a greeting before flipping pancakes onto a platter. Despite his love of good food, he was rail-thin.

"Storm coming in." Hammond pointed toward the peaks of the Tetons, layered in thick clouds.

He turned to his great-grandson. "Billy says he's packing food for your trek into the hills."

Casey nodded. "With the ranch buttoned up for the winter, I thought I'd get away. Maybe in my travels I'll get a glimpse of Storm's herd."

The elders in the family shared knowing looks. Through the years Casey had made it his business to keep track of the orphaned foal he'd rescued while pursuing a course of studies that was daunting. He'd chronicled Storm's passage from being assimilated by its mother's herd to reaching an age of independence. Now, all these years later, the stallion had a herd of mares and their young totaling more than two dozen.

Along the way, Casey had become something of an expert on the local wildlife, and was often consulted by ranchers and conservationists seeking his advice.

Meg caught Egan's hand and squeezed, as she studied their grandson. "Maybe you should wait a few days, to see whether this storm fizzles or grows."

Casey gave her a gentle smile. "Gram Meg, I don't want you worrying. I've been traveling these hills long enough to know how fickle Mother Nature can be."

"Fickle? Are we talking about you and your love life again, bro?" Brand and his wife, Avery, strolled into the kitchen, wearing matching smiles.

"It's a burden, but I've learned to carry it." Casey fist-bumped his older brother and bent to brush a kiss on his sister-in-law's cheek. "All the lovely ladies at Nonie's Wild Horses Saloon and Cafe will still be there, pining away, when I return."

That brought groans from the others.

Casey's aunt Liz, his father's younger sister, helped herself to a mug of coffee. "I spotted your bedroll and supplies out in the barn. You sure you want to head into that storm?"

"Now you're sounding like your mom." At Casey's remark, the others shared a laugh.

Liz winked at her mother. "You've always been the sensible one, Mom. But Casey, not so much."

Brand joined in the laughter before turning to his younger brother. "One of these days you'll return from one of your wilderness adventures to find that all your friends have married and your own personal herd reduced to a couple of toothless hags."

"And pigs will fly, bro. Look at Chet."

When his family members glanced at the ranch

foreman, Casey added, "Closing in on fifty, and still one of the area's most eligible bachelors." Casey gave Chet a thumbs-up. "You're one of my heroes, man."

Bo glanced over as his youngest son, Jonah, strolled in. "I thought you were up at your cabin, knee-deep in work."

"I was." Jonah helped himself to coffee. "But then I woke up this morning and realized all I had to eat was an apple and half a candy bar."

"And," Casey finished for him, "you figured why not grab a Billy special before tackling another chapter of your latest book."

"Exactly." Jonah turned to the cook. "What's on the menu this morning, Billy?"

"Steak and eggs, with a side of pancakes."

Jonah gave a sigh. "Did you do all that just for me?"

Billy grinned. "For all of you. But especially since the good doctor is about to go off on one of his mountain walkabouts. I figured I'd send him off with something memorable. Except for the few meals I'm sending along, he'll have to live with his own cooking for the next couple of weeks."

Brand dropped an arm around Avery's shoulders. "So we have Dr. Casey to thank for this fine meal."

Casey was grinning as they all gathered around the table. "You're welcome."

Bo looked over at his middle son. "Who's taking over your practice while you're in the hills?"

"I added Dr. Mercer's number to my service. He said he'd be happy to call on any ranchers who need a vet for the next week or so."

"Old Doc Mercer?" Jonah shared a grin with Brand. "Isn't he as old as dirt?"

Ham's head came up sharply and he fixed his great-grandsons with a piercing look. "Something wrong with being old?"

"No, sir." Jonah struggled to hold back a grin.

"That's right, boy. And don't you forget it." Ham turned to Casey. "I'm glad Will Mercer is still able to lend a hand."

"So am I. Otherwise, I'd never be able to enjoy some time away." Casey glanced at the sky outside the window. "Great send-off breakfast, Billy. But now I'm out of here."

Bo entered the barn just as Casey was loading his final supplies into his saddlebags. "I wish you'd consider taking one of the trucks, son."

"That was my plan." Casey nodded toward the snowflakes drifting past the open barn door. "But if it's snowing down here, it'll be waist-deep up in the hills."

Bo wrapped a muscled arm around his son's shoulders. "I know you're capable of taking care of yourself, no matter what the weather throws at you. But please check in from time to time, so my mother doesn't have to lose sleep."

"I will." Casey bit down on the grin that tugged at his lips. His father had been saying the same thing for years. And always, Bo Merrick pinned Gram Meg as the worrier. But in truth, the loss of Bo's wife, Leigh, had marked him for life. He was only truly happy when all his chicks were safe in the nest.

Bo hugged his son, who stood several inches taller. "Stay safe."

"You, too, Pa." Casey pulled himself into the saddle

and turned his mount, Solitaire, toward the door. "I'll check in as often as I can get service. But if you don't hear from me for a few days, you just have to believe I've taken shelter somewhere and can't get word to you."

"I understand, son."

As horse and rider started past the house, Casey spotted the entire family on the back porch, huddled in parkas, waving and calling their goodbyes.

With a nod to all, he turned Solitaire across a pasture and started up toward the distant mountains high above, which were wreathed in dark, ominous clouds.

Kirby Regan drove her truck to a lookout in the foothills of the Tetons and texted her boss with her location before stepping out. The crisp air had a bite to it, but that was to be expected in late October. It was perfect hiking weather. Warm enough by day to make good time into the hills, and cool enough at night to be comfortable in her insulated sleeping bag.

She had a rifle for protection and enough provisions to last a week, and if the weather held and luck was on her side, she'd be home in half that time.

Hearing the ding of a text, she dug her phone out from her pocket to check it.

Bring an approximate count of the mustang herds, and that promotion is in the bag.

With a smile, she slid her arms through the straps of her backpack, shouldered her rifle, and started out at a brisk pace.

When she'd left Wyoming after college, she'd

headed straight to Washington, DC, hoping to make her career in the big city. The minute she'd set foot in the nation's capital, she could feel the power in the air. The atmosphere there, so different from the small towns of Wyoming where she'd been raised, was like a drug. A by-the-books overachiever, she'd worked her way up the ladder in the Association of Land Management, and she probably would have continued the climb if she hadn't come home for her uncle's funeral. That brief visit had changed everything, bringing back a flood of happy memories that made her hectic life in the city suddenly unbearable.

Now she was back in Wyoming, and the silence and beauty of the countryside seemed all the more spectacular after her long absence. Oh, how she'd missed all this.

A cut in pay and a much lower rank in the Wyoming branch of the company made her more than willing to take on whatever tasks were assigned to her, just to prove to her supervisors that she had what it took to work in the field.

When this assignment had presented itself, she was thrilled to accept. As an expert hiker, she welcomed the task of heading into the hills to catalog the numbers of mustang herds she encountered. Since she was the rookie in the field office, her boss had told her this would go a long way toward cementing her position as someone who could deliver. As a carrot, he'd dangled the offer of a promotion in front of her. Not that she'd needed it. The thought of hiking alone in the Tetons was, to her, the assignment of a lifetime.

As she climbed, she adjusted her backpack, looking forward to a good workout. After spending the last few years exercising in a crowded, sweaty gym, she was back where she'd started, and loving every minute of it.

"You can do this," she muttered aloud. "Piece of cake."

By noon the misty rain-snow mix that had begun earlier had turned to snow in the higher elevations.

Kirby adjusted the hood of her parka and shouldered her backpack before following a trail that led into a heavily forested area. She knew by the fresh droppings that the herd wasn't too far ahead.

As she crested a hill and stepped out of the woods, she caught sight of the mustangs just disappearing over a rise. Kirby counted six or seven, and wondered how many more had already slipped away. The stallion, all black except for one white foreleg, stood watch as the last of the mares moved out of sight.

Quickening her pace, Kirby crossed the distance, noting idly that the snow had picked up and was beginning to form drifts. But she wasn't about to let a little snow keep her from cataloging this herd.

When she reached the top of the rise she looked down at the mustangs, which were moving more slowly now as they pawed the snow to graze on the range grass underneath.

She stopped dead in her tracks at the soul-stirring sight. From the time she was a little girl and caught her first glimpse of wild horses, it had always been this way. Though the Association considered them little more than numbers to be managed, she couldn't deny her love for these wild creatures. To see them living free, as their ancestors had, touched her deeply.

She counted the mares, logged the number into her phone, then took a photo. At the muted click, the skittish stallion, sensing something unknown, began herding his mares toward a line of trees in the distance. Within minutes they blended into the woods like ghosts and were no longer visible.

Kirby sat on a fallen log and allowed her backpack to drop to the ground.

By the time she'd finished eating her sandwich, she looked around and realized the snow had picked up considerably.

If this storm continued, she would have to re-adjust her thinking. Instead of getting home ahead of schedule, this little trip was liable to drag on for a week or more.

Not a problem, she assured herself. If her pace was slowed she could easily ration her supplies to stretch beyond her self-imposed deadline.

She drained her protein drink, stashed the empty bottle in her backpack, and set out at a hurried pace, keeping an eye out for shelter in the event the snow became impossible to traverse.

CHAPTER TWO

Casey was in his element. As he rode across a high meadow, the fresh tracks of deer, mustangs, and even a big cat were proof that the animals in the higher elevations were healthy and active.

Rather than being a problem, the snow just added to his sense of freedom. This wild stretch of land, inhabited by all kinds of animals, was his own private paradise, since no sane human would risk traveling it in such weather.

From his youngest years he'd always loved the solitude of the wilderness. Maybe it was because he'd spent all his time with so many family members. Not that he minded. Years ago he'd stopped resenting the elders and all of their rules and regulations. Like his brothers, he'd actually begun looking forward to his great-grandfather's musings about his early life in Wyoming, when Hammond Merrick had carved out a place for himself while successfully building one of the most prosperous ranches in the territory.

And he loved, as well, the romantic tale of how his grandfather, Egan, had first locked eyes with Margaret Mary Finnegan, the love of his life, whom he affectionately called his Meggie. Those two were still as much in love today as when they'd met.

He loved the sprawling ranch and sharing the chores with his brothers and foreman Chet Doyle. He loved watching his aunt Liz, a couple years younger than his father, and still single, as she pursued the great love of her life, photography. Like all his family, she was an inspiration. His father, Bo, nearing fifty, was his hero. Though he would carry his grief at the loss of his Leigh to the grave, he bravely carried on, teaching his three sons by words and actions how to be a man.

But what gave Casey the most pleasure was the knowledge that he could slip away by himself from time to time to savor the solitude he always found in high country.

When he encountered a herd of mustangs his heart filled with quiet joy. He loved the fact that they could live wild and free.

Wild and free. The thought had him smiling. It was what he'd wanted always for them. And for himself.

His smile faded as he caught sight of something out of place on the far side of the meadow. He urged his mount forward and noticed the snow up here had begun drifting.

"Hold on, Solitaire." He drew back on the reins, slowing his mount when he realized that the drifts were already as high as his horse's belly.

As they reached the other side, Casey recognized that what he had seen was a mustang on its knees. The closer the horse and rider got, the more the poor animal struggled to escape. But though it thrashed about in the snow, it was unable to stand and run.

"Easy now." Casey kept his tone low and his

movements slow, knowing this wild horse had probably never seen a human.

He easily dropped a lasso over its head and coiled the rope around the saddle horn, to keep the frightened animal from charging. Solitaire, trained for just such things, stood his ground, holding the rope taut as Casey dismounted and moved slowly and easily toward the injured horse.

"Let's see what's wrong, little filly." A quick exam revealed a deep, festering gash on its left foreleg. From the size of the wound and the amount of infection, this poor animal, which appeared to be not quite a yearling, was thoroughly drained of strength. No wonder she had given up and lay, panting and in pain, waiting to die.

Grateful that he never went anywhere without the tools of his trade, Casey retrieved a syringe from his black bag and injected an antibiotic into the filly's hide. The animal's ears flattened, and its sides were heaving, but it was clear she was too exhausted to do more than endure the touch of this human.

"We've got to get you to shelter." Casey removed the lasso, knowing the mustang was too weak to move.

He pulled himself into the saddle. Urging Solitaire through the snow, he rode a good distance in each direction until he found a cave big enough to shelter two horses. Satisfied that it wasn't inhabited by any predatory animals, he turned Solitaire back toward the place where the mustang lay, its breathing strained, eyes wide with panic.

Casey cut branches from the nearby trees and tied them in a crisscross pattern before covering them with his bedroll. It took all his strength to slide the helpless mustang onto the poor imitation of a travois. Then, walking alongside Solitaire, he guided him inside the cave before unfastening the straps he'd used to secure the conveyance to the stirrups.

He unsaddled his mount and led him toward the rear of the cave, where he set out food. After starting a fire, he placed a pan of snow over the flame and soon had water for both horses. While Solitaire noisily ate, Casey hand-fed the wounded mustang. When both animals were fed and watered, Casey opened a packet stashed in his saddlebag and silently thanked Billy for the container of beef stew. As the meal heated, Casey fashioned a bed for himself of evergreen branches to cushion his bedroll, which he slid out from under the mustang. Using his saddle for a pillow he leaned back, stretched out his long legs, and enjoyed his dinner, grateful to be snug and dry.

After administering a second injection of antibiotic into the mustang, Casey covered the animal with a blanket, pulled his hat over his head, and closed his eyes.

He was asleep almost at once.

Kirby trekked past the place where she'd seen her first herd of mustangs and climbed to the higher elevations. As daylight began to fade, she paused in a stand of evergreens. Assured that their branches provided enough cover from the snow to form a rough campsite, she dropped the heavy backpack and began to unload her supplies. With a campfire, a hot meal, and her insulated sleeping bag, she figured she would be more than comfortable for the night.

As she circled the area collecting tree branches for a fire, she reveled in the extreme silence. It was as though the snowfall had covered the whole world in a thick blanket, and all creatures in the universe had gone to sleep. She was alone in her own private winter wonderland.

She realized that this unexpected snowfall wasn't so much a hardship as a gift to be savored. After all, this was what she'd dreamed of after leaving the frantic pace of life in the city.

Hearing the ping of a text, she set the branches in a neat pile before retrieving her phone from an inner pocket.

Seeing that it came from her supervisor, Dan Morgan, she was smiling as she began to read. Her smile faded quickly at the words.

Authorities hunting an escaped convict in area. Be advised to cancel all plans and return to civilization asap.

An escaped convict? Here in the middle of nowhere?

Alarmed, she took up her rifle and stared around, her ears attuned to every sound. Now, instead of silence, she was aware of the howling of a coyote, the chorus of yips from a distant pack of wolves, and then a sudden, shocking crack, like a gunshot, as a tree limb broke under the weight of the heavy snow and fell to the ground with a shudder.

She couldn't stay here, out in the open, in plain sight of a man on the run. What he wouldn't do to get hold of her rifle, as well as her supplies. To a convict caught in these rough elements it could mean the difference between survival and surrender.

The isolation she had cherished just moments ago

had now become a real danger. She was alone in the wilderness, with no one but herself to count on, if she were to encounter a dangerous criminal.

With a sense of urgency, she began repacking her supplies. Shouldering the backpack, she kept her rifle at the ready as she trudged through the waist-high drifts and began her descent.

In her haste she stumbled over a boulder buried in the snow and fell face-first. Her rifle slipped from her hands and slid halfway down an incline. She heaved herself to her feet and stumbled as a knife's edge of pain shot through her ankle with such force, she dropped to her knees. On a hiss of breath she grasped at a tree limb to regain her footing and was forced to limp through the snow to retrieve her weapon. Her hands, she noted, were none too steady as she picked up the fallen rifle and continued inching along, fighting pain.

That tumble had taught her a valuable lesson. With darkness descending, she ran the risk of another, more serious fall. Despite her need to put safety first, her greater need was to find a safe shelter until morning, when she could return to the lower elevations where she'd left her truck.

She had a high-powered flashlight in her backpack but resisted using it. Though it would light her way, it would also make her an easy target for anyone hiding out in the darkness. Since she was forced to move slowly and carefully, she kept watch for any out-cropping of rock that offered shelter for the night. She hoped that by morning this pain would ease enough to allow her an easy descent from these hills.

* * *

Casey lay still for a moment, wondering what had just wakened him from a sound sleep.

Concerned that it might have been the mustang, he slid from his sleeping bag and crossed the cave to kneel beside the animal. Its breathing was labored, and though Casey kept his touch gentle, the mustang's nostrils flared, its eyes wide with fear.

He returned to his bag and was just removing a syringe when he sensed something at the entrance to the cave. A blinding light suddenly flashed on his face and he lifted his hand to shade his eyes.

"Don't move. I have a weapon, and I know how to use it."

At the distinctly feminine voice he got to his feet to see a figure at the mouth of the cave holding a rifle.

Solitaire whinnied, and the stranger turned toward the animal.

Casey used that moment of distraction to move quickly, striking out with his arm, sending the rifle flying across the cave. The flashlight fell and went rolling, its light still beaming. In that single moment Casey pounced, pinning the stranger's arms from behind, completely immobilizing her.

"You've got one minute to tell me who you are and what the hell you're doing pointing that rifle at me."

She sucked in a breath. "My name is Kirby Regan. I was warned about you."

"Warned about me?"

"I know of your escape. The authorities are on your trail. It's only a matter of time until they find you."

"What the hell?" With a muttered oath he released

his hold on her and retrieved her rifle and flashlight, which he now trained on her. "Turn around. Slow and easy."

Kirby turned, facing her worst nightmare. Though she was tall, this man towered over her. The sleeves of his flannel shirt couldn't hide the ripple of muscle. A dark stubble covered his cheeks and chin, adding to his look of danger. His eyes, she noted, were hot and fierce, and narrowed on her with a look of absolute fury.

His voice was low with anger. "I'm warning you. I don't suffer fools. You have one minute to explain yourself. And it had better be the truth, or you won't get a second chance to talk."

"I got a text warning me that the authorities are searching for you...for an escaped convict in this area."

His look changed from one of anger to one of thoughtfulness. "First, let me assure you I'm not an escaped convict."

Her head came up like a prizefighter. "And you expect me to believe you because...?"

He shrugged. "I don't care what you believe." He glanced at the mustang. "But I doubt an escaped convict would bother nursing a wounded animal while he tried to outrun the law."

Kirby noted the wrapping on the animal's leg and, beside the bedroll, a black medical bag. "You're a doctor?"

"Veterinarian. Casey Merrick. Why didn't you just head home when you got this warning?"

"I would have. But I got caught in the snowstorm and took a nasty fall in the dark. That's when I decided to look for shelter until morning."

"And you just thought you'd come in like Annie Oakley and hold an escaped convict until the authorities arrived to take him back to prison?"

At his sarcastic tone, Kirby's temper flared. "I was halfway inside this cave before I realized there was someone already here. It was too late to run, so I decided to just bluff my way through."

"You can see how well that worked for you."

He put the rifle down as he placed the flashlight on a boulder. When he turned back to her, he caught her gaze darting away from the rifle lying beside his bedroll. "You wouldn't get two steps toward it before I'd have you in a choke hold. But if it'll make you feel safer..." He tossed her rifle and despite her surprise, she caught it in midair.

When she took aim at him, he simply ignored her and moved toward his black bag. Without a word he picked up the fallen syringe, crossed to the mustang, and injected another dose of antibiotic into its rump. Running a hand over the frightened horse's muzzle he whispered, "You keep trying, little filly. You've got a long fight ahead of you."

His soft words toward the injured animal caused Kirby to lower her weapon and take a moment to look around the cave.

Casey set a fresh log on the dying embers. Soon the fire was blazing. He stood, wiping his hands on his pants. "How long have you been hiking?"

"I started early this morning."

"You have to be frozen." He nodded toward her backpack. "You got a sleeping bag in there?"

"Yes. Why?"

He shrugged. "Since we've established that I'm not

a dangerous criminal, and I doubt you're one, you might as well sleep close to the fire."

"You don't mind?"

He arched a brow. "From where I'm standing, you look like you could use a hot meal and a good, solid sleep."

At his words she gave a sigh of relief.

He set the last of the beef stew over the fire.

Kirby's limp was pronounced as she crossed to the fire, where she spread out her bedroll.

"That must have been some fall."

She nodded. "It was too dark to see the boulder until I fell over it."

"Want me to take a look? I could wrap it to reduce any swelling."

She shrank back, clearly uncomfortable. "I'll deal with it in the morning."

He shrugged. "Suit yourself." He handed her a container and a spoon.

Without a word she ate her fill before draining a bottle of water from her backpack.

Casey removed the blanket from the mustang and began draping it over the entrance to the cave.

Before she could ask any questions, he explained. "Now that you've told me about an escaped convict in the area, I wouldn't want anybody to spot the fire while we're asleep."

"I doubt I'll sleep much." She patted her rifle. "I'm happy to keep watch."

Without a word Casey checked both horses before climbing into his sleeping bag.

After a moment of silence, she said softly, "Thank you. For the food, the fire, and the shelter."

"You're welcome. Good night." He rolled over. "You might want to douse that light. If you're planning on keeping an eye on me, do it by the light of the fire."

Her face flamed. He knew that an escape convict wasn't the only one she'd be watching for this night. Veterinarian or not, he knew she intended to remain awake as long as possible throughout the night, rather than trust being alone in the wilderness with him.

CHAPTER THREE

At least twice during the night Kirby awoke to see the man kneeling beside the mustang, hand-feeding it a few morsels of food and tipping water into its mouth before returning to his sleeping bag.

Outside, the wind howled, flinging snow and ice against the outer walls of the cave. Hearing it, she was grateful for this shelter despite the fact that she was forced to share it with a dark, dangerous-looking stranger.

Though she'd been determined to stay awake and keep an eye on him, the warmth of the fire and her utter exhaustion conspired against her. Gradually her eyes closed. She drifted into sleep.

Kirby came instantly awake and sat up, shoving hair from her eyes, aware that her ankle was throbbing horribly.

Across the cave Casey was drinking from a mug while staring out at a gauzy countryside clothed in white. He'd removed the blanket covering the mouth of the cave in order to get a better view.

He turned. "'Morning."

"Good morning." She eased out of her sleeping bag, rolling it and fastening it before setting it aside. "How's the mustang?"

Casey nodded toward the horse, still lying in the corner. Though it watched with wary eyes, it was no longer straining with each labored breath. "Some better, thanks to the antibiotic. But the poor little filly has a long way to go. The infection is in the blood. She needs a lot more than I can give her out here."

"Will you call for help to move her?"

That had him smiling. "Have you checked your phone?"

Puzzled, she retrieved her cell phone and realized that there was no service.

"What was I thinking?" She tucked her phone away and limped toward the entrance of the cave. "Oh. Look at that." The pristine beauty of the snow-covered countryside had her sighing. "It's almost too pretty to be real."

"Yeah. A Christmas card in October." Seeing the way she favored one leg, Casey asked, "How bad is the pain?"

"Tolerable."

His eyes narrowed. "Maybe I'd better look at it."

"I'm fine." She gave a firm shake of her head, sending a signal that she didn't want him touching her.

He frowned but let it go. "Coffee?"

"Thanks." She accepted a mug from his hand and inhaled the wonderful fragrance before drinking.

As she started to turn away a sudden pain sliced through her ankle and she nearly fell. She let go of the mug and grabbed his arm.

"That does it." He helped her to sit down. "I'm taking a look at that ankle."

She had no choice but to lean back and watch as he untied the laces of her hiking boot and eased it from her foot. Her ankle was several shades of purple and began swelling as soon as it was free of the constraints.

As he began to probe the tender area, she couldn't contain a sudden intake of breath and she began to fight back tears.

"Sorry. I know this hurts. I've got some dressings in my bag. I'll wrap this and make a bag of snow to ease the swelling."

Without waiting for a response, he proceeded to do as he said.

Kirby took the moment to study him while he bent to his work. Despite his size, and the look of danger about him, his touch was surprisingly gentle. He was treating her much the same as he'd treated the mustang.

He got to his feet and left the cave, returning with a plastic bag filled with snow.

He smiled. "Lucky for us, there's an abundant supply of all this cold, white stuff to reduce the swelling." He handed her the bag and she pressed it against her ankle.

As he began to stand, she put a hand on his arm. "I'm sorry. Could we start over?" At his arched brow she managed a smile. "I must have looked pretty silly last night, barging in, rifle drawn, ready to do battle."

"At least you didn't shoot first and ask questions later." His grin told her that he didn't appear to hold a grudge.

She stuck out a hand. "First, thank you for this." She motioned toward the neat dressings on her ankle.

"I was trying to be brave, but I'm really grateful for your help."

"You're welcome."

She took in a breath. "So, for that new beginning, I'm Kirby Regan, and I work for the Association of Land Management."

He accepted her handshake. "Casey Merrick. Rancher and veterinarian."

Earlier, she'd thought his touch on her ankle was gentle and soothing, but the feel of his workworn hand on hers caused a very different kind of feeling. To cover her confusion, she asked the first thing that came to mind. "Is your ranch nearby?"

"Practically next door."

At her look of surprise, he explained, "It abuts this land we're on. It's been Merrick land for generations. Where do you call home?"

"For now I'm renting an apartment in Devil's Door. Do you know of it?"

He nodded.

"For the past few years I've lived and worked in Washington, DC. I just moved back home after my uncle's funeral. Actually, I'm here to buy his ranch, since I was raised on it."

"Your uncle has no other family?"

"A daughter. She's married and living in Idaho with her husband and two children. At the funeral she told me she'd inherited the ranch but wasn't planning on moving back. One of my uncle's wranglers told me Caroline was considering an offer to put it up for auction. I asked if he and the others would come back and work at the ranch again, and he assured me they'd love to. So I told my cousin I'd like to buy it." Kirby hesitated before saying shyly, "I think she was really surprised by my offer, but she promised to go over her father's financial affairs and get back to me with a fair price."

"And did she?"

Kirby nodded, and now her face lit with pleasure. "She asked a price higher than I'd hoped, but I told her it was manageable, if I'm frugal for a few years. Well," she added, "it'll be a struggle for a lot of years. But worth it, just to own the place where I grew up. I sold everything I could back in DC, bought a truck, and drove here, hoping to move in as soon as the papers are signed."

"Good for you. I wish you luck. There are too many ranches in the area going up for auction."

A thunderous sound broke the silence, and Casey helped her to her feet before offering his arm as they walked to the cave's entrance. Within minutes a Wyoming State Police helicopter came into view.

"Looks like they're searching for that convict." Casey's eyes narrowed as he watched the movement of the copter. "Which isn't good news for us."

He was frowning as he studied the mustang. "That little filly is still too weak to make it back to my ranch for treatment. Which means I'm going to have to risk spending at least another night out here. Hopefully by tomorrow she can walk."

Kirby's heart dropped. She chewed on her lower lip, mulling over her dilemma.

"Knowing there's a man still on the run out here changes everything." He paused. "Your ankle would never hold up if you tried hiking out of these hills. But if you're up for it, I could let you take my horse." He nodded toward Solitaire. "He knows his way home. If you're strong enough to stay in the saddle, you should be safely at my family's ranch by nightfall."

The thought of returning to civilization was oh-so-tempting. Still, Kirby quickly weighed the pitfalls of the situation. "I appreciate the offer. That's generous of you. And if I took you up on it, I could alert your family that you're up here in need of a horse or some other transportation. But there are no guarantees that I'd make it out without running into the man the police are hunting. And without the use of two good legs, even with a rifle, I wouldn't stand a chance of fighting him on my own. All he'd have to do is pull me out of the saddle and I'd be down for the count."

Casey nodded. "You're welcome to stay and share this shelter. We have more than enough supplies to be comfortable. Of course, a man on the run could stumble upon this cave and decide to fight us for it. You could be exchanging one problem for another." He gave her a long look. "I'll respect whatever choice you make."

The sound of the helicopter grew louder as it made another slow turn above them. Kirby lifted her head to watch its progress. When it faded from sight, she gave a long, deep sigh.

"In other words, damned if I do, damned if I don't."

He smiled, and she thought how handsome he was. "That's about it. Your call."

She nodded. "For now, I'll take my chances here. I guess, like your mustang, another day might be just what I need before tackling the long descent from the mountain. And there's strength in numbers. Two of us against one man on the run."

"One *desperate* man on the run. Don't forget that. If he finds us, he'll do whatever it takes to stay alive."

"That's my goal, too."

Casey gave her a quick smile. "That makes two of us."

He turned away and began rummaging through his supplies. "Are you in the mood for sausage or steak for breakfast?"

She gave a surprised laugh. "Are you serious?" At his grin she added, "Sausage. That way, we can have the steak for supper."

"Works for me." He lifted the lid of a container and set it over the fire. While the sausages heated, he opened a second container and set out an array of hard-boiled eggs and biscuits.

A short time later, Kirby was sitting beside him near the fire. "I'll give you this," she said, grinning. "You do know how to hike these hills in style."

He dug into his breakfast before admitting, "I can't take any credit for this. Our ranch cook, Billy Caldwell, is a genius in the kitchen. Billy keeps my entire family happy and well-fed with his creations."

"Wait. You have your own cook?"

"Doesn't everyone?" Casey gave her a sly smile that had her heart doing a sudden bounce.

She paused and took a long sip of coffee to steady herself. Now where had that unexpected reaction come from? Last night she'd thought of him as a surly stranger. How could one simple smile make such a difference?

"You mentioned a family. Wife? Kids? Just how many family members are there?"

"No wife. No kids. There's my great-grandfather,

Hammond. Everybody calls him Ham. He turned ninety this year and can still outwork all of us. Then there are my grandparents, Egan and Meg, both seventy. Their daughter, Liz, is a photographer, and their son, Bo, is my father. I have an older brother, Brand, and a new sister-in-law, his bride Avery. And a younger brother, Jonah. There's also our ranch foreman, Chet Doyle, who has been a friend to my dad since they were boys." He turned. "How about you? Are you from a big family, too?"

She gave a short laugh. "Afraid not. I mentioned my uncle Frank. He took me in and shared his home with me after the death of my parents."

"I'm sorry. How old were you?"

"Ten. I was feeling scared and lost and alone, and Uncle Frank seemed to know just how to ease me through all the grief and trauma. He put me to work in the horse barn, and before I knew what was happening, I had transferred all my love to those animals. For a girl from a small town, life on a ranch was just what I needed. And my uncle, who'd buried a wife and his only brother, bonded with me and became my best friend."

"That's nice. And you mentioned a cousin?"

"Caroline. She was off to college when I came to live with Uncle Frank, so I feel as though I barely know her. When she graduated, her job kept her far from home, and then she married a college sweetheart from Idaho. After the funeral, she told me she'd already made her peace with leaving the family ranch all those years ago."

Kirby turned away to refill her cup. "All my childhood memories are tied to Uncle Frank's ranch.

It just seems logical to try to continue to make it my home."

"Running a ranch alone can be an uphill battle."

She shrugged. "I'd like to think I'm up for it. Besides, I'll have Uncle Frank's wranglers, at least those willing to come back to work. I know a lot of them have already found other jobs. But if even half are willing to work for me, I think I can make it."

Casey studied her with new interest before setting aside his empty plate.

She held up the coffeepot. "Want a refill?"

He nodded and held out his cup. They drank in companionable silence. When he'd finished, he set down his cup and crossed to the mustang.

From her position beside the fire Kirby watched as he unwrapped the dressing on the horse's leg and administered ointment before wrapping it with fresh dressing. After administering another dose of antibiotics, he ran a hand over the mustang's mane.

For the first time the animal didn't react in fear. Its ears remained up, its gaze fixed on the man as he stroked and soothed.

Kirby set aside her coffee. "I'd say you've gained her trust."

"For now. That doesn't mean she won't revert to her old ways. But for now, she realizes that she needs me." He stood and crossed to his own horse, setting out fresh food and water. "I know you're restless, Solitaire. But I'm afraid you're stuck in here with the rest of us."

Hearing the sound of Casey's voice, the big horse tossed its head, as though understanding every word.

"You do have a way about you, Doctor."

At Kirby's words Casey turned and grinned. "At least with animals."

She felt the quick hitch in her heart and wanted to contradict him, but she held her silence.

Not just with animals, Dr. Merrick. That sexy smile is guaranteed to go straight to a woman's heart. As if you don't already know that.

CHAPTER FOUR

Casey pulled on his parka and made his way to the cave entrance before turning to Kirby. "I'm going outside to look around. Don't worry if I'm gone awhile. I'll be close enough to hear you fire off a shot if there's any trouble."

Kirby watched him leave and felt a momentary twinge. If not for this swollen ankle, she could have joined him. She had no doubt he was searching the area for any tracks that might have been left by a man on the run.

She tried to imagine what he was thinking. With a dangerous criminal in the area, was he frustrated to find himself stuck with a wounded animal and an injured woman? Without both, he could be safely home. Still, he hadn't shown any sign of impatience. In fact, he seemed perfectly calm, cool, and content, caring for her and the mustang as though he'd rather be here in the middle of a blizzard than sitting in front of a cozy fire at home.

She pressed the cold container against her swollen ankle and sank back against her bedroll, listening to the wind swirling outside the cave. With her rifle close beside her, she closed her eyes, grateful for the warmth of the fire, and the company of the horses, dozing in opposite corners.

Casey used his knife to cut off a low-hanging branch of an evergreen. For the next hour he walked around an area that encompassed all sides of the cave, searching for any sign of another human. With every step, he used the feathery branch to erase his footprints. No sense broadcasting to a desperate criminal the fact that there were other people out here.

Though he was fully aware of the danger he faced, another part of his mind was on Kirby Regan.

There was something sweet and vulnerable about her that had all his healing instincts on high alert. It was obvious that she didn't want to show any weakness. But that stoic nature had him all the more intrigued.

Part of her reticence probably came from losing her parents early and learning to depend only on herself. He knew from experience that losing a parent at an early age left plenty of marks on a child's soul. Fortunately, he and his brothers had one another, as well as a huge support system. And though Kirby's uncle opened his heart and home to her, she'd probably experienced plenty of times when she'd felt completely alone in the world. And so she had most likely learned to look out for herself.

She might have spent the past few years in a cushy job in the city, but she had the strength of a conditioned athlete. He could tell her ankle was a lot more painful than she let on. He marveled that she could even stand. In truth, he was glad she hadn't insisted on leaving with Solitaire. Unless she was able to make the entire descent unmolested, she would have been at the mercy of the weather, the animals, and the man the authorities were searching for.

The fact that she'd come here to buy her childhood ranch added another layer of interest. Casey wondered how it would feel to be separated from the ranch that had been in his family for generations. The ranch, and this land, were as much a part of him as the air he breathed and the food he ate. He hoped Kirby got her wish to buy the place. His hand fisted. There were far too many ranches going up for auction. And no way to save them. It was a fact of life across the West.

Beneath the shelter of evergreens, Casey put a hand up to shade his eyes as a police helicopter came roaring overhead. It veered off, only to be followed by a second helicopter. He watched as the two separated, each going in a different direction. Within minutes the sound of their engines faded.

This was proof that the convict was probably still at large.

When Casey was convinced that he hadn't missed any evidence of another human in the area, he returned to the cave. Instead of going inside, he walked around it, trying to see it from a passing stranger's point of view. Though it had a natural barrier on three sides, anyone searching for shelter would find it without too much trouble. Kirby had found it, even in the dark. The huge outcropping of rock and the overlarge entrance had been what drew him to use it to shelter two horses. Those were the same things that would lead a man on the run to take notice.

After cutting more evergreen branches, he began draping them over the top of the cave, and positioning some to hang down far enough to mask the entrance. When he was convinced that the cave was perfectly camouflaged, he stepped inside.

Kirby was standing to one side, leaning slightly against the cave for balance, her eyes narrowed on the entrance, her rifle aimed and ready.

Seeing him, she gave a sigh before lowering the weapon.

"Sorry." Aware that she'd been prepared to fire off a shot, he touched a hand to her arm. "I should have alerted you that it was me out there, and not a stranger."

"Yeah. That would've saved me a lot of worry." She put a hand to her heart. "I was gearing up for battle."

"Yeah. I see that. And cool as a cucumber."

She gave a weak laugh. "You wouldn't say that if you could feel the way my heart is pounding."

"If it's any comfort, I didn't see any sign of our convict around here. Apparently, neither did the police, since they left as quickly as they arrived."

"I heard the helicopters. Mind telling me what all that scraping overhead was?"

"Evergreen branches. Just a little camouflage in case anybody happens to come this way."

She sank down and set the rifle beside her.

Noticing her pallor, he turned. "I'll get you a blanket."

"No." She held up a hand. "If anything, I'm sweating."

With a dry laugh he sat down beside her and took her hand in his. "Sorry. I never gave a thought to what you must have been thinking with all that moving and scraping right over your head."

"I won't bore you with all the things I was thinking." She leaned her head back and closed her eyes.

Casey got to his feet and moved around the cave, adding another log to the fire, and checking the mustang. He noted idly that the animal barely flinched as he examined the leg.

When he began to remove the dressings, Kirby limped across the cave and knelt beside him.

He flicked a quick glance over her. "Need something?"

She shook her head. "I thought I'd hand you whatever you need from your medical bag."

Surprised and pleased, he smiled. "Thanks. You can grab that tube of salve and fresh dressings."

She did as he asked and watched as he gently applied fresh ointment to the deep gash before once more wrapping the mustang's leg. He finished up with his usual dose of antibiotics before closing up the bag.

Then he turned to her. "I suppose we should think about lunch—"

They both looked up as a roar louder than any thundering freight train interrupted him. It began at a distance, then drew closer until it passed directly over the cave.

Kirby's eyes went wide with fear as the cave was enveloped in darkness. If not for the fire, it would have been as dark as midnight. "What—?"

"Avalanche." Casey swore. "Probably induced by the warming temperature and low-flying copters."

Smoke began swirling around the cave, burning their lungs.

Coughing, Casey switched on a battery-powered

lantern before grabbing a saddle blanket and quickly smothering the flames. "We're going to miss the heat of the fire, but not the smoke." He reached for the longest log in the pile and turned to the mouth of the cave. "With nowhere to go, the smoke in this place would make breathing impossible."

While Kirby watched, he began poking and prodding the log into the wall of snow that had sealed the entrance to the cave.

The snow was so thick, the log couldn't penetrate. They were buried under a ton of snow. With no way to communicate to anyone where they were.

Casey rummaged through his saddlebags and removed anything that could be used to dig at the mound of snow that covered the entrance. Kirby did the same, searching through the meager things she'd bothered to bring.

Casey held up a small spade with a foldable handle.

Kirby produced a utensil, which combined a spoon and a fork. As she held it up she couldn't help sighing. "Aren't we a pair?"

Casey shrugged. "Something's better than nothing." He picked up a log and began jerry-rigging the spade to it, giving it a long, sturdy handle.

Kirby watched him before following his lead and doing the same with her utensil.

They stood side by side at the cave entrance, digging methodically at the snow and tossing it into whatever containers they could find.

"At least we'll have plenty of drinking water," Casey remarked as he poured the latest contents into the coffee pot. "And as long as we don't run out of coffee beans, we'll have enough caffeine to keep us wired for the job ahead."

"How will we make coffee without a fire?"

He pointed to his gear. "I carry an Insta-pot for camping. All the comforts of home."

Kirby managed a smile, though her fear was clearly etched on her face.

By midday, after they'd shed their parkas and struggled to ignore their aching muscles, Casey touched a hand to Kirby's arm. "You need a break. In fact, we both do."

Without a word she dropped down and leaned her head against the wall of the cave.

Seeing the pain etched on her face Casey moved toward their supplies. "I'll fix something for lunch." He sorted through the packets of food and lifted two containers. "I've got chili or beef-and-barley soup. Name your poison."

When he got no response he looked over at her. Her head had lowered almost to her chest, her breathing slow and easy.

With a smile he unrolled her sleeping bag and picked her up. Easing her down onto its inviting warmth, he covered her and knelt back to see if she'd stir.

With a sigh she rolled to one side, sound asleep.

Kirby awoke with a start. Sitting up, she saw Casey still digging at the snow-covered entrance.

"Sorry. I didn't mean to fall asleep—" she looked down at her sleeping bag and realized that he must have moved her while she slept "—and I certainly didn't mean to leave all the work to you."

"When a body is fighting an injury, sleep is healing." He paused. "How's your ankle?"

She looked away, to hide any pain that might be evident in her eyes. "It's okay."

"There's chili warming in that Insta-pot."

"Thanks." She hobbled across the distance and filled a bowl, practically inhaling it before setting it aside to join him.

She worked nonstop, determined to make up for the time she'd lost sleeping. If Casey noticed, he made no mention of it, and for that she was grateful.

In the corner of the cave Solitaire stomped a foot and snorted.

Kirby chuckled. "I think he's trying to tell you he's bored silly."

"I hear him loud and clear." Casey joined in her laughter. "Poor guy just wants to be free of this place."

"Do you think we'll get out of here?"

Casey nodded. "We're making progress. And since we have no choice, we'll just keep chipping away until we see daylight."

"Or moonlight." Kirby shot him a sideways glance. "With our phones out of commission, and no way to see outside, I'm feeling really fuzzy brained. Do you think it's still daylight? Or could it be dark outside?"

He shrugged. "It doesn't matter. The only thing that will dictate our staying or leaving this place, after we dig out, of course, will be that little filly." He indicated the mustang, watching them warily from a corner of the cave. "Once she can stand and walk, we'll head down the mountain."

Kirby tried not to let him hear her little sigh. Oh,

how she wanted to be out of this scary place and safely away from the threat of a convict on the run.

It might have been an hour or several hours later when their flimsy utensils broke through the last few inches of snow. Though it was a hole no bigger than a cup, they could see the gleam of moonlight on the crusted snow beyond.

"Look." Casey moved aside so Kirby could see what he'd just glimpsed.

"We did it." Kirby's sudden smile was as bright as her mood. Without thinking she wrapped her arms around his neck and gave him a fierce hug. "Oh, Casey. We did it."

"Yes, we did." His words, spoken against her temple, sent heat spiraling down her spine. "I'd say we're a damned fine team."

"Well..." Awkwardly she stepped a little away.

Aware of her embarrassment, he turned toward the fire. "To celebrate, we're going to have that steak I promised."

He removed several packages from the cooler. Now that there was fresh air, he started a fire, before tossing a steak and two twice-baked potatoes on foil over a small wire grill. While they were cooking, he rummaged beneath a layer of ice and retrieved two longnecks. Popping the caps, he handed one to Kirby before touching his bottle to hers. "Here's to..." He thought a minute before adding, "Here's to teamwork."

She smiled. "To teamwork."

Looking pleased, they tipped up their bottles and drank.

When their meal was ready they sat beside the fire

and enjoyed steak, potatoes, and a foil-wrapped package of peas and tiny carrots.

Kirby took one taste and gave a hum of pleasure. "Are these veggies homegrown?"

Casey nodded. "From Billy's garden. Actually it's a greenhouse we made for him for his birthday several years ago."

"A greenhouse. What cook wouldn't love his own greenhouse?"

"He told us it was the best birthday present ever. The man's a stickler for natural foods. And he's a wizard with everything he prepares. I don't think he ever serves the same meal twice. Except for his famous pot roast. That's become everyone's favorite."

"How lucky are you." Kirby tasted her steak and gave another sigh. "I haven't eaten anything this good in years. When I worked in the city, I never cooked. There was no time. It was either stop at a neighborhood restaurant or order carryout."

"How did you happen to move so far away?"

She shrugged. "Uncle Frank used to preach to me that I could be anything I wanted. And what I wanted was to spend the rest of my life right here in Wyoming, ranching like him. But he reminded me that he'd sent Caroline away to get an education, and he planned to do the same for me. He helped me pick the college, and when I interned for the Association of Land Management in DC, it seemed a natural progression to continue working there after I graduated." Her tone lowered and there was an edge to it as she added, "Besides, at the time, Caroline and her husband were considering making a move back to Wyoming to stay with her father."

"Was that your reason for remaining in DC?"

For a moment she didn't answer. Then, haltingly she said, "When I told Caroline that I would be happy to move home and lend a hand, she emailed me to say that she didn't want any additional stress put on her father, that his doctor had confided in her that Uncle Frank's health was failing."

"Stress? She actually suggested that your return might cause him stress?"

Kirby looked away. "I don't know if that's what she meant, but that's how I understood it. And so, I wasn't there when he passed."

Casey decided to put a positive spin on things. "Well, you're back now, and about to fulfill your dream of ranching like your uncle."

She managed a smile. "Yeah. That's true."

Casey leaned back against his saddle and crossed his ankles, enjoying the last of the meal and the beer.

Knowing they'd broken through the barrier of snow was reason enough to celebrate. And though the steak was perfection, and a cool longneck was an added bonus, the truth was, for Casey, the company of this pretty woman was pure frosting on the cake.

She was easy to talk to, and just as easy to listen to.

When he started to collect their dishes, Kirby stopped him. "You cooked. I'll clean up here. Besides, you need to check on your patient, Doctor."

While Kirby dropped their dishes in a pan of water heating over the fire, he crossed to the mustang.

A short time later Kirby was beside him, handing him the ointment and clean dressings as he removed the old ones. When she handed him a syringe, their fingers brushed, sending a quick sizzle of heat dancing along his arm.

When it had happened before, he'd tried to ignore it. Now he realized that he'd been anticipating it. And he had to admit, he was enjoying it way more than he should. Just as he'd thoroughly enjoyed her spontaneous embrace earlier.

Later, as they climbed into their sleeping bags, Casey lay watching the flickering shadows cast on the walls of the cave by the fire.

He'd never before shared his time in the wilderness with anyone. He'd always jealously guarded these treks into the mountains, away from all human contact. But as reluctant as he was to admit it, he'd enjoyed Kirby's company. And though he was eager to get this mustang to the barn, where he could give the poor animal more sophisticated treatment, he'd be sorry when this little idyll ended.

Kirby Regan was a damned fine companion. She'd been surprisingly easy to be around. He couldn't think of another woman, with the exception of Gram Meg, who would have endured so many unpleasant events. A blizzard, a sprained ankle, an avalanche, and the threat of a dangerous criminal hiding in the area. And all in the space of a couple of days. And she was still smiling.

That smile of hers played through his mind as he drifted into sleep.

CHAPTER FIVE

Kirby awoke to the incessant sound of dull, methodical thuds.

She opened her eyes to see Casey using a log to enlarge the opening of the cave. Kirby surmised that he must've been at it a while, since it was now big enough to allow a man to exit.

"Good morning." She eased out of her sleeping bag and was pleased to note that the almost crippling pain had lessened enough to allow her to stand without clenching her teeth. But just barely.

"'Morning." Casey turned. "How's the ankle?"

"Better than yesterday, I believe."

Seeing her bright smile, he relaxed. "That's good. Think you're up for a day of travel?"

She nodded. "And I'm betting Solitaire will be thrilled to leave his prison."

"So will our patient."

At Casey's words she realized for the first time that the mustang on the far side of the cave was standing. "Oh, look at her."

"Yeah. I think if it weren't for the snow barring the entrance, she'd make a run for it."

"If you turned her loose, would she survive?"

Casey shrugged. "It's hard to say. I've certainly pumped her up with plenty of antibiotics. But that cut was deep and infected, and I believe she'll need another week or more before it's healed enough to be considered infection-free for the long haul. Life in the wilderness is hard, but for a wounded animal it can be fatal. If she can't keep up, her herd will abandon her. And then there are the predators that are always watching for the weak and wounded, because they're easy prey. I don't intend to return her to the wild until she's strong enough to survive even the strongest threat."

He gestured toward the coffeepot on the hot coals. "There's coffee. And since you're awake, I'm going to stop and make breakfast." He set aside the log and crossed to the fire. "I've worked up a powerful appetite."

In no time Kirby and Casey were seated on either side of the fire, helping themselves to crisp bacon, biscuits, and hard-boiled eggs from a foil packet that Billy had packed.

After the hearty meal, Kirby sat back, contentedly drinking a second cup of coffee. "I wonder why food tastes so good way out here."

"Probably because we can't take it for granted. If we run out, we can't drive to a store and buy more."

She shrugged. "There's that. But I think it's more. It's the fresh air, the hard, physical labor, and"—she glanced at him—"the pleasant company."

He chuckled. "It has been pleasant, hasn't it?" He set aside his empty cup. "Considering our less-than-warm introduction, it's surprising how well we work together."

At his words, Kirby flushed. She'd been trying to make up for their rough start. "I'm sorry I slept while you did all that work."

"No harm done. You needed to rest. Now it's time to make our getaway." He picked up the log. "While I get the final few feet of snow out of the way, would you mind packing up our supplies?"

She nodded. "I'm happy to."

As she returned the food and utensils to Casey's saddlebags, and began saddling Solitaire, she kept sneaking peeks at Casey. He'd shed his parka. His sleeves were rolled to his elbows, his face beaded with sweat as he continued pounding the packed snow with the log until at last the entrance was open wide enough to permit both horses and riders to emerge.

With a smile of triumph he turned. "That should do it. Ready to face the trail?"

"I'm ready if you are." She poured the containers of melted snow on the last of the embers until she was certain the fire had been extinguished.

Casey tied a rope to the mustang's neck. "From the looks of these two, they're more than ready to stretch their legs."

Casey unrolled his sleeves and slipped into his parka before grabbing up his wide-brimmed hat. While holding the lead rope attached to the filly, he pulled himself into the saddle before turning to assist Kirby up behind him.

With a last look around the cave that had been their shelter, they faced forward toward the entrance. After the gloom inside, the sun was blinding as it reflected off a countryside covered in a snowfall so white it hurt to look at it.

As Solitaire moved out at a slow, measured pace, Kirby wrapped her arms around Casey's waist and felt the ripple of muscles beneath the parka.

When the wind picked up, blowing the snow in little eddies against their eyes, Casey pulled his hat low on his forehead. Kirby buried her face against his broad back.

As their mount plodded through the drifts, Kirby became aware of the fact that she felt not only warm but safe with this man. On her own, she would've been driven by panic, and a need to reach civilization as quickly as possible. But with Casey she had the feeling that the two of them could overcome any danger. Hadn't they survived a blizzard and an avalanche?

She touched a hand to her rifle, in the boot of the saddle along with Casey's. As they descended the mountain, they were both alert to any unusual movement, and were constantly watching for human footprints.

As they rode, Casey pointed out the various tracks in the snow. "Deer," he said as they emerged from a thick stand of trees.

When Kirby looked around and saw only wilderness, he pointed to the telltale prints. "A pretty big herd. And probably here less than an hour ago."

She began to follow his lead, noting the tracks and the droppings. Every so often, he'd point and call out, "Mustangs." Or, "Bobcat. And a big one, judging by those prints."

She glanced around, wishing she could see a big cat. Not up close, she thought, but it would be so exciting to spot one on a nearby cliff. Instead she saw only a dazzling white countryside for as far as the eye could see.

By the time the snow had thinned to a mere dusting in the lower elevation, they were both cold, weary, and eager for whatever comfort they could find at the end of the trail.

At long last they caught sight of outbuildings and, in the far distance, a plume of smoke from a chimney.

"There's my home."

Kirby could hear the affection in his voice. Her heart beat faster as she studied the sturdy, well-maintained barns, and beyond, a tall, three-story house of weathered wood and stone, looking as stately as the mountains that served as a backdrop.

Solitaire, sensing food and shelter at the end of their long journey, picked up his speed. The mustang was forced to keep up.

As the wind continued its assault, Kirby leaned her face against Casey's broad back and closed her eyes, absorbing the warmth and strength of him.

"Well, look what the storm blew in."

A man's deep voice greeted them as they rounded the barn.

Standing in the open doorway was a tall, muscular cowboy. He looked enough like Casey that he could have been his twin. Even the wide smile was the same, crinkling the corners of his eyes, lighting all his features.

"Didn't you say you'd be gone for a couple of weeks?"

Casey chuckled. "Now that's what I call a warm welcome. I thought you'd be happy to see me, bro."

"I am. Just puzzled. Since you're the guy who loves his solitude, what brings you back so soon?"

When Casey slid from the saddle, the man's eyes widened as he caught sight of Kirby, who had been hidden from his view.

With a nod of approval he gave Casey a thumbs-up. "Only you could ride into a blizzard and come home with a beautiful woman."

That had Kirby grinning.

"Kirby Regan, this is my brother Jonah. He prides himself on being a man of words."

"Hi, Jonah." Kirby descended from Solitaire's back and absorbed a sudden rush of pain when she put pressure on her ankle after so many hours on the trail.

Hearing the way she sucked in a breath Casey put an arm around her waist to hold her upright. "You okay?"

"Yeah." She allowed herself to lean into him for a moment before stepping away.

Casey handed his brother the lead rope. "Mind putting this mustang in a stall? Maybe that one in the corner, so she's isolated."

Noticing the way the mustang favored its left foreleg, Jonah arched a brow. "An injured mustang *and* an injured lady?"

"I found the filly on the trail, unable to walk. It has a deep cut that's infected."

"And he found me, or rather I found him, taking shelter in a cave."

"Sound like there's a story there." Jonah led the horse to a stall and removed the rope before stepping out and securing the stall door.

Though the mustang appeared skittish, the food and water soon snagged enough of her interest that she stopped her pacing to eat.

Before Casey could unsaddle Solitaire, Jonah took the reins from him. "You two look frozen. Why don't you go inside? I'll take care of this."

Casey shot him a smile of gratitude. "Thanks, Jonah." Keeping an arm around Kirby's waist, he walked with her toward the house.

She seemed embarrassed by his attention. "That first step caught me by surprise, but I'm fine now, Casey. Really."

He merely smiled. "Humor me. You're about to be overwhelmed by my family. Brace yourself."

As they crossed the distance from the barn to the house, both their cell phones began buzzing, letting them know that they were within range of service.

They paused to study their messages.

Kirby quickly read the half-dozen texts from her superior, each more frantic than the last. With a sigh she dialed his number and left a message when he didn't answer. "Dan? Sorry it took so long to get back to you. The storm knocked out service to my phone, but I want to assure you I'm safe. I found shelter in the mountains with Dr. Casey Merrick, and I'm currently at his family's ranch. Since we've just now arrived, I have no plans other than to read all my messages to catch up on what I've missed. I'll call you later and we can talk business."

As she tucked her phone in her pocket, Casey led her up the back porch.

They stepped into a big mudroom, with low shelves for boots, and hooks along the wall for coats and hats. They both hung their parkas, then sat on a wooden bench to remove their hiking boots.

As soon as her boot was off, Kirby hissed in pain.

She gathered herself for a moment, before following Casey's lead and crossing the room to wash in a deep sink that stood beside a table piled with fluffy towels.

From the other room came a chorus of voices and the low rumble of laughter.

The minute they stepped into the kitchen, the room went silent as everyone turned to them.

Kirby returned their stares as a white-haired cowboy called, "You're home early, boy. We weren't expecting you for a couple of weeks."

"I know I'm early, Ham. And I brought company." Casey caught Kirby's hand and led her toward the group, clustered around a fireplace at one end of the kitchen. "Kirby Regan, this is my family. My great-grandfather, Hammond Merrick."

"Everyone calls me Ham." The old man studied the visitor with interest. "Welcome to our ranch."

"Thank you, Ham." She extended a hand and he shook it with surprising strength.

"My grandparents, Egan and Meg Merrick."

They were both on their feet in an instant and hurrying over to hug Kirby.

Meg gave her a worried look before glancing at her grandson. "How long has this poor thing been in the saddle?"

Casey shrugged. "Most of the day."

"Why, you must be half-frozen. Here." Meg led Kirby to an upholstered chair by the fireplace and dropped an afghan over her lap. "We have hot tea if you'd like."

Kirby couldn't help smiling at her kindness. "Hot tea sounds heavenly."

"What about me, Gram Meg? No hugs for the weary traveler?"

His grandmother gave him a dismissive wave before throwing her arms around his neck. "You've been known to spend weeks in the saddle in the middle of nowhere."

He shot a grin at Kirby. "See? I get no respect."

While the others chuckled, a man crossed the room to hand Kirby a steaming cup of tea. He appeared to be in his midfifties, rail-thin, with sparkling blue eyes and fine brown hair in a bowl cut.

Casey handled the introduction. "Kirby, this is Billy Caldwell."

"Hello, Billy. Thank you for the tea. Casey told me you're the best cook in all of Wyoming."

"It's nice to meet you, Kirby. I didn't realize Casey ever bragged about me. I'll let you be the judge of whether or not he was telling you the truth."

She breathed in the wonderful fragrance permeating the air. "If what you're cooking is half as good as it smells, I can't wait."

Casey dropped an arm around his father's shoulders. "Kirby, this is my father, Bo Merrick."

Kirby's gaze darted from father to son. "Hello, Bo. You could never deny that Casey's your son. He looks just like you."

Casey nudged an elbow in Bo's ribs. "I consider that the highest compliment."

A handsome cowboy and a pretty blond woman wearing faded denims and a plaid shirt had trailed in behind Casey and Kirby, and were now coming over to offer their warm greetings.

Casey was quick to say, "Kirby Regan, this is

Chet Doyle, a longtime family friend and ranch foreman."

"Chet." Kirby accepted his handshake.

"And this is my aunt, Liz Merrick."

The blonde managed a shy smile before staring at the floor.

"Hello. You're the photographer." Seeing the way Liz colored, Kirby felt the need to explain. "We had a lot of time to talk while we were stuck in that cave, and Casey told me a little bit about his family."

"Wait." Hammond held up a hand. "Cave? You two were alone in a cave?"

"There was a blizzard raging." Kirby caught the sidelong glances being shared by the family as Casey continued, "And I had an injured mustang I was caring for."

"And my boss had texted me, warning that there was an escaped convict in the area." Kirby's words tumbled out in a rush. "I was racing to get down the mountain when I fell and sprained my ankle and went stumbling into Casey's cave, looking for shelter. But when I saw him, looking like some kind of trail bum, I thought he was the convict, so I held him at gunpoint and—"

"You pulled a gun on my great-grandson?" Ham's eyes narrowed.

"I'm afraid so. Of course, that didn't last but a moment before I was rudely relieved of my rifle and I was the one facing my own gun."

By now the entire family was leaning forward, eager to hear every word.

Seeing their reactions, Casey started laughing. "I wish you could see your faces. What the lady left out is the fact that we resolved our differences and agreed to work together to survive the blizzard, an avalanche, and an escaped convict."

"An avalanche? I'm afraid you left that out of your narrative." Meg looked horrified.

"It sealed the entrance to the cave, but we managed to break through the barrier, as you can see."

"That's some story," Jonah said. He'd just come in from the barn, trailed by his brother and sister-in-law.

Casey turned. "Kirby, you've met my younger brother, Jonah. This is my older brother, Brand, and his wife, Avery."

Kirby shook her head. "Casey told me about his big family, but until now I didn't realize just how many of you there are."

"We're big, we're noisy, and we'll expect you to remember all our names," Jonah said with a grin.

That had the others nodding and laughing.

Noticing Kirby's empty cup, Meg took it from her hands. "Do you have somewhere you need to be?"

Kirby shook her head. "There's nobody waiting for me."

Meg smiled. "Good. Then I suggest you consider spending the night."

It was on the tip of Kirby's lips to offer a protest. Instead, she merely smiled. "Thank you. I'd like that."

Meg turned to her grandson. "Casey, why don't you take Kirby upstairs and show her the guest room? I'm sure after all the two of you have been through you'll both welcome a hot shower and a chance to relax before dinner."

"Thanks, Gram Meg." Kirby followed behind Casey. As soon as they stepped out of the kitchen he caught her hand. "Is your head spinning from all the names and faces?"

She laughed. "Does it show?"

"Not at all. You handled it like a pro. Come on." He led the way up the stairs, while she tried not to limp as she climbed beside him.

He opened a door and stepped aside. "I think you'll be comfortable here. If you need anything at all, let me know. My room is next door. Right now, I'm going to take the longest shower in the universe."

"Oh, that sounds heavenly."

"Take all the time you want to settle in. I'll see you downstairs." He winked before pulling the door closed behind him.

CHAPTER SIX

When the door closed, Kirby turned to study her new surroundings.

A big bed was covered with a pale down comforter. Tossed carelessly at the foot was a throw of soft heather. Across the room were floor-to-ceiling windows that afforded a view of the Grand Tetons looming in the distance. On the other side was a desk and chair, and along another wall was a series of bookshelves holding bound leather volumes of what appeared to be a collection of CDs. Mounted opposite the bed was a flat-screen television.

At a knock on the door she opened it to find Avery holding a pile of clothes. "We thought you might need these." With a smile she handed them to Kirby and turned away.

"Thank you," Kirby called before closing the door and setting them on a chair.

She opened the adjoining bathroom door and paused, trying to take in the expanse of marble, on the floor, the shower, even the vanity. And across the room a jetted tub invited her to soak.

In mere minutes, she was out of her clothes and

into the warm water, reveling in the jets spewing more warmth, until she was purring with pleasure.

She scrubbed her hair until it gleamed, then just sat back, letting the warm water lull her until, afraid she might fall asleep, she climbed reluctantly from the tub and wrapped herself in a bath towel.

She opened drawers and doors in the vanity and found everything she could ever need: combs, brushes, gels, lotions. After blowing her hair partially dry, she slathered as much lotion on as she could before leaving the bathroom to climb into the inviting bed.

She was asleep as soon as her head hit the pillow.

Kirby jerked awake, feeling more than a little confused. A glance around reminded her that she was in the luxurious guest room of Casey Merrick's ranch. The fading light outside the windows assured her that at least she hadn't slept away the night.

When she climbed out of bed, still wearing the towel, she glanced at the pile of clean clothes on the chair. She held them up, pleased to find a pair of denims and a soft, long-sleeved shirt in pale peach, as well as a pair of soft, knitted slippers.

With gratitude for this thoughtful family, she dressed and ran a brush through her hair before stepping from the room.

The sound of voices grew louder as she descended the stairs and made her way to the kitchen.

"Hey." Casey separated himself from the others and crossed the room to take her hand. "You look rested."

"And you look—" she stopped, suddenly embarrassed at what she'd almost blurted out in front of his entire family "—fresh."

There was no trace of the trail bum she'd first met. He'd shaved, and his hair, curling at the collar of a crisp plaid shirt, still bore the evidence of his shower. His long legs were encased in clean denims. On his feet were scuffed boots. He looked rested and relaxed, and entirely too handsome and sexy to be the scruffy man she'd just spent time with in a cave in the middle of nowhere.

As he drew her toward his family, she felt herself blushing. "Thank you all for these clothes."

Meg looked over. "You're welcome. Avery and Liz contributed the clothes, since they're close in size to you, Kirby. I have to take credit for the slippers. I thought, since you're dealing with a sore ankle, they would feel better than stiff shoes or boots."

"Well, I thank all of you." Kirby accepted a glass of pale wine from Casey's hand. "For the clothes, the lovely room, and your hospitality. It's so much more than I expected, and I'm so grateful."

"You'll be even more grateful when you taste Billy's pot roast," Casey said with a wink.

"I can't wait."

She took a seat beside Liz and Avery, enjoying the warmth of the fireplace and the conversation that swirled around her. When Liz held out a tray, she accepted what was offered and began to nibble on a cheese roll fresh from the oven that had her sighing with pleasure.

When she looked at Casey, he winked, and she felt her heart take a sudden bounce. Oh, the man looked good enough to devour.

When Billy announced that dinner was ready, the

family moved across the room to take their places at a big trestle table.

Before Kirby could wonder where to sit, Casey was holding a chair out for her. When she was seated, he took the place next to her.

With Hammond at the head of the table, and Egan at the opposite end beside his Meg, the others gathered around, passing platters of tender roast beef and another of garden vegetables—potatoes, carrots, snap peas, and tender green beans. There was a salad of various greens and tomatoes tossed with a light dressing of oil, red wine vinegar, and lemon, along with rolls still warm from the oven.

Kirby helped herself to salad. "These greens look like they just came from a garden."

"They did." Billy said proudly.

"Oh, yes. Casey mentioned your greenhouse."

While they ate, the family took a moment to praise Billy's cooking before carrying on an animated conversation about the latest problem with one of the plows they'd had to abandon on a stretch of road acres from the barn.

Jonah was shaking his head. "It stopped cold. No warning."

"You sure you didn't forget to fill the tank?" Hammond's tone was a growl of displeasure.

Instead of taking offense, Jonah simply shook his head. "I'm old-school, Ham, just like you taught me. That's always the first thing I check."

"How old is the battery?" Egan nudged his wife. "Not that there's anything wrong with being old."

The two shared a laugh.

"The battery's new this season." Jonah helped himself

to another roll before glancing at Casey. "I'm hoping the good doctor will take a look at it tomorrow and figure out what's wrong. Otherwise, it may just have to sit out there until next spring."

Casey was grinning. "You can drive me out there first thing in the morning and I'll have a look at it."

Brand turned to Kirby, who hadn't said a word through the entire meal. "In case you're wondering, Casey isn't just good at doctoring animals. He's the one who usually ends up doctoring most of the equipment around here, too."

Casey shared a smile with Kirby. "That's me. A jack-of-all-trades."

"And master of none," Ham said smugly.

"You didn't say that that when you asked me to figure out what was wrong with your favorite truck, Ham."

At Casey's taunt, the old man nodded. "You're right. When it comes to that old pile of nuts and bolts, no one's better at fixing it than you, boy." The old patriarch turned his attention to Kirby. "Where're you from, girl?"

"I grew up not far from here on my uncle's ranch. You may have known him. Frank Regan."

Ham's eyes widened. "I knew Frankie. Come to think of it, I remember seeing him in town years ago with a skinny little girl in tow. Rumor was that he'd brought his brother's girl to live with him."

Kirby smiled and nodded. "That's me."

Ham's tone lowered. "I heard he passed away not long ago. They say his ranch is standing empty."

"Not for long, I hope." Kirby ducked her head.

The old man pinned her with a steely-eyed look.

"Rumor is his daughter isn't willing to come back to work it."

Kirby shook her head, hoping to defend her cousin. "It isn't that Caroline doesn't care about the ranch, but she's made a life for herself, with a husband and three children, far from here. It wouldn't be right to ask them to leave all that behind for the sake of her childhood home."

"So she'll just turn her back on it?"

Casey looked up from his meal. "I recognize that tone, Ham. Kirby's hoping to buy the ranch from Frank's daughter."

The old man gave her a long look. "You thinking about running Frank's place on your own?"

Kirby nodded. "Of course, I'll need help. But I met with a couple of his wranglers at the funeral, and they told me they would welcome the chance to come back."

Hammond's tone softened. "It's nice to know someone's willing to try to save both the ranch and its employees, girl."

Meg gave her a smile. "Where did you go when you left your uncle's ranch, Kirby?"

"Washington, DC. I got a job with the Association of Land Management."

At that Hammond's lips thinned. "Bean counters. All of them."

Ignoring his great-grandfather's disdain, Jonah asked, "What did you do there, Kirby?"

She kept her tone level. "Bean counting."

That had everyone except Hammond bursting into laughter.

The old man, she noted, shot her a look guaranteed

to freeze her blood before returning his attention to the food on his plate.

"As you can see, the ALM isn't one of Ham's favorite government agencies." Jonah shot her a grin.

"Technically, it isn't government owned. It was put together by ranchers to be a counterpoint to the government agencies."

"It's still a bloated bureaucracy," Ham said with a tone of anger.

Jonah interrupted. "So where are you working here in Wyoming?"

"I'm still with the Association. When I left DC I found a temporary apartment in Devil's Door. But leaving the city meant I'd have to take a demotion." She sighed. "As the newest member of the team here, I was given the assignment nobody else wanted."

Brand passed a platter of beef before looking over. "And what's the job nobody wanted?"

"I was sent to the hills to identify as many mustang herds as possible."

"Like I said." Ham's frown deepened. "A bean counter."

"I'm afraid so." Kirby wondered why the old man's words didn't bother her. Maybe it was because of the roast beef, so tender it melted in her mouth, along with the mashed potatoes so creamy and yummy she was almost humming with pleasure. How could anyone feel anger while indulging in such a meal after a long day on the trail?

She looked at the cook. "Billy, Casey wasn't exaggerating. This is the best I've ever tasted."

While Billy smiled in pleasure at the compliment,

Casey nodded. "Told you. Even those fancy DC restaurants can't hold a candle to this."

"I absolutely agree." She helped herself to another biscuit. "And this..." She gave a sigh. "Pure perfection."

Around the table, the others smiled and nodded.

Casey looked around at his family. "I haven't heard the sound of helicopters for a while now. Have you heard anything about the missing convict?"

Brand shook his head. "No word on his capture yet. But I noticed a number of state police officers up in the hills on all-terrain vehicles."

Bo frowned. "We've been warned to be careful while going about our chores, especially if we have to go any distance from home. And the authorities asked us to report anything out of the ordinary." He glanced around the table. "With so many of the ranchers around here having range shacks in the hills, most of them empty once the herds have been brought down for the winter, the fear is that a man could survive for months on the supplies stored at any one of the camps."

The others nodded in agreement.

Bo muttered, "Think about it. A lone man finding shelter, heat, food, and all far enough from civilization where nobody would ever intrude for months."

Ham's gravelly voice lowered with feeling. "You mark my words. Sooner or later that escapee's bound to make a mistake. Whether he tries to steal a vehicle, or just gets cabin fever and decides to make his way to a big city, he'll leave a trail. In the end, these guys always get caught."

Bo looked at his three sons. "That may be true, but it's the destruction he could cause before getting caught that worries me. I don't want any of you taking foolish chances. Remember, desperate men will do whatever necessary to survive. And the authorities have already said this guy is dangerous. Ray Keller was doing time for murder, and the media is calling him Killer Keller. I guess, according to them, he enjoys killing. His last victim was a prison guard who left behind a young wife and three kids."

With a shudder, Meg turned to Billy. "With all this talk of trouble, I think a change of scenery is in order. We'll take our dessert and coffee in the great room."

Egan offered his hand, and the two led the way from the kitchen, with the others trailing behind.

Casey walked beside Kirby. "In case you haven't noticed, Gram Meg is the peacemaker in the family."

Kirby smiled. "I noticed. I'm glad she changed the subject. Just thinking about an escaped convict hiding somewhere in the hills makes me uncomfortable."

He closed a hand over hers. "You're safe here."

She felt the quick rush of heat at his touch and felt a shiver along her spine.

Safe here?

She nearly laughed out loud. In this cowboy's company, *safe* wasn't at all the word that came to mind.

Tempted was more like it. Very, very tempted to let down her guard and simply enjoy whatever this cowboy was offering.

"Let's all sit by the fire." Meg and Egan took their places as the family gathered around the big stone fireplace that dominated the room.

Egan picked up the TV remote.

Kirby settled on a sofa, with Casey beside her. There

were two more matching sofas along with several comfortable chairs and ottomans. A round basket holding a variety of knitted lap robes stood guard near the hearth. A cheery fire blazed on the grate.

As everyone settled into their favorite spot, a picture of a man with long, stringy dark hair and a hound-dog face that bore a puckered scar on the left side from his temple to his jaw filled the television screen. The reporter was saying that Ray Keller, a lifer with nothing to lose, had earned his scar in a prison fight, killing one of the other inmates with his bare hands.

At a look from Meg, Egan turned off the TV just as Billy entered the room pushing a rolling cart holding a three-tiered chocolate cake, along with plates, cups, coffee, cream, and sugar.

After passing the dessert around, the family turned to Casey, eager to hear about his time spent in the hills.

Bo spoke first. "I saw your wounded mustang out in the barn. She's a beauty. What do you think happened to her?"

"It looked to me like she may have tangled herself up in some barbed wire and then thrashed about until she did damage, or maybe an animal trap some rancher had set out. Whatever got her, she was beyond being able to fight it. When I found her, she was lying in the snow, waiting to die."

"Poor thing." said Liz, her tender heart obviously going out to the animal. "I'm so glad you found her in time, Casey."

"I *hope* I found her in time." Casey gave a shake of his head. "The jury's still out. Even though she's up and walking now, if that infection got into the blood, she'll need a lot more help before it's completely cleared up."

Brand polished off the last of his cake. "I want to hear about the avalanche."

"It sounded like a freight train roaring overhead." Casey glanced at Kirby. "Once the opening to the cave was sealed, we were trapped. We had to douse the fire so we wouldn't choke on the smoke. If we hadn't had a battery-operated lantern we'd have been in total darkness."

"How long did it take to break through?" Jonah asked.

Casey shrugged. "We both lost track of time. But we used whatever tools we had and kept chipping away at it until we could see daylight. That was the hard part. By this morning I knew we'd be able to make our way out in plenty of time to reach the ranch before supper time."

"What do you think caused an avalanche so early in the season?"

Casey shook his head. "I'm only guessing, but I think the police helicopters flying low overhead may have contributed to it."

Ham clenched a fist. "Another thing we can blame on that damnable convict. He better not come around here, or I'll teach him a thing or two."

That had his family sharing smiles. The old man's temper was legendary.

Brand got to his feet and caught his wife's hand. "Morning chores come early. We're heading up to bed."

As they said their good nights, the others began setting aside their empty plates and cups and doing the same.

Casey turned to Kirby. "Ready to call it a day?"

She nodded before saying to Billy, "Casey had every right to brag about your cooking. The dinner was amazing. And so was this dessert."

The cook beamed with pleasure. "I'm glad you enjoyed it."

She wished everyone good night and followed Casey up the stairs.

At the door to her room he paused. "Is there anything you need?"

She made a sound of protest. "Not a thing. I can't believe how thoughtful your family has been." She put a hand on his arm. "They're amazing. They've made me feel so welcome."

He looked down at her hand, then up into her eyes. "It's obvious that they like you."

"Now how could you possibly know that?"

"I can tell by their reaction to you."

She chuckled. "Even your great-grandfather? Could he possibly like an Association of Land Management bean counter?"

He shared her laughter. "That's just Ham's way. He's known around these parts as a stern bear of a man. Ham was here in Wyoming before all the rules were even written, and he resents them, even those put in place for his protection. But believe me, once he bonds with a person, he becomes their fiercest protector. Give him time. You'll see. He's the original free spirit."

"A free spirit?" She arched a brow. "He reminds me of someone." She grinned. "I think you're a lot like him."

That had him returning her smile. "Guilty."

As she turned to push open her door she felt his

hand at her shoulder. Turning, she was caught by complete surprise when Casey bent close to press a kiss to her cheek.

It was the merest touch of his lips on her skin, as soft as a butterfly's wings. And yet she could feel the shock waves all the way to her toes. Especially when she could sense him breathing her in.

"Sweet dreams, bean counter." He tugged on a lock of her hair before giving her one of those heart-stopping smiles.

"'Night." It was all she could manage over a throat that was suddenly as dry as dust.

She stepped inside and closed the door before leaning weakly against it.

A half hour later, as she lay in bed, she wondered what in the world was wrong with her. Her reaction had been over the top.

After all, she'd been thanking him for his family's hospitality, and he had probably wanted to add his own lukewarm welcome.

Except...

There had been nothing lukewarm about her reaction to it. Even now, just thinking about the simple brush of his lips on her cheek had her toes curling.

It was as she'd thought earlier. This cowboy was too sexy for his own good. And hers.

CHAPTER SEVEN

The next morning, Kirby lay perfectly still in bed, listening to the alien sounds. Cattle lowing. A door closing down the hall. A man's deep laugh.

A glance at the floor-to-ceiling windows revealed the soft glow of dawn beginning to color the sky with streaks of pale pink and mauve and crimson just above the peaks of the Tetons.

After her years in the city, she'd grown accustomed to the sounds of traffic from early morning until late in the night. Of elevators signaling a workforce on the move. The street lights outside her apartment obliterated the night sky, making it impossible to differentiate between dawn and dusk.

She bounded out of bed and crossed the room to watch as the sunrise turned everything to rose-gold over a land that lay hushed and silent.

This was why she'd come back to Wyoming. That brief visit for her uncle's funeral had reminded her of all the things she'd left behind. She'd sacrificed so much for the sake of a career that hadn't lived up to its promise.

Bean counter.

Ham's words played in her head. Living and working in the District, she'd become a numbers manager. And now she'd been assigned the task of counting mustang herds, instead of being a manager of the land she loved. The irony of her situation had her shaking her head as she turned and made her way to the shower. But at least, she consoled herself, she was counting animals instead of crunching bottom-line numbers for a bureaucracy.

A short time later, having dressed in her own clothes, which she'd found carefully folded on a chair in her room, she descended the stairs and followed the voices to the kitchen, where the older members of the Merrick family had already assembled for breakfast.

Brand, Jonah, and Casey could be heard laughing in the mudroom as they washed up after their early-morning chores in the barn.

"'Morning." Casey strolled into the kitchen and gave her a long look before helping himself to a mug of coffee.

"Good morning." She felt herself flushing under his scrutiny as she sipped orange juice. "I'm sorry I wasn't up early enough to lend a hand with the chores."

Casey grinned at Jonah. "That's what they all say."

Jonah nodded. "That's all right, Kirby. We left a couple of stalls for you to muck after breakfast, just so you'd feel at home."

"Gee, thanks."

"You're welcome. Besides, since you're hoping to buy your uncle's ranch, you may as well dip your toe—"

"—in the manure," Casey finished for him.

That brought a round of laughter from the others as they gathered in the kitchen.

"Breakfast is ready," Billy called as he began carrying platters of food to the table.

They needed no coaxing as they took their places and began passing plates of eggs scrambled with onions and green peppers, as well as roasted potatoes, thick slices of ham, and a basket of cinnamon toast.

The family fell silent as they satisfied their hunger brought on by morning chores.

Ham sat back, sipping strong, hot coffee, looking pleased. "A breakfast fit for a king."

Egan nodded. "It never gets old, does it?"

The two men shared a smile.

They all looked toward Kirby when her cell phone rang.

She glanced at the screen before pushing away from the table. "Sorry. This is my boss. Excuse me."

She stepped from the room, and after a brief conversation she returned.

Casey looked up. "Everything all right?"

She nodded. "I hate to ask for yet another favor, but my boss wants me to come into the office, and I parked my truck miles from here in the foothills of the Tetons before I started my hike."

Before she could say more, Casey held up a hand. "I don't mind driving you to the spot."

"Thank you. I really appreciate it."

Casey turned to Billy. "If you need anything from town, give me your list before I head out."

"I will." Billy was already scribbling on a notepad.

As the family began pushing away from the table, Kirby put a hand on Avery's arm. "Thank you for the use of your clothes. If you'll tell me where the laundry room is, I'll see that they're washed before I leave."

"There's no need for that." Avery grabbed her hand. "Just leave them in the hamper in the guest room and I'll pick them up later." She squeezed both of Kirby's hands. "It was so nice getting to know you, Kirby. I wish we'd had more time."

"Me too." Kirby was smiling as she turned to include the others. "You've all been so warm and welcoming. I hope you know how much I appreciate all your kindnesses."

Meg hurried over to give her a hug. "I just want your word that you'll come back to visit soon, Kirby."

"I'd like that. Thank you for everything, Miss Meg."

Brand and Jonah couldn't help teasing as they paused beside her. "We'll keep a pitchfork ready with your name on it, Kirby. Next time you come to visit, we'll put you to work."

She was laughing as they walked away.

Egan gave her a warm hug. "You hurry back now, you hear?"

"Yes, sir." She returned his embrace.

"And take care of that ankle, Kirby." Bo stared pointedly at her foot. "I know you're trying to hide it, but it's still paining you, isn't it?"

She nodded and said softly, "More than I care to admit."

"I thought so. As the father of three, I learned early how to spot someone in pain." He gave her shoulder a squeeze. "You might want to see Dr. Peterson at the Devil's Door Clinic when you get to town."

"I will. Thanks, Bo."

Chet Doyle paused to shake her hand, while Liz stood a little apart and gave her a shy smile.

It occurred to Kirby that she and Casey's aunt hadn't shared more than a word or two. She hoped it was just simple shyness on Liz's part.

Her thoughts scattered as Hammond Merrick walked up to her and gave her a measured look. "Bye, girl. Let us know when you settle in to your ranch."

Your ranch.

She hugged those words to her heart.

"And don't spend all your time counting beans."

She managed a smile. "Yes, sir. But as long as my boss orders me to count mustangs, I guess I have no choice."

He arched a brow before walking away.

Kirby turned to Billy, busy at the sink. "Thank you for those memorable meals, Billy. I won't soon forget you."

"I'll remember you, too." He crossed the room and gave her a warm embrace. "Like Miss Meg said, you come back soon."

"Thanks. I hope I get the chance."

With a smile, Kirby hurried up the stairs to collect her backpack.

When she stepped out the back door, Casey was already waiting by a ranch truck. He held the passenger door open until she'd settled inside before circling around to the driver's side.

As they started along the curving driveway, she studied his profile. When she'd first met him in the cave, she'd thought he'd looked dangerous. And now, having spent enough time with him and his family, she realized she hadn't been too far off the mark. Though he had a silly sense of humor and had proven himself an excellent veterinarian and caretaker of a wounded animal, there was still an air of danger about him. In the way he moved, like a big cat stalking its prey. In the way his dark gaze seemed to assess everyone and everything he studied. In the way he made her feel...safe, and yet oddly vulnerable. In a fight, she'd want Casey on her side. But when he'd kissed her cheek, she'd found herself swept up in something so unsettling, she'd felt as though she'd lost her way.

As though sensing her strange mood, he turned and smiled. "A penny for them."

At her startled look, he winked.

There it was again. That sudden jolt to her heart.

"Just thinking about all the things I'll have to catch up on." A lie, she knew, but she couldn't possibly admit her true thoughts.

"I don't know." He reached out to touch a finger to the little frown line that creased her forehead. "I was sensing some pretty deep thoughts."

She glanced down at her hands, clenched together in her lap. With effort she unclenched them and managed a smile while changing the subject. "You're lucky to have such a big, loving family."

He nodded, but she knew he'd seen through her little deception. "I suppose to someone without family, we come on a little strong."

"No. Not at all. I really enjoyed my time with them."

"Even Ham?"

She laughed. "Your great-grandfather is very stern. But I can't help admiring him for all he's done in his life and continues to do. How many men still put in a full day of work at that age?"

Casey shrugged. "Sometimes I forget how old he is. I've grown up watching him work circles around all of us." He slowed when they reached a fork in the road. "Which way to your truck?"

"Left." She pointed. "I drove along this road for about twenty miles until it ended with a circular lookout. That's where I parked my truck and started my hike."

During the entire drive, they never passed another vehicle.

Casey was grinning. "I'll bet this isn't something you ever saw in DC."

She laughed. "You're right about that. There isn't a single street in the entire District that isn't clogged with cars."

As they came up over a rise Kirby was still smiling as she fished her key out of her pocket.

When Casey pulled into the deserted area, he turned to Kirby with a puzzled look. "Are you sure this is where you left your truck?"

She was staring open-mouthed. The lookout was empty.

"I don't understand. It was right there."

The snow had obliterated all trace of a vehicle. If there had been tracks, they were now completely covered.

"If you're certain…" Casey pulled his cell phone from his pocket and pressed a number before saying, "Noble? Casey Merrick. My family's houseguest would like to report the theft of her truck from the mountain lookout on Old Teton Trail. I'll give her the phone and she can give you the details while I drive her to town."

"This is police chief Noble Crain." He handed his phone to Kirby and drove the entire way to town in silence, listening to Kirby's answers as the police chief peppered her with questions.

"I'm renting a room above Myrtle Fox's bakery in Devil's Door."

There was a pause before she said, "I work for the Association of Land Management. I recently transferred from Washington, DC. I was assigned to count and record the number of mustang herds in the hills. My boss texted me with the news of an escaped convict in the area and ordered me to forego the mustang count and return home. The sudden blizzard changed my plans."

Another pause. "It's not a company truck. I bought it in DC and drove it here." She described the make, model, and license number before swallowing hard. "It's insured."

She listened before saying, "Yes. Of course I'll come to your office and sign any necessary papers." She glanced at Casey for confirmation.

At his nod, she added, "Thank you, Chief Crain."

When she handed over Casey's phone, he tucked it in his shirt pocket and then surprised her by taking her hand in his. "I know you're shocked. I am, too. But if your truck is still in Wyoming, I'm betting Noble Crain will have it back to you in no time."

She was shaking her head. "This could have happened right after I left it. That would give the thief plenty of time to drive clear across the country."

"Or not." He kept her hand in his. Squeezed. "Maybe, by the time we get to town, Noble will have heard from the state police that it's already been found abandoned somewhere."

She looked at their joined hands and realized that even this simple connection made her feel better somehow. "From your lips, cowboy."

"Trust me." He shot her a warm look that had her heart going into overdrive.

CHAPTER EIGHT

Casey drove slowly through town, pointing out to Kirby some old familiar places, like Harvey Spriggs's farm equipment sales, and Ben Harper's Grain and Feed and adjacent hardware. As they drew near the bank and courthouse, he paused to allow people to cross Main Street.

He waved to Julie Franklyn and her son, Greg, before shifting to face Kirby. "They own Julie's Hair Salon and Barber Shop. As soon as Greg finished school, he joined his mom in the business. See that couple chatting with them? That's Carrie and Ray Spence. They just opened a spa next door to the salon, offering manicures, pedicures, and massages." He winked. "I'm betting Julie is hoping they'll join forces to offer their customers some specials that will bring more people to both places."

"Sounds smart to me."

He pointed to a store up ahead. "Have you been to Stuff yet?"

Kirby shook her head. "Not yet. I haven't had the time."

Casey nodded. "Sheila Mason is a fourth-generation owner. She carries everything from clothes for the entire family, to new and used household goods."

"I'm glad nothing about it has changed. I'll be sure to stop by. I haven't even started furnishing my apartment yet. All I have are a bed and a lumpy sofa left over from the last tenant."

Casey pulled over to the curb. "This is the police station." He stepped out and made his way quickly to the passenger's side, where he held her door before taking her hand.

At her arched brow he merely smiled. "You didn't think I'd send you in there alone, did you?"

She returned his smile. "Thank you."

He pushed open the door and greeted the pretty woman behind the desk. "Hi, Maryanne. This is Kirby Regan."

To Kirby he added, "Maryanne is Chief Crain's wife."

Maryanne got on her feet to offer a handshake. "Hi, Kirby. I'm sorry to hear about your truck. You two go right on back. Noble is expecting you."

As they walked toward the rear of the office, Kirby shot a sideways glance at Casey.

He was grinning as he whispered, "Small towns and gossip. Half the town will know about the theft by noon. The other half by tomorrow, after they pay a call to Nonie's Wild Horses Saloon."

She sighed as she stepped into the chief's office, knowing he'd spoken the truth. Small towns and gossip, indeed.

The chief stood up and offered his hand to the both of them. "Casey. Miss Regan."

"It's Kirby."

"Kirby." He gestured to the two chairs facing his desk. "I'm sorry about the theft of your truck. I've already contacted the state police with the description and license number. Since it's an out-of-state plate, it should be easy to locate. Were there any valuables in the vehicle?"

She nodded. "I left a gold chain with a locket hanging on the mirror."

At his questioning look she pressed her hands together so tightly in her lap the knuckles were white. "The locket holds a picture of my parents. It's special to me, and I didn't want to wear it while I was hiking. When I realized it was around my neck, I took it off and hung it on the mirror, intending to put it back on when I returned from the hills."

Noble made a note of it before asking, "Anything else?"

"Nothing of value. Some loose change in a cup holder."

"How did you happen to park your truck in that location?"

"I let my GPS decide for me. When I reached the lookout, it told me the road ended there."

He managed a quick grin. "So it does. After that, it's just foothills and mountains. Did you begin your trip there from the office, or from home?"

"My apartment. Why?"

Noble Crain steepled his fingers and lowered his head before asking, "You told me you've rented an apartment above Myrtle Fox's bakery. Did you stop there on your way here?"

The question caught her off guard. "No. We came

directly here from the lookout when we discovered my truck missing. Why?"

"Since you used your truck's GPS from home, that would mean that anyone who plugged in a location would know where the truck's journey began." He gave her a long, steady look as his words began to sink in. "And if he had control of your means of transportation, he could be fairly certain you wouldn't get home before he did."

"My apartment...?"

"The thief may have paid a call." He got to his feet. "I'll go with you."

They were less than half a block from Myrtle's Bakery and the apartment above it.

Leaving their vehicles behind, they walked the short distance. As they climbed the stairs at the back of the building, the chief held out his hand for the key. Kirby handed it over and waited with Casey as Chief Crain inserted it in the lock. Before he could unlock it, the door opened.

Noble Crain lifted his hand, palm up. "You may want to wait a moment, Kirby, while I look around."

As he stepped into the apartment, Kirby gave a little gasp. From her vantage point she could see the mess inside. Every door and drawer in the tiny kitchen had been left open. As she moved further into the room, she could see into the cramped sitting area, where the sofa cushions had been slashed open. In her bedroom, the bed linens had been tossed aside and the mattress upended and slashed, with stuffing tossed about everywhere.

The closet doors were ajar, and every article of clothing had been torn from hangers and strewn about the room. Coat pockets were turned inside out. The drawers of a small chest had been removed, their contents dumped unceremoniously about.

Seeing the stricken look on her face, Casey put an arm around her shoulders and led her away from the rooms and out onto the landing just outside the apartment.

She'd been holding herself together by a thread. The minute Casey's arms went around her she crumpled and allowed the tears to fall. Tears of rage, of horror, of shock. Once started, there was no way to stem the flow. Her body shook with bitter tears, weeping until they'd run their course.

When she finally pushed away, Casey handed her his handkerchief.

"Sorry." She wiped at her eyes and blew her nose.

"Don't be. This has to be a shock."

She nodded. "I was so angry about having my truck stolen. But this—" she swept a hand to indicate the chaos inside "—this is personal. A thief went through all my things." A shudder passed through her at the thought of some stranger opening drawers and cupboards, touching her things, tossing them aside like so much trash. She began to cry again, softer now, as she struggled to compose herself.

"You have every right to be mad, Kirby. I'm mad, too."

The chief stepped out onto the landing. "I'm sorry, Kirby, but I'm going to ask you to look around and see if you can think of anything that might have been taken. I know with all the mess in there, it won't be easy."

With his hand beneath her elbow he helped her navigate around the littered floor, allowing her to take her time looking. After nearly half an hour she said, "My laptop is gone. It was sitting on top of my desk. And some antique picture frames..." As her voice trailed off, a little wobbly, Chief Crain saw her looking sadly at the old, torn photos of a man and woman in clothes from the turn of the century.

"Grandparents?"

"My great-grandparents. My uncle told me the picture frames were handmade by my great-grandfather. Like my locket, they have no value except to me, but they can't be replaced."

"Anything else you can think of that could be missing?"

She sighed. "My bank book and a credit card were in my top dresser drawer. They may be in that pile of clothing, but if he saw them, I'm sure he took them. And a little satin case of my mother's jewelry. I've had it since I was a kid."

With each pronouncement, the chief made a note. Finally he steered her back to the landing, where Casey had patiently waited. "I'm sorry to tell you this, Kirby, but I'm going to ask you to stay away from here until I can have the state police assist in getting any evidence they can. Prints. DNA. There's a good chance that after he stumbled upon your truck, he came here hoping to get enough cash and valuables to get as far away as possible." He looked truly contrite as he added, "When they're finished, I'll ask Myrtle Fox to call her insurance agent about compensation for the cleanup, and installing new locks."

Kirby was shaking her head. "I'm new here in town. I have no family. Where am I supposed to go?"

Before the chief could respond Casey spoke up.

"That's not a problem, Noble. Kirby will stay at our ranch until this is resolved."

"But I—"

He gave a quick shake of his head, cutting off her protest. "My family will have my head if I don't bring you back."

Noble gave a smile of satisfaction. "And that's a fact, Kirby. The Merrick family is like that. They're good people. You can trust them to make you feel welcome."

"But I've already overstayed—"

Casey took her cold hand. Now that the shock of processing all that had happened was setting in, she was actually trembling. "I'll call them. The minute they hear what's happened, they'll insist that you come and stay at the ranch. And after I call them, I'll take you to your office. Your boss has a right to know what's going on."

She stared down at her foot, tapping a nervous tattoo, her mind in turmoil.

On the one hand, she resented the fact that her hard-won independence had just been snatched from her. She felt like Alice falling down a deep, dark tunnel, wondering what sort of craziness was awaiting her at the end. On the other hand, she was so grateful that Casey was here during this terrible tumble, to offer aid and comfort as she crash-landed. At least she wasn't alone in this crazy mess.

Noble Crain watched the play of emotions on her face. He'd seen it before, whenever an innocent was thrust into a situation completely out of their control. "I have your cell phone number, Kirby. As soon as the state guys have finished, I'll share all the information

I have with you. Hopefully, by then, we can recover your truck and identify the thief."

"Thank you, Chief." She paused. "Is it all right if I take some clothes with me?

At his nod of approval she returned to her apartment and gathered up several changes of clothes, stuffing them into an overnight case she found tossed in a corner of the room.

As she and Casey descended the back stairs behind the police chief, she felt Casey's hand at her back, and shivered slightly.

When he led her toward his truck, she thought again how she would have handled all this alone.

Alone.

It wasn't the first time she'd had to deal with life's troubles on her own. But her uncle, bless him, had stepped in and taken her under his wing, making her feel safe and loved at the most vulnerable time in her life.

And now, though she didn't want to dwell on it too deeply, she'd happened upon another angel, Casey Merrick, just as her life had begun to unravel.

Fate? she wondered. Or sheer luck?

At the moment, she was too overwhelmed to sort it all out.

Casey opened the door to his truck and settled her inside before turning to shake the police chief's hand. In tones she couldn't hear, the two men carried on a brief conversation.

Casey met the chief's narrowed gaze. "You think it's the convict?"

Noble Crain arched a brow. "Despite scouring the

countryside, there hasn't been a trace of him. It makes sense, if he's the one who got hold of her vehicle. He might have made it out of Wyoming, and even out of the country. I'm sure, since it has out-of-state plates, we'll find it abandoned somewhere in exchange for something less traceable. Right now, it could be in some rancher's barn where a battered old truck is missing. But that could explain why our teams couldn't find as much as a footprint in the snow. I'd say Miss Regan is damned lucky she wasn't still inside her vehicle when he came across it. A man that desperate would have had no problem eliminating her for her wheels."

"Sooner or later she's bound to come to the same conclusion."

Noble nodded. "Right now, she's feeling lost and confused and angry and sad over all this. She's been personally violated. I figure there's no sense adding to her misery. But you're right. In the next day or so it will dawn on her that with the theft of her truck, the vandalism of her apartment, and a desperate escapee, she's lucky to be alive."

Casey climbed up to the driver's seat before giving Kirby a warm smile. "Okay. Let's stop by your office and bring your boss up to speed."

She pointed toward the end of Main Street. "We could have walked. It's just up there."

He winked. "I don't mind driving. This will give you a minute to gather yourself." He closed a hand over hers. "Now breathe."

She gave him a sideways look. "Yes, sir."

He softened his words with a sexy grin that did strange things to her heart. "Doctor's orders."

"Is that what you tell your patients?"

He chuckled. "Yeah. And the funny thing is those damned cows and horses never listen to me."

She couldn't help laughing along with him.

Content that he'd eased her burden, at least for the moment, he put the truck in gear and headed toward her office.

CHAPTER NINE

Casey parked outside the small string of buildings that shared space with an insurance agency and a local Realtor.

He looked at Kirby, relieved to see that some of the color had returned to her cheeks. "Are you okay to do this?"

She took in a breath. "I'm fine."

He stepped out of the truck. Before he could circle around to open her door she'd already gotten out and started toward the office, moving determinedly ahead of him. Taking this as a cue to step back, he trailed behind her as she entered her office, and noted that her limp was more pronounced, probably due to all the tension.

"Hey." A man holding a cell phone to his ear turned with a smile. He waved a hand and said a few more things into the phone before setting it aside to hurry toward her. "Glad to see you survived the storm."

"Me too." Kirby turned to include Casey. "Dan Morgan, this is Casey Merrick."

"Nice to meet you, Casey." Dan offered a firm handshake while giving him a long look. "I've heard of the Merrick family. I hear you go way back around these parts."

"Four generations." Casey smiled. "And still going strong. How about you, Dan? Are you from around here?"

"My folks have a place in Oklahoma." He smiled to soften his words. "I know you and your family are all ranchers. I tried my hand at ranching. It wasn't for me."

"It's not for everybody."

"An understatement." Dan turned to Kirby. "I noticed you favoring your right foot when you came in."

"And I thought I was hiding it so well."

"Something happen during the hike?"

"Yeah. I took a fall in the dark and sprained my ankle."

"Have you had it x-rayed?"

She shook her head.

"Then I suggest you make a stop at the Devil's Door Clinic. If anything happens on the job, it's fully covered. But I'll need signed forms from the doctor to submit to headquarters."

She nodded. "Okay." She swallowed before going on. "When Casey drove me to the lookout to pick up my truck, it was gone. Stolen. I just met with Chief Crain, and he's already filed a report with the state police."

"Wow." Dan shook his head. "I'm sorry. This has not been a very warm welcome as you start your new job. I hope you're not regretting your decision to come to Wyoming."

"Of course not. But there's more."

At his arched brow Kirby took a breath before saying, "Apparently the thief used my truck's GPS system to figure out where I live. The chief accompanied me to my apartment and it had been torn apart. There wasn't a single thing left in there that he hadn't shredded."

"Hey." Hearing the pain in her voice, her boss put a hand on her arm. "That's a whole lot of misery to come back to. Again, I'm really sorry, Kirby. Have you got a place to stay?"

"Casey has invited me to stay with his family. It's where I went after my fall."

"Good." Dan looked past her to Casey. "That's generous of you and your family." He returned his attention to Kirby. "Look, you need a few days to sort all this out. Why don't you stop by the clinic and have that ankle x-rayed? Then deal with finding new wheels and cleaning up the mess in your apartment. And when you get the all clear from the doctor that you're able to work, and the pressure of what to drive and where to live gets cleared up, we'll go from there."

"But the herds of mustangs—"

He held up a hand. "They'll still be there when all this blows over. Besides, until we get word that the convict is back behind bars, none of my field operatives are going near those hills, so take some time for yourself. According to your files, you have paid vacation due."

"Dan, I can't thank you enough for understanding."

"Life happens." He gave her a reassuring look. "Besides, I'm thinking this will give us a chance to try something new when you're back on your feet."

"New?"

He nodded. "I just sent DC a request to authorize the purchase of a drone." He gave her a steady look. "I got the idea when I read in your file that you're qualified to operate one. Just how much experience have you had with drones?"

"No field experience. But I passed the qualifying test to operate them."

"That's more than I can say for anyone else on my team. I figured I'd send a request for purchase and hope for the best. Hopefully I'll get the okay and then as soon as our new piece of ultraexpensive equipment arrives, we'll test it with you in charge and see how well it works. You may be able to count those mustang herds from a nearby hill, without ever having to hike to the high country again."

When his phone rang, he reached for it and studied the caller ID. "I have to take this. Why don't you head over to the clinic, and then get settled at the Merrick ranch? I don't need to see you back here until I hear from DC. Agreed?"

Kirby nodded. "Sounds good. Thanks, Dan. I'll let you know what the doctor says."

He waved a hand to Kirby and Casey before speaking into his phone. "Association of Land Management. Dan Morgan here. How can I be of help?"

When they got back to the truck, Casey opened the passenger door and guided Kirby in. Once he'd settled in the driver's side, he looked over at her.

Kirby leaned her head back and exhaled slowly.

"Feeling better now?"

She managed a smile. "Much. With all that had gone wrong, I was so afraid my new boss was going to regret hiring such a loser."

"And now he knows he's hired a winner. Not to mention the only one on staff who can operate an expensive drone. That's bound to earn you points."

Her smile grew. "Yeah. Who knew it would come in handy?"

Instead of starting the truck, Casey returned her smile. "I like your boss. And I agree that it's time to pay a visit to the clinic. Dr. Peterson should take a look at that ankle and see if it's healing properly."

"Okay."

"And then..." He turned the key and backed out of their parking slot. "Maybe while Ben Harper's loading supplies in the back of my truck, you and I can grab some lunch at Nonie's. A cold longneck and some hot chili. What do you say?"

Her smile matched his. "I like the way you think, cowboy."

They were both laughing as he drove toward the Devil's Door Clinic.

Jenny Swan, Dr. Peterson's efficient assistant, entered the consultation room where Kirby and Casey waited.

"The doctor will be here in just a moment."

Kirby was jiggling her good foot, the only sign of nerves. "I figure he'll just give me a prescription for pain before sending me on my way."

Just then the doctor walked in and immediately took Kirby's hand in his. Looking into her eyes, he gave her a gentle smile. "I've met some strong women in my life. My wife, bless her, was one of them. She could carry a baby at her hip while cooking supper, and clean up the kitchen afterward, still carrying that wiggling child like he weighed nothing at all." He glanced across the room at his assistant, who nodded in agreement. "But you take the cake."

At Kirby's look of confusion, he patted her hand.

"This is my way of saying that the X-rays show that the sprained ankle you've been walking on would have sent most of us to our beds."

"Is there a problem with it?" Kirby looked at Casey. "I thought...that is, we both thought I'd soon be free of pain."

Dr. Peterson shot a grin at Casey. "I bet this young lady told you it was getting better, and you never thought to argue."

Casey shrugged. "You're right. But then, animals are my area of expertise, not humans."

Kirby was quick to defend him. "Actually, he'd been busy treating an injured mustang during a raging blizzard, and on top of that, we had to deal with an escaped convict said to be in the area, and then an avalanche. So Casey might have been just a bit distracted to worry about something as simple as a sprain."

Dr. Peterson merely smiled. "It wasn't simple. In fact, it was a hairline fracture. Fortunately, there seems to be no further damage from all the walking you've been doing. The wrapping Casey applied might have helped hold the foot rigid enough inside your hiking boot that the swelling is going down nicely and the tiny fracture is mending. But to ensure that it continues to mend, I'm going to give you some rules to follow."

"Rules?"

He began carefully wrapping her ankle. "Minimal walking, and only while wearing this soft walking boot." He motioned toward the boot his assistant was holding. "Ice when you can. Soothing baths. And whenever you're sitting down, elevate that leg." He accepted the boot from Jenny and showed Kirby how to fasten the Velcro strips. "Not too tight. Not too loose. Got it?"

Noting the way her smile faded he added, "I'll see you back here in a week. If the healing continues, I may ease up on the rules a bit."

She took in a breath. "Thank you, Dr. Peterson."

"You're welcome." He turned to his assistant. "Jenny will give you a printout of everything I've told you, as well as a prescription for the pain if you need it. And one more thing." He looked toward the hallway. "Avery. In here."

They all looked up as Brand's wife, Avery, paused just inside the doorway. "Kirby, I assume you've already met Avery Merrick, Brand's wife."

Kirby nodded. "I didn't realize she worked here."

The doctor exchanged a smile with Avery. "Since her marriage to Brand, I keep wondering how we got along without her. Folks here in town used to drive more than thirty miles to see a physical therapist. Now we have our very own." He smiled to soften his words. "And you'll be glad of it. I told Avery what I'd seen on your X-rays and that I might need to prescribe a little physical therapy when your ankle heals. But only if you have any problems."

Avery squeezed Kirby's hand. "I'm glad it wasn't anything more serious, though Dr. Peterson said it must have caused you considerable pain. You'll let me know if I can help, once you're out of that boot?"

Kirby nodded, looking slightly dazed. "Thanks, Avery."

"You're welcome." She kissed Casey's cheek before turning back toward the door. "See you guys. I have a date with a patient out at his ranch."

A short time later, Kirby was wheeled through the sliding doors in a wheelchair pushed by Jenny Swan just as Casey was pulling in to a spot in front of the clinic.

Casey helped Kirby into the truck. "Still up for a cold longneck and some hot chili at Nonie's?"

"More than ever."

As he drove, Kirby rested her head against the seat and closed her eyes. So far this day had been nothing but bad news. How she yearned for something good.

She felt the strength of Casey's hand as it closed over hers. Opening her eyes she looked over at him. Her poor battered heart took a sudden dive, and she found herself smiling in spite of her fears.

"While you were being x-rayed, I talked to my family. The minute they heard about your troubles, Gram Meg insisted you come and stay with us."

Kirby felt warmth spread through her like a soothing balm. "Have I told you how amazing your family is?"

Casey nodded as he backed his truck into a loading dock at Tremont's Grain and Feed. "Yeah. They're pretty special."

He parked and turned to her with his best imitation of an old movie cowboy. "Here we are, little lady. I'll leave my truck here and we'll head across the street. You're about to experience the best thing the town of Devil's Door has to offer. I hope you're prepared for the experience of Nonie's Wild Horses Saloon. Or as we like to call it, cowboy heaven."

She was still laughing as he rounded the truck and lifted her out of her seat. Instead of setting her on her feet, he continued carrying her across the street and through the door, where he stood a moment, allowing them both to adjust to the dim lights, the smoky interior, and the sound of the jukebox cranked up to an ear-splitting volume.

Before he could set her on her feet, a pretty woman who looked more like a nursery school teacher than a saloon owner sauntered up. She wore a prim white blouse and black tailored slacks. Her short auburn hair was curled softly around a face with minimal makeup, warm blue eyes, and a welcoming smile. "Casey Merrick, I hope that sweet young lady in your arms is here willingly, and not being carried in against her will."

He turned up his megawatt smile. "Nonie, you get prettier every day."

"And you get more charming, Casey." She eyed Kirby, still being held easily in his arms. "Who's your friend? Or should I say 'prisoner'?"

"This is Kirby Regan. She's new to town, so you'll want to make a good impression on her."

"Don't I always?" She smiled at Kirby. "Regan? Any relation to Frank Regan?"

"My uncle. He used to bring me here when I was little."

"Of course. Kirby. I remember. I'm sorry for your loss."

At her words Kirby swallowed hard.

"How Frank doted on you."

That had the smile returning to Kirby's eyes.

"Welcome back home. Are you just passing through, or are you thinking about staying?"

"I'm hoping this will be permanent. I took a transfer from the DC office of the Association of Land Management back to my home state of Wyoming."

"I'm not surprised you've come back." Nonie glanced around and spotted an empty booth in the rear of the room.

Indicating that Casey should follow her, she led the way, all the while continuing her conversation with Kirby as though it wasn't at all strange that she was being carried in Casey's arms. "Most folks who thought they'd like to see Wyoming in their rearview mirrors usually end up coming back home, and are so happy to do so."

Kirby took advantage of a break in conversation and leaned close to whisper into Casey's ear. "Isn't she going to ask why you're carrying me?"

He was grinning from ear to ear. "What makes you think I don't carry in all my women this way?"

She gave a little giggle and was still laughing when they reached the booth. Casey paused to set Kirby on the empty seat before sliding in beside her.

Taking that as her cue, Nonie slid onto the seat across from them.

"Now then." She glanced around, as though checking if anyone was near enough to overhear. When she leaned across the table, Kirby was certain she would ask about why she wasn't walking.

Instead, Nonie turned to Casey. "How's your daddy these days?"

Casey reached across the table and took Nonie's hand in his. "He's still the same. Working hard. Playing even harder. And as far as I know, still alone." He winked at her. "Anything I've missed?"

Nonie slapped his hand playfully. "That's enough for now." She paused before adding, "At least the alone part. He doesn't need to be. There are...some ladies in this town who wouldn't mind keeping him company."

"Anyone I know, Nonie?"

She got to her feet, suddenly all business. "What'll you two have?"

Casey exchanged a look with Kirby before saying, "Two cold longnecks, and two bowls of your hottest chili."

She turned to Kirby. "You letting this cowboy order for you?"

Kirby couldn't help laughing. "Is there anything else you'd rather recommend?"

Nonie gave a shake of her head. "My chili's the best thing on the menu."

"Then I'll have what he ordered."

"Done."

As Nonie walked away, Kirby looked at Casey incredulously. "She still hasn't asked why you carried me in."

"Told you." He closed a hand over hers. "And here you thought you were the first. You should just be glad you're not built like Georgia Preacher. I had to toss her over my shoulder like a sack of Georgia peaches. It was that or order a honey wagon, but then I'd have had to wheel her back out after she polished off three bowls of Nonie's chili."

"You're making this up."

"You don't believe there's a girl named Georgia Preacher here in town?"

"If there is, you never carried her into this place the way you just said."

He sat back with a satisfied grin. "You can ask Nonie when she comes with our order."

Kirby shook her head. "The way Nonie looks at you, she'd probably swear to any lie you told."

He merely smiled. "That's nothing compared to the

way she looks at my dad whenever he comes in here. You'd think he was the best thing on the menu."

They were both chuckling as Nonie returned with their drinks, two bowls of steaming hot chili, and all the trimmings. There was a little bowl of chopped onions, a bowl of grated cheese, and two separate hot sauces, one marked HELL HATH NO FURY and the other marked DON'T EVEN ASK, as well as a basket of crackers.

With sighs of pleasure, they clinked their bottles and took long pulls of cold beer before digging in.

CHAPTER TEN

Nonie settled onto the bench across from them and sipped from a tall glass of water.

Casey looked around between bites. "Looks like business is good, Nonie."

"It's picked up some since the snow. The minute we get a storm, folks think about hot chili and a burger on the grill."

"Nothing wrong with that."

She smiled. "Nothing at all. When I first heard about that escaped convict, and the order to shelter in place, I worried that folks around here would lock their doors and stay put. But after a day or two, I guess they were suffering cabin fever. With each passing day business has just gotten better and better."

Casey nodded toward the identical twin servers with long blond hair falling straight past their shoulders, wearing snug denims tucked into tall boots and T-shirts that read: FOR THIS I WENT TO COLLEGE. They were kept busy moving between tables delivering plates of burgers and fries, bowls of steaming chili, and trays of longnecks. "That has to make Gina and Tina happy."

"You bet." Nonie beamed as she watched the two young women laughing and talking with the customers.

At a signal from one of them she slid from the booth. "Okay. I knew this wouldn't last. Back to work." Before leaving she said, "If you want anything more, just give me a holler."

"Will do." Casey gave her a thumbs-up as she walked away.

Kirby glanced at the two pretty servers. "Her daughters?"

Casey shook his head. "Her nieces. Her brother's girls. He and his wife died when the twins were five. Nonie took them in and made a home for them. They're in their last year of college now. They take online classes so they can help out with the lunch and dinner crowd, but Nonie's determined that they take their final semester in Laramie so she can watch them receive their degrees with the rest of their graduating class."

"That had to be a big commitment on both sides. Nonie took on the care and feeding of the two, and they have to be overwhelmed by juggling work and college classes."

"They're all up for it. But I think raising them was a much bigger commitment than Nonie bargained for."

At Kirby's questioning look he shrugged. "According to my dad, Nonie was engaged at the time. The guy called off the wedding and left town, saying he didn't sign on to raise somebody else's kids."

Kirby huffed out an angry breath. "I'd say Nonie got a lucky break when he left."

At Casey's arched brow she shook her head. "He

sounds like a selfish loser. She's better off without him. Who needs a guy who can't handle a few bumps in the road?"

Casey looked at her thoughtfully. "I never thought about it that way. Most folks in town figure she paid a high price for opening her home to her brother's girls."

Kirby watched as one the girls whispered something to Nonie that had them both convulsing in laughter. She shook her head. "I'm betting she got back every bit as much love as she gave."

Casey followed her gaze and broke into a wide smile. "Yeah. They're as devoted to Nonie as she is to them."

As Kirby and Casey lingered over their lunch, the two girls found time to amble over. "Hey, Casey."

He looked up with a big smile. "Hey, Gina. Tina. This is Kirby Regan."

They both greeted her enthusiastically.

"It's so nice to meet both of you. Casey told me you're going to graduate college this year."

Two heads nodded in unison.

"And then what? Got any plans for the future?"

The two exchanged smiles before Gina said, "Aunt Nonie wants us to go into business for ourselves. But we're not sure we'd ever be happy leaving here. We love working with her."

"Yeah." Tina nodded. "Besides, this place is our second home."

"And that's the best feeling in the world." Kirby arched a brow. "Who knows? Maybe if you stay, you two will use what you've learned to grow this business." She glanced around. "Maybe bring in some live music on the weekends. Open up that high ceiling all the way back to the beams and turn that second story into balcony seating."

Gina's jaw dropped. "We've been talking about that very thing." She peered at Kirby. "Are you a mind reader?"

Kirby gave what she hoped was a witchlike smile. "I'll never tell."

At that, they all joined in the laughter.

A request from a table nearby had the two sisters turning away. "Nice to meet you, Kirby. Maybe someday we could pick your brain. But right now, we need to get back to work."

As they hurried away, Casey put a hand on Kirby's. "My great-grandfather would call what you just did 'planting before harvesting.'"

At her curious look, he explained. "You just planted a seed in their minds. Maybe, if you stick around long enough, you'll see if it grows into something that can produce a good harvest."

"I like that." She met his steady gaze. "How I wish someone would plant a seed in my mind about how to deal with all my losses."

"One step at a time." Casey drained his beer. "Let's pick up the supplies Billy ordered and head back to the ranch. I'm betting my family will have plenty of suggestions on how to move forward."

As they slid from the booth Casey surprised her by once again scooping her up in his arms.

"Hey." She put her hands on his shoulders, attempting to draw back. She went along with it earlier but was unwilling to wrap her arms around his neck again. It seemed too intimate. "I'm not an invalid."

"Humor me." His voice, murmured against her ear, sent an electric current sizzling through her system.

Before she could argue he began threading his way among the tables, and she had no choice but to wrap her arms around his neck and hold on.

"Hey, Casey. What've you got there?"

At the deep voice, Casey paused. "Hey, Ben. This is Kirby Regan. Kirby, Ben Harper. He owns the hardware store and grain and feed store."

"Hello." Her face flaming, she could do nothing more than nod a greeting.

"Just picked her up, did you?"

"Something like that."

"Your order's all loaded."

"Thanks, Ben." Casey moved on until a portly man with a drooping mustache stood in his way.

"'Afternoon, Casey. I see you picked yourself a pretty flower."

"That I did, Wilson. This is Kirby Regan. Kirby this is Wilson Tremont. He is the mayor of Devil's Door."

"Mayor Tremont."

"Just Wilson," the man said with a grin. "'Mayor' sounds too stuffy. Besides, I'd happily resign the job if I could talk anybody else into taking it. Nice to meet you, Kirby."

"And you."

Casey turned away. "See you soon, Wilson."

As Casey strode toward the exit, he heard his name again and turned to see the police chief seated with a couple.

"Noble."

"That ankle giving you some trouble, Kirby?"

She looked down at the police chief from Casey's

arms. "No more than when I saw you earlier. But Casey is convinced I need to be carried."

"I don't blame him one bit. Nothing like having a pretty woman in a man's arms to make him walk taller and straighter." The chief motioned toward his companions. "Kirby Regan, this is Carrie and Ray Spence. They own the new spa in town."

She nodded a greeting. "It's nice to meet you."

Ray Spence couldn't resist the urge to hype his business. "If you're in the mood for a soothing therapeutic massage, Kirby, come see us."

"Thank you. I'll keep that in mind."

After that quick exchange Casey carried her outside and across the street to his truck before setting her in the passenger seat.

Once he settled into the driver's side and turned the ignition on, he looked over and saw the flush on her cheeks. "Something wrong?"

"I feel so silly, meeting all those strangers while being carried like a baby."

"I'm sorry, that wasn't my intention. I just want to make sure you don't reinjure your ankle. But look at it this way. They won't soon forget you. And they won't think of you as a baby, but a babe."

He winked, and whatever complaint she'd been about to voice was forgotten.

After composing herself she thought about the past few minutes. "Do you realize that not one of them asked why I wasn't walking?"

"They were being polite. Besides, I'm sure Chief Crain's lovely wife already told them all about your fall in the hills, the theft of your truck, the trashing of your apartment, and the fact that you're staying at my ranch.

Maryanne considers it one of the perks of her job. She gets the news first and feels it's her obligation to pass it along as quickly as possible. You'd be surprised at how warmly she's welcomed everywhere in this town whenever there's good gossip to share."

He drove from the loading dock and started along Main Street, with the radio cranked up to Willie Nelson wailing about the perils of loving a cowboy.

Kirby found herself singing along as the truck ate up the miles back to the Merrick ranch.

When they parked alongside the trucks lined up by the back porch, Kirby felt a lightness in her heart. All the troubles of the day, which had felt so overwhelming, now seemed to melt away. She was aware that she would have a lot to deal with in the coming days. But knowing she had a place to stay relieved so much of the pressure. Especially since the Merrick family was so easy to be around.

It wasn't, she told herself, because she'd been given a little more time to spend with this easygoing cowboy. But there was something about Casey Merrick. Just being with him, and enjoying that zany sense of humor, and that easy-as-Sunday-morning attitude, had her feeling that no matter what went wrong in her life, it would somehow turn out all right.

CHAPTER ELEVEN

Casey opened the passenger door and reached for Kirby.

Realizing what he intended, she shrank back. "You can't carry me into your house, Casey."

His grin was quick and sexy. "Says who?"

"Your family will think I've been hurt again."

"Not again. Still."

When she assented, he easily scooped her into his arms and carried her up the steps, through the mudroom and into the kitchen, where most of the family was gathered.

The conversation ended in midsentence as soon as they walked in.

Egan was on his feet at once. "Another fall, Kirby?"

"No. It's your grandson's idea of a joke. I told him to let me walk."

"Just following the doctor's orders." Casey crossed the room and settled her in an overstuffed chair by the fireplace. "Dr. Peterson said she should stay off her feet as much as possible." He pulled a footstool close and lifted her two feet onto it. "And to elevate the leg whenever she could."

Meg's look turned serious when she caught sight of the walking boot. "So this wasn't a simple sprain?"

"A fracture." At her look of concern, Kirby hurried to add, "But it's healing nicely—the doctor is just taking precautions to see that it continues to do so. He said in a week or so he'll take another X-ray to determine that everything's proceeding as it should. If it is, he'll remove the boot and allow me to resume normal activities."

"I'm glad he's not taking this lightly." Meg accepted a kiss on her cheek from her grandson. "When I was a young nurse-in-training I saw a lot of simple medical situations go wrong because so many people got impatient and pushed themselves too far, too fast."

Kirby blushed. She knew she was being gently reprimanded.

Bo put a hand on her shoulder. "Casey called and told us what happened with your truck and apartment."

Egan's hand fisted at his side. "That's a heap of trouble for one person, Kirby. I hope you know we're all here for you."

She ducked her head, afraid their kind acceptance would make her embarrass herself by weeping. "Thank you."

Bo reached for a longneck. "Noble Crain considers any crime committed in his town to be a personal insult. I'm sure he'll be working overtime to locate your truck and find out who vandalized your place."

Billy paused beside Kirby's chair. "Hot tea?"

She nodded gratefully and he handed her a steaming cup.

"Thank you." Kirby knew, by the sympathetic smile he gave her, that he was aware of her discomfort at being the center of attention. It only brought more color to her cheeks.

"Well, look who's back." Jonah nudged Brand as they walked into the kitchen. "There's a pitchfork with your name on it hanging in the barn."

That brought a round of laughter from the others, easing the tension.

Relieved to have something else to talk about, Kirby smiled. "I guess I've finally found a reason to thank Dr. Peterson for grounding me."

"Grounding you?" Jonah pounced on the word. "Have you been a naughty girl, Kirby?" He shot a look at his grandmother. "When we were kids and we gave Gram Meg any trouble, she would tell us we were grounded." He lifted his right hand as though swearing an oath. "Worst punishment ever."

Brand and Casey nodded in agreement.

"This feels like a punishment. But the doctor said it's only for a week or so. Just enough time for the bone to heal properly."

"Good." Jonah rubbed his hands together. "And then you can join us for barn chores."

Bo, watching the interaction between Kirby and his three sons, was grinning. "See what you came back to?"

Kirby nodded. "I'd say these three are determined to find a sucker to share the dirtiest jobs around the ranch."

"You got that right. You need to stay in shape for whenever you take over your uncle's ranch." Jonah turned to Casey. "I've been doing as you asked and checking on your mustang. She's still limping, but that wound is clean and healing."

"That's a good thing. Thanks, bro."

Jonah turned to Billy. "Do I have time for a shower before supper?"

"More than enough time."

"Great." Jonah snagged a beer before heading toward the stairs.

Billy looked up from the stove. "Brand, are you and Avery joining us?"

Brand shook his head. "I'm meeting Avery at the Powel ranch. She's working with Jamie until six. We'll grab something at Nonie's before heading back here."

"I heard about Jamie Powel's tractor accident. How is he doing?" Meg asked.

"Healing nicely. Avery and Dr. Peterson think he's doing all the right things. Another week or two of therapy, and he should be good as new." Brand turned to Kirby. "You might want to ask Doc if he thinks you'll need a little physical therapy when that ankle can take your full weight."

"He already suggested it. Avery met us at the clinic."

"See there?" Bo clapped a hand on his oldest son's shoulder. "She's a step ahead of you. But I like the way you were drumming up business for your bride."

"Always." Brand laughed. "Actually, there's no need, Pop. The truth is, Avery's got more business than she can handle. Dr. Peterson suggested she put out a call for some assistants."

"I can understand why." Hammond's remark got everyone's attention. He stared at Kirby. "After I took a fall, I wanted nothing to do with Avery's offer of physical therapy. But that woman made a believer out of me."

Gram Meg nodded. "She did indeed. As I recall, you were convinced that therapy was a waste of your time."

He shrugged off her remark and aimed his words at Kirby. "Just don't push yourself, girl. I know it's hard to take it easy when all you want to do is get back to how things were. But if you follow Doc's orders and give your body time to heal, you'll be glad you did." He paused before changing the subject. "Does Noble Crain think there's a connection between what happened with your truck and apartment, and that escaped convict?"

His words caused a sudden silence.

Casey was the one to answer. "That was his first instinct. He'll know more when the state police check for prints at Kirby's place."

The thought of a team of investigators going through her personal belongings had Kirby's heart lurching. She glanced at Casey, seeing his frown of concern.

As the conversation swirled around her, she found herself hoping with all her heart that whoever had done this was caught, and soon. Hammond's words played through her mind.

I know it's hard to take it easy when all you want to do is get back to how things were.

She'd come home to Wyoming to start a new chapter in her life. And ever since, it had all gone so wrong.

Before she'd left DC her life had been never-ending stress, and she'd grown weary of the schedule, the congestion, the frantic pace of life. She'd allowed herself to believe that if she returned to Wyoming, life would fall into the simple rhythm she remembered from her childhood.

What if she'd been fooling herself, and this was life's way of reminding her that she couldn't come home again?

What if she had just made the biggest mistake of her life?

She looked up as the family burst into laughter, and she realized that Casey had said something funny.

He caught her eye and winked, and she once again felt that crazy reaction she always had whenever they connected.

Casey gave her one last grin before he addressed the family. "I'm heading to the barn to check on my patient."

Kirby drained her tea and willed herself to relax. The very thought of these good people lifted her up.

For now, this evening, she had food, shelter, and friends who would see to her comfort. And she would hear from her cousin Caroline soon and find out when she could take possession of her uncle's ranch.

Her ranch, she reminded herself. With the money she'd saved, and enough hard work, she could one day call the ranch hers.

She would concentrate on only the good things in her life. Tomorrow was soon enough to deal with whatever troubles came her way.

"A lovely dinner, Billy." Meg turned to Kirby. "I think we'll take our dessert and coffee in the great room. Are you up for it?"

Kirby managed a weary smile. "Thank you, but I think I need to lie down."

"Of course you do." Meg looked concerned. "You've had quite a day. The guest room is all ready for you, Kirby."

Before she could push away from the table, Casey was there, lifting her in his arms.

Heat rushed to her cheeks. "Dr. Peterson said I could walk in this boot."

"Humor me." He paused at the doorway. "Save me a piece of that chocolate cake, Billy. I'll be back."

The others called their good nights as he walked away.

With her arms around his neck, and her face so close she could breathe him in, Kirby forced herself to relax in his arms, though it seemed an impossible task. The nearness of this man did strange things to her, speeding up her heart rate along with her breathing.

She tried to keep things light. "Aren't you afraid I'll get used to this?"

Outside her door he turned his face so that his mouth was almost brushing hers. She felt the soft whisper of his breath on her face as his gaze traveled down to her lips, and she was almost afraid her heart would burst out of her chest.

For what felt like an eternity, they shared a heated look before Casey broke the moment, saying, "Maybe you ought to be the one to worry that I'll get used to this. You may never get to walk on your own again."

There was that devilish smile again, melting all her resistance.

He nudged open the door and carried her across the room, placing her gently on the edge of the bed. Without a word he knelt in front of her and began removing her hiking boot from her uninjured foot.

She bent down to stop him. "I can do—"

At that same moment he looked up. "I told you—"

For the space of a heartbeat, they froze. Then, she

brought her hands to his shoulders, unsure if she was going to pull him in or push him away, but he was already moving in. In slow motion they came together in a hesitant kiss.

The minute their mouths touched, everything changed. Though she'd been determined to resist him, her fingers curled into the front of his shirt, aware of the solid flesh she could feel beneath the fabric. Her eyes fluttered closed, and she wasn't even aware of the little sigh that escaped her throat.

The kiss deepened, and Kirby wondered if he could hear the thundering of her heart as it beat a wild tattoo in her chest.

"Casey..."

He drew back, his eyes steady on hers. "I know. I need to go."

She hadn't even known she'd whispered his name. And now that he'd misinterpreted her meaning, she thought about dragging him back for one more drugging kiss, but he was already getting to his feet.

With a sigh of regret she watched him walk to the door.

He turned. "If you need me, I'm—"

She nodded. "I know. Next door."

"Or I could..." He stared meaningfully at the bed.

She managed a throaty laugh. "Not going to happen, cowboy."

"Yeah. That's what I figured. Good night."

When the door closed behind him she fell back on the bed and rubbed a hand over her eyes.

Of all the things that had happened today—her truck, her apartment, the doctor's diagnosis—she ought to be drowning in the depths of depression. Ought to. But

right this minute the only thing that mattered was what
had just happened between her and Casey.

What kind of magic did he possess? How was it
that a simple kiss from that cowboy could lift her
up and make her believe everything would be better
tomorrow?

CHAPTER TWELVE

Kirby limped down the stairs, taking care to keep as much weight as possible off her injured ankle. After a night of solid sleep, she was feeling a renewed sense of purpose.

Though the walking boot made her gait clumsy, she was grateful the injury hadn't been any worse, requiring a cast and a pair of crutches. Today she intended to concentrate on all the good things in her life, rather than dwell on what had gone wrong.

Her apartment would be cleaned. Her truck was insured. She had a sympathetic, understanding boss and, best of all, a place to stay until she could return to her apartment. Or, if Caroline made a decision soon enough, she might even be able move into Uncle Frank's ranch. And best of all, she'd fallen asleep with the taste of Casey still on her lips. That kiss, though fleeting, had done more than anything else to lift her spirits. And, to be perfectly honest, she wanted more.

When she entered the kitchen, she found Liz and Avery sipping coffee, their heads bent in quiet conversation.

"Hey, Kirby." Avery beckoned her over. "Coffee?"

"Yes. Thanks." Kirby accepted a steaming mug of coffee and took a long, satisfying drink. "Oh, I needed this."

The deep rumble of masculine voices could be heard in the other room, signaling the return of the men from their morning chores.

One by one they drifted into the kitchen, making their way to the counter where tall glasses of freshly squeezed orange juice rested on a tray, along with a carafe of hot coffee.

Casey paused beside Kirby, his big hands wrapped around a steaming mug of coffee. His voice was low. Intimate. "How are you feeling this morning?"

Her smile at the sight of him could have lit up the room. "Much better. Thanks to you."

As soon as the family had gathered at the table Billy began passing platters of bacon and eggs, sliced tomatoes from the greenhouse, and a basket of sourdough toast.

Hearing the slam of the back door, everyone looked up as Chet stepped into the room, slapping his wide-brimmed hat against his leg. "Sorry to interrupt your meal. As soon as you all are finished, I'm going to need some help on the South Road."

Hammond looked up. "More snow?"

Chet shook his head. "Ice. Yesterday's sun started a thaw, but then last night's cold made the melted snow slick. We have a truck on its side. We'll need the dozer. And maybe a backhoe."

"Anybody hurt?"

"No. Two of the wranglers were carrying supplies, but they got out without a scratch. I sent a crew up to transfer the supplies to another truck. But we'll need heavy equipment to get that truck upright. And while we're at it, we may as well make some repairs to the road and get a load of sand to cover the ice."

"Do you have time to eat?" Bo asked.

Chet shrugged. "I'll make time." He snagged a mug of coffee before taking a seat at the table.

Meg looked over. "How long have you been out there?"

He flexed his cold hands. "Since sunup, when I got the call."

Hammond remarked, "That's the life of a rancher. Nothing ever happens at a convenient time. I remember back in fifty-nine or sixty, I was hauling a load of feed in a snowstorm, and my old truck went off the road halfway between town and home. I walked miles to my barn and saddled my old plow horse Jenny. Took me until midnight to right that truck, load up the sacks of feed that spilled all over hell's half acre, and make it back home. I was barely asleep when it was time to get up and start another day."

While he reminisced about an incident that had happened more than fifty years before, Kirby listened with rapt attention, loving the image of this lone cowboy taming a slice of wilderness. The others, having grown up hearing Hammond's stories, ate quickly, nodding from time to time without comment. Soon they were draining their coffee and pushing away from the table, deciding among themselves who would operate the bulldozer and who would drive the backhoe.

Casey paused beside Kirby. "Sorry, but this could take most of the day."

"Casey, I don't need a keeper."

"I know. But I feel—"

"—responsible. I get it. I'm a big girl." She touched a hand to his. "I know a thing or two about keeping a ranch going, so go and take care of business."

"Yes ma'am." He grinned, then followed his brothers and Ham out the door.

When the men were gone Meg said to Avery, "What's on your agenda today?"

"I'm not seeing any patients until this afternoon. Liz and I thought Kirby might enjoy seeing Liz's studio." She turned to Kirby. "It's out back in the vehicle barn. Care to have a tour?"

"I'd love to." Kirby got to her feet. "Should we go now?"

"If you'd like." Avery looked at Liz, who nodded.

"What a grand idea." Meg brightened. "Mind if I tag along?"

Without waiting for a reply she linked her arm through her daughter's. "Since this is your tour, Liz, lead the way."

With a wave to Billy, the four women made their way to the mudroom to pull on parkas and boots before heading toward the barn.

Avery took hold of Kirby's arm. "We'll follow a bit slower." She added with a smile, "And since Chet warned of ice, I intend to keep hold of you until we're safely inside. You can't afford another fall."

"Here we are." Liz left the others standing in the doorway of her studio while she flipped switches, flooding the space with light.

"Oh." Kirby spoke the word on a sigh as she took in the bright, airy studio lined with shelves containing hundreds of photographs.

As she began walking slowly along the length of the room, she noted that most of the photos were of the Grand Tetons in full color, showing off the four distinct seasons.

There were herds of deer or wild horses in fields of wildflowers, or surrounded by fiery autumn foliage, while other pictures were in stark relief against a background of endless white snow-clad mountains.

One section of the studio was devoted to black-and-white photographs, which seemed even more dramatic because of their lack of color.

Kirby leaned close to study a portrait of Hammond leading a horse toward a corral. She could see his work-worn hands, the lines etched deeply into his leathery face, framed by a battered, wide-brimmed hat.

"Oh, Liz, this is so beautiful."

Liz crossed to her, and her smile grew as she saw what had caught Kirby's eye. "Ham is one of my favorite subjects."

"I can see why."

As she continued to wander around, she suddenly stopped in midstride to sigh at a photo of Casey kneeling in the mud, tending an injured mustang. This one, in color, exposed a look of tenderness in his eyes as his big hand rested on the horse's neck.

Liz paused, more interested in Kirby's reaction than in the photo. "That was used on the cover of *My Wyoming*. A reporter wrote a beautiful article about Casey, describing him as the local vet who watches out for the herds of mustangs on his family's land."

"I'd love to read it some time."

"I'll find you a copy."

At a little squeal from the other side of the room they looked over.

Avery picked up a box from a worktable. "What are you doing with these old childhood photos of Brand?"

Liz hurried over. "I'm planning on making an album for each of my nephews, starting with their earliest days." She pointed to the three boxes filled with an assortment of pictures. "There are photos from the old Butcher ranch, where Bo and Leigh had settled with the boys. Then later pictures of Bo and the boys back here after the fire."

Seeing the question in Kirby's eyes Liz turned to her mother. "Maybe you'd like to fill Kirby in on the family history."

Meg nodded. "Years ago, the Butcher property adjoined our land. My son Bo and his wife, Leigh, bought it and were building a new house while living in the original one that was more than a hundred years old. We'd all just left after a lovely Sunday dinner with the family. During the night sparks from the chimney ignited some shingles. It quickly spread through the old wood, and though Bo and the three boys escaped, Leigh didn't make it."

"How terrible." Kirby put a hand over Meg's.

"What made it even worse was the fact that Bo believed that the fire might have been helped along by Des Dempsey, whose father owned the bank in Devil's Door."

"Why would Bo think such a terrible thing about the local banker?"

"Des and Leigh were engaged, until Leigh met Bo. When she and Bo married, the Dempsey family let it be known that their banking services were closed to our family. That could mean death to a rancher, who often has to take out hefty loans to operate in hard times. To survive, we've been forced to do our banking in Stockwell, more than fifty miles away."

"Did Bo report his suspicions to the police?"

Meg nodded. "Even though an insurance inspector deemed the fire 'of unknown origins,' without a police force or regular fire department in those days, nothing was investigated, and the incident forgotten by everyone except us. To this day, Bo believes the fire was set by Des Dempsey, though he can't prove it."

Meg blinked to hold back tears. "Bo and the boys were devastated. They moved back to our ranch to recover, but Bo couldn't bring himself to rebuild, so we merged the two ranches into one, and he and the boys continued on here." She sighed. "It was good for them, but also for us. We drew together in our grief, and I believe we've become stronger over the years."

"I'm glad you were able to be here for them. I guess…" Kirby paused, feeling suddenly shy.

"What, Kirby?" Meg caught her hand.

"I guess that explains why you're so good at making me feel welcome. You've had years of experience."

"Indeed." Meg squeezed her hand. "I'm glad you feel welcome. You've been through enough."

"I'd say your family could write the book on that."

The four women shared a sweet bond of understanding as they continued looking over the photos that took up every inch of space in the studio.

Kirby paused in front of a glass case. Inside were several shelves filled with awards, some local, but many more from national and international organizations.

Avery sidled up beside her. "Pretty impressive, wouldn't you say?"

Kirby nodded. "What impresses me the most is that a shy woman like that—" she paused to glance across the room to where Liz and her mother were holding a black-and-white photo up to the light "—can express so much emotion in her work."

Avery gave a soft laugh. "Liz may be shy, but as I've come to know her, I've learned that she's a passionate woman. Especially about her work."

Meg walked over to the two young women. "Have you seen enough?"

Kirby shook her head. "I doubt I'll ever see enough. What a gift your daughter has. I envy her."

Meg put a hand on her arm. "A wise teacher once told me that we're all gifted. Our real purpose in life is to uncover our gifts and use them wisely."

Kirby arched a brow. "I like that. I just hope I live long enough to discover what mine are."

"I have no doubt you will." Meg tucked her arm through Kirby's before turning to her daughter. "Thank you for letting us invade your space, Liz. But I think it's time we get back to the house."

"I'll be along later, Ma. I have a little work to see to here first."

After thanking Liz for the tour, Kirby started toward the house with Meg and Avery.

As the two chatted, Kirby fell silent. Everyone, it seemed, had something they were passionate about. Liz had her photography. Avery was in constant demand for her skill as a physical therapist. Meg's gift was her generous spirit and warm hospitality.

All Kirby could claim was a job. Oh, she liked it well

enough. And was good at what she did. But it certainly wasn't something she was passionate about.

So where was her passion?

"I wonder if the men have cleared that ice."

At Meg's words Kirby blinked.

"I think I'll take one of the trucks up to the ridge and see how they're doing." Avery looped her arm through Kirby's. "Want to go with me?"

"I'd love to."

Avery turned to Meg. "Want to join us?"

The older woman halted at the back porch. "You two go along. After that walk in the cold air, I'd prefer joining Billy in the kitchen for a cup of hot tea." She paused. "That reminds me. As long as you're joining the men, why don't I fetch a container of hot coffee for them?"

Avery nodded. "Good idea. I know they'll be grateful. I'll bring the truck around to the back door."

CHAPTER THIRTEEN

Kirby climbed up to the passenger's side of the truck while Avery took the wheel. Snugged between them on the seat were a giant container of coffee and several disposable lidded cups.

They followed a winding road that climbed steadily past outbuildings and fenced pastures, weaving through stands of evergreens.

"So you were Brand's physical therapist? Is that how the two of you met?"

Avery nodded. "Miss Meg hired me after getting a recommendation from Dr. Peterson. She called our hospital director, and from my name assumed she was hiring a male therapist who would bond with her grandsons and enjoy doing guy things with them for the six weeks of the contract, since the ranch is so isolated."

"Wow. Not a great way to start. How did you handle it?"

"Better than Brand. He was annoyed with his grandmother, and with me for wasting his time."

"From what I see, the two of you found a way around those early problems."

"You wouldn't say that if you'd been at our first meeting." Avery laughed. "It's funny how love can sneak up at the most unexpected time."

As she drove, Avery kept her eyes on the twisting road as she asked Kirby, "What do you think of Casey?"

Caught by surprise, Kirby tried for humor. "Is this a trick question?"

Avery chuckled. "Not really. I'm just asking because he seems . . . so attentive."

"Is that out of character for him?"

"Not at all. At least not with animals. When he's treating one of them, there's a tender side to him that's really touching. But watching him with you, he's . . ." She shrugged, leaving the rest of her words unspoken.

"Are you saying he's not this way with other women? Because he strikes me as a guy who's very comfortable with the opposite sex."

"Oh, he is. Don't misunderstand. A guy as fun-loving as Casey is bound to attract women. But he seems—" another shrug "—he just seems different with you."

"Good different? Or bad different?"

"Definitely good. In fact, he seems pretty intense."

Kirby felt a little tingle of awareness and had to admit to herself that Avery's words had certainly brightened her day. "Thanks for letting me know."

"Don't tell me you haven't noticed the attraction."

"Oh, I've noticed. But I keep telling myself it could all be a game to a guy as sexy as Casey."

"I guess that's something every couple has to figure out for themselves." Avery slowed the truck and pointed. "Here we are."

The damaged truck had already been righted and moved off to one side. As Brand sauntered over, Avery lowered the driver's side window. "Making progress?"

"Yeah, babe." He nodded before opening the door. When Avery shifted over, he slid in beside her.

He brushed a kiss on her cheek and she laughed. "Your nose is cold."

"Sorry. It's raw out there today."

She cranked up the heater. "Can you stay awhile and warm up? We came bearing gifts." She pointed at the container of coffee.

"My hero." He kissed her again before accepting a steaming cup. "I guess I can stay a few minutes. We'll be wrapping things up here soon."

They watched through the windshield as Casey and Jonah worked in tandem to complete the repairs on the slick road. Each time Casey deposited a load of dirt with the backhoe, Jonah was there with the dozer to smooth it out. Chet and Bo manned shovels, tamping down the edges of the road.

After a few minutes Brand opened the truck door and climbed down. "Time to put this job to bed. The guys will be grateful for this." He tucked the container under his arm and juggled the stack of cups. "If you're willing to wait, I'll ride back to the house with you."

Avery looked over at Kirby, who nodded and smiled back at her before responding, "I'll be here."

When the final mound of dirt was in place, both Avery and Kirby stepped out of the truck and joined the cluster of men, who were gathered around hollering words of encouragement or, in Ham's case, shouting orders.

"Over to the right, Jonah. You missed a spot."

The dozer turned and rumbled over the already smooth earth, flattening it even more.

"That's better." Hammond gave him a thumbs-up, and his great-grandson nodded before moving on.

Casey stepped down from the backhoe and ambled over to give a hand gathering up the shovels and assorted tools before stowing them in the back of their truck.

Brand turned to his father. "If you don't mind driving Gramps and Ham, I'll ride back to the house with Avery and Kirby."

Bo nodded in agreement while wrapping his hands around the warmth of the cup. He turned to Avery. "Thanks for the coffee. It's just what I needed."

Casey stopped beside Kirby. "Want to ride back with me?"

She looked past him to the backhoe. "On that?"

"There's room for two. Come on. Life's short. Take a risk." He held out his hand.

With a laugh she caught his hand and allowed him to lead her to the big machine that stood idling.

Casey helped her up to the cab. Though it was a tight squeeze, they managed to fit on the seat behind the control panel.

Kirby looked around with interest. "Pretty fancy. I used to drive my uncle's backhoe when I was in high school. But he didn't have a heated cab."

"Not just heat. This baby has air-conditioning, too."

She shook her head. "All the comforts of home."

"You bet. Nothing but the best for our ranch hands. If we could, we'd add a refrigerator and a microwave, and we could rent it out as a bunkhouse."

They shared a laugh as he began fiddling with levers.

The machine grew louder as the feet that anchored the backhoe to the ground were lifted. Another lever caused it to go in reverse, beeping as it backed away. After a slow turn, it began lumbering across the frozen meadow toward the barns in the distance.

"Want to drive?"

"You'd let me?"

"You said you drove your uncle's."

"That was years ago. And it didn't have even half the dials and controls of this."

"That's all right. I'm right here beside you to make sure you use the right control. I won't let you crash."

"Gee, thanks." With a laugh she took the wheel.

While she steered, Casey wrapped his arms around her waist.

She shot him a look. "Did you just let me drive so your hands would be free?"

"You bet. I'm no fool." He leaned in to press his face to her neck. "You smell good."

When she gave a husky laugh and started to wriggle away, he said, "Both hands on the wheel, woman. You wouldn't want us to have an accident way out here, would you?"

She looked over at him, seeing the amusement bubbling up. "You're a devious man, Casey Merrick."

"So they tell me. Sly like a fox."

"In that case—" she lifted her hands "—I think you'd better drive."

"Spoilsport."

He put a hand on the wheel, while wrapping his other arm around her waist and tucking her up closer beside him. "We'll both steer."

With a laugh she put a hand on the wheel. As the

vehicle moved across the snow-covered ground, she felt deliciously warm and content.

"Jonah and I raced to the equipment barn, but I got there first and grabbed the keys to this baby."

"Why?"

"The enclosed cab. Heat. The old dozer is open to the elements. By now Jonah's—" he paused dramatically before bursting into laughter "—Jonah's backside is a block of ice."

She joined in the laughter.

They were doing nothing more than driving a piece of heavy equipment across a Wyoming field, and she was having the best time.

"What did you do after I left?" Casey nuzzled her ear.

She absorbed a curl of pleasure all the way to her toes. "Your aunt gave me a tour of her studio."

"She did?" He gave her a surprised look. "She must trust you."

"What does that mean? I would think she'd be proud to show off the photographs that have won her so many awards."

"She's proud of her work, but in case you haven't noticed, she's shy about letting anyone into her private world."

"Oh, I've noticed. I was beginning to think she didn't like me." Kirby turned, and realized that their faces were almost touching. "But she didn't seem reluctant about giving me a tour."

"That's a good thing." His gaze was focused on her mouth. "See that lever beside your leg?"

She nodded.

"Pull it back as far as you can."

She did as he directed and the big vehicle came to

a sudden, lurching stop. She arched a brow in silent question.

He gave her one of those irresistible smiles that went straight to her heart. "Now if you'd put your hand—" he took her hand and placed it on his shoulder "—here."

Before she could react, he gathered her close and covered her mouth in a kiss hungry enough to devour her.

As he lingered over the kiss a rush of heat started at her fingertips and spiraled straight to her core.

He lifted her slightly and turned her so that she was straddling him, her body pressed so firmly to his she could feel his heartbeat inside her own chest.

Her arms were around his neck, though she couldn't recall how they got there. She returned his kisses with an eagerness that caught her by surprise.

"Mmm." He hummed with pure pleasure against her mouth. "Now this makes all the bone-jarring work of the past hours worthwhile." He kissed her again, long and slow and deep, before running openmouthed kisses down the column of her throat.

He fumbled with the zipper of her parka. "You're wearing way too many layers. Think you could slide this off?"

Laughing, she managed to get one arm out of the sleeve when a loud rumbling beside them had them both looking up.

Jonah shifted the gears of the dozer, allowing it to idle beside the backhoe.

Two heads whipped around to see him laughing.

Casey's eyes narrowed as he cranked open the window. "Beat it, bro. Go on up to the barn."

"And miss the hottest scene around? Not on your life." Jonah crossed his arms over his chest and leaned back. "Don't let me interrupt. You two have that cab so steamy, it's drifting over here on a wave of heat. Of course, all that steam makes it a struggle to see you."

"And I'm not letting you see anything more." With his hand on the small window Casey called, "Except maybe my fist in your face." He rapped his knuckles against the glass for emphasis before closing it.

Jonah merely grinned.

Kirby couldn't hold back her giggles. "Oh, Casey. You should see your face."

"Don't laugh. It'll encourage him. He thinks he's so funny."

"I can't help it—he is." She pressed her forehead to his, her body shaking with mirth.

"We could try ignoring him. Maybe he'll go away." Casey ran his hands up and down her back, but she only laughed harder, knowing his brother was watching every little movement.

"How can I feel romantic when I know he's watching?"

"He's like a cold shower." Casey gave a sigh of disgust. "Jonah's arrival is about as amusing as a skunk at a barbeque."

Kirby zipped her parka up to her chin and settled herself beside Casey on the seat. At his direction she pushed the lever, sending the backhoe into a lurching forward motion.

Beside them, the bulldozer began inching along, keeping pace with the backhoe.

Casey caught her hand, lacing his fingers with hers. "Think you could give me a rain check on that romantic interlude?"

She chuckled. "Is that what that was?"

"Well, that's the way it started out. Of course, it ended like a comedy, thanks to Jonah." He paused. "How about it? Would you consider a rain check? If we can ever be alone, that is."

She returned his sly smile with one of her own. "I'll consider your offer. In fact, I like your odds, cowboy. If we ever manage to be alone."

CHAPTER FOURTEEN

When the backhoe was parked in the equipment barn, Casey caught Kirby's hand and helped her down.

Beside them, the dozer's rumbling ceased. Jonah climbed from his seat and crossed the barn to hang the keys on a hook along the wall. "Next time we have to go out on one of these runs, I call dibs on the backhoe. I nearly froze on the way here. You two were generating enough heat that you didn't need an enclosed cab."

Casey paused to hang his set of keys up, too. "Sorry about your bad luck, bro." He tousled his brother's hair before dropping an arm around Kirby's waist and starting toward the house. Over his shoulder he called, "You ought to think about giving up writing all alone in that little cabin in the woods, and spending more time doing research at Nonie's."

"That little cabin helped me produce a best seller."

Casey barely paused. "Let's see how that best seller keeps you warm tonight."

Jonah hooted with laughter.

Kirby suddenly dug in her heels and Casey paused beside her. "What's wrong?"

"What did you mean about a best seller?"

"I told you he's a writer."

"You never said he was published."

Casey shrugged. "I guess I thought that went with the territory. His book is the talk of the town. And not just Devil's Door, or even Wyoming. He's a national bestselling author."

"Why haven't I heard the name Jonah Merrick?"

Casey was grinning. "How about J. R. Merrick's book *Overload*?"

Her mouth dropped open. "*That's* Jonah? Your brother is J. R. Merrick?"

"I thought you figured it out."

"I didn't have a clue." She began walking again, feeling slightly dazed.

A minute later, just as Casey and Kirby were heading up the steps of the back porch, a giant snowball landed with a splat against Casey's head.

Jonah taunted, "Let's see if that cools you off, bro."

Casey spun around, brushing away snow. Seeing Jonah's arm lifted to lob another, he nudged Kirby out of the way with a snarled warning and dropped to the ground to gather ammunition of his own.

Kirby watched with growing concern as the two brothers tossed a dozen or more snowballs at one another, hurling vicious oaths that sounded more like soldiers in mortal combat than brothers unleashing pent-up energy. Both brothers looked a mess, with their hair plastered to their heads, faces bright red from a combination of the energy exerted and the cold from the snowballs hitting with deadly accuracy. She debated the wisdom of stepping between them to keep this from escalating into an all-out war.

Before she could do anything, the two were smearing

snow on each other's faces, and laughing hysterically as they slapped shoulders. They walked side by side until they reached her at the top of the steps.

"Good aim," Jonah was saying.

"You too, bro. That last one went right down my neck." Casey opened the front of his parka and shook snow from his soggy shirt.

"Exactly where I aimed it."

Laughing like loons, they stepped into the mudroom, still complimenting each other on their skill.

Kirby observed and listened in astonishment.

Since she'd grown up without siblings, she hadn't known what to expect. But from the fierceness of their snowball fight, she'd expected them to continue the rivalry. Instead, they were practically patting each other on the back.

Men, she thought. She had a lot to learn about them—especially these brothers, who continued to surprise her. Scrapping one minute, laughing together the next.

After a long, hot shower and a change of clothes, Kirby strode into the kitchen and found Bo and Chet standing by the fireplace, each holding a longneck and talking in low tones.

She paused. "Sorry. I didn't mean to disturb—"

"You're not disturbing us." Bo waved her over. "Billy's looking for something in the pantry, but he left a tray of drinks. Help yourself."

She picked up a tulip glass of white wine and noted the loaves of fresh bread still warm from the oven, lined up in a basket on the counter. Something bubbled on the stove and the heavenly fragrance had her mouth watering.

"...going to have to replace that culvert under the road next spring," Chet continued. "But after the work done by Casey and Jonah, it should hold through the winter."

"Good." Bo tipped up his bottle and drank. "Maybe you should put up a notice of some kind along that stretch of road so the wranglers remember to slow down."

Chet nodded. "I'll get at that tomorrow."

Bo turned to Kirby. "So you've driven a backhoe before?"

She arched a brow.

Before she could say a word, he added, "I saw Casey turn over the wheel to you. Quite a compliment, since he rarely allows anyone to drive his baby. He treats that machine like it was made of pure gold."

She knew her face was flaming. He'd seen that? What else had Casey's father seen?

Just then Casey strolled into the kitchen and gave her one of his sexy smiles, sending her heart into overdrive.

His dark hair still bore droplets of water from the shower. His jeans were clean, the sleeves of his flannel shirt rolled to the elbows. Even his boots looked as though they'd been freshly polished.

He reached for a longneck and took a long pull on his beer before saying to his father, "What's this about gold?"

"The backhoe. I was telling Kirby that I've never known you to trust anybody to drive it."

Casey shot her a quick grin. "Kirby's not just anybody."

To cover her embarrassment, she rushed to explain.

"I told Casey I drove my uncle's backhoe when I was in high school. Of course," she added, "it had an open cab and only a couple of controls. As different from that fancy machine out in the barn as flying a kite and thinking that could make me a jet pilot."

Casey touched a finger to her cheek. "Don't sell yourself short, Sunshine. I bet you would've had that sweet machine mastered in a couple of hours."

"In your dreams, cowboy."

The two shared a laugh as Bo and Chet joined in.

By the time the rest of the family had drifted into the kitchen, the talk had turned to the weather, and the fact that more snow was predicted in the coming week.

Casey and Kirby stood sipping their drinks, shoulders touching, smiles filled with secrets as the conversation swirled around them.

"Great dinner, Billy." Casey shoved away from the table, grateful that the meal had finally ended.

Not that he didn't love Billy's pot roast with all the trimmings. Garlic mashed potatoes. Orange-glazed carrots. And those lighter-than-air biscuits. But his blood was still hot from that interrupted scene on the backhoe, and he'd come up with the perfect excuse to get Kirby away from his never-ending family, and hopefully back into his arms.

He turned to Kirby as she got to her feet. "Have you heard from Chief Crain?"

She shook her head. "Not a word."

"Would you like to head into town? On Fridays he always works late, since so many wranglers spend their paychecks at Nonie's. Noble can always count on one or two cowboys drinking too much. He likes to stick around and see that nobody gets out of hand."

His grandmother touched a napkin to her lips. "Why not wait until morning? Kirby can call Noble at his office. Besides," she added, "You wouldn't want to miss dessert. Billy's made your favorite. Black Forest chocolate layer cake."

She looked around the table. "Why don't we take dessert around the fireplace in the great room?"

Egan took his wife's hand. "Sounds perfect, Meggie."

As she and Egan led the way, the others began to follow.

Casey put a hand on Kirby's arm. "I'll leave it up to you. A long, moonlight drive into town, or dessert with the family?"

Before she could answer there was a knock on the door. Everyone paused while Bo hurried through the mudroom and returned moments later trailed by the police chief.

Noble greeted all of them before directing his words to Kirby. "'Evening, Kirby. I hope you don't mind this interruption. I thought I'd bring you up to date on what we've learned."

"Good." Meg gave him her most welcoming smile. "Your timing is perfect. You just saved Casey and Kirby a long drive to town. Please join us in the great room, Noble. I do hope you like Billy's Black Forest chocolate cake."

The chief's smile widened. "I've never been known to turn down an offer to sample one of Billy's special desserts, Miss Meg."

As Casey trailed the others from the kitchen, he

gave a strained smile and watched his evening's plans going up in smoke.

"Hold on." He put a hand on Kirby's arm, allowing the others to go ahead. "Maybe," he whispered, "we'll find time after Noble leaves to check on the mustang out in the barn."

"Didn't you do that before dinner?"

He gave her his most potent smile. "Yeah. But an injured animal can never have too many visits from the doctor and his assistant. Especially if the assistant needs to be carried to the barn and back, giving said doctor the perfect excuse to hold her in his arms."

She laughed aloud as the truth dawned. "Why, Casey Merrick. I do believe you're a very devious man."

"Guilty as charged, ma'am. Does this mean you approve?"

Her smile held a thousand secrets. "I think it would be a good thing, once the chief leaves, to pay a visit to that mustang. Just so she knows we haven't abandoned her, of course."

He leaned close enough to brush her cheek with his lips, sending a shiver of anticipation along her spine. "A woman after my own heart."

CHAPTER FIFTEEN

Noble Crain polished off a generous slice of cake and downed his second cup of coffee while keeping up a steady stream of small talk. It was obvious that he'd had years of experience putting anxious people at ease in his company.

"Billy, I haven't had cake this good since the last time I paid a call here."

The cook smiled his pleasure at the chief's compliment.

Then Noble lamented the weather with Hammond and Egan. Talked crops with Chet, Bo, and his sons, and remarked on a photo of Liz's that had appeared in a recent nature magazine, causing both Liz and her mother to beam with pride.

At last Noble turned to Kirby. "You'll be happy to know that Myrtle has hired someone from town to clean the apartment. She wanted me to tell you that she'll replace anything that was damaged, and she promises that all the clothes that were tossed everywhere will be carefully returned to the closet. She knows that you're renting on a weekly basis, until you can take possession of your uncle's ranch, but she insists she'll need at least another week before you can move back into the apartment. Of course, there will be no rental fee for the time you had to spend away."

"I'm happy to give her whatever time she needs, as long as I can find someplace in town where I can stay."

At once, Meg waved a hand to dismiss her suggestion. "You're not going anywhere. You're like family now, Kirby."

"But it could be another week—"

Meg merely smiled. "I heard Noble. You're welcome to spend as much time here as you need."

"Thank you, Miss Meg."

Kirby shook her head in wonder at so many kindnesses before turning to the police chief. "Between the Merrick family and Myrtle Fox, this is so much more than I'd hoped for. I'll be sure to call Myrtle and thank her."

"Good. Good." Noble Crain's manner turned serious. "Now then. The state police have sent me their report. The fingerprints lifted at your apartment match those of the escapee."

There was a collective gasp. All eyes were on the chief now. Though no one spoke, there was a sudden hum of electricity in the room. Kirby felt it as surely as though sparks were shooting off. Though she'd been warned that the escaped convict was probably behind all of this, it seemed so much more sinister hearing it confirmed by the police chief.

"There's no trace of your truck yet. By now our convict could be hundreds of miles away in another state, and that may be where they'll find your truck."

Noble looked around at the others. "Finding a vehicle

to steal in that stretch of wilderness must have been like a gift to a desperate man. And using the truck's GPS was a real bonus." He turned back to Kirby. "I'm sorry to say the few belongings he stole from your place have probably already been pawned. The authorities will distribute a description of the items in the hope that someone will recognize them and give us a lead."

He crossed the room and took her hand. "I'm really sorry for all your troubles, Kirby. I know it's not the sort of welcome you were hoping for when you returned to Wyoming."

"Thank you, Chief." She took in a breath. "I'll admit it was a shock. But now that I've had time to think it over, I realize how fortunate I am. All he stole were things. And things can be replaced."

"Exactly." He squeezed her hand before releasing it. "Some folks who've been victimized never get to that point. They get stuck in the what-if and the why-me. I'm glad you're able to move on."

Hammond cleared his throat. "So, Noble, have the authorities given the all clear around here?"

The chief nodded. "As far as we know he has no family here in Wyoming. He's Southern-born. Mississippi. Now that the FBI is on the case, they're watching that part of the country, expecting him to try to make contact with relatives or old friends willing to help him with food and shelter."

"That's a relief." Meg closed a hand over Egan's, her eyes crinkling in a smile. "Now my men can feel safe going back into the high country."

Egan brushed a kiss on her cheek. "You mean *you* can feel safe when we go there."

"Exactly."

Their remarks brought smiles to everyone's lips.

Noble got to his feet. "If there are no more questions, I'll head on back to town. Being Friday night, I like to be there in case a wrangler with money in his pockets starts feeling a little too frisky."

With Meg and Egan leading the way, he called his goodbyes to the others before leaving the room.

After his departure the family remained, discussing the excitement of having had an escaped prisoner in their vicinity, and their relief that things could get back to normal.

Finally Hammond got to his feet, stifling a yawn. "Morning comes early. I'll say good night."

As he passed Kirby he paused to give her one of those direct stares. "I'm sorry that fellow helped himself to your things, but like you said, things can be replaced. Good night, girl."

When he left, the others began to follow suit, drifting off to their rooms.

Casey announced to no one in particular, "Think I'll head out to the barn and see how the mustang's doing." With a smile he turned to Kirby. "Maybe you'd like—"

Bo crossed the room and dropped an arm around his shoulder. "I'll go with you. Every time I see you doctoring an animal, I'm reminded that my rebellious son is now an honest-to-goodness veterinarian and it gives me a real jolt of pride and pleasure."

"Thanks, Pop. If you're sure you're not too tired...?"

"Never too tired to watch my son the doctor in action."

"Well then." Casey looked at her. "'Night, Kirby."

"Good night, Casey. 'Night, Bo."

With a last, wistful glance at Kirby, Casey turned away as he and his father headed to the mudroom for parkas.

"That's a nasty wound." Bo leaned on the railing as Casey knelt in the stall and examined the mustang's leg.

Though the animal was still skittish and backed into a corner at the sight of humans, Casey was able to determine that the injury was healing nicely.

"About fifty percent better than when I found her." Casey wiped bits of straw from his hands as he got to his feet. "The antibiotics are doing their job. And it doesn't hurt to have her confined so she can't re-injure that leg. Add to that a healthy diet, and she's soon going to be strong enough to have a good life."

"I'm glad you found her when you did. She probably wouldn't have survived that snowstorm."

Casey nodded and stepped out of the stall to stand beside his father. "If cold and starvation didn't do her in, I'm sure the predators would have smelled the blood and moved in for the kill, knowing she was too weak to fight."

"Speaking of predators..." Bo tucked his hands in his pockets. "I'm relieved that Noble and the state police have given the all clear about that escapee. I'm just sorry he happened upon Kirby's truck. That poor young woman has had her share of misery since coming home to Wyoming."

"Yeah." Beside him, Casey couldn't hide his smile. "But she's stronger than she looks, Pop."

Bo kept his gaze fixed on the mustang. "The two of you looked pretty cozy in the cab of the backhoe."

Casey's grin widened. "Something you want to ask, Pop?"

His father shrugged. "Just want you to remember she's a guest in our home, son."

"A really pretty guest."

That had Bo turning to him with the stern look he'd perfected over a lifetime of raising three young hellions. "Pretty or not, she's to be treated with respect." After a moment of silence he arched a brow. "Now would be the time to say 'yes sir.'"

Casey managed a straight face for another second before his teasing grin broke through. "Yes sir."

Bo made a fist and playfully punched Casey's shoulder. "Okay. I get that she's pretty. And it's obvious to anybody with half a brain that she stirs your blood. But just remember that your grandmother will have your hide if she thinks you're overstepping the line with one of her houseguests."

"So this is all about Gram Meg, right?"

"That woman's like a dog with a bone if she thinks one of her grandsons is misbehaving."

"And what about you, Pop?"

"I'm my mother's son. If she doesn't bust your hide, I'll do it for her." For a moment he managed a stern look before his lips curved into a smile that was so much like his son's, it was like looking in a mirror. "So if you cross her, don't say I didn't warn you."

"Yes sir."

In a perfect imitation of Ham, Bo growled, "Say it like you mean it, boy. And mean it when you say it."

That was all it took for the two men to burst into hoots.

As they turned and made their way from the barn, the frigid night air rang with the raucous sound of their laughter.

CHAPTER SIXTEEN

'Morning, Dan. I hope you don't mind my calling on a Saturday." Kirby prowled her room while holding her cell phone to her ear, watching snowflakes drifting past the window.

Snow in October. And not just a few flakes. The sight of all the snow reminded her of something Uncle Frank used to say to her.

Looks like the angels are shaking a canister of snow up in heaven.

Ever since then, she'd loved snow even more.

Dan's voice broke through her musings. "Not at all. How's the ankle, Kirby?"

"A little better every day. I'm hoping to be rid of this boot as soon as Dr. Peterson gives me the thumbs-up."

"When do you see him again?"

"Early next week. But if you'd like, I could come into the office Monday and do something that doesn't require me to walk a lot. Do you have any paperwork I could handle?"

Her boss's laughter boomed over the phone. "Kirby, you are officially on paid sick leave. That means you don't come anywhere near the office until you get cleared by your doctor." He paused. "Are you still at the Merrick ranch?"

"Yes."

"Sounds like it's starting to feel a little crowded out there."

She chuckled. "Not at all. This place is so big and rambling, it's like being in a hotel."

"Then why are you in such a hurry to get back to work?"

"I guess it's just part of my DNA. I grew up on a ranch. I'm used to hard work. I'm not very good at sitting around being pampered."

"Wait. Are you serious?" He gave an exaggerated, drawn-out sigh. "Do you know how many people would stand in line to be in your position?"

Kirby laughed. "Okay. I get it." She assumed a lazy drawl. "If you need me, I'll be at the spa, having my cuticles oiled."

"That's more like it." He joined her laughter before saying, "Now on another topic, that drone I was hoping for is on back order. Washington said it could be a couple of months before it arrives. In the meantime, since the townspeople have decided that the escaped convict is no longer a threat, and since you're itching to work, you may want to ask Dr. Peterson when he thinks you can resume walking and hiking. Whenever he approves, you can get back to counting the mustang herds in the high country. But only when that ankle is completely healed and ready to withstand a strenuous workout."

Kirby took a moment to consider his words before saying, "I'm not sure if that's good news or bad news. Have you looked out your window lately?"

He chuckled. "Yeah. I see the snow. Welcome to Wyoming."

"I hear you. I'll call you next week after my visit to the clinic."

"Great. And Kirby, once you get cleared to return to work, it could prove to be a long, cold winter. So my advice is to enjoy this downtime. It may be the last you get until next spring."

"Thanks, Dan. I'll do my best to be lazy."

As Kirby disconnected, she caught sight of Casey and Jonah leaving the barn and hunching deep into their parkas as they faced the snow.

Just seeing Casey got her heartbeat racing. Last night, when his father had innocently spoiled an opportunity to spend time with her in the barn, he'd looked as abject as she'd felt. In fact, it would have been comical if she hadn't been so disappointed. Bo had unknowingly ruined the evening for both of them.

Hearing the doors opening and closing downstairs, and the low hum of masculine voices, she hurried from her room, eager for whatever the day brought.

She found Casey and Jonah in the kitchen, drinking coffee.

When she entered the room Casey's head came up. "Hey, Sunshine."

"Hey, yourself. Is it as cold outside as it looks?"

"Colder." He and Jonah shared a laugh. "Looks like we'll have to brave the cold after breakfast and start plowing snow."

Casey wiggled his brows like a villain. "If you play your cards right, little lady, I may let you ride along."

"Only if the snowplow is heated."

Jonah shot her a wicked grin. "I don't think heat is a

problem for the two of you. You generate enough that you don't have to worry about freezing."

"Hey." Casey punched his arm. "If you keep mouthing off like that I may not include you in our plans for later."

"Plans?" Jonah nudged Kirby, and the two of them looked at Casey.

He merely smiled. "I'm thinking it might be a good day to take the afternoon off and head into town. We could have lunch at Nonie's."

He turned when the rest of the family came ambling into the room. "In fact, maybe we could all take a snow day in town."

Bo shrugged. "It's been a while since I took time off from chores."

"There you go." Casey was smiling. "Afterward, I know what Gram Meg will want to do."

At her arched look he said, "It wouldn't be a good day in town for you without making a stop at Stuff."

"You know me so well." Meg laughed. "I was just thinking that it's been too long since I had a visit with Sheila Mason."

"Maybe you should ask Jonah to do some shopping, too." He teased his brother. "Sheila lights up every time she sees you, bro."

Jonah dismissed him with a shake of his head. "If we're going into Devil's Door, I intend to spend some time checking out the new computers at Tech Stop."

Casey nudged Kirby. "Where high tech meets small town."

"Is that their motto?"

He shook his head. "If it isn't, it should be." He looked around. "Is everybody up for a day in town?"

As they took their places around the big table, everyone was nodding, except for Liz, who took her time stirring cream into her coffee.

Even Billy joined in the excitement. "I think it's a good day to visit Ben Harper over at the hardware store and see what's new in kitchen gadgets."

As Liz took her seat Meg put a hand over hers. "How about it, honey? Want to go with us?"

Liz carefully dropped a napkin on her lap, keeping her eyes averted. "Sorry. I can't spare the time. Too much to do in my studio."

"Oh well. Another time." Meg accepted a platter of eggs from Egan and held it out to her daughter before passing it on.

Kirby watched in silence as the family picked up the familiar threads of conversation about the early snowfall, the fact that the plows would be out in full force on the interstate, and all the things they planned on their visit to town. And though she wondered why Liz couldn't spare the time to join them on a rare family outing, she decided it was none of her business.

"Okay, Sunshine." On his way to the mudroom Casey paused to tug on a strand of Kirby's hair. "Time to plow snow. Want to ride along?"

"Sure." She studied the row of parkas and wide-brimmed hats hanging on pegs above pairs of sturdy boots. The shelf above held an assortment of work gloves and woolen caps. "What should I wear?"

"Bring winter gear. Even though it's warm in the truck, you need to be prepared in case we get stuck somewhere and have to walk home."

She shot him a look. "Have you been stuck in snow before?"

He winked. "Often enough that I'm always prepared."

"A regular Boy Scout."

"You got that right." After pulling on a heavy parka he selected a set of keys from a long line of hooks and led the way out the back door.

In the equipment barn Jonah was already climbing into one of the trucks outfitted with a plow. He turned to say, "I'll clear the north ridge. You can take the south."

"Got it." Casey held the passenger door for Kirby before circling around to the driver's side.

Minutes later, with the plow engaged and snow flying past their windows, they moved along the driveway, clearing it as they headed toward the highway.

Casey looked over. "Warm enough?"

Kirby nodded.

As they listened to Patsy's familiar wail about being crazy, he reached over and put a big hand over hers. "Alone at last."

She laughed.

"You may have noticed that around here, with so much family, it isn't easy to get much alone time."

"I've noticed. But they're all such fun, I can't imagine wanting to get away from them."

"Really?" He frowned. "How about last night? By the way, I'm sorry all my well-made plans went up in smoke because of Pop."

"Just what sort of plans did you have?"

"Oh, the usual. Wild, crazy sex in an empty stall, followed by wild, crazy sex in the hayloft."

"Wow. And I had the misfortune of missing all that."

He grinned. "I'd like to make it up to you. How about wild, crazy sex right now in a big old truck?"

"In your dreams, cowboy."

"I figured as much. Your loss, little lady. You don't know what you're missing."

She managed to sound stern. "I'm sure you're dying to tell me."

"I'd rather show you."

That had her laughing, despite her best intentions. "Casey Merrick, you have a vivid imagination."

"I do when it comes to you. We could have had quite a night if it hadn't been for my dad stepping on all my plans."

Her tone softened. "He's so proud of you, Casey."

"Yeah. It's a good feeling, knowing I'm doing something he approves of." He squeezed her hand and turned his attention to the snowplow as it moved slowly and steadily through the mounds of snow, clearing the miles of asphalt from the highway back to the ranch.

Beside him Kirby thought of the traffic jams that this much snow would create in the District. She and her fellow workers would be tied up for hours, while surrounded by anxious, frowning faces tight with worry, and horns blasting while emergency sirens blared.

She hummed along with Patsy and realized that she was doing nothing more than riding in an old truck and having the time of her life. And all because of the fun-loving, sexy cowboy beside her.

And while she was pretending not to notice the attraction, it was growing by the day. He made her laugh. He made her feel special. He made her feel safe.

The unbidden thought was like a bolt of lightning. Even though she tried to deny it, she was, as the song said, crazy, and falling head over heels for Casey Merrick. And not giving a care in the world to the possibility of a painful landing,

CHAPTER SEVENTEEN

With the area plowed, Casey dropped Kirby off at the back porch. "Round up the family and tell them we leave in half an hour."

She nodded and hurried inside.

True to his word, Casey returned from the barn shortly to gather the family for their trip to town.

In the mudroom he tossed a set of keys to his father. "We'll need two trucks, Pop. Brand, Avery, and Jonah can ride with Kirby and me. I figure you can drive Billy, Ham, Gram Meg, and Gramps Egan."

"Great." Bo caught the keys, and father and son headed out to the equipment barn.

Scant minutes later they returned, trucks idling by the back porch, as the family members trooped down the steps and climbed aboard.

Brand and Avery settled into the back seat and snuggled close, while Jonah sat in the front beside Kirby. As she moved closer to Casey to make room, their shoulders brushed, and they exchanged a quick smile.

"Okay, bro." Jonah fastened his seat belt. "Let's stir up some dust in Devil's Door."

From the back seat Brand chuckled. "The only thing we'll be stirring up today is snowflakes."

Avery tucked a hand in Brand's. "It isn't even officially winter yet, and I'm already tired of all this snow."

Jonah looked over his shoulder. "Haven't you ever had snow in October back home in Michigan?"

"Probably. But I doubt that we've ever had this much."

Brand kissed the tip of her nose. "Don't worry, babe. You're going to learn to love all this snow. And remember, I'll always keep you warm."

That had Jonah groaning. "You know what I think about all that lovey-dovey stuff? I should have gone in the other truck."

Casey was grinning. "Not a bad idea. You'd fit right in with the old geezers."

Jonah hooted. "If Pop heard you call him a geezer, he'd blister your hide."

"With one arm tied behind his back," Brand added.

After joining in their laughter, Casey nodded. "You're right about Pop. Not only could he beat any one of us in a fight, he's still got that thing with the women."

Kirby blinked. "That thing?"

"Sex appeal. You'll see how the women in Devil's Door flock around him whenever he comes to town."

"Especially Nonie." Jonah winked at Kirby. "Everybody thinks her boyfriend left her years ago because she took in her brother's twins. But I've always suspected she was the one who tossed aside her boyfriend because she had a crush on Pop, and still does after all these years."

"Wow." Kirby laughed. "Romance and drama in a small town."

Brand shared a smile with his bride. "When it comes to love, there's no difference between small towns and big cities."

Avery sighed and squeezed her husband's hand. "I can attest to that." She brushed a kiss to his cheek. "And I'm so thankful for the love I found in this small town."

Jonah lowered his window and pretended to suck in gulps of frigid air. "Man, after all that gooey sugar I need to fill my lungs."

They were all still laughing as they arrived at Devil's Door and rode slowly along Main Street.

Their first stop was the grain and feed store. After backing into the loading dock, the men went inside to fill out an order and arrange for it to be loaded into their trucks while they were busy in town.

The women strolled along the Main Street sidewalk, knowing the men would find them when they'd finished with their business.

As predicted, Meg led them directly to Stuff. As they stepped inside, Sheila Mason looked up from the counter.

"Miss Meg." Her smile brightened. "How nice to see you in town."

"Sheila. How have you been?" Instead of a handshake, Meg gathered the young woman in a warm hug, which was affectionately returned.

"I'm just fine. Thank you."

Meg turned to include the others. "You know Avery. Have you met our houseguest, Kirby Regan?"

"It's been years. You used to come in here with your uncle." Sheila paused. "I'm sorry for your loss."

Kirby nodded. "Thank you." She looked around. "You've made some changes since I was here years ago."

"Mostly cosmetic. Are you back for good?"

"I am. I'm hoping to take over my uncle's ranch."

"That's great news." Sheila glanced at Kirby's foot. "How're you doing?"

"Great." Kirby pointed to her orthopedic boot. "Except for this thing, but my ankle is getting stronger every day."

"That's even better news." Sheila hesitated before saying, "Myrtle Fox was in yesterday, and said she's getting that apartment cleaned up as good as new."

Kirby nodded. "Chief Crain told me the same thing."

Sheila looked beyond her to Meg, who went over to leaf through a rack of women's shirts. "Those just came in, Miss Meg. And when I unpacked them, I figured they had your name on them."

Meg chuckled. "You know my style, Sheila." She removed several and draped them over her arm. "I believe I'm going to have to try these on."

Sheila took them from her. "I'll hang them in a fitting room." As she walked away she called, "Feel free to try on anything you like, ladies."

For more than an hour the three women enjoyed themselves trying on a mountain of clothes, exclaiming as each stepped from the fitting room to model her choices for the others.

When the men arrived, they headed toward a back room where Sheila sold an assortment of new and used household items and assorted farm tools.

It was the usual gathering spot for the men of town who were waiting for their women to finish shopping.

A short time later Meg, Avery, and Kirby finished making their choices. On the floor by the counter stood half a dozen large handled bags.

Casey sidled up to Kirby, who was signing a receipt. "I see you got in some shopping."

"Just a little."

"Uh-huh." With a grin he nodded toward the bags. "How many are yours?"

"Just that one. And that one." She pointed. "Oh, and that one."

"Just a little shopping? Looks like you're planning on being the best-dressed rancher in these parts."

She merely smiled. "A girl can never have too many jeans."

"Or boots," Avery added as she admired her reflection in the mirror. She was wearing new jeans tucked into a pair of hand-tooled Western boots.

"Or hats." Meg picked up a black woolen Western hat and perched it on her head. It made a pretty contrast against her white curls.

"You have to have that, Meggie." Egan walked up behind her, wrapping his arms around her waist.

She laughed at their dual reflections before turning to him. "You're right. I have to have it."

With a laugh he walked to the counter and asked Sheila, "What's the damage today?"

"I'll tell you in a minute." She tallied the shirts, along with a pretty, ankle-length blue denim skirt Meg had chosen, as well as the hat.

When Egan read the total and handed her his credit

card, he turned to his wife. "Not a bad day's haul, Meggie. And you're worth every penny."

With a delighted laugh she rewarded him with a kiss on his cheek.

Hammond came out from the back room, holding a magnetic flashlight he'd found. Before he could pay for it, Bo stepped up beside him. "I'll get it, Ham." He set down a pair of sturdy work gloves. "That and these, Sheila."

He dug out cash from his pocket, wrapped in a rubber band.

When Sheila had given him his change, she looked around with satisfaction. "If you folks have other things to do while you're in town, why don't you leave these packages here, and pick them up on the way home?"

Meg spoke for all of them. "How thoughtful of you, Sheila dear. As long as you don't mind, we'd love to." She glanced at the others for confirmation. "I guess we should be back for them in a couple of hours."

At their nods of agreement, she hugged Sheila one final time before they took their leave.

As they left the store, Avery looked around. "Where did Billy go?"

Jonah answered. "He's still in Ben Harper's Hardware. To browse."

"Which always leads to some major buying," Casey added.

Everyone laughed as Casey explained to Kirby, "Billy is like a kid at Christmas whenever he has a chance to shop for the latest kitchen gadgets. The man has drawers filled with things we've never heard of."

Kirby arched a brow. "Like what?"

"Ever see a lemon zester?" Jonah asked her.

She shook her head.

"Or a melon baller? An apple corer?"

She chuckled. "Can't he just use a spoon or a paring knife? Or are you pulling my leg?"

"Swear it." Casey lifted his right hand. "Billy loves crazy kitchen gadgets that nobody has ever heard of."

"But you have to admit," Bo said. "Billy knows how to use every one of them. And I say, if those little things make him happy, they're worth whatever they cost."

"You got that right, boy." Ham led the way, nodding and pausing to lift his hat in a courtly gesture each time he met a woman passing by.

In turn they all greeted him like a long-lost relative, asking about his health, and exclaiming on how fine he was looking.

Kirby, trailing behind the family with Casey, turned to him. "Now I see where you get all that charm. Ham certainly knows how to turn it on."

"When it suits him. Of course, we all know he can turn it off as quickly as he turns it on."

She lowered her voice. "Like a certain cowboy when a stranger points a rifle at him."

"Hey now, I've apologized for the rough intro-duction." He took her hand as they crossed the street, then continued holding it as they trailed behind the others. "I've noticed that you haven't pointed a rifle at me since then."

"Only because you've behaved. But be warned, cowboy. If you should get out of line..."

He held up his free hand in mock surrender while keeping his other hand linked with hers. "Yes, ma'am. I hear you and I don't want to get you riled up."

They shared a laugh as they approached Nonie's

Wild Horses Saloon and Cafe. The yellow-and-orange neon sign was a beacon in the curtain of snow.

When Ham pushed open the big wooden door, it squealed in protest.

He made an impatient sound. "I wish someone would pour some oil on that hinge."

"And stop alerting Nonie that patrons are entering?" Bo clapped a hand on his grandfather's shoulder. "I think Nonie is so used to hearing the squeaking door, she's stopped noticing it."

The old man shook his head. "It just purely grates on my nerves."

Bo leaned close. "Okay, Ham. Next time I'm in town, I'll see that it's fixed."

Hammond nodded his approval before stepping aside to make room for the rest of the family.

As they crowded around inside, Nonie looked up. Seeing them, she set down her tray and hurried over to greet everyone.

"Well, aren't you all looking fine today."

Though she spoke to all of them, she was staring directly at Bo, as he whipped his Stetson from his head and held it in his hand.

"'Afternoon, Nonie. You're looking fine, as well." While he spoke, he turned the hat around and around in his big hands, as though needing something to do while he returned her stare.

For the space of several seconds the two of them merely smiled. Then, directing her words to the others she said, "That table in the middle of the room is just the right size to accommodate all of you. If you'll follow me."

She led them across the restaurant, where they

paused half a dozen times to greet old friends seated nearby.

As Kirby was swept up in the introductions, it became more like a reunion than a simple lunch in town. Everybody knew everybody and seemed genuinely pleased to exchange friendly greetings.

Several of the ranchers called out, "It's good to see you walking, Kirby. Last time you were in here, you arrived and left in Casey's arms."

That had his family turning to stare.

Casey feigned innocence. "We'd just come from the clinic. Doc Peterson warned Kirby to stay off her foot."

Jonah clapped a hand on his brother's shoulder. "How much did you pay the doctor to say that?"

"The advice was free. But I figured I'd get as much mileage as possible out of it."

The two shared a laugh.

By the time the family was seated at their table, additional chairs and place settings had been added, as well as glasses of water and menus.

Billy joined them and hung a small bag on the back of his chair.

Ham noticed. "I see you did some shopping, Billy. What'd you buy?"

"Oh, just this and that." He smiled, clearly savoring the moment before he reached back and opened the bag. "I can't believe my luck. Look what I found."

They all stared at the strange object that looked like a set of huge tongs and a sharp knife.

Ham scratched his head. "What do you call that thing?"

"A vegetable gripper and slicer. Specifically for

tomatoes." At their blank stares he explained, "It's used to hold a tomato firmly in place while making uniform slices." He looked at Nonie, standing by Bo's chair. "I'm sure I don't have to tell you how handy that can be."

Nonie smiled and shook her head. "Sorry, Billy. I've never had an occasion to use a tomato slicer. I just use a sharp knife and don't give a thought to how uniform the slices turn out to be."

"That's how I used to feel about slicing tomatoes. But now, I can use my handy-dandy tomato slicer and have perfect slices every time."

"Let me know how you like it." Nonie gave him another bright smile before returning her attention to the others. "Anybody want a beer or wine before ordering lunch?"

The men ordered longnecks, and the women opted for tea and coffee. A short time later Nonie's twin nieces, Gina and Tina, assisted her in serving the bowls of steaming broccoli-and-cheddar soup along with the special of the day, roast beef sandwiches on sourdough bread, and Nonie's famous coleslaw with wine vinegar dressing.

As the family remarked over the food, Billy fell silent, taking small sips and bites while looking thoughtful.

Seeing him, Meg chuckled. "You're doing it again, Billy."

He turned to her with a quizzical look.

"I see the way your mind is working. You're trying to figure out just what Nonie put into each part of this meal."

He broke into a wide smile. "I didn't realize I was so transparent."

"I'm sure it's a professional hazard. You can't simply enjoy a good meal. You have to dissect every ingredient that goes into it, especially if it's something that appeals to you."

He nodded. "Guilty as charged. I'm already thinking ahead to what I can add to this soup to make it my own."

"And then," Casey said with a grin, "you'll do the same with the roast beef sandwich."

"I've already decided it's the perfect dish for my homemade horseradish," the cook said with a straight face.

CHAPTER EIGHTEEN

During lunch Chief Crain ambled over to their table.

He doffed his hat and greeted everybody before addressing Kirby. "The state police haven't found a trace of your truck yet."

"Is that unusual, Chief?"

He nodded. "We expected our guy to ditch something so obvious for a vehicle that would be harder to spot. So now, the state boys are thinking he may have sold it to a chop shop for some quick cash. If that's the case, it will be untraceable. Those places strip the valuable parts before they cut up what's left into a pile of scrap metal."

Kirby tried to erase the sudden vision of her new truck cut into a pile of rubble.

"Are the authorities any closer to catching this guy?" Ham asked with a trace of annoyance.

"They think so. There have been over a hundred reported sightings of someone who resembles the escaped convict all the way from Chicago to Memphis. And no matter how far-fetched it may sound, they have to investigate every lead." Noble Crain put a hand on Kirby's arm. "I have no doubt he'll be found, and soon, especially since they're showing his photo on TV stations across the country."

At the ringing of his phone, he turned away to glance at the caller ID. "Sorry, folks, it's work. I'll stay in touch."

He walked away, speaking into his phone.

When Nonie passed their table, Casey held out a hand for the bill.

Ham frowned. "I'll get it, boy."

Casey shook his head and took the bill from Nonie. "It's my treat, Ham. Besides," he added with a quick grin, "it doesn't even make a dent in the debt I racked up in veterinary school."

"That was money well spent, son." Bo gave him a warm smile.

"Thanks, Pop." Casey handed several bills to Nonie, saying, "Great lunch, as always, Nonie."

"Thanks, Casey. That means a lot." She angled her head toward Billy, across the table. "Especially knowing I'm being critiqued by an expert."

Billy chuckled. "It takes one to know one, Nonie. My compliments."

As the family got to their feet, Nonie put a hand on Bo's arm. "Don't be a stranger now, you hear?"

"I promise. Now that winter's coming, things will slow down a bit on the ranch, and I should be able to make time for... old friends."

As they made their way to the door, Casey said in an aside to his brothers, "What did I tell you? The old man still has it."

Once outside, Egan turned to Meg. "Ham and I are due for a haircut. Any of you in need of a trim?"

Casey ran a hand through his hair. "Billy always does a great job on my hair."

"He did mine yesterday," Jonah admitted.

"I'm good." Brand turned to his father. "How about you, Pop?"

Bo nodded. "I could use a trim."

Egan turned to his wife. "Why don't all of you head on over to that new sweet shop, Katie's Kitchen, and sample the goodies? Pick up a few of your favorites and then meet us back at Julie's Hair Salon in an hour or two. By then we'll be ready to head back to the ranch, and we can enjoy whatever new desserts you folks pick out for us right after dinner tonight."

Billy chuckled. "Smart move, Egan, since you know I won't have time to do any baking today."

The older man grinned. "You know Ham and I don't like to miss a dessert if we can help it."

"Sounds good." Meg brushed a kiss over his cheek before leading the way toward the new bakery in the middle of town.

Bo, Egan, and Ham headed in the opposite direction, while pausing every few steps to speak to friends and neighbors.

As Kirby strolled beside Casey she couldn't help asking, "Billy cuts your hair?"

"And has since I was a kid."

Beside them Jonah nodded. "In fact, I don't think the three of us have ever had anyone else cut our hair." He turned to Brand for confirmation.

Brand nuzzled Avery's cheek. "Actually, bro, I've been letting my bride trim my hair whenever she thinks I need it."

Jonah put his hand to his ears. "Too much information, big brother. Next you'll be telling me she dresses you."

Brand and Avery shared a smile. "Maybe not so much dresses me as un—"

"That's it." Jonah sprinted ahead, leaving the others watching and laughing.

Jonah held the door to Katie's Kitchen as their group stepped inside. A little bell announced the new arrivals, bringing a pretty young woman out from the back room.

"Hello. I'm Katie Clark. Welcome to my pastry shop."

"Katie, I'm Meg Merrick." Taking charge, Meg introduced the others before saying, "We've been hearing good things about your new shop. Since we're in town for the day, we had to stop by and see it for ourselves."

Katie gestured to a fancy crystal plate atop the counter. "Today's specialty is my chocolate peanut butter bars. Please help yourselves to a taste."

Amid murmured words of approval, the tray was soon empty, as they nibbled the treats while peering into glass display cases containing cakes, pies, cupcakes, and cookies.

Billy pointed to a tray of Italian pastries. "Did you bake the shells of your cannoli, or buy them?"

Katie's voice rang with pride. "I personally make everything that I sell in my shop. Would you care for a taste?"

Billy shook his head. "You can't keep giving away your profits. Let me buy one." After a moment's hesitation he said, "In fact, I'll buy two. One to eat and one to pass around."

He took his dessert to a round table across the room.

Following Billy's lead, each member of their group made their choice and bought two of it. They moved tables together to taste and pass half a dozen different pastries, all the while singing the praises of Katie's treats.

Afterward, Meg ordered a selection of cannoli, éclairs, brownies, and Katie's chocolate peanut butter bars, which everyone had agreed were the best ever.

"Poor Ham doesn't stand a chance tonight," Meg said as she picked up the bag of goodies. "He'll need to take a walk after dinner just to make up for this sugar intake."

They were all in good spirits when they met up with Bo, Egan, and Ham outside Julie's Hair Salon.

Casey caught Kirby's hand. "Come on. I want you to meet Julie and her sons."

Inside the hair salon he introduced Kirby to a dark-haired woman busily trimming the hair of an elderly woman. "Hey, Julie."

Her eyes crinkled. "Hey, yourself, Casey. Who's your pretty friend?"

"Kirby Regan, this is Julie Franklyn, owner of this salon."

"Hi, Julie." Kirby looked around. "What a pretty place."

"Thanks." Julie's smile widened at the compliment. "My sons, Hank and Greg, did the work remodeling this old building."

"This is Greg." Casey introduced Kirby to a handsome young man who was busy trimming a rancher's hair. "And this is Hank." A smiling, younger version of Greg stepped from around the register to offer a handshake.

It was then that Kirby noted his prosthetic hand.

"It's nice meeting you, Hank." Kirby turned to his mother. "It has to be satisfying to work with your both your sons."

"It is."

Hank returned to the register to answer the phone. Greg and Julie continued working while Julie said, "After their father died, I wanted to do something that would offer us the opportunity to earn a living without keeping up the ranch."

Kirby nodded in understanding. "Ranching is hard work. Still, knowing that, I'm really eager to take over my uncle's ranch. Maybe you know of it. Frank Regan's ranch."

"Of course I know of it. I was sorry to hear about Frank's passing." Julie gave her a long look. "I hope you know what you're in for."

"I do. At least I think I do."

"Then I wish you luck."

"Thanks, Julie. It was so nice meeting you. Meeting all of you," she added with a smile for Greg and Hank.

The two young men returned her smile.

Seeing the others waiting for them outside the shop, Kirby called her goodbyes and trailed Casey out the door.

As they made their way toward the Grain and Feed Store where they'd parked their trucks, Casey once again took her hand.

Something about that simple gesture warmed her like nothing else.

She turned to him with a smile. "You certainly have friendly people here in town. Could you tell me about Hank's hand?"

"He picked up some sort of bacteria from Devil's Creek when we were kids. All of us swam there, but something infected an open cut, and the doctors couldn't treat it in time. Hank lost his hand almost to the elbow."

"That had to be hard on him, and on his family."

Casey nodded. "Dr. Peterson sent him to a specialist in Casper, and when he returned he became a wizard with his new prosthetic. Hank could handle every baseball that came his way, out-throwing and out-catching everyone else. And in no time he was back working the ranch alongside his dad and brother."

"Good for Hank."

"Yeah. And when they sold the ranch and moved to town to open the shop, we started calling him Henry Scissorhands. That guy can cut, shape, and do fancy hairstyles with the best of them. He always claimed it was the prosthetic that gave him the advantage. He was our very own bionic man."

That had the two of them sharing a smile.

When they reached their trucks, already loaded with supplies, Casey called to his father, "If you want to go ahead, I'll drive back to Stuff and pick up those bags."

"Sounds good. Thanks, son."

Minutes later the trucks separated, one heading back to the ranch, the other heading toward Stuff to collect their things.

On the way home, Casey turned up the volume on the radio. They all sang along with Carrie and Reba and Dolly at the top of their lungs.

CHAPTER NINETEEN

When they arrived home the women unloaded their shopping bags and hurried off to their rooms to store their purchases in closets and drawers.

The men drove to the barn to unload supplies, while Billy cautioned them to expect a late and lighter-than-usual supper. After Nonie's satisfying lunch, that plan pleased all of them.

When the others returned to the house, Casey remained in the barn and let himself into the mustang's stall, where he dropped to his knees to inspect the horse's leg.

"I thought I'd find you here."

At the sound of Kirby's voice, he looked up. "I figured you'd lock yourself in your room and enjoy being free of the gang."

"Hey, I enjoyed being with your gang."

His smile grew. "I'm glad. I know we can be overwhelming at times."

"Maybe at first. But now that I'm used to having so many people around, I've learned to love it." She shook her head. "I'm not sure I'll be completely comfortable being alone in my uncle's ranch house."

"You could always stay here with the Merrick gang."

"I think I've already overstayed my welcome."

"Don't ever think that. I see the way my family enjoys your company."

"Not nearly as much as I enjoy all of them. But sooner or later I'm going to have to get used to being on my own again."

"It's a good thing your uncle's wranglers have said they're willing to come back and work for you."

"Some of them." She chuckled. "That's not the same as being surrounded by the loud, opinionated Merricks."

"Loud and opinionated?" He wiggled his brows. "Those are fighting words, woman. Take it from one very loud, opinionated member of this family."

"Yes, you are. Of course I mean it in the very best way." Laughing, she nodded toward the mustang. "How's she doing?"

"Better than I'd hoped. This wound is completely healed." Casey stood, brushing straw from his knees.

Instead of backing away as it had in the beginning, the mustang merely stood watching as Casey let himself out of the stall.

Once latched, Casey halted next to Kirby and leaned his arms on the rail. "I think she's ready to return to her herd."

"Really?"

He nodded. "I'll take her back to the hills where I found her and turn her loose. But not for a few days. I intend to give her extra portions of food to fatten her up for the looming winter, when she'll have to forage for food through a lot of snow."

"Her herd could be miles away by now."

"It doesn't matter. Instinct will take over. She'll find them. Or they'll find her."

Kirby smiled up at Casey. "I hope Dr. Peterson gives me permission to remove this boot. I'd love to go with you when you head up to the hills."

"In that case, I'll wait until you visit the clinic."

"You mean it?"

He tugged on a lock of her hair. "I can't think of anybody I'd rather have along on my hike than you, Sunshine." He dipped his head and brushed a quick kiss over her mouth.

She absorbed a rush of heat that left her weak.

His hands moved to her shoulders and he gathered her close before lowering his head. "That was nice. Mind if I try that again?"

She lifted her face in invitation.

His mouth moved on hers, setting off an explosion of fireworks behind her closed eyelids.

Her hands automatically wrapped around his waist. Holding on for fear of falling, she gave herself up to the pure pleasure.

He changed the angle of the kiss, taking it deeper.

Oh, the man knew how to kiss; his mouth firm on hers, his hands moving along her back, lighting fires everywhere he touched.

As the kiss spun on and on, Kirby was engulfed in a wave of heat that had her knees buckling.

She took a quick step back while continuing to hold on to him. "Wait."

He lifted a hand to her cheek. "What's wrong?"

"Nothing." She swallowed, and it sounded overly loud in her ears. "We need to...I need to think."

"Okay." He paused. "Is it something I said? Something I did?"

"No." She looked away.

He cupped her chin, forcing her to look at him. "Want to talk?"

She shook her head. "Not yet. I just...need some time."

He seemed to give that some thought before saying, "Okay. Come on." Taking her hand, he led her out the barn.

On the walk back to the house, she waited for his questions, but he remained as silent as she. The only sounds were the crunch of their footsteps in the snow and the wild thundering of her heart.

They paused in the mudroom to deposit their boots and parkas before walking to the stairway.

He took her hands. "I'll see you at dinner."

She nodded and turned away, hating the questions she could read in his eyes. She was grateful that he didn't push her for answers.

Once in her room she dropped to the edge of her bed, her mind in turmoil.

Hearing voices downstairs, she marveled at how this group of strangers had become like long-lost friends. And one among them had become much more than that, though she didn't want to dwell on that fact, for fear of jinxing it.

That kiss in the barn had been simple enough. And yet it had rocked her world. She'd felt the sexual jolt all the way to her toes.

She'd like to think Casey had felt it, too. Or was it different for him?

Oh, how she wished she'd had siblings to talk to.

She hoped she wasn't making too much of this. But a cowboy as confident as Casey Merrick would be an expert on women. And though she'd had her share of boyfriends, she'd had no experience with the conflicting emotions she'd been experiencing since meeting Casey.

Maybe it was because of all the things that had happened in such a short span of time. Her uncle's death. Her move back to Wyoming. The fall in the hills. The avalanche.

Those experiences should have been enough for a lifetime. But then there'd been the theft of her truck and the trashing of her apartment, all done by an escaped convict still on the loose.

And yet, whenever she thought about everything that had occurred, the most amazing thing of all was simply...that handsome cowboy downstairs.

He was funny and smart and thoughtful, and when they were together, she felt happy and hopeful.

Careful, she warned herself. Things were moving too fast. If she didn't use her common sense, she could find herself in over her head and drowning. With no lifeline to latch on to.

That was why she'd pulled back, out there in the barn. She knew if she hadn't, they'd still be out there, taking that kiss to its inevitable conclusion. And though she'd wanted that, a part of her knew she wasn't ready.

Why? What was it about Casey Merrick that forced her to push the pause button?

Because, she thought, he was unlike any guy she'd ever known. And though she thought of herself as sane and sensible, the truth was she was head-over-heels crazy about him.

There. She'd admitted it. And though she didn't know what to do about these feelings, she knew one thing. If this was love, it wasn't the warm, fuzzy feelings poets wrote about. Instead she felt scared, confused, and honestly miserable, all at the same time. She loved being with him. In fact, she cherished every minute they had together, but she felt edgy, too, as though she were on the very edge of something monumental.

Maybe that was part of the problem.

A part of her wanted to just give in to the feelings and see where they took her. Another part of her wanted to continue to be the smart, strong, independent woman she'd always been so proud to be. And she was terrified that by giving in to these wild yearnings, she would somehow lose herself.

She stood and began pacing. Why couldn't she be like her girlfriends Kat and Evie and Remmy back in DC? Her friends had gone through a string of boyfriends, and they seemed more than happy to simply enjoy the journey, no matter where the train finally stopped.

Why did she have to be so damned cautious?

Annoyed at where her thoughts had taken her, she stripped and stepped under the shower, hoping some of those new clothes would lift her spirits.

Over a late supper Chet turned to Casey. "Your dad and I are heading up to the highlands in the morning to winterize the range shacks. Want to lend a hand?"

Casey nodded. "I'm in."

"Hey." Brand looked up. "What about me?"

Chet shrugged. "I figured you'd want some alone time with your bride."

"I love my alone time." He brushed a kiss over Avery's cheek. "But heading into the hills to close up the range shacks for the winter is a family tradition."

Jonah nodded. "I agree. And I'm available, too."

"Good." Chet was grinning. "The more willing workers, the faster we get it done." He turned to Billy. "You might want to send along some chow. We never know what sort of weather we'll find up in the hills."

"You bet." Billy sipped his coffee, and the others could see the wheels turning in his mind, already mentally planning what to cook and pack.

Casey turned to Kirby. "When do you meet with Dr. Peterson?"

"Four days and eight hours."

Her words had everyone around the table laughing.

"Not that you're keeping score," Casey said with a wink.

Their laughter grew, while Kirby's heart hitched at that simple wink of an eye.

"I'll be back in plenty of time to drive you," Casey assured her.

"If you're not," Avery said, "I'm happy to take her to town."

Kirby merely smiled, hoping Casey would be back in time, but aware that she'd just been given several days to clear her mind, without having that sexy cowboy around to muddy the waters.

Kirby awoke to doors slamming, voices calling, and the sound of engines revving. As she descended the stairs, she glanced outside to see a horse trailer hitched to a stake truck. The men were busy loading supplies and several horses were being led up a ramp. In the back of the truck, snowmobiles were secured, as well as bales of hay, tools, and coolers neatly labeled and secured with bungee cords.

When she arrived outside, the first thing she saw was Avery and Brand standing close together. At the look in their eyes, Kirby felt a shiver of warmth. They were so in tune, it seemed as though they'd been together for a lifetime, rather than still newlyweds.

Casey ambled over to tug on a lock of Kirby's hair. "You going to miss me, Sunshine?"

"I'll probably be way too busy having fun with your sister-in-law, your aunt, and your grandmother. We're going to have several days of girl time."

"Yeah," he agreed, smiling into her eyes.

Though his smile remained, something flickered in his eyes before he ducked his head and brushed a kiss over her mouth.

It was the briefest of kisses, but it shot an arrow clear through her heart, leaving her stunned.

She put a hand to his chest. "Hey. Watch what you're doing, cowboy."

His sexy grin was back. "Just hoping it'll give you a reason to miss me, at least a little, because I'm going to miss the hell out of you."

Before she could respond he sauntered away and climbed into the truck.

As the trucks pulled away, everyone called out their farewells. Casey waved to his family, then looked beyond them to where Kirby stood alone.

She could feel the heat of his touch as surely as if he were still kissing her. She couldn't help touching a finger to the warmth of her lips.

She caught his quick grin before the vehicle turned and all she could see was the back of his head.

He lifted a hand out the open window and she had the crazy urge to race alongside the truck and grab hold.

She stood until it was out of sight before turning away.

She was going to have to do something about her foolish heart.

CHAPTER TWENTY

The men gathered around a blazing campfire, polishing off a supper of Billy's beef stew, biscuits, and beer. Leaning their backs against their saddles, or the logs neatly stacked for winter, they stretched their long legs toward the warmth of the fire, ignoring the snowflakes that dusted their hair and clothes.

Bo looked around with pride. "This was a good day, boys. We got a lot done."

Chet nodded in agreement. "Yeah. I figure another day at the north cabin, and we can rest easy for the winter."

Jonah gave a dry laugh. "Or as easy as possible while we use the next couple of months repairing our equipment, taking stock of our herds, and gearing up for spring calving, which always seems to come before we've had a chance to catch our breath."

The others chuckled.

Bo gave a solemn shake of his head. "Ham always warned me: Nobody ever said ranching would be easy. If it was, we wouldn't have so many ranches going up on the auction block."

"Ranching. You either love it or hate it," Chet muttered.

"Good thing everyone here loves it." At Casey's statement, the others grinned.

Feeling mellow, Brand took a long pull on his beer. "I'm loving it a whole lot more since Avery came into my life." He shook his head, "And that's quite a statement, considering how good I was at being alone until I met her."

On the other side of the fire, Bo smiled as he stared at the dancing flames. "Love is a crazy emotion, son. One minute you're alone, without a thought to anything but today. Then you meet a woman who turns your life completely upside down, and you find yourself making plans for the future. And instead of resenting this intrusion in your life, you find yourself using any excuse to be alone with her. And then, once you know she's the one, you can't imagine your life without her."

Hearing the unexpected emotion in his father's voice, Casey couldn't help asking, "How did you survive losing Mom?"

Bo continued staring into the fire, as though seeing his beloved Leigh's face in every dancing flame. "I'm still hanging on by my fingernails, son. There are days when it doesn't seem possible that she's been gone since you boys were just tykes. Other days, it feels like a bad dream that will end when I wake up and she'll come walking in the door. Even now I can see her so clearly, and smell that perfume she always wore." He slowly shook his head in disbelief. "From the first day I met her, I knew she was the one."

The others fell silent, knowing that for this very

private man to bare his soul was something so rare that he was probably already regretting his words.

He tipped up his beer, draining it before getting quickly to his feet. "It's been a good day, but a long one. Think I'll turn in now."

Chet stood. "Time for me to do the same. 'Night, all."

Within minutes Brand and Jonah followed their lead, heading toward their beds.

At the door to the range shack Jonah turned to see Casey sitting alone, staring pensively into the flames. "You coming?"

"I'm going to finish my beer. I'll be along in a minute."

When the door closed, Casey remained sitting against his saddle while thoughts of Kirby filled his mind, as they had so often lately.

What was it about her that had him so tied up in knots? Maybe it was the fact that she'd come out of nowhere. He'd taken himself off to the high country to be alone, and then suddenly there she was, bursting into his cave, intruding on his privacy. But what should have felt like an invasion had felt instead like an unexpected treat. And when he'd brought her home, she'd fit right in with his big, noisy family. Living alone with an uncle would not have prepared her for the Merrick family flash mob, and yet, she'd been able to go with the flow.

He downed the rest of his beer and grinned at the snowflakes tickling his face. Kirby was like those snowflakes. Soft, gentle, cool. He loved the way her eyes danced with humor at the strangest times. Like when Ham started in on one of his rants. All Casey had to do was glance over at Kirby, and he could almost hear the soft lilt of her laughter, though her features remained completely composed.

He loved the fact that she was comfortable being with him and his brothers. Ranch life didn't intimidate her. Neither did things like shopping with Avery and Gram Meg. She fit in so easily with his family, it was as though she'd been born here.

But it wasn't any of those things that he thought of when he was with her. What he thought of—all he thought of—was taking her in his arms and driving her slowly mad with the passion he could sense simmering just below that calm surface.

The way she responded to his kiss and his touch told him, more than any words, that she was doing her best to hold him at arm's length in order to keep from losing control.

What would it be like, he wondered, to see her let down her guard completely and just ride the wild tide of passion?

He was having a hard time controlling his own desire when he was around her. The thought of lying with her, doing all the things he wanted, made him restless. But the choice had to be hers. And if she didn't choose soon, he'd probably go stark raving mad.

He crushed the can in his hand before he realized what he'd done.

Slowly he got to his feet and turned toward the cabin. He knew his body craved sleep, but his mind was running on overdrive, and all he could think of was Kirby. The way she looked. The way she tasted. The way she felt in his arms.

He knew it was going to be a long, sleepless night.

*   *   *

After saying good night to the others, Kirby and Avery retired to the family room. Drawing their chairs close to the fireplace, they propped their feet on a shared footstool.

"Oh, this is nice." Kirby leaned back, enjoying the warmth of the fire while she sipped her tea.

Avery smiled. "Have I told you how happy I am that you're here?" At Kirby's look of surprise she added, "It's nice to have someone my age to talk to. Since moving to Wyoming I've been burning up the internet gabbing with girlfriends back in Michigan."

"Was it a hard adjustment moving here?"

Avery chuckled. "You mean, being loved by my very own sexy cowboy? Living in this fabulous house that's as big as a hotel, and having gourmet meals served on a daily basis? What's not to love?"

Kirby shrugged. "When you put it that way…"

The two women shared a laugh.

"But still," Kirby persisted, "you left a part of your life behind."

"Not really. I probably talk to my father more now that I've moved across the country than I did when we were working in the same hospital. Then, we were barely speaking. Now, he's like a new man, asking my opinion on everything from when he should plan on a visit here to whether or not I think he should try dating at his age."

"What did you tell him?"

"Visit next summer, when the hills are alive with wildflowers. And as for dating, he'll never know until he tries it." She brought her hands to her eyes. "But

I'm hoping he doesn't share that part of his life with me. Too much information for a daughter."

The two giggled merrily.

"Speaking of too much information..." Avery stirred sugar into her tea. "I've never seen Casey so... mellow. The two of you seem to be getting along."

Kirby looked at her. "Is there a question in that statement?"

Avery held up a hand. "Sorry. I know it's none of my business. But I can't help it. Now that I'm part of the family, I just have to ask. Are you two getting serious?"

Kirby frowned. "I wish I knew."

"What does that mean?"

"I don't know what we are." Kirby ran a finger around the rim of her cup. "There's a definite attraction. But I have no idea if it means anything, or if Casey is just another good-looking guy only interested in the chase. I'm afraid that the minute we act on our feelings, he'll be ready to move on."

"Maybe he's thinking the same thing about you."

Kirby's head came up sharply as she stared at Avery in surprise. "Why would he think such a thing?"

Avery shrugged. "Why would you?"

"Most of the guys I know see commitment as another word for being tied down."

"Says the girl who's about to move away to her uncle's ranch and start a new life."

The two remained silent a long time before Avery said gently, "As for commitment, from what I've seen since joining this family, I'd say the Merricks commit to everything. The hard work of ranching. The pleasure of working together. The satisfaction of supporting one another. Commitment is their middle name."

Kirby grew thoughtful. "It's what I most admire about them. But I'm talking about long-term commitment, as in an exclusive relationship. I've watched Egan and Miss Meg. Their bond is so special. I want that kind of love, but I'm afraid it isn't possible, and I don't want to settle for less."

Avery smiled. "I know what you mean. They're a joy to be around." Her voice lowered. "I'm no expert on love. And I remember thinking much the same thing when I first came here and found myself attracted to the man I'd been hired to help with physical therapy."

Kirby couldn't help interjecting, "Talk about 'physical' therapy."

"Yeah." Avery joined in her laughter. "It's physical. And mental. And emotional. As for love, I think it's a crapshoot. Either you stand on the sidelines so you won't get hurt, or you risk it all by diving in and figuring things out a day at a time, knowing your heart could get broken in the process."

She could see Kirby digesting her words. "Not that I'm an expert. Just giving you my two cents." Yawning, she tossed aside the afghan covering her lap and leaned over to brush a kiss on Kirby's cheek. "I loved having this time with you, Kirby. Good night. See you in the morning."

"Me too. 'Night." As the fire burned low, Kirby sipped her tea while mulling Avery's words. Love. Risk. Heartbreak.

Pretty heavy stuff.

Thoughts of Casey filled her mind unbidden.

She loved his loyalty to his family, and his determination to carry his share of the work. She loved the gentle way he treated the injured mustang. He was dedicated to healing, and it showed.

She loved the care and respect he showed Ham and his grandparents and his father, and the strong bond he had with his brothers. He treated Chet and Billy like members of the family. And he was so careful with his shy aunt Liz.

Kirby tried to think of anything she didn't like, but nothing came to mind.

Maybe Avery was right. Maybe it was time to stop putting up barriers, and questioning everything he said and did, or didn't do, and admit that she was just plain crazy about the handsome, sexy, easygoing cowboy who seemed to be taking up way too much of her time.

CHAPTER TWENTY-ONE

Kirby stepped out of the shower and checked her phone. There was no message from Casey. The trek to the high country, which they all expected to take only two days, had now turned into four, with no word on when to look for their return.

As she dressed, she reminded herself that she'd seen firsthand how cell service in the hills was affected by weather disturbances. The dark clouds obliterating the peaks of the Grand Tetons for the past several days were a clear message that another storm had blown in, trapping anyone caught in it. Here in the lower elevations, it had been merely rain and sleet, but in the mountains, it would surely be a blizzard. Fortunately, the men had shelter and plenty of food, along with enough experience dealing with the whims of nature to ride out the storm.

Hearing a commotion in the mudroom, Kirby brightened before racing down the stairs. The eager, expectant look on her face faded when she saw Egan and Ham depositing their boots and parkas in the mudroom.

Ham's eyes twinkled. "From the way you came

blowing in here, I'd say you were expecting one of those rock stars. Sorry to disappoint you."

She blushed, knowing her face had betrayed her. Hadn't Uncle Frank always told her she wore her emotions on her sleeve? She looped her arms through both of theirs. "You two are my rock stars. Why didn't you wait for me? I told you I'd give you a hand with the barn chores."

"You've got to be quick, girl. Chores wait for no one." Ham grinned at Egan over her head. "Don't you have an appointment with Dr. Peterson today?"

She nodded and walked with them to the kitchen, where Meg was sitting at the table.

Inside she crossed to the counter and helped herself to a glass of juice, while the two older men grabbed some mugs of steaming coffee.

Egan kissed his wife's cheek before sitting down beside her. "Feels more like February out there, Meggie."

"I could feel the chill when you opened the back door." Meg patted his hand before glancing over at Kirby. "What time is your appointment with Dr. Peterson?"

"Ten o'clock."

"If you need a driver—"

Avery interrupted. "I'm on it."

Kirby shook her head. "You don't need—"

"I do. Besides, I promised Casey before he left that if he wasn't back in time, I'd see to it."

"Thanks, Avery."

When Billy announced that breakfast was ready, Meg caught Avery's hand as she started toward the table. "Something tells me you're missing that handsome husband of yours."

Avery nodded. "I know they're just waiting out the storm, and there's safety in numbers. But I'll feel better when he's home."

"Of course you will, honey." Meg squeezed her hand. "We all will."

As Kirby moved her food around her plate, she realized that she had no appetite. Looking around and seeing the somber faces, it gave her some small measure of comfort to know that this entire family felt the same way she did. It wasn't so much that they worried. After all, unexpected weather wasn't new to any of them. But they wouldn't truly relax until all of them were together again.

When had this happened? How had she allowed a man, who'd been a stranger not even weeks ago, to become so important in her life?

Though she resented the nerves that fluttered, she couldn't deny the truth. Casey had begun to matter to her. Much more than was comfortable.

Damn the man.

"We should do something to celebrate." Avery backed the truck out of the parking slot at the Devil's Door Clinic. "You're finally rid of that clumsy boot."

Kirby's smile brightened. "Dr. Peterson said the X-rays showed the bone was completely mended. He saw no sign of the fracture or any other trauma." She touched a hand to Avery's arm. "Best of all, he said I could resume my normal activities."

"All good." Avery shot her a grin. "But don't forget he wrote a scrip for six sessions of physical therapy. I'm thinking we could manage a couple a week until you're as good as new."

Kirby was already shaking her head. "Only if you can schedule them at my uncle's ranch...I mean *my* ranch."

She had to stop a moment and take the words in. Her smile touched her eyes and lit up her entire face. "My ranch. Do you know how lovely that sounds? This is the first time I've said those words. But the last time I spoke with my cousin, she'd said she'd talked with her lawyer, who would begin the paperwork. She did warn me to be patient, since these things take time. But very soon now, I'll be moving into my own place."

Avery reached over and caught her hand. "I wish you weren't leaving. It's been fun having you here."

"Thanks. I've loved it, too. You're like the sister I always wished I had."

"Are you and your cousin as close as sisters?"

Kirby looked away. "I would have liked that. But she was older, and away at college when I moved to the ranch."

"What about holidays and summers? Didn't you two spend any time together?"

Kirby shook her head. "When Caroline came home for holidays, she pretty much ignored me. I had assumed it because of our age gap. But I was never certain whether that was the reason that she seemed so cool to me, or if it was the fact that she resented having to share her father with someone."

A thought had Kirby turning to Avery. "You're an only child. How do you think you'd have felt if your father had brought a relative into the family?"

Avery chuckled. "You'd have to know my father. He didn't even have enough time for me, so there was no way he would ever make room in his busy life for a relative, no matter how painful the circumstances. As for me, I would have loved having someone to share things with. I was so lonely after my mother died. But I'm not sure I really knew just how lonely my life was until coming here. Seeing Brand with his brothers and this big, loud, loving family made me realize just how much I'd missed."

Kirby nodded in understanding. "The Merricks are an amazing family, so warm and welcoming. As for my cousin, once she had a boyfriend, she started spending her holidays with his family. Then she got a summer internship in Casper, and we hardly ever saw her."

"How did your uncle react?"

Kirby shrugged. "If he was sad, he hid it well. We grew closer than ever, and because I was such a tomboy, he included me in all the ranch chores and even on his trips to neighboring ranches to visit his cronies. He used to brag to his friends that I was the son he never had."

"He said 'son'?" Avery shook her head. "Not 'daughter'?"

"He already had a daughter. I think he didn't want word to get back to Caroline that I had become her substitute."

"I see." Avery thought about it a minute before saying, "Your uncle was a smart man."

"Yeah." Kirby fell silent as the truck ate up the miles away from town. "And a really good man. I miss him."

"Oh, my gosh." As they drew near the ranch, Avery pointed.

Parked near the barn was the stake truck and trailer.

Casey and Jonah were leading the horses down a ramp while Brand and Chet were unloading empty coolers.

Bo was talking to Meg and Egan, while Ham watched the frantic activities from the back porch.

Avery parked her truck behind the others and the two young women went racing across the distance that separated them. Avery flung herself into Brand's arms, and he swung her around and around before setting her on her feet to kiss her.

Kirby skidded to a halt inches from Casey. With a smile he tipped his hat. "Gram Meg said you were in town."

She nodded, feeling suddenly tongue-tied.

"I see you've lost the boot."

"Everything's mended just fine." Instead of glancing at her foot, she kept her gaze fixed on the handsome cowboy standing in front of her.

"Well…" Casey's voice died.

"I'll take care of this, bro." Jonah took the lead rope from his brother's hand and led the two horses into the barn.

While everyone around them asked a million questions and bustled about unloading, Casey and Kirby stood very still without saying a word.

After an awkward moment, they both tried to fill the silence.

"Sorry I was gone so—"

"We could see the storm—"

"I meant it when I promised to take you to your doc—"

"I really wanted to be here before you got back—"

They stopped, then burst into laughter.

Casey grabbed her hand and led her inside the barn just as Jonah stepped out.

"Okay." Casey lifted a palm toward her. "You first."

"No. You go ahead."

He surprised her by dragging her close. Against her temple he murmured, "I'm so happy to see you."

She drew in a ragged breath and turned her face slightly until their lips were almost touching. "Me too."

He shot her a sexy grin. "Did you miss me?"

She avoided his eyes. "Hardly at all."

He cupped her chin in his hands, forcing her to meet his laughing gaze. "Liar."

"What about you?" She felt the heat of his touch all the way to her toes. "Did you miss me?"

"Only every minute I was gone."

At his unexpected admission, the teasing retort she'd planned fled from her brain. Instead she spoke the only words she could think of. "I missed you, too."

He pressed his forehead to hers and exhaled slowly. "Thank you. Now, finally, I can breathe."

"... snow was piling up against the wall of the range shack until even the windows were covered." At the sound of Bo's voice, their two heads came up sharply.

"You don't say?" Ham, who was walking beside Bo, paused to stare at Casey and Kirby.

A slow smile touched his lips. "I see our rock star is back."

He and Kirby shared a grin.

When he moved on, Casey narrowed his eyes at her. "You called me a rock star?"

With a perfectly straight face she arched a brow. "Is that what you thought you heard? I believe your great-grandfather called you a rock head." She touched a finger to Casey's temple. "Yep. Just as I thought. Filled with rocks."

"Uh-huh." Still grinning, he held her hand again. "If you're looking for a fight, look somewhere else. I already got you to admit you missed me. And that's enough to make my day, woman."

The two of them were still laughing as they walked hand in hand toward the house, where the wonderful smells of Billy's roast beef and garlic mashed potatoes wafted on the air.

Apparently even the cook realized the return of half the family called for a celebration.

CHAPTER TWENTY-TWO

A fat moon hung in the midnight sky as Kirby made her way to the barn. It was strange, she thought, how quickly she'd let go of the sounds of the city. Here in Wyoming, she had already become completely accustomed to the familiar, comforting sounds of her childhood on her uncle's ranch. The distant lowing of cattle. A coyote calling to its mate.

Inside the barn she heard Casey's voice coming from the corner stall.

"Well, just look at you." Casey got to his feet in the mustang's stall and brushed his hands down his pants. "You're looking fat and sleek and well healed, little girl."

"I could say the same for her doctor."

At Kirby's voice Casey looked up with a smile. "I thought you went up to bed."

"I did. Then I saw the light on in the barn and realized you were out here checking on your patient."

He stepped out of the stall and secured the latch before joining her at the rail. "That gash on her leg is completely healed."

"Thanks to the good doctor."

"It's a nice feeling." His voice was hushed out of deference to the nighttime silence enveloping them. "When I found her, she was close to death. I wasn't sure I could help, but I had to try."

"And now look at her."

"Yeah." He was smiling when he turned to Kirby. "I can't put it off any longer. She's been cooped up too long. Time to take her back to the hills and turn her loose."

Kirby nodded. "I called my boss today and let him know that Dr. Peterson signed a release allowing me to resume my normal activities. So Dan said any time I want to head back to finish counting the mustang herds, I've got his permission."

Casey drew an arm around her shoulders. "Perfect timing. So, are you up to hiking in the snow-covered hills?"

"Are you? After all, you just got home."

"Around here, there's a short window of opportunity. I know the family can spare me a day or two in the highlands, and then it'll be time to lend a hand repairing the equipment and celebrating holidays before it's time again for spring calving." He paused. "Want to head out tomorrow?"

She nodded. "I can't wait. I'm not good at killing time and feeling lazy."

"I've noticed." He smiled down into her eyes. "I'll tell Billy to load us up with enough supplies to keep us from starvation. We can probably get on the trail right after chores."

"I'm happy to lend a hand with them."

"No need. Save your strength for the hike. With more than a foot of new snow up there, it'll be slow going.

But we'll take horses so we won't have to navigate the snow on foot. That'll be our insurance that you don't put too much strain on that freshly healed ankle."

He kept his arm around her shoulders as they left the barn and returned to the house.

In the mudroom they pried off their boots and hung their hats and parkas before heading toward their rooms.

At the foot of the stairs he turned to her, and for a moment she thought he might kiss her. Instead, he merely touched a finger to her cheek. "'Night, Sunshine. See you in the morning."

"Yeah. Good night." She turned and climbed the stairs.

When she paused outside her door she looked back. He was standing where she'd left him, watching in silence.

With a smile she opened the door and entered the room.

As she prepared for bed, she wondered at the way her heart felt. Though she'd hoped he would kiss her, she wasn't so much disappointed as intrigued. From the look in his eyes, it wasn't disinterest she'd seen, but patience.

Patience. It wasn't something she'd expect from a hard-driving, hard-living cowboy. But then, Casey was constantly surprising her.

She climbed between the covers and lay in the darkness, feeling a quick rush of excitement. By this time tomorrow night she would be back in the hills, where it had all started. But this time, she had an even more compelling reason to feel this little rush of quiet expectation.

This time she wouldn't be alone.

*   *   *

Casey led the mustang from the stall. Outside the barn two horses were ready and waiting, their saddlebags bulging with supplies.

The family gathered around Kirby and Casey to wish them well before they set out.

"Text when you can, bro." Brand clapped Casey on the shoulder.

"Will do." With a quick embrace to his aunt and grandmother, he pulled himself into the saddle.

Beside him, Kirby accepted hugs from everyone before following suit.

Billy caught Kirby's hand. "I put some mac and cheese in with the supplies. You're going to love it."

She laughed with delight. "Thanks, Billy. You know the way to my heart."

Jonah tugged on her horse's reins. "I know somebody else who does, too."

She merely arched a brow and held her silence, aware of Ham's sharp-eyed gaze fixed on her. There wasn't much that got by the family patriarch.

Casey nudged Solitaire into a turn, and Kirby's mount followed. As the two horses forged a path across a pasture, the family waved and shouted. And then, as they rounded the big barns, the voices died and they began an upward trek toward a high meadow, already deep with fresh snow.

Casey slowed his mount and waited for Kirby's horse to pull alongside. He reached out for Kirby's hand. "You're looking mighty happy, Sunshine."

"I am. I called Dan this morning and told him I was back on the clock."

"I'm sure that made his day."

"Yeah. He said it would be good to check one more thing off his to-do list." She took in a breath. "And Caroline called to say she's sorry for the delay, but the bank was asking for a lot of paperwork. She hopes everything will be in order in a few days."

He squeezed her hand. "Even better news."

She nodded. "So when Myrtle Fox called to say the apartment has been thoroughly cleaned and that it's ready for a tenant, I had to tell her that I won't be coming back, except to pick up my things."

"How did she take the news?"

"She said she has two other people asking to rent it, so she'll hold my things in the back room of her bakery until I can pick them up. She plans on signing a new tenant today."

Casey chuckled. "Leave it to Myrtle to have a Plan B. She doesn't let any grass grow under her feet."

Kirby shared his laughter as they continued climbing and wondered at the lightness around her heart. She had the feeling that the dark cloud of disaster that had followed her from DC was finally gone for good.

"Look." Hours later, Casey spotted a herd of mustangs.

While the mares foraged in the snow for grass, the leader stood atop a hill keeping watch. When he spied the mustang behind Casey's mount, he reared up and issued a warning whinny.

Kirby turned in the saddle. "Is this our filly's herd?"

Casey shook his head. "Afraid not."

"How do you know? Is speaking mustang another one of your claims to fame?"

He chuckled at her little joke. "What that stallion had to say to our filly was definitely not a welcome-home greeting."

As if to prove his words the herd, driven by their leader, drifted into the shelter of a nearby woods. All that was left of them were their prints in the snow.

Casey nudged Solitaire up the hill, leading the mustang.

Kirby's horse followed.

When she drew abreast Casey nodded toward her cell phone. "You recorded the herd?"

She nodded. "I wonder how many more we'll see."

Casey shrugged. "Hard to say. With so much snow, a lot of the herds will be forced to travel long distances from their usual rangeland looking for food and shelter. But I'm betting we'll encounter more than a dozen separate herds before we head back."

Kirby was smiling as she tucked away her phone. It felt so good to be back doing what she'd come here to do. What was even better, she was sharing it with Casey.

In the woods, where the snow wasn't as deep as in the open fields, they were able to dismount and lead their horses.

Casey turned. "How's the ankle holding up?"

"Not even a twinge so far."

"You'll let me know if it starts giving you any trouble?"

"I will. But I don't want you to worry. Dr. Peterson said everything looked perfect."

He paused beside her. "I'm just reminded of my brother. When Brand broke his leg, he did some damage by not getting therapy before resuming his activities, and he paid a price for it."

"As I understand it, his break was serious. Avery told me the surgeons had used titanium rods and pins to repair the damage. Mine was considered a hairline fracture. Barely visible, even with X-rays."

"I know." He put a hand on her arm. "But humor me and give me your word that you'll let me know if you start to feel fatigued."

"Yes, Dad."

"Okay. I get it. I won't nag." At her little laugh he arched a brow. "Well, maybe just a little."

"I promise to tell you if I need to rest."

"Good." He pulled himself into the saddle as they entered a high, snow-filled meadow. "Time to let our horses do the work."

Kirby mounted and looked around, giving a sigh of pleasure at the scene spread out before them.

The snow-covered hills gently folded into one another, dazzling like a sea of diamonds beneath a blinding sun.

"Look." Kirby pointed behind them. "Ours are the only prints. This is like our own private world."

Casey nodded. "It's why I love coming up here whenever I can get away. There's a sense of order and timelessness. No schedules. No chores. Just nature, the way it's always been."

He paused, his attention caught by something in the distance. "Look up there."

On a distant hillside stood a black stallion, watching over his herd of mares.

"That stallion is one of the reasons why I became a vet."

At her questioning look he explained. "He was a newborn, and I found him shivering in a snowstorm. With Ham's help I brought him to our barn and gave him food and shelter until he was able to make it on his own. I named him Storm, and though I turned him loose, I've charted his progress through the years. His herd numbers almost two dozen at last count."

"Storm." Touched by his story, Kirby turned to Casey. "Could this be our mustang's herd?"

When the scent of the herd reached the wild horse, she lifted her head and gave a sharp whinny.

The stallion answered, and the mustang reared up, pawing the air and tugging sharply on the rope.

Casey smiled. "I'd say we have our answer."

He dismounted and ran a hand over the mustang's head before removing the rope.

The stallion gave another whinny and the mustang started toward the herd. Though her first steps were hesitant, as though relearning how to navigate through the deep snow, she was soon galloping at full speed.

Caught up in the moment, Kirby dismounted and stood beside Casey, watching with rapt attention.

When the filly reached the herd, the stallion raced to challenge her. For a moment Kirby held her breath as the two beautiful animals made a slow turn around one another. Then the filly stepped into the circle of horses, nuzzling one or the other before pawing the ground and dipping her head to nibble range grass.

Kirby turned, wrapping her arm around Casey's. "At long last, she's home with her family."

"Hey, now." Seeing tears streaming down Kirby's cheeks, he put an arm around her and drew her close. "There's no reason to cry. She got her happy ending."

"I know. These are happy tears." She was blubbering, but she couldn't stop. "That was so simple, and so beautiful."

He gathered her against him and murmured against her temple, "Yeah. Wouldn't it be great if everything in life could be that simple?"

She felt the deep rumble of his voice vibrate through her, and her tears continued. The rough, scratchy collar of his parka rubbed against her cheek and she welcomed it, as she welcomed his arms, his voice, his breath warming her face.

Sensing her tension he framed her face with his big hands. "You all right?"

"Yeah." She sniffed before continuing. "Just feeling a little overwhelmed. I wanted her..." She shrugged. "I wanted her to stop and look back, maybe. I wanted her to be torn between the kind human who saved her life and the family she'd always known. Like they do in the movies."

"Ah." He drew out the word before his mouth curved into a wide smile. "I didn't realize what a romantic you are."

She managed to smile through her tears. "Yeah, that's me. A hopeless romantic."

"Not hopeless, Kirby. Not you. I believe a little romance is good for the soul." He lowered his face to hers and brushed a soft kiss over her lips.

Despite the fact that he kept the kiss soft and easy, she could feel the heat of it.

Before she could react, he stepped back. "We won't need to find a cave tonight. There's a range shack not far from here. We'd better move. Darkness comes early in the hills."

He waited until she mounted before coiling the mustang's rope and pulling himself into the saddle.

By the time the sun had made its arc across the sky, and the snow-covered hills were shadowed by the peaks of the Tetons, they arrived at one of the family's cabins.

After securing their horses with plenty of food and water in the lean-to shelter out back, they paused on the long porch, where a fresh stack of firewood stood waiting.

Kirby watched as he unlocked the door. "Did you know we were close to this?"

He nodded. "I know every inch of this land."

"So this was part of your plan."

His smile was quick and dangerous. "You bet. A cave can be handy, when there's no other shelter available. But nothing beats a roof over your head and a cozy fireplace when two people are out in the cold."

He held the door open and said in a mock villain's voice, "Welcome to my web, said the spider to the fly."

She couldn't help laughing, even though she felt a quick sexual jolt as his hand brushed hers.

CHAPTER TWENTY-THREE

Casey coaxed a thin flame to the kindling, and soon a log was blazing on the grate.

Grateful for the warmth, Kirby shed her parka on a hook by the door before crossing to the fireplace.

"Hungry?" She nodded toward the bulging saddlebags he'd deposited in the tiny galley kitchen.

Casey stood, wiping his hands down his pants. "Not yet." He continued staring into the flames, as though deep in thought.

She nudged him with her elbow. "A penny for them."

He turned, staring into her laughing eyes. "I'm thinking how hungry I am."

"But you just—"

"Not for food." He touched a finger to her cheek. Just the slightest brush against her skin, but she felt the tingle all the way to her toes.

Again, he fell silent, and it was on the tip of her tongue to say something to break through his thoughts.

Before she could speak, he lifted his hands to frame her face. "It's you I'm hungry for, Sunshine."

He plunged his hands into her hair before leaning close to nuzzle her jaw.

She thought of all the things she wanted to say, but the only sound she could form was a little hum of pleasure as his mouth continued a lazy exploration of her face.

His voice was a growl against her skin. "What's that? Did I hear you say, 'Yes, Casey, I'm hungry for you, too'?"

She laughed, a clear sound in the quiet of the cabin. But then she looked up into his eyes. Though they were dark with need, she realized that he was as quiet as a wild creature, awaiting an invitation to come closer.

She shouldn't have been surprised. Hadn't she watched him step back from her whenever they got too close, just as she herself had kept some distance between them? Still, his reaction had her intrigued. She had never known a man quite like him. Part rough, tough ranch hand; part gentle healer.

Hoping to keep things light she reached up, running her hands along his arms. "Why yes, Dr. Merrick. As a matter of fact I happen to be very hungry for—"

The light-hearted words she'd been about to say were smothered by a kiss so hot, so hungry, she could taste his carefully banked passion, simmering just below the surface. It caught her by such surprise, she was filled with a wild yearning that left her knees weak and her blood heating by degrees.

"Casey—"

"One word, Kirby. Yes or no."

She felt her heart stop.

"Yes. Oh, y—"

"Thank heaven." His mouth quickly covered hers

while his arms came around her, drawing her close. He kissed her with all the force of a raging storm, pouring out all the feelings he'd kept bottled up inside.

She returned his kiss with equal passion, pressing herself against him, desperate to share those feelings.

For the longest time he lingered over her lips, as though to satisfy a deep hunger. Then, needing more, he tugged her sweater over her head and tossed it aside.

Beneath it she wore a wisp of lace that revealed more than it covered.

"You're just full of surprises." There was a smile in his voice as he reached behind her, unhooking it and watching as it drifted to the floor. "Sunshine." The word was torn from his mouth. "You're so beautiful."

He dipped his head to run kisses down her throat, then lower to capture one erect nipple with his mouth.

A spear of heat shot through her core, and she was dizzy with need as she clung to him.

She reached for the buttons of his shirt, needing to feel him, flesh to flesh.

"Casey." With a little sigh of pleasure, she ran her hands across his chest and lower, to the flat planes of his stomach.

On a hiss of impatience, he backed her up against the wall, his hands, his mouth avid, eager. The wild throbbing of his heartbeat matched her own. She returned kiss for kiss, touch for touch, desperate with the need to feel him inside her own skin.

She managed to whisper, "The bunk..."

"Too far." He dipped his head, running hot, wet kisses down her throat until she nearly sobbed from the pleasure that was building.

"Casey, the floor's too cold."

"You think so? I'm burning up. But if you need heat…" In one frantic burst of adrenaline he scooped her into his arms and carried her across the room to the bunk. When he set her on her feet, they both scrambled out of the rest of their clothes, trembling like children on Christmas morning.

He lifted her onto the cot and stretched out beside her. They came together, hearts pounding, bodies straining.

"Kirby." He ran soft kisses over her face, down her throat, then lower, devouring her inch by inch.

Now that she was free to touch him at will, she couldn't seem to get enough. The muscles of his arms fascinated her. His hair-roughened chest held her enthralled. And as her fingertips moved lower, she heard his quick intake of breath and thrilled to the knowledge that she had such power over him.

He buried his lips in the sensitive little hollow of her throat and heard her moan. With a laugh she returned his kisses with a hunger that matched his. But when his lips moved lower, to take her breast, her sighs turned into a gasp of raw need.

Oh, this was what she'd hungered for. This giddy feeling that her world had tipped upside down, her head spinning, her heart pounding wildly out of control. And all because of this man.

He moved over her, kissing her, touching her as she lay, too steeped in pleasure to do more than sigh.

Soon the pleasure became a sharp, gnawing ache and she rose up, clutching at him.

"Now, Casey."

"In a minute. I've waited so long. And wanted you for so long. Wanted you like this." His eyes were hot and fierce as his mouth, that clever mouth, and those strong, workworn fingers, drove her higher, then higher still. "Just like this. All that cool control gone. I've been waiting for you to want me the way I've wanted you."

She felt her body go taut as she reached the first crest. Her hands fisted in the blanket beneath them, but he gave her no time to recover as he took her up and over again.

"Casey." His name was torn from her lips.

Seeing her wild with need shattered the last of his resolve. Claws of desire shredded his composure. He could wait no longer.

"Kirby. Oh, God, Kirby."

As he entered her, she gripped his shoulders, her fingers digging into his flesh as she began moving with him, climbing with him.

Hearts pounding, lungs straining, they moved together in a desperate dance, climbing higher then higher still, until they reached a shuddering climax that had them drifting back to earth like millions of glittering stars.

As Kirby lay very still, waiting for her world to settle, she became aware of the little things she never had time to notice. The rattle of the wind against the cabin door. The hiss and snap of the log on the fire. Casey's uneven heartbeat keeping time to her own. The strength in the arms still locked around her. The way Casey's damp hair fell over his forehead in a sweet, boyish way.

She lifted a hand to brush an errant strand but he stopped her, pressing a kiss to her palm.

His eyes were intense and fierce. "You okay?"

"Yes. You?"

"Mmm."

"I guess that's a yes."

His teasing smile came, crinkling his eyes. "Do you know how long I've wanted you?"

"How long?"

"Since you stormed into that cave like Annie Oakley, ready to do battle."

"You're making that up."

"I swear." He lifted a hand before brushing hair from her cheek. "I never thought I'd admit this, but seeing you holding that rifle really got me hot."

"If only I'd known. But I'll remember that for the future."

"No need." He stroked her face. "You could get me going just by breathing."

"Really? Does this mean I'm really sexy, or does it mean you're just easy?"

"Both."

They chuckled.

"So." She put a hand on his chest. "You had this little...seduction here in your cabin all planned?"

"Not exactly." He paused. "Sort of. I thought the range shack would be more comfortable. And I was really hoping our being alone up here could lead to..." He shrugged.

"Hot sex?"

That had him laughing. "I was going to say a romantic interlude."

"Says the blunt-spoken cowboy who didn't even wait to feed me."

"Sorry about that. Let me make it up to you."

As he made ready to roll off the bunk, she stopped

him with a hand to his arm. "I'm just having fun with you. I'm not really hungry, at least not for food."

He turned back to give her a long, appraising look. A slow smile spread across his face. "Why Miss Regan, what a little glutton you are."

"It takes one to know one." She batted her lashes. "But I wouldn't mind some more of those deep kisses."

"Yes, ma'am. Happy to oblige, ma'am."

He gathered her close and kissed her until she was humming. And then for good measure he kissed her again and again, until they lost themselves in their very own private paradise.

Casey, barefoot and naked to the waist, his jeans un-snapped, set a blackened coffeepot on a metal rack positioned over the fire, and soon coffee bubbled, filling the little cabin with its wonderful aroma.

Kirby had pulled on his flannel shirt, which fell to her thighs. Working alongside him, she filled two plates with thick slices of beef in gravy and several scoops of Billy's macaroni and cheese, while Casey added rolls browned on a rack over the flames.

They shared a wooden bench positioned in front of the fireplace, over which they'd placed a warm woolen blanket.

Their feet were propped on the hearth.

"All the comforts of home," Casey murmured as he dug into his meal.

"It's really cozy. A little home away from home." Kirby looked around as she enjoyed her dinner. "My uncle's ranch wasn't big enough to need something like this. How many of these cabins do you have?"

"Just two. Over the years we built them as we

acquired more land to accommodate the growing herds. Most of the wranglers work on a rotating basis, up here for two weeks, then closer to the ranch so they can get some time in town. Touching base with civilization from time to time keeps them sane. But when they're up here, this place offers them a place to bunk and shower whenever they're not with the herd."

"I'm sure the wranglers appreciate it."

"Most." He grinned. "Some of the old-timers actually prefer sleeping out under the stars."

She set aside her empty plate and sipped strong, hot coffee. "I used to love it when Uncle Frank would let me accompany him to the hills overnight. I can't think of anything prettier than falling asleep beside a campfire and looking up at a sky full of stars."

"Yeah." He crossed one foot over the other. "The first time my dad allowed me to go along with him and Gramps Egan and Ham, I thought I'd died and was in heaven. I remember sitting by the fire listening to Ham talk about his childhood in the wilderness, and the things he had to do to survive. I'd fall asleep to the sound of his voice, and dream that I was doing the things he'd talked about. I was this brave action hero, fighting blizzards and fending off bears and wolves."

Kirby smiled at the image. "What a wonderful childhood."

He nodded. "Looking back, I realize that the older folks were doing everything they could to ease us three boys over the loss of our mother. But at the time, I didn't have a clue. I resented Gram Meg for forcing us to study. I resented my dad and Gramps and Ham for being so strict with us, never letting us out of their sight. Now, of course, I realize they must have been half mad with the reality that it was possible to lose a loved one and have to live with the pain. And that it could happen again."

Kirby went very still. "I never thought about that. No wonder my uncle took me with him everywhere, even when he was visiting old cronies. I wonder what it did to him to lose his wife, his only brother, and his sister-in-law. And once his daughter left for college, he must have realized that his world was shrinking. All he had left was me."

"And all you had left was him. That's a pretty lonely life."

She shook her head. "He was enough. Whether I was mucking stalls beside him, or riding in the hills, or making a visit to town to load up supplies, he made it all fun." She looked over. "The same way you and your brothers make everything fun."

He grinned. "Maybe some things, but I draw the line on barn chores. Making them fun is a stretch."

"But you do it. All of you. And I hear as much laughter in the barn as I do in the house."

He grew thoughtful. "They say laughter's good for the soul."

"I laughed a lot with Uncle Frank."

"Why did you leave him and go to DC?"

"I've asked myself that question a lot. I haven't made a lot of good choices. I guess I thought life would be glamorous in a big city."

"Was it?"

She shook her head. "Honestly? I found myself spending hours in rush-hour traffic, doing a job that didn't challenge me, rushing to my tiny one-room walk-up with a takeout supper, and then getting up the next morning to do it all again." In a flurry of frustration Kirby got to her feet and picked up their empty dishes before walking to the small galley kitchen.

She filled the sink with water she'd heated over the stove.

Casey's voice sounded behind her. "Laughter isn't the only thing good for the soul. Know what else is?"

Before she could respond he said softly, "Good loving. Especially when the soul is troubled."

With her hands in the sink she felt his arms encircle her waist from behind. "Casey..."

He pressed his mouth to the little hollow between her neck and shoulder, nuzzling the soft skin until she shivered. "Sunshine, you have to know what you're doing to me."

She turned in his arms, unmindful of the water that dripped from her hands onto his shirt. "Washing dishes turns you on?"

"Yeah. And you in my shirt, looking better than I ever could. Hell, everything about you turns me on."

She flushed before admitting, "It's the same thing you do to me."

There was that sexy smile that always managed to squeeze her heart.

He pressed his forehead to hers. "Let's leave the dishes for later. I have something much better in mind."

"I just bet you do." She smiled dreamily as he lifted her in his arms and carried her to the bunk across the room.

As they undressed each other and tumbled into bed, their lovemaking wasn't rushed, as the first had been. Now it was slow and easy, as though they had all the time in the world.

CHAPTER TWENTY-FOUR

Kirby awoke to the wonderful fragrance of coffee.

For a moment she lay very still, getting her bearings, as she recalled her amazing night with Casey. They'd made slow, delicious love, before washing the dishes and banking the fire. Throughout the night they'd dozed, then woke up for more loving, before sharing all the little things about their childhoods that they'd never shared with anyone else.

He'd been as interested in her history as she'd been in his, and they were surprised to find so many similarities in the lives they'd lived growing up just miles apart.

She'd learned so many new and fascinating things about him. Not only his love for this land, and the animals he tended, but the high regard he had for his family. Despite the teasing, there was a deep well of love here. He'd regaled her with tales of his childhood escapades with his brothers, and she loved seeing the bold, brash boy he'd been.

"'Morning, sleepyhead." Casey settled on the edge of the bunk and held out a steaming mug. "Coffee?"

"Oh, yes. Thank you." She sat up, oblivious to her nakedness, and accepted the coffee, taking a long drink before handing it back. "Something smells wonderful. Did you make breakfast, too?"

"I did." He set aside the cup and brushed her hair from her eyes. "But you're going to have to wait awhile to eat."

She arched a brow. "Why?"

"Because I have something else in mind first."

As his words penetrated her sleep-fogged brain, her smile grew. "Oh, you mean…Now who's the glutton?"

"I see we're on the same wavelength, Sunshine." He settled himself beside her and gathered her into his arms.

Against her mouth he murmured, "It's the perfect beginning to a really special day."

And then there were no words as they lost themselves in their newly discovered passion.

Kirby finished the last of her steak and eggs. "That was fantastic. Bless Billy."

Beside her, Casey finished another mug of coffee. "The man can cook."

"You're not bad yourself."

He grinned. "It's easy, as long as I have the right supplies and a fire to cook them on."

"I'm impressed by your camping skills."

"I had good teachers." He caught her hand. "Are you fortified for a hike in the hills?"

She nodded. "Maybe we'll run across some more mustangs."

"That's the plan." He followed her to the kitchen

where they washed their dishes and set them aside before pulling on their hiking gear.

After banking the fire, they left the little cabin behind and saddled their horses. Soon they were high in the hills, looking out on the snow-covered land where it was easy to imagine that they were the only people in the world.

"That makes four more herds." Smiling, Kirby clicked off as many photos as she could before the mustangs drifted into the cover of the forest.

"We'd better think about getting back to the cabin. It'll be dark soon." Casey held the horses' reins as Kirby tucked away her phone and pulled herself into the saddle.

As they crested a hill and looked down at the range shack, Casey reached over and held Kirby's hand.

At the tender gesture she turned to look at him. The smile he gave her had her heart swelling inside her chest. How was it possible that this cowboy had the power to turn a simple day in the hills into something special?

"Last one to reach the cabin has to make dinner," he called as he let go of her hand.

Unable to resist the challenge, she dug her heels into her mount. Though the snow was belly-deep in places, both horses, sensing food and shelter, made a valiant effort to run.

With Casey's horse just a fraction behind her, Kirby spurred her horse on, reaching the cabin's porch first. She leapt from the saddle and stood laughing as Casey dismounted.

"Looks like I get to be a lady of leisure tonight."

He was grinning, and as they led their horses into the lean-to behind the cabin, she had the distinct impression that he'd held back just enough to allow her to win.

She decided to humor him. After all, a win was a win.

When the horses had been tended to, they walked arm in arm to the cabin, grateful for shelter from the biting cold.

Casey added kindling to a couple of logs and soon had a fire burning on the grate.

He started toward the galley kitchen. "Are you up for some grilled chicken?"

"Sounds perfect."

Kirby rummaged through the saddlebags and discovered some sliced vegetables and some wooden skewers. "Look what Billy prepared for us."

"Great. We'll grill them with the chicken." Casey popped the tops of two longnecks and handed one to Kirby.

He took her hand and led her to the blanket-covered bench. "Since you won the race, you get to sit here and watch while I slave over a hot fire."

They were laughing as he set the food on the wire rack over the flames before joining her on the bench. As they stretched out their legs toward the warmth of the fire, they tipped their beers and sighed with the pure pleasure of it.

Kirby put a hand on his. "I love this cabin."

He twined his fingers with hers. "I know what you mean. I've loved it since I was a kid. Of course now I'll love it even more, because of what we shared here."

"It has been special, hasn't it?"

"You made it special."

She glanced at their joined hands. "*We* made it special."

He leaned close to brush a kiss over her mouth. "What would you say about holding off our supper for a while?"

Seeing the smoldering heat in his eyes she stood and began leading him toward the bunk. "I think cold chicken sounds perfect."

"I overcooked the vegetables."

They were sitting side by side under the covers, enjoying a lukewarm supper.

"I think they're fine." She opened her mouth as he offered her a bite of his grilled red pepper.

"Want another beer?"

She shook her head. "I think I'll make a pot of coffee."

She scrambled out of bed and filled the pot with water and coffee before setting it over the glowing coals.

When it finished brewing, she held up a mug. "Want some?"

He nodded, and she poured some into two mugs before carrying them to the bunk. They sipped in companionable silence.

"I could get used to this," Casey said.

She chuckled. "I was just thinking the same thing."

"Maybe, instead of just another day or two, we should throw out all the rules and stay up here for the winter."

"What would we do for food?"

"I guess I'd have to roam the hills and hunt."

"And I'd have to dress whatever game you brought home and cook it."

"Or..." He grinned. "We could just head home and let Billy worry about all that."

She was laughing. "I like the way you think."

"Good." He set aside his mug before placing hers beside it and gathering her into his arms. "Because what I'm thinking is—"

"You're worse than a glutton. You're insatiable."

"All your fault. Once you let me taste the forbidden fruit, I was lost."

Her laughter ended in a sigh as, with soft, easy kisses and slow, practiced touches, they slipped away to a world of pleasure beyond belief.

CHAPTER TWENTY-FIVE

'Morning, Sunshine."

Kirby awoke to find Casey perched on the edge of the bunk, watching her. "Good morning. How long have you been awake?"

He brushed a strand of hair from her eyes. "Just long enough to make a fresh pot of coffee." He frowned slightly. "And to check on the weather."

She smoothed his forehead. "And...?"

"There's a storm rolling in. I know we were hoping for another day at least, but this one looks big. The snow's already falling, and the clouds over the Tetons are thick enough to suggest a blizzard that could trap us up here for a week or more."

She lowered her finger to his cheek. "Would that be so bad?"

He closed a hand over hers. "It would be heaven. But I can't spare that much time away."

"I know." She felt the sharp sting of reality crowding in. "And I need to call Caroline to see if her lawyer has the papers ready to sign."

"There you are. Let's cling to the positive." He drew her up beside him. "We'll need to get on the trail soon."

He leaned close and brushed his mouth over hers. "But if we skip breakfast there might be time for one more…"

"Talk about looking for something positive." She couldn't help laughing. "I guess we could eat later, along the trail."

"A woman after my own heart. Thank heaven." He stretched out beside her, all the while brushing soft, wet kisses along her throat until she was humming with pleasure. "I'll make it up to you. I promise. And if we're lucky, we'll make it home in time for a hot dinner with the family."

She wound her arms around his neck and pulled him close. Against his lips she whispered, "Right now, I'd rather have my hot cowboy."

"Your wish is…"

Neither of them needed the words.

Several more inches of snow had fallen overnight, forcing them to be cautious as they made their descent.

Gusts of snow stung their faces, nearly blinding them at times. As the north wind picked up speed, they hunched deeper into their parkas and lowered their heads to avoid the worst of it.

As the horses picked their way through the drifts, Casey looked over at Kirby. "I'm glad we aren't on foot or you'd be buried under all this snow."

She laughed. "And you'd have to put me on your shoulders."

He shot her a surprisingly solemn look. "I wouldn't mind in the least. I hope you know I'd do whatever necessary to keep you safe."

Touched, she reached over to take his hand. "I know that, Casey. It means the world to me."

He looked at their joined hands. "You're special to me, Sunshine."

"I'm glad. Because you're special to me, too." She thought about saying more, but the time wasn't right.

When her horse stumbled, she released his hand to concentrate on the difficult journey ahead of them.

Though they hoped to make it back to the ranch in time for supper, the severity of the storm had her narrowing her goal. It would be enough to simply make it back safely, no matter how long it took.

As they broke free of the woods and entered Merrick land, the blizzard raging in the higher elevations was only a memory. Here in the flat meadow, there were no more than a few inches of fresh snow, and the wind had grown calm.

When the horses rounded a bend, Casey pointed. "Look. Down there. Home."

Kirby had long ago stopped feeling her fingers or toes. But the moment she caught sight of the ranch in the distance, her flagging energy was revived, and for some strange reason she didn't want to probe too deeply, she felt like weeping.

The horses, now in familiar territory and sensing food and shelter at the end of their long journey, began to strain against the reins in their eagerness.

Kirby turned to Casey. "Should we give them their heads?"

He laughed. "Why not? They're as eager as we are." He couldn't resist adding, "Last one there has to unsaddle and feed them."

With their riders urging them on, the two horses began to lengthen their strides until they were running full out toward the barns looming up in the early evening shadows.

They rounded the barn and came to a halt nearly neck and neck.

Casey was grinning. "You don't give up, do you? I call it a draw, Sunshine."

"I'll concede." Kirby slid from the saddle. "Though I think I was a nose ahead."

"Too close to call." He reached for the reins of her horse, but she shook her head.

"If it's a draw, we both win. Why don't I unsaddle these two and towel them down while you find fill their troughs with food and water?"

"Done." With an admiring look at the way she handled things, despite the long hours in the saddle, he strolled into their stalls and began measuring out food and water.

When the horses were comfortably stabled, they walked to the house, eager to shed their frozen boots and gloves and parkas.

Hearing the chorus of voices in the kitchen, they made their way in, breathing the wonderful aroma of freshly baked bread and hearing the unmistakable sizzle of steaks on the grill.

"Well." Bo saw them and lifted his longneck. "We were just wondering if the two of you were caught in that blizzard in the highlands."

"We saw it coming and got out just in time." Casey took Kirby's hand and led her toward the warmth of the fire.

As soon as she was seated beside Meg, Billy came over to hand her a steaming cup of tea.

"Oh, bless you, Billy." She wrapped her hands around

it and inhaled the delicate perfume of the cinnamon stick he'd used to stir it.

"The two of you look half-frozen," Meg remarked.

Kirby nodded. "It was a long, cold ride home."

Home.

The word slipped easily from Kirby's lips, and though she wasn't aware of it, Meg met Egan's gaze and the two of them shared a knowing smile.

Casey took a long pull on his beer before setting it aside. "Do we have time to shower and change before we eat?"

Meg glanced at Billy, who nodded and said, "We'll make time."

Casey turned to Kirby. Following his lead, she set aside her teacup. When he offered his hand, she took it and the two of them hurried away.

As soon as the door closed behind them Jonah turned to his family. "I don't know about the rest of you, but I'm practically blinded by the light in my brother's eyes. If that's what a couple of days in the hills can do to a guy, I'm swearing off all hiking until I'm past the age of temptation."

Egan shared a look with his son, Bo. "And what age would that be?"

Jonah shrugged. "I guess when I'm old and gray."

"Don't let the wrinkles and gray hair fool you, boy." Ham kept his tone steely, although a hint of a smile tugged at the corner of his lips. "A man's never too old to be tempted by a beautiful woman."

"Twelve separate herds." Kirby, her hair damp and curling around a face devoid of makeup, was animated as she described the mustangs she and Casey had encountered in the hills. "My boss is going to be so pleased. And I took as many pictures as I could for his file, so Dan's superior in DC will be impressed."

"Sounds as though you're impressed, too." Avery, seated next to Brand, was enjoying Kirby's enthusiasm.

"I am." Kirby looked around with a bright smile. "There's something almost mystical about seeing horses living wild. Dan told me that none of the other employees wanted to hike the hills and count the herds. They consider it drudgery, but I'm so glad I had the chance to do this. They're magnificent."

She couldn't seem to stop herself. "And being up in the hills, away from civilization, is the most amazing feeling. It might seem silly to you guys because you have all this around you whenever you want to enjoy it. But for years now, whenever it snowed in DC, I'd watch it turn to black slush within days." She sighed. "It's so beautiful in the hills. Not another footprint anywhere in those acres of snow."

Without thinking she lay a hand over Casey's. "It felt like we were the only humans left on the planet."

"Wait. Hold on now." He smiled down into her eyes. "Are you saying we weren't?"

They shared a laugh while the others watched in silence.

Ham cleared his throat. "How did that little mustang filly do, boy?"

"Even better than I'd hoped. As soon as she spotted her herd, she let us know."

"Casey told me it was Storm's herd."

Kirby began talking again before Casey could answer. "He told me all about how Storm came into his life, and how he still keeps track of him and his herd." She went on to describe the scene of the frantic whinny, the tender reunion, and then the filly disappearing into the woods with her herd.

"She was back with her family, and it was so heart-warming."

"Except for one minor detail you left out," Casey added.

Everyone waited.

He shared an intimate grin with Kirby before adding, "The ungrateful little filly didn't even give me a backward glance before running off, and that, according to Kirby, spoiled the moment."

At the blank stares Kirby felt the need to explain. "I told Casey that in the movies, she would have run back to nuzzle her hero one last time, and then return to her herd."

Jonah shared a grin with Brand. "I suppose you'd like me to write a scene like that in my next book."

Her eyes widened. "Would you?"

He was already shaking his head. "In case you've forgotten, I write gritty mysteries."

"But you could insert a tender scene."

"Not going to happen." He added with a smile, "But maybe you can persuade Casey to try his hand at writing a romance. I'd say that's right in his wheelhouse these days."

Instead of a clever remark, Casey merely remained silent, still wearing that silly grin that had been on his face since his return.

The family remained around the table for the longest time, enjoying Billy's apple pie and ice cream, as well as many cups of coffee, while Kirby continued relating details of the mustangs they'd encountered in the hills.

Beside her, Casey seemed content to just sit and listen to the sound of her voice.

The ringing of her cell phone startled her.

Laughing, she picked it up, saying to the others, "I haven't heard that sound for days now." She glanced at the caller's identification. "Oh. It's my cousin." She pushed away from the table. "This is the news I've been waiting for. Excuse me."

Her voice softened as she crossed toward the door. "Hi, Caroline. I'm so happy you—"

Before she could step out of the room she paused, her words fading, along with her smile.

Casey was the first to note her stricken look as she stood frozen in the doorway, listening to her cousin's voice.

"I see. But I…" Kirby's words died as the voice on the other end droned on before halting abruptly.

She leaned a hand against the wall, as though needing help to remain standing. "That's it, then. I guess there's nothing I can say or do to change your…"

Casey was on his feet in an instant, crossing the room to her side. Her call had ended before he even reached her, and she stared at the phone in her hand as though not really seeing it. Then, as he approached, she held out her arm stiffly, to keep him away.

"I can't… I need to…" Tears flooded her eyes.

"What's happened? What did she say?"

Kirby swallowed. "Caroline said her father left too many debts. Her lawyer advised her to ask the bank in town to take possession. When she told them of my offer to purchase, they claimed they have a buyer willing to pay much more, and that would go a long way toward clearing the outstanding debt."

"Des Dempsey's bank." Casey's voice was filled with scorn. "But you're family. Won't your cousin reconsider—"

She gave a firm shake of her head. "Caroline said the deal is already done, the papers signed. The bank now owns my uncle's ranch. The buyer will take possession in the spring."

"Sunshine…"

She gave a shake of her head and backed away. Glancing toward his family she managed to say, "I'm sorry. I can't talk now. I really need to…"

She turned and fled.

In the silence that followed they heard her hurried footsteps on the stairs, and the sound of the guest room door opening and closing.

And then an ominous silence settled over the house and the family.

CHAPTER TWENTY-SIX

Though she'd been awake for hours, Kirby waited until she heard sounds of activity before making her way down the stairs. She paused to take a deep breath and force a smile to her lips before entering the kitchen, where the Merrick family was already gathered around the fireplace.

Meg looked up and called, "Good morning, Kirby."

Casey set aside his mug of coffee and met her halfway across the room. "Did you sleep?"

"A little." Despite the telltale red, puffy eyes, she managed to keep her smile in place.

Meg studied her with concern. "We all know how much you sacrificed just to return home to make an offer on your uncle's ranch. We're so sorry about your cousin's unhappy news."

"Thank you. I appreciate your concern." Kirby helped herself to a cup of coffee from the tray and turned to face them. "It's a new day, and I took some time to consider my options. I've already emailed a copy of my report on the mustang herds to my boss, along with the photos I took. When I told him I'm in need of a place to stay, he mentioned that Julie Franklyn has a room above her shop that she's been thinking of offering for rent, and it's close enough that I can walk to work, which is important, until I can arrange to buy another truck. When I phoned Julie she said she'd love to have me as a tenant, but she needs a day or so to clean it up."

"If she gets busy, that could stretch into more than a few days." Meg looked at Egan before saying, "We'd like you to stay here until it's ready. And maybe we can use our powers of persuasion to get you to stay on longer."

Kirby couldn't hide her delight at this offer. "That's kind of you, Miss Meg, and I'm so grateful to all of you for your hospitality. But I need to consider my...my new normal." The words stuck in her throat, and she had to swallow hard before adding, "It may take a while, but I'll sort it all out. But if you wouldn't mind loaning me one of your trucks for today, I'd like to drive over to the ranch for a last visit." She shrugged. "I guess it's my way of saying goodbye to my dreams."

Bo was quick to say, "I'll fetch a truck right after breakfast, honey."

"Thank you, Bo. I appreciate it."

Just then, Billy announced that breakfast was ready.

As the others started toward the table, Casey held back. "I'd like to go with you. Could you hold off the visit until tomorrow?"

She paused. "Why?"

"Because I got an emergency call from Buster Mandel. He wants me to take a look at one of his cows. From the symptoms he described, I could be stuck there for a couple of hours."

"Casey." She shook her head. "That's your job. I

don't want my trip to be a problem for you. I'm certainly capable of going alone."

"But—"

"Shhh." She put a finger to his mouth, then just as quickly withdrew it as though it burned. Would the touch of him always have this effect? Would she always go weak at the knees every time he got close?

With a sigh she said, as calmly as she could manage, "Of course, I was hoping you could come along, but it's probably better if I do this alone. I'm sure I'll get all emotional and blubber like a baby. I'd rather shed my tears without an audience."

"But I want to be there for you."

"That means the world to me. But you have your patients to think about. And this is just some silly sentimental journey I'm taking, in the hopes that I can put those old dreams away for good and get on with my life."

She marched to the table, and he trailed after her more slowly.

The conversation was subdued, and though Kirby tried to follow along, she was distracted, and offered little except an occasional nod or tight smile.

As the family began to disperse for the day, Meg took Kirby's hand. "I hope you know how much I admire the way you're dealing with this, Kirby. You came back to Wyoming with such high hopes, and you've been through enough trials to crush some people. But I do hope, after a visit to your uncle's ranch, you'll come back here in time for supper."

"But Julie Franklyn's apartment—"

"—isn't ready. And besides, we're not ready to let you go yet." Meg squeezed her hand. "Please say you'll come back here in time for supper with our family. Tomorrow will be time enough to pack up your things and head to town."

Across the room Casey remained silent, but the pleading look he shot her went straight to her heart.

Seeing it, Kirby nodded. "Thank you, Miss Meg. I'd love another night with all of you."

"Oh, I'm so glad." Meg drew her close and hugged her fiercely before letting her go.

After breakfast, Bo pulled up by the back porch and left the ranch truck idling.

Kirby walked down the steps to find Casey waiting for her. He held the driver's side door until she'd settled herself inside. He reached through the window and took her hand. "I'm glad you're coming back here tonight. There are things . . . I want to say. Things I need to tell you."

She felt the curl of heat along her arm and withdrew her hand from his. "There are things I want to say, too. I'll never be able to thank you . . . your family for all their kindnesses."

His tone roughened. "The things I want to say have nothing to do with my family."

"Well . . ." She felt a sudden stirring in her heart even though her mind had already leapt ahead to the journey before her. She put the truck in gear. "I'll see you tonight."

As she started along the driveway, she studied Casey in the rearview mirror. So handsome and rugged. So fierce and yet so tender. Everything about him tugged at her.

How was she going to say goodbye? They'd just

finally connected, and had shared an experience that was already beginning to feel like a dream. Surely she'd imagined it. It had been too perfect to be real. The long, lazy night hours of loving. The laughter and teasing. But, like all the good things in her life, it had ended too soon.

She dragged in a deep breath. Time for a reality check. His job as a rancher and veterinarian demanded all his time. Hadn't he said he had a very small window of time to play before getting back to the family business? That time was now past.

She was a low-level employee who'd burned a lot of bridges to chase a dream. And now, with that dream in tatters, she needed to figure out her next step in this messy life that just seemed to unravel more with every decision she made.

Was it her? she wondered. Were her decisions always so wrong? Or had she been born under a dark cloud?

Kirby left the interstate and drove along an old familiar ribbon of asphalt until she turned onto a patch of dusty road. The snow-covered fields looked bleak and neglected. Portions of the wooden fence that meandered up and over and across the hilly land were broken, the rotted wood lying in the snow. Her uncle had always taken such pride in that fence, spending precious hours each spring replacing any boards that needed fixing after they had been battered by winter's blast.

As she drove up to the house, she was thrust back in time to her childhood. This was the place where she'd arrived, alone and afraid after her world had shattered. And within weeks she'd felt safe and loved. Because of Uncle Frank. How he must have mourned the loss of his brother and sister-in-law. And yet he'd swallowed his grief and made a home for their lost little girl, who had come to him broken and in need of repair.

He had jokingly referred to himself as a repairman. How true. He could repair anything. Even a little girl's heart.

She sat staring at the snow-covered roof, the old faded curtains on the windows, the wide steps of the side porch, with a door that always slammed behind her. No matter how many times her uncle warned her to close it softly, she always forgot until it slammed, and his voice would drift out to her, *Gently, Kirby. Gently.* And then would follow his words with that wonderful throaty rasp of laughter that told her he didn't really mind.

He taught her to muck stalls, and how to wield a hoe between the rows of corn and beans and tomatoes in the garden. He'd taught her to drive a truck and a tractor, and how to play poker with his cronies on Saturday nights. And on Sunday mornings he'd taken her to church, and afterward they would stop at Nonie's for eggs. Uncle Frank would have Nonie's special coffee, which she later learned was coffee with a shot of brandy. And Nonie always had hot chocolate for Kirby, with a mound of whipped cream out of a can.

Feeling the sting of tears, Kirby let herself out of the truck and walked across the yard to the corral. There were no horses there now, but this was where Uncle Frank had patiently taught Kirby how to ride a horse. As a girl she'd been afraid of them. They seemed so big—these giant animals that he wanted her to sit on. But she did, at his urging, and slowly, like a toddler taking those first steps, she'd learned to be as comfortable in the saddle as she had once been on a bike. And when she'd mastered the art of riding, Uncle Frank had surprised her with her own pony, Tulip. A silly name for a horse, but he'd given it to her in springtime, when the tulips were just blooming.

Oh, how she'd loved that pony. She and Tulip grew together, running wild across the fields. If her uncle worried about her, he kept it to himself. She would dance into the house, all pink cheeks and windblown hair, to tell him about her day with Tulip, and he would listen as though what she had to say was the most important thing in his life. If he had debts, or troubles of any kind, he never let it show.

Thinking about those lovely days brought a smile to her lips. Though she would have to say goodbye to her dreams of living here, at least she had her memories. No one and nothing could take them away from her. Not her cousin, who had never warmed to her. And not a bank consumed with the business of making money.

This had been the most amazing place to grow up. A child's playground. Horses and cows, tractors and trucks. Half a dozen elderly ranchers and their families who accepted her and her uncle with the open arms of friendship. Nights under the stars up in the hills with the herd. Unexpected trips to town with a stop for a burger and fries and a big scoop of vanilla ice cream with fresh strawberries on top.

She walked around the corral to wander across a field no longer planted. Instead of neat furrows where crops had been harvested, there was just flat land dusted with snow.

She trudged up a hill to the meadow where the herd would spend their summers grazing on the lush grass that grew there. An area that had once been black with cattle was now empty.

She stood and looked around, remembering it as it had been in her childhood. How long had her uncle struggled to keep up with the never-ending work of ranching, while trying to stay one step ahead of the debts? From the looks of things, it had been too over-whelming, even for a Superman like Frank Regan.

With a sigh she walked down the hill. An aged tractor, its parts strewn about it, lay behind the barn, growing rusty from being abandoned out in the elements.

She circled around to the front of the barn. The huge door protested loudly as she leaned her weight into it. With an effort she managed to force it open.

Inside, it took her a moment to adjust to the gloom. The stalls, which used to be filled with stock, now stood empty.

In a corner of the barn she caught sight of a vehicle. Walking closer she realized it was a newer-model truck. Odd, she thought, that it looked a lot like hers.

Curious, she pulled open the driver's side door and let out a gasp of shock and surprise.

It didn't just look like hers; it was hers. There in the cup holder was the red, white, and blue mug she'd brought with her from DC. On the passenger seat lay the pretty yellow scarf she'd discarded.

For a moment she could do nothing more than stare, while her mind tried to process what she was seeing.

No wonder the authorities hadn't found her stolen truck.

How did it get here? How long had it been here?

Had the thief exchanged it for one of her uncle's vehicles?

No matter. She reached into her pocket and withdrew her phone. As she began scrolling through her contacts for the police chief's number, she felt the cold steel muzzle of a gun against her temple. Behind her, a man swore loudly and fiercely, before growling, "Stupid bitch. You had to come in here, didn't you? Being nosy just sealed your fate."

CHAPTER TWENTY-SEVEN

"Casey Merrick, you're one damned fine vet." Buster Mandel walked beside Casey as he made his way to his truck. "I figured that old cow was so sick you'd have to put her down."

"She's got plenty of years left, Buster." Casey tossed his black bag in the truck before turning to offer a handshake. "I'll be back to check on her in a couple of days. In the meantime, if she's not able to join the herd by tomorrow, you call me."

"I will." Buster pumped his hand. "I'm going to start calling you the miracle worker."

Casey laughed. "The miracle is in the drugs."

He climbed into his truck and waved. As soon as he left Buster's ranch, he reached for his cell phone and called his grandmother.

"Casey." Meg answered on the first ring. "How are Buster and Trudy?"

"They're good, Gram Meg. They said to say hi. And the cow's on the mend. She'll be good as new in no time."

"That's good. About the cow, I mean. But ever since Trudy's fall, I worry about her."

"She said not to worry. Now that Avery's got her on the right track with her physical therapy, she's feeling even better."

"Oh, I'm so glad. I'll pass that along to Avery." There was a smile in Meg's voice.

"I'm going to head on over to the Regan ranch to be with Kirby, in case she's feeling down."

"I'm glad. My heart broke for that sweet thing, traveling alone to say goodbye to her uncle's ranch. You'll be sure to bring her back here in time for supper?"

"Count on it."

He rang off and headed down a dusty road. In less than an hour he'd be with Kirby. Maybe that was why his heart felt so light. If the time was right, he intended to tell her how he felt about her, and what he hoped for their future.

Their future.

Before meeting her, his future had seemed, like his past, to be centered around his family, the ranch, his career as a veterinarian. Not a bad life at all. But ever since Kirby walked into that cave, everything had changed. He couldn't imagine a life, a future, without her in it.

He hoped and prayed he didn't spoil everything by springing this on her. It certainly wasn't the best timing for a soul-baring confession. He knew her life was in turmoil right now. But he wasn't willing to wait. Especially after their time alone in the hills. He was already missing her with an ache that couldn't be soothed with a kiss or an occasional tumble in bed. He knew now that he wanted what he'd never dreamed of. He wanted it all. Marriage.

Kids. Maybe someday their own ranch nearby, close enough to lend a hand and ease the burden of endless chores on his dad and grandfather and great-grandfather, but far enough away to give them a life of their own.

Like the old Butcher ranch his father had bought when they were kids. *Before the fire.*

It was so long ago, it no longer brought the pain of loss, as it did to his father. In fact, the thought of the old ranch house had him smiling. He could vaguely recall nights with his parents spent around the big old fireplace in the parlor, with Gram Meg and Grandpa Egan, and Ham and Aunt Liz, all gathered for Sunday supper. Though that life had ended abruptly after the fire that took his mother, the images were indelibly inscribed in his mind.

He wanted that with Kirby.

With an air of anticipation, he turned up the radio to sing along with Rascal Flatts about life being a highway. And wasn't that the truth?

More than anything, he wanted to ride it for a lifetime with Kirby by his side.

"Move it." The gunman had Kirby's arm in a viselike grip as he dragged her to the ranch house.

With a gun to her head, she didn't fight him.

Inside the kitchen he bound her hands and feet so tightly the rope cut into her flesh, leaving her wrists and ankles numb with pain.

"If you even try screaming, I'll finish you off. Got it?" He stuck his face closer. "Got it, bitch?"

She managed to nod her head.

He kicked her legs out from under her, sending her

sprawling on the cold linoleum floor of the kitchen. With her hands bound, she couldn't stand, or even sit up.

When he turned away, she struggled to calm the terror that had her by the throat, threatening to choke her. She could hardly catch her breath.

She'd never been so afraid in her life. The minute she'd seen this stranger she'd known he was the escaped convict they'd dubbed Killer Keller, recognizing him from when his image had been plastered all over the TV.

All those leads the authorities were following, from Wyoming to clear across the country . . . and yet, here he was, within miles of where they'd been searching.

Practically in their backyard.

Oh, why hadn't she run the minute she'd spotted her truck? If even half of what they'd said about him on the news was true, he would have no reason to spare her life.

She watched as he tossed her phone onto the kitchen counter before stirring something on the stove.

He glanced over at her. Seeing her watching him, he said, "There's only enough here for me. Not that it matters. The dead don't eat. And that'll be you as soon as it's dark enough to haul your ass to that old well out back."

Something perverse made her say, "What's the matter? You don't want a bloody mess here in the house?"

He smirked then, and she realized he looked even more evil than when he frowned. The smile gave him the chilling look of the devil himself. "That's right. When I finally leave here, nobody will be the wiser.

Once they stop looking for me under every leaf, I'll disappear forever. As for you, you'll just become another missing female who's never found."

She felt a shiver convulse through her body, knowing it was true. Her cousin would never miss her. Her boss would file a missing person report, but he would soon replace her. And Casey? Her heart took a heavy bounce. Casey would be half mad with worry and try to move heaven and earth to find her. But in the end, he would be forced to move on with his life.

She felt a sudden rush of tears at the realization that she hadn't even said a proper goodbye to the Merrick family. She'd accepted their amazing hospitality and had walked away this morning, blindly assuming she'd be back with all of them tonight.

Worst of all, she'd been cool to Casey, dismissing his offer to come with her if she'd wait until tomorrow.

Tomorrow.

Her heart sank as the truth dawned.

There would be no tomorrow. Today was all she had left. And she had squandered it.

Ray Keller ate directly from the pan of canned stew he'd heated on the stove. While he ate, he glanced at the woman lying on the floor across the room.

"I got you to thank for finding this place."

He saw her eyes widen. When she didn't respond, he went on as though it didn't matter one way or the other. "I found a bunch of papers in your truck."

"My truck? What makes you think the truck is mine?"

"I saw your picture in that miserable apartment in Devil's Door. A crummy place, by the way, but I figured I'd find something of value." He chuckled to himself. "Having a GPS is the same as having a map that says, 'Hi there. Here's where I live. Come on over and take whatever you want.'" He chuckled again at his little joke. "So I did. When I stumbled on that truck up at the lookout, I saw you just disappearing over a hill and figured I had a couple of hours at least before you'd return and realize it had been stolen. That gave me plenty of time to use the GPS to locate your place and help myself. That picture on the night table showed you standing next to your brand-new truck, looking like you just won the lottery. I wish you had. That place wasn't worth risking a drive to town. It was slim pickin's."

He paused to take a bite of his stew. "When I didn't find any cash, I knew I'd have to look elsewhere. Reading through those papers, I put two and two together and realized this ranch was your family's place, so I decided to see what I could grab. I figured it would be an easy matter to get rid of anybody living out here in the middle of nowhere. But when I found it deserted, I realized it would make the perfect hideaway. There's plenty of food in the cupboards. A choice of beds. Change of clothes. Everything I need until the authorities give up and stop looking for me. When that happens, I plan on heading out, then ditching your truck. I'm sure I can hitch a ride with some stupid rancher, dispose of his body, and make it across the border.

"So." He mopped up gravy with a piece of bread. "What were you doing here?"

When she remained silent he growled, "I spotted you as soon as you drove up. Watched you walking around like you owned the place."

Kirby shivered at the creepy knowledge that he'd been watching her the entire time she'd been here. She'd been so caught up in her memories, she hadn't had a clue. If she'd left before entering the barn, she would be safely away now, and on her way back to the Merrick ranch.

"So, was I right? This is your family's ranch?"

She swallowed down her tears and refused to give him the satisfaction of an answer.

"Okay. Keep your secrets. Doesn't matter." He thought a minute before saying, "Was the old codger in all those pictures your father or grandfather?"

"Old codger?" The words were out of her mouth before she could think.

"Got your attention, did I?" He laughed. "I guess the only way to get you to talk is to insult some old geezer who means something to you."

"That old codger was my uncle. He was the kindest man in the world."

"Yeah? Where is he?"

"Dead." She nearly choked on the word, and the reality of it was like a blow to her heart.

Uncle Frank was gone, and the ranch he loved would be sold to a stranger who wouldn't have a single memory of the life that had been lived here. And someday, years from now, someone would discover bones in the old deserted well, and the mystery of her disappearance would be solved. But it would be too late for any sort of justice.

"So that's why this place is abandoned. But if this

ranch belongs to your family, why did you move to a cheesy walk-up in town instead of living here?"

"It isn't mine." Another blow to her heart. Just saying the words out loud made it seem more real, and had tears burning the backs of her eyelids.

"Well, it's mine. At least for now." He spooned up more stew. "Now we just wait until dark and have us some fun."

CHAPTER TWENTY-EIGHT

Kirby watched as Ray Keller paced around the room, his eyes darting often to the clock on the wall, then out the window, then to Uncle Frank's gun lying on the counter beside her phone.

She knew without a doubt he was anxious for night-fall so he could finally dispose of her.

Dispose. Such a simple word for the complicated mess she'd made of things. This convicted killer would use her own uncle's gun to shoot her before dumping her body down an old, unused well. And though she'd fought the ropes that bound her until her wrists and ankles were raw and bloody from the effort, she hadn't been able to budge them. She was tied tightly, and all she could do was wait helplessly to be killed.

Helpless. Hopeless. Useless. The words played through her mind.

The tears she'd shed earlier were now dry. She had no tears left. Now she was forced to admit the fact that only a miracle could save her.

That knowledge burned like a hot knife in the pit of her stomach. She knew it was a slim chance, but her desire to live was so strong, she clung to it. While she was forced to lie silently on the cold floor, feeling desperately alone, she whispered a prayer that something would happen to change her fate.

"What the hell...?" With a string of oaths Ray Keller rushed to the side of the window, drawing aside the curtain just a bit to peer out without being seen.

Kirby strained to hear anything out of the ordinary.

Gradually she heard the crunch of wheels on gravel, and the hum of an engine.

Keller crossed the room and dragged her to her feet, using a knife to slice cleanly through the rope at her ankles and wrists.

With a beefy hand around her neck he hauled her to the window. "Know this cowboy?"

She saw Casey descend from his truck and look around before starting toward the door.

She nodded her head, too choked up with emotion at the sight of him to manage a single word.

"Now you listen and listen good. See what he wants and get rid of him fast. If you don't, I have no problem putting a bullet through his head right where he stands." He jammed the gun to the back of her head. "You understand me?"

Terrified, she nodded.

With the gun pressed firmly against her she could hear Casey's booted feet on the porch. Every step brought him closer to death, and the thought of it had her heart beating a wild tattoo in her chest.

At the knock on the door she jerked as though she'd been shot. Keller's hand tightened, and he slammed the gun against the back of her head hard enough to have her seeing stars before whispering, "One wrong move and he dies."

There was no time to think. No time to plan. All she knew was that she had to get Casey to leave, or he'd be dead along with her.

If she couldn't save herself, at least she could do this one thing. She had to convince him to leave. Had to.

Keller reached around her and opened the door no more than a few inches, allowing Kirby to remain hidden while revealing only her face to their visitor.

Casey was smiling. "I saw the truck and was glad to know you were still here. I thought I'd try the house first. If you weren't here, I figured I'd check the barn or out in the fields."

Her mouth was so dry, she wondered if she could get a word out. "Casey. I...wasn't expecting you."

"I finished my work at Buster Mandel's ranch, so I thought I'd drive over so you wouldn't have to be alone."

Keller's mouth was so close, she could feel the sting of his breath as he whispered, "Cut the small talk."

The press of the gun was enough to have her hardening her tone. "I told you I could handle this alone."

Casey's smile faded. "Yeah. You did. But I wanted to be here for you. Especially now. I figured you'd welcome some company."

She had to blink hard to fight the tears that welled up, knowing the sacrifice he'd made to be here for her. Just for her.

Not now, she thought. There wasn't time for any tender feelings. Though it was tearing her heart to shreds, she had to get through this and force him to leave by any means possible. "Casey, you're not listening." She swallowed and, clenching her teeth, she said as harshly as she could manage, "Don't you get it? I told you not to come. I don't want you here."

He winced at her words.

His smile was wiped away, replaced by a sudden frown. "Sorry. I guess I overstepped. I thought I could help lift your spirits."

She heard the hiss of fury from Keller's lips. The gun was rammed so hard against her head, she could feel his hand trembling with the desire to pull the trigger. She realized he was at the end of his patience, and at any moment he would step around her and fire at point-blank range at Casey. He would die suddenly, violently, without any warning.

She couldn't bear the thought.

Lifting her chin for courage, she reached out, gripping the edge of the door as she said, in her most imperious tone, "How do I make you understand? I want you to go, Casey. Right now."

For an instant his eyes widened, and she thought she saw something like a glimmer of knowledge in them. Then his eyes narrowed, and she was certain she'd only imagined it.

"Yeah. Sorry to be a bother. See you." He turned away and stormed down the steps to his truck.

Kirby watched his retreat with naked hunger. It took all her willpower to keep from calling out to him. But the only way she could save his life was to hold her silence and let him go free.

Free. Right now, that mattered more to her than her own fate.

Without a backward glance Casey drove away, leaving a trail of snowflakes blowing in his wake.

When he was gone Keller swore loudly, his hand

shaking with such frenzied violence, she thought he would surely pull the trigger on her. She could feel the raw fury radiating from him in waves.

He pointed the gun at her temple, and she closed her eyes, waiting for the explosion. "I've always hated guys like that. So smooth, so sure of themselves. Do you know how much I wanted to waste that cowboy?" A shudder passed through him, and he visibly shook it off before dragging her across the room.

As he bound her wrists and ankles once again, he muttered, "I wanted to watch his eyes when he realized I was standing behind you. I'd have given anything to put the gun right up to his forehead and pull the trigger."

He shoved her to the floor with such force she cried out. She flinched when he snarled in her direction, "Listen girly, nothing gets me higher than the thrill of a kill. And I'm in the mood for a killing. Lucky for your cowboy, I had to play it smart and get rid of him. But I'll get my kicks in a couple of hours when I get to watch you die."

While he moved about the room Kirby laid there filled with dread, feeling the violence building, priming him for what was to come.

As the minutes ticked by, she began going over and over the hateful words she'd hurled at Casey. It no longer mattered that she'd been forced to say them in order to save his life. It mattered only that these would be the last things he would ever remember about her. Words that had cut deeply, leaving scars on his heart forever.

She would give anything to be able to call them back. To explain just why she'd said them. But it wasn't to be. Instead, Casey would always remember that she'd coldly, heartlessly cut him out of her life for good, just before she went missing forever.

Casey plucked his phone from his pocket as he drove like a madman. Once the dirt road curved out of sight of the Regan ranch, he brought the truck to a lurching halt and dialed a number, waiting anxiously as it rang once, twice, three times. Finally, the call connected.

"Chief Noble Crain."

"Noble, it's Casey Merrick. I just left the old Regan ranch."

"You don't say? How's it looking, Casey?"

"I don't have time for that. Listen to me. Kirby is in the house, and when I arrived, she acted funny."

"Can't blame her for that, Casey. I just heard the news here in town that her uncle's ranch is now owned by Des Dempsey's bank. She's got to be feeling pretty let down that she didn't get a chance to buy it the way she'd planned."

"You don't understand. This isn't about feeling sad. She was determined to make me leave. As though someone was coaching her. And there's more. She wouldn't open the door more than a crack, but just for a second I spotted blood dripping from her wrist."

"Did you ask her about it?"

"There was no time. She was closing the door in my face."

"Maybe she cut herself. Look, son, I don't see what I can—"

"Listen to me, Noble. Something's all wrong here. I'm asking you to come out and investigate. But whether you do or not, I'm going back."

There was a long silence, and Casey knew Noble was trying to process what he just told him. Finally he said, "If you really believe something's wrong, you need to stay away until I can get there."

"Something's very wrong. And I'm not waiting around for you or anyone else. I'm not leaving until I find out what's going on. If Kirby is in trouble as I suspect, I intend to be there for her." Casey disconnected, before dialing his family ranch.

When Billy answered, Casey asked if the family was around. Hearing that they were having lunch, he said, "Put me on speaker, Billy. Everyone needs to hear this."

As quickly as possible he described the brief meeting with Kirby. After listening in silence, Bo spoke for them.

"What do you think, son?"

"I feel in my gut that she's being held against her will, Pop."

"Then you call Noble Crain and ask for police protection."

"I've already called him. Noble's in town. An hour away. I intend to go back there and see for myself. But this time I'm not going to drive up and announce my intentions."

Egan's voice interrupted. "Is there another way to get there?"

"I didn't get much time to study the lay of the land, Gramps. But there's a barn not far from the house. I plan on leaving my truck here, at the end of the road, and walking back. I'll use the barn for cover until I can manage to get closer to the house. I need to see why Kirby was being so secretive."

Ham's gravelly voice broke in. "You listen to me, boy. We're heading over there right now. I know you can't wait for us, but you be smart. If that girl's in trouble, you could make things worse."

"That might be true, Ham. Or I could make it bad for whoever is threatening her. All I know is this. I have to be there for Kirby."

"Of course you do, boy. Just don't go getting yourself killed."

"I'll do my best."

Casey rammed his cell phone in his pocket and reached for his rifle before stepping out of the truck and sprinting in the direction of the ranch.

As he ran, he prayed that what he feared was all wrong. Maybe Noble was right, and Kirby had simply cut herself. But there had been too much blood. And it had encircled her wrist like a ribbon...or a rope.

A rope that had rubbed her flesh raw.

He nearly dropped to his knees as the thought took hold and gripped him like icy shards.

She'd been tied up.

There was suddenly no more doubt. He knew, deep in his heart that someone was holding Kirby against her will. And she'd sent him away rather than have him share her fate.

CHAPTER TWENTY-NINE

Casey followed a circuitous route back to the Regan barn, taking care to remain well hidden from view from the house.

It took him some time to navigate the dips and hollows. For some time, he managed to keep to the dense woods, but once he was in the clear, he made a dash to the rear of the barn for cover.

Just as he was about to slip around to the front, he heard the sound of an engine. Peering around the corner of the building he saw the ranch truck his father had loaned Kirby rolling toward the entrance of the barn. In the driver seat was a man.

Casey ducked back, hoping the driver hadn't spotted him.

While the truck was being driven inside the barn, Casey moved quickly along the rear of the building looking for any cracks in the wood that might allow him to see the stranger when he exited the truck. Though the barn was ancient, the paint faded and peeling, and much of the wood old and scarred, Casey realized with rising frustration that there were no cracks or holes big enough to let him peer inside.

Hearing the squeaking protest as the great door was being closed, he crept to the side of the building and was able to catch a glimpse of a tall, heavyset man with long, dark hair striding toward the house.

Something vaguely familiar about the man triggered the thought that Casey had seen him before. But he couldn't think of anyone from town who looked like that. Furthermore, no one he knew would be a threat to Kirby.

He waited until the front door slammed shut before creeping closer to the house. Once there he ducked below a window, listening for voices.

Hearing none, he slowly straightened, and decided to risk looking through the glass.

What he saw nearly stopped his heart. Kirby was lying on the floor, her ankles and wrists bound with rope.

It gave him no satisfaction to see the proof of his suspicion. Instead, he felt a terrible, simmering fury building inside him.

The man from the barn was standing across the room, with only his back visible. Beside him on the kitchen counter was a gun.

Though Casey's first instinct was to kick in the door and confront the man holding Kirby hostage, he struggled to remain calm, cool, and collected. He needed to look at this from every angle. He wasn't concerned for his own safety, but he couldn't risk putting Kirby in further danger by getting her caught in the crossfire if he came in with guns blazing. Especially since that pistol was just inches away from her captor.

*   *   *

When Kirby had heard the back door slam, she'd been puzzled. Had Keller left? Why? For how long?

It didn't matter. Knowing she was alone, if only for a minute, had her looking around frantically for anything that could be used to cut through the ropes.

She rolled across the floor until she bumped into the cupboard. Like a contortionist she lay facedown and pressed her forehead to the hard floor until she gained enough leverage to get to her knees. She knelt a moment to get her bearings, then with a supreme effort, jumped up and managed a wobbly stance that had her weaving like a drunk.

Out the window she could see Keller getting into the Merrick truck and heading toward the barn. Now she understood. He'd heard Casey say he knew she was here because he'd seen the truck parked outside. It was obvious that Keller had no intention of allowing that to happen again.

Aware that she had only a few minutes, she turned, and with her hands bound behind her, began feeling around in the drawer for a knife. At last finding one, she nudged the drawer closed with her hip and began sawing at the ropes.

She saw Keller stepping out of the barn and began sawing harder, faster.

Nerves had the knife slipping from her fingers. She gave a cry of distress as it clattered to the floor. She looked up to see Keller approaching the porch with his head down.

Desperate, she fell down and began fumbling around for the knife.

She could hear his heavy footsteps on the porch, and then the door opening.

At last she felt the cold press of the knife and gripped it between her fingers, rolling across the floor and hoping she was close enough to wherever she'd been when he left that he wouldn't notice she'd moved.

Keller didn't even glance her way as he kicked the door closed and flopped down at the kitchen table.

"Cold." With a muttered oath he picked up the half-eaten pan of stew and dumped it into a bowl before setting it in the microwave.

Minutes later he carried it back to the table and finished eating. When he was done, he sat back and tilted the chair on its two back legs, propping his feet on another chair. He helped himself to one of her uncle's cigars and held a match to the tip.

As smoke curled over his head, he crossed one foot over the other in a lazy pose and gave a smile of contentment. "This is as good a place as any to hide out until the heat's off."

He took another puff. "The old geezer who lived here had good taste."

At the contemptuous way he dismissed her uncle, Kirby felt tears well up and spill over. "The man who lived here had a name. Frank Regan. And he was like a father to me."

Keller took another drag on the cigar and gave her a chilling smile. "No sense crying over a dead man. You'll be joining him soon enough."

After fielding Casey's call, Noble Crain got ready to head out to the Regan ranch. Before leaving he sorted through the pile of emails and messages. As always, those from the state police garnered the most attention.

One in particular, with the heading ESCAPED CON-VICT in bold letters, caught his eye. Killer Keller had been loose way too long. Every day authorities across the country held their breath, expecting to be alerted to a string of murders left in his wake. So far, there had been none. No news of any sort.

Noble scanned the message, which stated that the trail had gone cold. Not a single lead had panned out. It was as if Ray Keller had vanished into thin air.

He tapped a pen against his desktop. Nobody vanishes. As a trained lawman, he knew that every criminal left clues. A good police officer followed his instincts to spot those clues in time to prevent further crimes.

Distracted, he thought about Kirby Regan. For a while, at least, he'd thought her truck would lead them to Keller.

No such luck.

He tossed aside the paper and shoved away from his desk. Time to get out to the Regan ranch and see what had Casey Merrick so riled up.

He was halfway to the ranch when he got a call from Bo Merrick.

"Hey, Bo. I was just—"

Bo's voice was a low growl of nerves. "Noble, I just heard from Casey."

"Yeah, he called me a while ago—"

"We're on the way to the Regan ranch."

" 'We'?"

"My family. Casey wanted me to tell you he saw Kirby bound hand and foot in the kitchen."

The chief felt a wave of remorse for not taking

Casey's call as seriously as he should have. His voice lowered with anger. "Does he know who did this?"

"He couldn't see the guy. Said he's big, broad shouldered. Long, dark hair. But he only saw his back."

"That could be anybody."

Bo swore. "I don't care who he is. He's holding Kirby captive, and my son says he's going to confront the guy. And we're hell-bent to back him up."

"Now you listen, Bo—"

"No, Noble. You listen. Get up here as fast as you can. And if I were you, I'd call the state police to lend a hand."

"But—"

Before the chief could respond, the line went dead.

Big, broad-shouldered, long dark hair.

His thoughts flashed back to the notice on his desk. Could it be...?

He punched in the direct line to the state police and reported what he knew, and what he suspected, before requesting backup. After giving general directions, he was assured they would have a helicopter in the air within minutes.

He hung up and floored the accelerator. Since he was on country roads, he decided to forego the siren. He wasn't likely to run into any other vehicles way out here. And he could avoid alerting the guy holding Kirby hostage that the law was coming.

He tried dialing Bo Merrick's number, to warn the family of his suspicions, but he didn't answer. He let loose with a string of oaths. The Merrick men might consider themselves tough guys, but they were amateurs against an escaped lifer with nothing to lose by killing anybody who got in his way.

*   *   *

Kirby watched in silence as Ray Keller smoked the cigar down to a nub before stubbing it in an ashtray. When he stood and picked up the gun from the kitchen counter, she couldn't swallow the fear clogging her throat.

She held her breath as he walked toward her. A glance at the window told her it was still daylight. Had Casey's visit changed his mind? Had he decided not to wait until dark?

Without a word he stepped over her and dropped into her uncle's favorite rocker set in a little alcove between the kitchen and parlor, where he could see both the television and his captive. He picked up the TV control and scrolled through the channels until he found one to his satisfaction.

As the true crime show profiled a teen who had killed his parents, grandparents, and little sisters, Keller started chuckling.

"See that?" He pointed with the control. "That could've been me. Except I didn't have grandparents or a sister. No relatives at all that I knew of. Just two parents who were the meanest drunks in the world. They spent my childhood ignoring me, unless one of them wanted a punching bag. No matter how bad things got, I had nobody to turn to for help. But then one day I was all grown up. One night, when they came home drunk and mean, I didn't shoot them. I waited until they wore themselves out beating me black-and-blue. And while they slept it off, I hacked them to death with a knife and a hatchet." He gave a small, chilling laugh. "And I enjoyed every minute of it."

Kirby felt icy fingers of dread crawling along her spine. Everything about this man repulsed her. Was he deliberately trying to ramp up the terror, just to add to her misery? If so, he was accomplishing his goal. She couldn't control the sick terror that had her in its paralyzing grip.

She closed her eyes, willing herself to breathe. She wasn't dead yet. And now, though it was slim, there was hope.

She waited. And watched. And hoped desperately that he would become distracted enough to ignore her.

As soon as she saw that he was once more caught up in the drama, she began working the blade of the knife against her ropes. Though it was slow and painful, she could feel a few of the rope strands beginning to unravel. As she worked, she prayed she didn't drop the knife again. Despite the television being on, Keller was bound to hear if it hit the floor.

He chuckled, and she used that moment of distraction to work faster until, though she couldn't believe it, she felt the rope begin to fall away from her wrists. She caught it between her fingers, hoping that if he should check her bindings he wouldn't see that her hands were free. Then she lay as still as her uneven breathing would permit.

Now to find a way to work at the rope at her ankles. She risked a glance at Keller, wishing he would doze. Instead, he seemed more alert and excited than ever as he watched the show like a rabid fan. The smile on his ugly face told her that he was enjoying this portrayal of a juvenile killer. Instead of being repulsed by the very real violence, he was probably envisioning himself in the starring role.

Kirby kept her eyes fixed on his face, waiting for any hint of his eyes closing. She was desperate to free her ankles, to flee this monster before he could carry out his threat. Every minute she waited felt like an eternity.

Peering through the window, Casey saw the man finish his cigar and disappear.

Had he left the room? Since Casey had never been inside the house, he had no idea of the layout. Craning his neck, he could see Kirby still bound, and still on the floor.

He needed to find out where her abductor had gone. He began circling the house, peering into windows. Seeing no one, he pulled himself hand over hand up an ancient trellis to the upper floor and looked in other windows. Again, he came up empty.

Where could the man be?

Casey glanced at the sky, cursing the fact that daylight was fading. If he didn't act soon, he might miss the element of surprise.

He debated his choices. If he stormed in, he took the chance that the abductor had easy access to his gun and might shoot Kirby before Casey could save her.

If he found a way to sneak inside and free Kirby first, he could send her outside before confronting the abductor.

Knowing he couldn't risk putting Kirby in even more harm than she already was, he climbed back down and circled around the house again, determined to find a way inside without smashing a window and alerting the man to his presence.

With each minute he felt his frustration growing. For

Kirby, being held against her will, every minute must be an eternity of agony. He couldn't bear the thought of how she must be suffering at the hands of this guy.

Why had he taken her hostage? Who in hell was he?

As he peered in yet another window, he saw the man walking into the kitchen, steps away from where Kirby lay bound on the floor.

In the man's hand was a gun. When he turned slightly, Casey felt a lightning bolt of recognition.

He knew instantly where he'd seen him before. His face had been on all the television news broadcasts for days.

He was the escaped convict known as Killer Keller.

CHAPTER THIRTY

Whatever cautious move Casey had planned was instantly forgotten when he saw Kirby's captor standing over her with the gun. The only thing that mattered right now was that Kirby was being held against her will by a cold-blooded killer who would have no problem killing again.

Desperate, he pressed his father's number on speed dial and said, "I have no choice. I'm going in."

He dropped the phone into his pocket before using the barrel of his rifle to smash the floor-to-ceiling window, sending shards of glass raining across the kitchen floor. He charged inside, with no regard to the jagged pieces of glass that raked his face and his arms, leaving blood dripping from half a dozen cuts.

At the first sound of breaking glass Keller wheeled around, taking aim with his pistol and firing off a shot in one quick motion.

The bullet missed Casey by a hair, hitting what was left of the window and sending more glass crashing down.

Casey was just taking aim with his rifle when Keller fired again. This time Keller hit his target and

Casey absorbed a burning pain in his left arm. A scant second later the arm went limp, dangling helplessly at his side.

For a split second Casey glanced at his arm as though it didn't belong to his body. And then, sheer determination kicked in and he started across the room toward Keller, the rifle clenched in his right arm, his finger on the trigger.

Seeing what he intended, Keller turned and aimed the gun at Kirby, who was still lying helplessly on the floor.

"Come on, cowboy." He actually smiled as he waved his hand. "One more step and I waste her."

Casey stilled immediately, his heart nearly stopping at the look of absolute terror on Kirby's face.

"It doesn't matter, Casey." Kirby's voice was strong, despite her fear. "He's already said he intended to kill me after dark."

"Now he won't have to kill you." Casey looked first at Kirby, then at Keller. "Kill me instead."

"You trying to be a big, brave hero, cowboy?" The convict's smile grew. "Okay, hero. Prove it. Drop the rifle and kick it over here."

Casey did as he said even as Kirby protested again. "You can't trust him. He's a—"

"I think we all know what I am." Keller's gaze darted from Casey to Kirby before he threw back his head, laughing maniacally. "Looks like I'm going to have myself a real good time tonight. Two killings are always better'n one. Especially when each stupid victim wants to save the other."

He picked up the discarded rifle and swung the barrel against Casey's temple with all his might.

With a grunt of pain, Casey dropped to the floor in a heap. Getting to his knees, he shook his head and stumbled up, only to have Keller's booted foot connect with his groin. He doubled over, but before he could straighten again Keller followed up with another rifle-butt blow to his head.

This time, when Casey fell to the floor, he was silent as he slipped into oblivion.

"You've killed him." Filled with blinding rage and absolute terror, Kirby almost revealed her freed hands before clenching them firmly behind her back as she twisted and turned, inching herself across the floor until she was beside Casey's still body.

"I hope you're wrong. I'd like to use him for a punching bag a few more times before I shoot him." Keller touched a finger to Casey's throat. "Good. Still alive. For now. That means I can have some more fun with this cowboy when he wakes up. I prefer an opponent who won't give up too soon. It makes the game more interesting."

After binding Casey's wrists and ankles, Keller walked back to the comfortable recliner and picked up the TV remote. Keeping both weapons beside him, he began scrolling through the channels until he found another crime show. Humming a tune, he settled in to wait for dark.

Two trucks headed toward the Regan ranch at break-neck speed. Bo drove the first truck, with his grandfather beside him and his parents in the back seat.

His argument that his grandmother should remain

at home with Liz and Avery had been loudly overruled by the women. They'd insisted that the family would stand together, no matter the danger.

Ham turned to his grandson. "I hope Casey isn't foolish enough to go storming in like J. Edgar Hoover and his band of agents. They always got hit with a volley of bullets in those movies."

Bo stared straight ahead, his hands clenched tightly to the wheel. "Casey's always kept a cool head when there's trouble, Ham."

"That was before."

Bo glanced over. "Before what?"

"Before he fell head over heels for the bean counter."

In the back seat, Meg huffed a breath. "Kirby is much more than a bean counter, Hammond."

"That she is, Margaret Mary." He looked over his shoulder, pinning her with a look. "But you can't deny it. Our Casey has fallen hard."

"You're right about that." Meg reached over and caught Egan's hand before saying to her father-in-law, "And seeing the two of them together, it's something we can all understand. I imagine he's in agony right now, worrying about Kirby, and how to free her from this stranger."

Her words had the others nodding in silence.

Brand was driving the second truck, with Avery beside him and Jonah next to her. In the back seat were his aunt Liz, Chet, and Billy.

Theirs was a somber group, their voices, when they spoke, muted.

Avery, recalling her own near-death assault at the hands of a woman with a fatal attraction, felt a chill along her spine. "I know what Kirby is feeling. I wish I could be there to comfort her."

Brand took one hand off the wheel long enough to squeeze her hand. "Don't go there in your mind, babe."

"I can't help it. The minute Casey told us about seeing blood on Kirby's wrist, I keep thinking about the lengths an attacker will go to in order to control the victim. In my case Renee Wilmot used drugs to subdue me, but at least I had a fighting chance. It must be so hard to have your hands and feet bound, knowing you can't escape."

"Okay." Brand's tone was rough. "Let's not get ahead of ourselves here. Let's hope that when we get to the Regan ranch, Casey and Kirby are just fine and it was all a misunderstanding."

From the back seat came Liz's voice. "From your lips, Brand."

Chet, seeing her hand trembling, put a big hand over hers.

All of them fell into an uncomfortable silence.

Kirby watched and waited, until she was certain Keller was deeply involved in the TV show. Letting go of the pieces of rope she'd been holding behind her, she moved slowly and carefully, inching her hands toward the rope at her ankles. While she worked the knife she kept watch over Keller, desperately afraid he would see her movements and realize what she was doing.

And then there was Casey. There was so much blood. His arms. His poor face. She knew he'd been shot, but she didn't know which was worse, the bullet wound or the blow he'd taken to his head and body. He was so still it tore at her heart. For a moment she stopped what she was doing to assure herself that he was still alive. When she saw the slight rise and fall of his chest, she managed to breathe. Keller had been right. He was alive. At least for now. She would cling to that and do whatever she could to thwart this madman.

She returned to the rope with renewed vigor. She had to get free. Had to. Even though she had no idea what chance she had against a man armed with both a pistol and a rifle, she held on to the hope that if they were freed of their bonds, at least they stood a small chance. If they remained bound, they had no chance at all.

Noble Crain was in constant contact with the state troopers as they made their way from the police post thirty miles east of town. "The Merrick family is ahead of me somewhere. I tried to convince them to wait for us to do our job, but their son is on the Regan property and they're not about to wait for anyone."

There was a short laugh on the phone before a deep voice said, "No need to explain, Noble. Ranchers are a breed apart. They're used to doing what they have to do, and to hell with the rules."

"Yeah. That's the Merrick family. How soon will you be here?"

"We're coming up on you right now."

He looked in his rearview mirror and saw the convoy of state police vans. They must have set a new speed record.

"And the helicopters?"

"Any minute now."

He stepped out of his SUV and waited until the state police walked closer, their assault weapons drawn.

They had already agreed to leave their vehicles out of sight while they made their way to the ranch house on foot.

If what he suggested turned out to be true, and the man holding a hostage inside was escaped convict Ray Keller, they wanted to be certain that he didn't get away again.

It was a matter of pride to all of them. If they were successful, they would be hailed as heroes. If they made a mistake that allowed him to escape yet again, the blame would lie squarely on their shoulders.

Not one of them was willing to consider failing, especially with an innocent hostage at his mercy.

Killer Keller would be stopped, or they would die trying.

The real job was to make sure that the hostage emerged from this siege alive.

CHAPTER THIRTY-ONE

Casey awoke to fireworks going off. Bright neon red-and-yellow flashes, brighter than the sign over Nonie's Wild Horses Saloon. The only trouble was, they were going off inside his brain, causing him to wince in pain.

At least, he thought, it was proof that he wasn't dead. Yet.

For a moment the fireworks ended, and he began to relax. But then they started up again and he clenched his teeth as pain radiated from his brain to his left arm, before exploding through him. His entire body was bathed in sweat.

Maybe death was better, he thought as he clenched his teeth against the pain.

"I'm sorry." He heard the softest whisper and wondered how he knew that voice.

He opened his eyes and tried to focus on the beautiful woman who floated in and out of his vision.

She put a finger to his lips and gave the slightest shake of her head before her finger disappeared from view. He wanted to tell her to touch him again. For that one instant he felt warm, and now he was cold. So cold.

Fresh pain radiated along his left arm. White hot pain. He opened his mouth but no sound came out. Yet in his mind he was screaming in agony.

What in hell was happening to him? When he tried to move his hands, they wouldn't budge. The same with his feet.

He looked down and realized that his ankles were tied with rope. His wrists were bound behind his back, as well. And then a fresh thought speared through his mind. He'd been shot. Trying to save Kirby.

Kirby. She was being held hostage by that convict.

He had to save her. *Had to.* He tugged desperately at the rope binding his wrists, and felt it fall away.

In that same moment, Kirby swam into his line of vision again as she gave a firm shake of her head, her finger back on his lips.

Moments later he felt her move away slightly as she began working a knife through the rope at his ankles.

Despite the pain, he was suddenly awake and alert.

For a brief moment he'd thought he had some sort of mystical powers that could disintegrate rope. Now he realized that he hadn't mysteriously broken free. This was all Kirby's doing. By some miracle she had taken possession of a knife and was trying to free him.

When the rope she'd been working on finally fell away, she wrapped the ends lightly over his ankles, and pointed to the man in the recliner, who was intent on the television screen.

He understood her signal. If Keller looked over, he would assume that both he and Kirby were still bound, hand and foot.

He gave her a quick nod of his head, and for the first time she managed a smile of relief as she hid the knife beneath her body and lay perfectly still beside him.

Now, free of his bonds, he would have to concentrate all his energy on staying alert. Whenever he saw their chance, he had to be ready to take it, no matter how much it cost him. Including his own life. His only goal now was to save Kirby from this killer.

The Merrick family huddled behind the barn, holding a frantic whispered conference.

Bo's voice was husky with agitation and fear. "All Casey said was that he was going in. Then the line went dead."

Brand touched a hand to his father's arm. "We've all got rifles. I say we just follow Casey's lead. If we storm the house, this guy can't hit all of us."

Bo was quick to shake his head. "But he can hit some. I'd like to leave here with my entire family intact. There has to be a better way."

Jonah tossed his rope and lassoed a beam above the hayloft window.

At his father's arched brow, he shrugged. "I figure I'll see if there's any equipment inside that could be useful. Like a backhoe that we could use to smash through a wall or two."

Bo nodded. "Good thinking. That would certainly distract whoever is inside with Kirby and Casey."

Jonah began climbing hand over hand, with Brand following right behind him.

The two brothers forced the window open and climbed inside, while the family waited in silence below.

Minutes later, though it seemed more like an hour, they slid down the rope to announce that there was no heavy equipment left. But they'd found the ranch truck Kirby drove, along with a newer-model truck that had Washington, DC, plates.

Bo's eyes went wide. "It has to be Kirby's truck."

Meg looked puzzled. "But it was stolen."

"Yeah." Bo's face turned into a frown of doom and gloom. "This changes everything."

Ham shot him a stern look. "You thinking what I'm thinking?"

Bo nodded. "If Casey's stolen truck is here, that means the guy who stole it is here, too."

"But I thought it was stolen by that escaped convict…" All the color drained from Meg's face as she realized the truth. "Oh, sweet heaven." She felt Egan's arms come around and draw her close. Against his chest she managed to cry, "Oh, Egan. Kirby and Casey are in there with a convicted killer."

Chief Noble Crain led the team of police sharpshooters over a rise and came to a sudden halt when he spotted the Merrick family behind the Regan barn.

He turned to Lieutenant Barrow, the officer in charge. "That's the family of the man who phoned me. I'll have a talk with them and explain your plan."

As he approached, Bo started forward. "Kirby Regan's truck is parked inside this barn, Noble. We believe that the escaped convict is the one holding her hostage."

Noble nodded. "The state boys and I have reached the same conclusion." He glanced around. "Where's Casey?"

"Inside. He called and said he was going in. Then the line went dead. We plan to follow his lead."

Noble swore and held up a hand. "You're not going anywhere until you get your marching orders from the state police." With a worried expression he turned away to speak to the lieutenant.

Minutes later he returned to make introductions, only to find the Merrick men ignoring his order and loading their rifles.

He lifted a hand for their attention. "We have a team of state police sharpshooters who are already surrounding the house. When Lieutenant Barrow gives me the signal, I'll use the bullhorn to alert Ray Keller that his only chance of staying alive is to release the hostages and surrender. I want all of you to stay here, far from danger, until you get the all clear."

When he walked away Ham drew himself up to his full height and turned to his son, grandson, and great-grandsons. "That's all well and good, and I'm sure those sharpshooters are the best around. But from what I've heard about this convict, he's not going to just release Kirby and Casey and walk out with his hands in the air like a good little boy." He turned to the women. "You three will stay here where it's safe. We're going in after Casey and Kirby before this killer realizes he's surrounded and panics, then shoots up everything in his path."

He started to march away when he turned to see the women moving along beside them. When he began to protest, Meg stopped him with a hairy eyeball. "Hammond Merrick, I've stood beside your son for fifty years, and I've never hid from danger. I don't

intend to start now. Those hostages inside are as much
my family as yours."

Behind her, Avery and Liz nodded their agreement.

Realizing it was a waste of time to argue, he spun
away and continued toward the house, with the others
following.

The Merrick family was halfway to the ranch house
when a voice, amplified by a bullhorn, announced,
"Ray Keller. The house is surrounded by Wyoming
State Police sharpshooters. If you release your hostages
and come out with your hands in the air, you will not
be harmed."

Inside the house, Keller leapt from the chair where he'd
been watching a true-crime reenactment of a brazen
gang of bank robbers shooting half a city's police force
as they made good their escape to a waiting van.

After his time on the run it took him mere seconds
to react. He tucked his pistol in the waistband of his
pants and aimed the rifle at the man and woman lying
on the floor.

"Looks like the rules of the game have changed."
Instead of his usual smirk, his face was contorted with
fury. "They think they've got me cornered. But I've
still got an ace up my sleeve." He stepped closer, pointing the rifle downward toward Casey. "Sorry I can't
dump your body down the well like I'd planned, but
you'll be just as dead in here. That'll let them know I
mean business. And then the woman will be my shield
when we walk out of here together. And if they try to
stop me, I'll let them know they've signed her death
warrant, too."

*   *   *

Casey's mind was working feverishly. Thanks to Kirby, he had an ace of his own. Though he knew it was a gamble, he needed Keller to get close enough to overpower. Otherwise, the first bullet out of that rifle would bring on his last moment on earth.

"You think that gun makes you a big man, don't you?"

Keller blinked before stepping closer. "This gun makes me the man to beat. And if you think I'm dumb enough to toss this aside and fight you with my fists, think again, cowboy. I'm nobody's fool. Killing you is going to be a real pleasure. I just wish I had time to make you suffer first."

As he took aim, Casey kicked out with his foot to hook Keller's ankle, catching the convict completely by surprise as he lost his balance and fell forward. The motion caused him to fire off a shot. The bullet went wild.

Casey used that moment to pounce, bringing his fist to the back of Keller's head, stunning him for an instant. Casey grabbed a handful of the man's hair and slammed his face to the floor.

Keller swore and twisted free, kicking viciously at Casey's left arm, causing blood to spurt from the bullet wound and Casey to suck in a breath on the crippling pain. Even before he could straighten up, Keller took aim with the rifle and fired again at close range, sending Casey slamming against the wall before sliding slowly to the floor. Barely conscious, he watched helplessly as Keller advanced, rifle aimed and ready to fire a final, fatal shot.

At the sound of voices, Keller's head came up sharply as a group of men and women came racing through the same shattered window Casey had used earlier.

He swore. "More heroes. Now you're all going to die."

As he turned and took aim at them, he heard a female's voice cry, "No!"

There was a blur of motion to one side as Kirby came at him like a wildcat, her raised arm holding a knife.

Before he could react she jammed the knife into his shoulder again and again, forcing him to drop the rifle and clutch at the fountain of blood that spurted.

With a savage oath he fell to his knees. Seeing that the Merricks were still advancing, he made a grab for the pistol at his waist. Just as he freed it, a booted foot made contact with his hand and the pistol went flying through the air. He looked up to find Kirby standing over him, tears of pain and rage flowing down her cheeks.

"You killed Casey," she shouted. "For that, I'll never forgive you. Never." She continued pummeling him with her fists, until he was forced to cover his head with his hands as the Merrick family jumped into the fray.

The sound of gunshots inside the house had the police quickly changing tactics. With a group of them maintaining their positions to keep the house surrounded, in case the fugitive tried to break away, the rest of the officers were ordered to proceed inside.

With Noble Crain and the lieutenant in the lead, they entered to find Brand and Jonah Merrick standing over a bloody Ray Keller with rifles pointed at his head. The others had gathered around Casey's bloody figure lying in a corner of the room.

"He's alive." Meg's voice had Noble hurrying over to see for himself as he yelled for medics.

"Are you sure?" Kirby was clinging to Casey's hand, while tears flooded her eyes.

As paramedics approached, the family was ordered to move away and make room.

"I've got a pulse," one of the paramedics shouted. "Erratic but strong."

Another inserted an intravenous needle into Casey's arm.

All the while, Kirby continued holding on to Casey's hand, as though afraid to let go for even one second.

"You need to step back, Miss," one of the paramedics said.

"She...stays." Casey managed the words through a haze of pain.

"Oh, Casey." Kirby's tears flowed even faster. "I was so afraid he'd killed you."

Across the room, Ray Keller had been restrained before medics began assessing his wounds.

"Damned female stabbed me clear to the bone," he was shouting as the police led him away.

Casey gave a thumbs-up to his family. "She's... hero."

"You both are." Noble gave the Merrick family a look of amazement. "I don't know how these two managed to survive, but I'm betting they'll have quite a story to tell. As for the rest of you..." He shot a look at the lieutenant before adding, "We weren't pleased to have you ignore our orders, but I suppose, since it ended well..."

"Thanks to that little firebrand." Ham pointed at Kirby, who was busy admonishing the medics to handle Casey with care as they lifted him onto a portable gurney and began rolling it toward the door.

One of them turned to her. "You'll have to stay behind, Miss."

"Stays...with me," Casey said as firmly as he could with the sedative beginning to take effect.

Noble nodded to the medic. "You heard him. The young lady goes with him." He turned to the others. "I'll want statements from all of you."

Ham started toward the door. "Stop by the ranch later, Noble. Right now we need to follow along to town."

As the family disappeared, the state police lieutenant watched with a frown before turning to the chief. "Are you just going to let them walk away like that?"

Noble couldn't suppress a grin. "You saw how they follow orders. They barged in here ahead of our shooters. They were ready to stop a killer's bullets in order to save one of their own. You think a little thing like asking for their statements is going to keep them here now?"

The lieutenant chuckled. "I see what you mean. So that's the famous Merrick family. I understand the old man is a legend."

"Hammond, the Hammer. Yeah. That's one tough old bird. And the rest of them are just as tough."

Noble looked around at the officers bagging evidence, while outside the team of sharpshooters was busy putting away their weapons in the convoy of vehicles that had rolled up after the all clear.

"Thanks to the Merrick family, we got our man."

"Without a fatality."

Noble nodded and shook the officer's hand. "Now I'd better head back to town to watch the circus."

At the lieutenant's questioning look he said with a laugh, "I can't wait to watch the Merrick family take charge of poor Dr. Peterson at the Devil's Door Clinic. In fact, I'm betting it'll be better than a circus."

CHAPTER THIRTY-TWO

Billy had been busy in the kitchen since early in the morning. From the amazing aromas perfuming the air, it was clear he was preparing all of Casey's favorites.

Meg and Egan sat by the fire with Ham, talking softly. Every so often they would glance out the window, hoping to spot the truck that had left for town hours ago.

Liz had locked herself in her studio in the barn, explaining that working on her photographs would help pass the time until her brother and nephews returned with Casey and Kirby.

Kirby. The thought of her had Meg lowering her voice. "I'm worried about Kirby. She wouldn't even come back with us last night to shower and rest."

Ham shot her a look. "Would you, if that was Egan in that hospital bed?"

"Of course not. But that's different. Egan has been part of my life for over fifty years."

In his typical brusque manner Ham said, "I think once you've found the right one, the number of years doesn't matter. Love's love, whether for a minute or a lifetime."

Meg nodded. "I'm just not sure those two really know what they're feeling. Especially Kirby. That poor young woman has been through an ordeal. She needs time. And some pampering."

"And she'll get it. First things first, Margaret Mary. You could see that she was worried sick about Casey, after seeing him shot at close range, and believing him dead. How could she leave him, even for a night?"

Egan added, "Dr. Peterson said the bullets hadn't hit any vital organs or arteries. The wounds were clean. Besides the gunshots, much of the blood was from the glass when he'd burst through that window. But Casey was looking pretty scary when we got there."

"Thank heaven, he was so lucky." Meg touched a hand to Egan's. "But poor Kirby went through a trauma of her own. I saw Dr. Peterson's face when he examined the cuts made by those ropes around her wrists and ankles. The cuts were deep, proving that she'd fought them until she couldn't fight anymore. Her flesh was so torn and bloody, it looked like she'd been caught in one of those cruel animal traps. I almost think she'd have chewed off her own hands just to get free, in order to save Casey."

Ham gave a grunt of acknowledgment. "Still, Doc wouldn't be releasing her and Casey if he didn't think they were healing."

"I'm sure they are." Meg sighed. "Still, I'm a firm believer in therapy."

"We've got Avery for that."

Meg shook her head. "Not physical therapy. Kirby experienced terrible fear at the hands of that killer. It isn't something she can simply forget overnight.

Trauma like that could haunt her for years without the proper care."

Billy crossed the room and handed Meg a cup. "Herbal tea, Miss Meg. It'll soothe you."

"Thank you, Billy." She fell silent as she sipped her tea and joined the men in listening for the sound of a truck.

"I want to see the two of you back here at the end of the week." Dr. Peterson handed Kirby a printout of his notes on the proper care of their wounds, along with several prescriptions. One for pain medication for Casey, and another for ointment for Kirby's wrists and ankles, which had already begun scabbing over. "And Kirby, you may want to talk to a counselor about any lingering fears or bad dreams."

"Yes. Thank you."

As the doctor's assistant, Jenny Swan, wheeled Casey toward the door, Kirby walked along beside him in a mental fog as she kept a hand on his arm.

With Brand and Jonah trailing behind them, ready to assist Casey into the back of the truck, their father, Bo, remained behind in the clinic.

As soon as they were alone Bo turned to the doctor. "What's bothering you, Doc? Is there something about Casey's wounds you haven't told me?"

The doctor shook his head. "It's not about Casey. His wounds are fine. I'm worried about Kirby. She barely slept last night. Just kept watch over Casey, as though she expected him to stop breathing at any minute."

"Don't you think that's typical? They were both held hostage by a man bent on killing them."

Dr. Peterson shrugged. "There's just something…" He paused. "I can't put my finger on it, but Kirby seems in a kind of limbo. That's why I suggested some counseling. I want her to be able to put this behind her and get on with her life."

Bo nodded. "After all that young woman has been through, I'd think it strange if she wasn't feeling anxious."

The doctor managed a smile. "I could be overreacting. But keep an eye on her, Bo."

"I will." The two men shook hands and Bo made his way to the truck, in front of the entrance of the clinic.

He climbed up to the passenger seat and glanced in the back, where Casey and Kirby sat, shoulders brushing, both looking everywhere but at one another.

On the long drive home they seemed content to let Brand and Jonah carry the conversation, while they stared out the side windows, watching as a light snow fell, dusting the highway before them.

The minute the truck pulled up to the back porch, the family spilled down the steps to greet Casey and Kirby with fierce hugs and tons of kisses.

"Here's our little spitfire," Egan said.

He and Meg kept their arms around Kirby, while Ham led the way inside with Casey.

In the kitchen both Casey and Kirby were urged to sit by the fire where they were bundled under afghans. Billy handed Kirby herbal tea and offered Casey a mug of hot chocolate.

"You'd better be careful," Casey warned. "With all this pampering, I may decide to give up ranch chores altogether and just sit around watching the rest of you work."

"Not likely." Brand shared a grin with Jonah. "You try it, bro, and we'll haul your—" he shot a glance at his grandmother before saying quickly "—we'll haul your hide out to the barn and tape a shovel to your hand so you can't stop until the job's done."

That had everyone laughing and beginning to relax.

Casey looked around. "Where's Aunt Liz?"

"Out in her studio. Chet went to tell her you're home."

"He could've phoned her."

Jonah gave his brother a sly look. "Then he wouldn't have had an excuse to walk back with her."

The two shared grins.

When Kirby finished her tea Meg said gently, "Would you like to go up to your room and shower?"

For the first time Kirby seemed to realize how she must look. "I guess I should."

She climbed the stairs, hearing the familiar murmur of voices below.

Once in her room she stepped into the bathroom and caught her reflection in a mirror. She was dismayed to see the bloody stains on her filthy shirt and pants.

For a moment she gripped the edge of the counter, seeing again in her mind the way Casey had looked after being shot. So much blood. So much pain. And all she could do was watch in absolute terror as his life seemed to be draining away.

She stripped and got into the shower, feeling the sting of the spray as she scrubbed away all traces of blood and let the warm water beat down on her. She stepped out and dried herself before wrapping her hair in a thick towel.

From the closet she withdrew a suitcase and began packing her meager belongings. During her time at the clinic she'd had time to think. To plan on what she ought to do next.

Tomorrow she would move into the apartment above Julie Franklyn's hair salon. Though she hadn't had a chance to see it, she knew it would suit her simple needs. After all, she'd survived in the big city for years, even though her heart had always been in Wyoming. Now she was back, and though it wasn't turning into the life she'd envisioned, she'd made her peace with it. If she couldn't have a full loaf, she'd settle for half.

What had Uncle Frank always said?

No sense crying over spilt milk. Clean up the mess and enjoy what's left in the jug, and then get on with it.

When she'd finished packing, feeling exhausted beyond belief and unable to ignore the lure of the big bed any longer, she climbed beneath the covers and was asleep almost as soon as her head hit the pillow.

At a knock on her door Kirby awoke with a jolt and sat up. It took her a moment to get her bearings. Slipping out of bed, she hurried to see who it was.

Casey couldn't help smiling at the sight of her wearing nothing but a towel. "You look rested. Not to mention really hot." As he watched her flush, his smile widened. "I figured once you came upstairs, you'd grab some sleep."

"Sorry." Caught unawares, she suddenly felt shy.

He gave her a steady look. "Every time I woke last

night in the clinic you were sitting beside me. I don't think you slept at all."

She gave a negligent shrug of her shoulder. "That doesn't matter. What does matter is that you slept."

"I had no choice. Dr. Peterson had me so full of sedatives, I'd have slept through a tornado." He lifted her hand to his lips. "Besides, my fierce little warrior was there beside me, ready to protect me."

She shivered at his intimate touch. "Just returning the favor."

He made no move to leave. "Billy said dinner will be ready in a few minutes. But we have time—"

She pulled away. "Give me a minute to dress, and I'll join you downstairs."

Casey looked beyond her to the open suitcase. "What this?"

She turned away to avoid the censure in his tone. "I thought I'd get a head start on packing. I'll be ready to move into Julie Franklyn's apartment in the morning."

His voice lowered. "You in a hurry to leave?"

"Of course not." She kept her back to him. "But I've imposed long enough. Thanks to me, your family almost lost you."

He dropped a hand on her shoulder. "Kirby—"

She whirled, then stepped away, evading his touch. "Give me a minute, Casey."

"Of course. Sorry. I'll be downstairs."

She struggled to ignore the pain in his eyes as he turned and walked from the room.

Closing the door, she dressed quickly and ran a brush through her hair.

A short time later she descended the stairs. The

sound of voices drifted from the kitchen. When she stepped into the room the voices halted for a moment, and then Billy called them to supper.

She took the seat beside Casey. And though the meal was a joyful celebration, filled with typical Merrick jokes and teasing, she and Casey remained subdued.

From his position at the head of the table Ham looked around with a smile of satisfaction.

Watching him, Bo muttered, "It feels good, doesn't it, Ham?"

The others fell silent as the old man nodded. "There was a moment when I worried that we might never get this chance again."

Bo lifted his longneck in a salute. "Here's to family."

Around the table, they lifted beer and water and cups of tea to intone, "To family."

Casey glanced at Kirby, who managed a weak smile while lifting her cup with the others.

As the meal dragged on, though, Kirby moved her food around her plate, Casey gave up all attempts to pretend to eat. While the teasing and laughter swirled around them, they held themselves stiffly, as though avoiding even the merest touch of hand or shoulder.

Just then Ham announced, "I'm thinking we should take another day off and head into town for a celebratory drink at Nonie's. I'm sure by now the folks in town have heard about Casey and Kirby and their wild adventure, and they'll be hungry for details from the horses' mouths."

When the others nodded, and Jonah made a smart remark about how many pretty girls he could impress by admitting he was part of the rescue team, Casey's smile was wiped from his lips.

He pushed away from the table so suddenly his chair tumbled backward.

He took no notice as he grabbed hold of Kirby's hand. "Come with me."

Startled, she simply stared, her eyes wide. "What? Where?"

"I don't know. Away from here." He thought a moment. "To the great room."

"Now?" She held back.

"Right now." His tone was pure ice.

While the family watched and listened in silence, Billy called, "I made your favorite dessert. Brownies with hot fudge sauce and ice cream."

"No thanks, Billy." Casey was staring intently at Kirby. He gripped her hand tightly. "Come with me." Seeing that she was about to refuse, he managed to growl, "Please."

Kirby slowly got to her feet.

As the others watched with looks that ranged from curiosity to amusement, Casey and Kirby left the room.

CHAPTER THIRTY-THREE

Kirby's heart was thumping inside her chest so loudly she wondered if Casey could hear it.

She risked a quick glance at his face. So stern. So serious. He looked, if not angry, at least determined. As though he had things to say that were about to burst out of him. Things he couldn't wait another minute to say. Things he couldn't hold back another minute.

Painful things she didn't want to hear?

As the thought formed, her heartbeat began thundering painfully, making it hard to breathe.

He didn't let go of her hand, even after they stepped through the doorway. He led her across the room where a fire burned on the hearth. He gestured toward two chairs close together and waited until she settled into one before taking the other, perching on the edge as though unable to settle. The look he gave her was direct and piercing.

She had to lick her dry lips before she could say a word. "What's wrong, Casey? You look so...fierce."

"I know you've packed your things. That must mean you've made plans. So, what do you want, going forward?"

She shrugged. "I guess I'll try to figure it out the way I always have. One step at a time."

"When we were alone up in the hills, you confided in me. You told me when you left Wyoming, you found yourself doing a job that wasn't what you'd hoped for, living in a big, impersonal city rushing from traffic jams to hurried takeout meals, to waking up to do it all over again the next day."

"Maybe I was being too dramatic. It wasn't that bad."

"Bad enough that you sold everything to come back home. That tells me you'd had enough of city life. How about now? You came back to Wyoming with a dream to buy your uncle's ranch. Do you intend to fight for that dream?"

She shook her head. "After what we went through there, I don't think it would ever feel the same. There are too many bad memories now."

His tone lowered. Softened. "Can we talk about what happened at your uncle's ranch? Specifically, what happened when I got there?"

She looked down at her hands. "I know I hurt you, saying all those ugly things when you came to surprise me. You looked so happy to be there, and I..." She swallowed. "Keller said if I didn't get rid of you, he would kill you."

Casey nodded. "That's what I figured. He was standing right behind the door, wasn't he?"

"Yes."

"With a gun to your head?"

A shudder passed through her. "I don't want to think about that. But I had a lot of time to think after you left. I realized that I should have found some other way to make you leave. I realized that once I was dead, those awful words would be the last things you'd remember about me. But it all happened so quickly, I couldn't think…"

He leaned close to touch his finger to her mouth. "Kirby, I figured it out when I saw the blood on your wrist."

"You did?" She lifted her head to stare at him.

"I didn't know all of it, but I figured you were in trouble. That's why I drove away as fast as I could, so I could alert the family and the authorities, before coming back."

"I thought you were so wounded by my words, and so mad at me, you couldn't wait to get away. And then everything started getting out of control, and all of it so horrible, there wasn't time to sort through it all. I just knew that the most important thing of all was getting you to leave. If Keller managed to kill you, it was all on me."

"Why would you think that?"

"Because it's the truth. If not for me, you would have never been there. If not for me, your family would have never had to go through all this. Don't you see? You've all been so kind to me from the first time you met me, and I repaid all of you by almost getting you killed. I can't stand thinking about what almost happened. And I think, the sooner I can get out of all your lives, the better you'll all—"

Again he touched a finger to her mouth. "Okay. You've had your say. My turn. You want to know what I was thinking while I was lying in the clinic?"

"I don't think I want to hear this."

"I was thinking it's time I take another trek up into the hills."

At that sudden turn in the conversation, Kirby found herself having to make an adjustment. She nodded numbly. "It will be good for you. You told me it's where you can completely relax. And where you do your best thinking, away from everybody. After what you've been through, I'm sure it'll feel like heaven."

"Only if you're there with me."

"What? That's just silly. I have to be practical now, Casey. I've neglected my job. I need a place to stay. I've got to figure out my future."

"Maybe, up in the hills, we'll both have time to figure out our future."

At the hushed tone of his voice she couldn't find her own.

"Think about it, Kirby. Nobody around for miles. No escaped convict to watch out for. No wounded mustang to care for. No timetable forcing us to cut short our time, even if a blizzard blows through. Just the two of us. Alone together."

"Alone together." She couldn't help almost smiling. "How can two people be alone *and* together?"

"Two people who love each other can find themselves alone together, away from family, work, responsibility, and all the cares of the world, so they can simply...love."

"That's a nice dream. But reality—"

"Not a dream. It can be our reality, for the rest of our lives. Tell me something, Kirby. Could you be happy way out here, on my family's ranch?"

"Honestly? This place is heaven."

"Then heaven can be ours. Do you love me, Kirby?"

She drew back. "Why are you asking me this?"

"Just answer. Do you love me?"

"I..." She took in a deep breath. "Are you asking this because I brought you all this trouble?"

"You brought me something so special, I didn't even recognize it until I almost lost it."

She began shaking her head and moving back, away from his touch. "You're not making any sense."

He caught both her hands in his and held them tightly. "When I thought I might lose you forever, I realized the truth."

Ham's voice played through his mind.

Say it like you mean it, boy. And mean it when you say it.

His voice lowered. Softened. "I love you, Kirby Regan. Desperately. More than anything in this world, I want you to be part of my life. And if you say that you love me, too, that you want to be with me forever, you'll make me the happiest man in the world for the rest of my life."

She felt those damnable tears welling up and spilling over, and couldn't stop them. "For the rest of your life. Oh, Casey, there was a moment, when Keller shot you at close range, that I thought I'd seen your life end. And I wasn't sure I could bear it." She swiped at her tears and flung her arms around his neck. "I couldn't bear seeing you hurt...or worse. I want the same thing you want. Just you, Casey Merrick, for the rest of my life."

"About damned time," Jonah shouted as the door burst open and the family spilled inside, offering words of congratulations while grabbing both Casey and Kirby in fierce hugs.

Billy produced a bottle of champagne and began passing around filled flutes of bubbly.

As the family milled about, thumping backs and bumping fists, Casey made his way to Kirby's side and took her hand in his. "Sorry. I'd hoped to propose in the traditional way, and give you some time, but once again the Merrick family decided to intrude and do it their way. Do you mind?"

"Mind?" She wrapped her arms around his neck and pressed her mouth to his. "I can't wait to be part of this crazy family."

"Really? You mean it?"

"With all my heart."

"I wouldn't settle for less than all your heart, Sunshine."

"You've got it. I think you've had it since the first time I met you and saw how tenderly you cared for that wounded filly."

Ham strode over and stepped between them before catching Kirby's hand. His look was direct and fierce. "I thought maybe you'd had enough of us."

"I'll never have enough of you and this family, Ham."

"Good, because you're about to become part of this family. And we'll always be here for you, girl."

He turned and pinned Casey with a look that he'd perfected through the years. "For a while there, I was afraid you'd lost your senses, boy. I see now you finally figured things out."

"I did. Just the way you taught me, Ham."

The old man stepped away, allowing Casey and Kirby to draw together as he lifted his glass and proposed a toast to the couple. Brand and Jonah added naughty jokes, while Meg and Egan stood beaming.

Through it all Casey and Kirby stood smiling their

secret smiles, feeling a rare sense of peace settle over them as they realized just how happy they were to be sharing their joy with this rowdy, funny, amazing family.

Life didn't get much better.

EPILOGUE

Snow was falling in a gauzy curtain outside the windows. The prediction for the month of November had come true. So far there'd been a record snowfall in Wyoming. The countryside around the Merrick ranch was a picture postcard.

In the kitchen Billy was preparing a wedding lunch. Both Casey and Kirby had asked for a simple ceremony here at the ranch, and the family had agreed to honor their wishes. But that didn't mean the meal had to be simple.

Beef tenderloin, cooked to perfection, was resting on a sideboard. Potatoes were bubbling on the stove and would soon be mashed with butter and sour cream. A salad of fresh lettuce and tomatoes from the greenhouse awaited Billy's special balsamic dressing. Steam arose from a basket of sourdough rolls fresh from the oven.

Billy put the finishing touches on the wedding cake. At Casey's request it was four layers of strawberry shortcake, mounded on top with freshly whipped cream. Billy set in place the wedding figures, a man and woman in full hiking gear, the man's figure holding a black medical bag in his hand.

With a sense of pride Billy stepped back to admire his creation.

"Looks great." Jonah dipped a finger in the whipped cream and was smacked with Billy's wooden spoon.

"No fingerprints."

"Okay." With a wicked grin Jonah ran a finger around the rim of the plate before tasting. "See? No prints."

Brand stood in the doorway. "Time for us to fetch the bridegroom."

"Isn't he in his room?"

Brand shook his head. "Out in the barn."

"I hope he took the time to muck some stalls. It's the least he can do since he intends to be gone for a couple of weeks."

The two brothers sauntered out together, their laughter ringing in the air.

"Oh, Kirby," Meg sighed.

She, Liz, and Avery gathered around Kirby as she stood before the full-length mirror in the upstairs guest room. "You're such a beautiful bride."

Kirby wore an ankle-length denim-and-lace dress with long sleeves inset with lace, and a deep V neckline with a stand-up collar. Simple, yet elegant. On her feet were Western boots. She wore her hair long and loose, with one side tucked up behind her ear and pinned in place with a jeweled hair clip.

Meg studied Kirby's reflection in the mirror. "Reverend Lawson is downstairs."

"I just need a minute." Kirby produced three small bags and handed them around.

"What's this?" Meg stared at the bag.

"You're the grandmother of the groom, Miss Meg. But since you're Casey's grandmother, I figure after today, you'll be mine, too. I hope you don't mind?"

"Mind? Kirby, honey, I'm honored." Meg opened the bag to reveal a tissue-wrapped wood carving of a woman with three boys and a girl at her knee. All were looking up with matching smiles.

Meg's eyes were damp as she kissed Kirby's cheek. "Thank you. I'll treasure this."

"Not as much as I treasure you."

Liz opened her bag to find an oval brooch with a mustang rearing on its hind legs.

She looked up with a smile. "Where did you find this?"

"On the internet." Kirby beamed her pleasure. "It reminded me of one of the pictures in your studio."

"Thank you." Liz gave her a fierce hug. "I love it."

They turned to watch as Avery opened her bag and found a ceramic statue of two women with their arms around one another. It was inscribed, "To the sister of my heart."

Avery couldn't stop the tears. "I never had a sister until today."

"Neither did I. But I'm so happy to have you."

The two women fell into each other's arms and hugged.

There was a knock at the door. The two women stepped apart just as Meg opened it to find Casey standing outside.

"I understand there's a bride hiding in here."

The women laughed as they started past him.

Avery leaned close to whisper to him, "I don't

think she's hiding. Just waiting for her true love to claim her."

"That's why I'm here."

As the door closed, Casey stood a moment, drinking in the vision across the room. When he managed to find his voice he said, "I see you've returned to your roots."

Suddenly shy, Kirby nodded. "I hope you don't mind that I didn't choose a traditional wedding gown."

His smile was quick and sexy. "Sunshine, ours isn't a traditional wedding. But I do believe our marriage will be."

"Oh, I hope so. I see your grandparents, and I want the love they have."

"We already have it. Now all we need is a lifetime together." He moved closer, keeping both hands behind his back. "I brought you some things. Which door would you like to open first?"

She tapped his left shoulder.

"Okay. Door number one." He handed her a small jeweler's box.

She opened it. Nestled inside she caught the glint of a chain and a familiar gold locket. She shot him a look of amazement. "Is this...?"

He nodded. "The one with your parents' pictures inside."

"But I thought it was gone forever."

"The police found it in Ray Keller's supplies. He admitted that he intended to pawn it whenever he got the opportunity." Casey turned away to hide something in the nightstand before turning back to lift the locket from the box and fasten it around Kirby's neck. "Now it's back where it belongs. And your parents are here with us, to witness their daughter's wedding."

She felt the moisture of tears and blinked them away. "Casey. This is a miracle."

"I like to think the miracle is us. You and me, Sunshine."

He went again to the nightstand before saying, "Now for door number two."

She touched a hand to his right shoulder, and he pulled his arm from behind his back to hand her a nosegay of bright orange Indian paintbrush.

She let out a little gasp of surprise. "The state flower."

"To celebrate the fact that you're back in Wyoming to stay."

"Where did you find any in bloom in this weather?"

"Julie Franklyn's friend owns a flower shop. She forced the blooms in a hothouse."

"I love them."

"And I love you, Sunshine." He didn't need Ham's reminder to say it like he meant it. It was the absolute truth.

He gathered her close and kissed her until they were both breathless.

As they came up for air, he caught her hand and started toward the door. "Come on. The preacher's waiting, and I'm in a hurry. Once this party's over, we can head on up to the hills where I can have you all to myself forever and ever."

Forever and ever.

The words sang in her heart as she descended the stairs beside her sexy cowboy. She'd come so far. All the way across the country and back to her roots, to find her home with this wonderful man and his rowdy, fun-loving family.

In Casey's arms she'd found all the joy and love she'd ever dreamed of.

What an amazing adventure they'd had so far.

And she was sure that this was just the beginning of the adventure of a lifetime.

BILLY'S SOURDOUGH ROLLS

Ingredients

½ cup sourdough starter
1 cup lukewarm water
2½ cups all-purpose flour
1½ teaspoons salt
2 tablespoons sugar
6 tablespoons unsalted butter—room temperature
¼ cup nonfat dry milk
¼ cup potato flour
1½ teaspoons instant yeast

Directions

Combine all the ingredients, mix, and knead, adding more flour or water if necessary to make a soft, smooth dough.

Place the dough into a lightly greased bowl, cover, and allow to rise at room temperature until it's nearly doubled in bulk (approximately 1 to 1½ hours)

Lightly grease two 8-inch round cake pans.

Transfer the dough to a lightly greased work surface, gently deflate, and divide into 16 pieces.

Shape each piece of dough into a ball. Place 8 balls

in each round pan, and space evenly so they aren't touching.

Cover the pans and allow the rolls to rise until they touch and are puffy (approximately 1 to 1½ hours).

Preheat the oven to 350 degrees F.

Bake for 24 to 26 minutes, until they are a light golden brown on top. (Thermometer should read 190 degrees.)

Remove the rolls from the oven and after a couple of minutes transfer them to a rack to cool before serving.

Don't miss Jonah's story in the next Wranglers of Wyoming story, *Meant to Be My Cowboy*.

Coming in Summer 2021

ABOUT THE AUTHOR

New York Times bestselling author R.C. Ryan has written more than a hundred novels, both contemporary and historical. Quite an accomplishment for someone who, after her fifth child started school, gave herself the gift of an hour a day to follow her dream to become a writer.

In a career spanning more than thirty years, Ms. Ryan has given dozens of radio, television, and print interviews across the country and Canada, and has been quoted in such diverse publications as the *Wall Street Journal* and *Cosmopolitan*. She has also appeared on CNN News and *Good Morning America*.

You can learn more about R.C. Ryan—and her alter ego, Ruth Ryan Langan—at:
    RyanLangan.com
    Twitter @RuthRyanLangan
    Facebook.com

FOR A BONUS STORY
FROM ANOTHER AUTHOR
THAT YOU'LL LOVE,
PLEASE TURN THE PAGE
TO READ

WILDFLOWER RANCH BY
CAROLYN BROWN

Shiloh never knew what it was like to have sisters. But
suddenly the father she never knew leaves his ranch
to Shiloh and her two half siblings. The only catch: to
fully inherit, they must live together on the ranch for a
full year. Shiloh couldn't be more different from Abby
Joy, a former soldier, or Bonnie, a true wild child. But
the three soon find they have more in common than
they could've imagined. When a neighboring rancher
catches Shiloh's eye, she'll have to decide exactly
how much she's willing to sacrifice for her shot at
the ranch.

FOREVER

CHAPTER ONE

Spring was Waylon's favorite season, when the wild-flowers painted the Palo Duro Canyon with their brilliant colors. That evening, the last rays of sun lit up the red Indian paintbrush, almost the same color as the dress Shiloh was wearing. The centers of the black-eyed Susans reminded him of her dark hair, and the blue bonnets scattered here and there were the color of her eyes.

"Wildflower Ranch," he whispered and liked the way it rolled off his tongue. He'd been looking for a brand for his new ranch ever since he bought it. "I like it. Wildflower Ranch," he said again with a nod, and just like that, he'd named his place.

Since most of his friends were married, Waylon had been to lots of weddings. Like always, he found a corner where he could watch the people without having to mingle with them. He wasn't really shy or backward, but though he didn't like crowds he did like watching people. And he liked to dance some leather off his boots at the Sugar Shack, the local watering hole, on Saturday nights.

Shiloh breezed in and out of the house, appearing

under the porch light to talk to someone for a few minutes, and then disappearing for a little while, only to return again. She looked different from the way she did at Ezra's funeral not quite three months ago. That day Waylon had stood off to the side as the sisters arrived one by one. Abby Joy was the last one to get there, and she looked like she had just left a military exercise in her camouflage. Shiloh might have come from a rodeo in her western getup, and Bonnie could have been a biker's woman in black leather and sporting a nose ring and tattoo. At that time he had wondered if Ezra hadn't been right when he sent all of them away right after they were born.

But ever since that morning, he hadn't been able to get Shiloh out of his mind.

Now there were only two sisters in the running to inherit the Malloy Ranch—Shiloh and Bonnie. When the sisters first came to the canyon, Waylon would have sworn that Shiloh would be the first to leave. Bonnie would follow her within a week, and Abby Joy would be there until they buried her beside old Ezra in the Malloy family cemetery right there on the ranch.

He'd sure been wrong, because that very evening Abby Joy had married his good friend Cooper and moved off Malloy ranch and over to his place. It wasn't the first time Waylon had been wrong, and it most likely wouldn't be the last time, either. He watched the two remaining Malloy sisters out of the corner of his eye. Shiloh was the taller of the two and had long dark brown hair.

In her cowboy boots and tight jeans at her father's funeral, she had looked like she was the queen of Texas. Maybe that confidence and sass was what had drawn him to her from the beginning. Not that he'd act on the attraction, not when there was so much at stake for her. Ezra had left a will behind, saying that the three sisters had to live on the Malloy Ranch together for a year. If one of them left, then they received an inheritance, but they could never have the ranch. If none of them left, then they inherited the place jointly. If they all moved off Ezra's massive spread, then Rusty, his foreman, inherited it.

Waylon had always thought that deep down Ezra wanted Rusty to have the place anyway. He'd just brought the sisters together to satisfy his own conscience for sending them away at birth because they weren't sons.

Waylon was a patient man. He didn't mind sitting back in the shadows of the wide porch and waiting for another look at Shiloh in that dress that hugged her curves. When she came back again, he sat up a little straighter so he could get a better view of her. The full moon lit her eyes up that evening like beautiful sapphires. His pulse jacked up a few notches and his heart threw in an extra fast beat. He could only imagine what kissing her or holding her in his arms would feel like—but he sure liked the picture in his head when he did.

The reception had started in the house and then poured out onto the porch and yard. That's where Shiloh was headed right then. She met up with Bonnie, and the two of them talked with their hands, gesturing toward the house and then back at the piano under a big scrub oak.

Maybe they were trying to figure out how to get the piano back inside. Waylon would be glad to help them with that, just to be near Shiloh for a little while. The chairs that had been arranged in two rows for the wedding were now scattered here and there, and Shiloh picked up one with each hand and carried them from the yard to the porch.

"Need some help?" Waylon asked when she was close enough that the porch light lit up her beautiful eyes. Ezra Malloy's three daughters hadn't gotten a physical thing from him, except the color of his eyes, and even then they were all three slightly different shades of blue.

"Hey, what are you doing hiding back here?" Bonnie, the youngest Malloy sister, pulled up a chair and sat down beside him.

"Just watching the people," Waylon answered. "You look right pretty tonight, Bonnie. When I first saw you at Ezra's funeral, you looked like maybe you were into motorcycles."

"I might have been, but they cost way too much money for me to own one. My boyfriend had one back in Harlan." Bonnie sighed. "If I'd known Abby Joy was going to wear combat boots, I would have worn my comfortable lace-up biker boots." She kicked off her shoes. "He bought me the jacket and boots, and then we broke up. He didn't want me to come out here to Texas when Ezra died. He said I was too wild to live on a ranch. I'm proving him wrong." She stopped, as if waiting for him to say something, but she hadn't asked a question. After a few seconds she went on, "Have you ever been a groomsman before? This was my first time ever to be a bridesmaid."

"No," he answered. "I've been to a lot of weddings, but I'm not usually one for big crowds."

Shiloh pushed the front door open and motioned to her sister. "Bonnie, come on. Abby Joy is getting ready to throw the bouquet."

Bonnie put her shoes on and got up, but Waylon stayed in his chair. Shiloh's high-heeled shoes made a clicking noise on the wooden porch as she crossed it, and she crooked a finger at Waylon. "You too, cowboy. Cooper is about to take Abby Joy's garter off, and he's calling for all single men."

"Oh, no!" Waylon held up both palms. "I don't want that thing."

"I'm not catching that bouquet either. I'm superstitious, and I refuse to be the next bride in the canyon," Bonnie said. "I'm going to own a ranch in nine months. I sure don't have time for romance."

"You'll own the Malloy ranch over my dead body." Shiloh did a head wiggle. "The best you'll ever do is share it with me."

"Wanna bet?" Bonnie stopped at the door.

Shiloh stuck out her hand. "Twenty bucks?"

"How about a hundred and a bottle of good Kentucky bourbon?" Bonnie asked.

"Deal!" Shiloh shook with her.

Waylon didn't have a doubt in his mind that Bonnie would be forking over money and bourbon. Next to Abby Joy, he'd never met a woman as determined as Shiloh—or as sassy for that matter.

Shiloh surprised him when she grabbed his hand and tugged. "Come on. You can put your hands in your pockets, but you're one of the wedding party. It wouldn't be right for you not to be in on the garter toss."

He stood up, thinking she'd drop his hand, but

she didn't. Sparks flittered around the porch like fireflies on a summer night. Sure, Waylon had been attracted to Shiloh since the first time he laid eyes on her, but this tingly feeling was something he'd never felt before.

She led him into the foyer, where the men were gathered over toward one end. Abby Joy was sitting about halfway up the stairs, and Cooper had begun to run his hand up her leg, searching for the garter. When he found the blue satin and white lace thing, he slipped it slowly down to her ankle. Whoops and hollers filled the room from the guys who were gathered up in a corner with their hands up. They were putting on quite a show for the lady who was filming, but then the garter wouldn't stretch far enough to go over Abby Joy's combat boot. The noise died down slightly as Cooper slowly untied the strings, pulled her boot off, and then slowly removed the garter from her foot. It got loud again when Cooper turned around backward and threw it over his shoulder. Several of the young unmarried men did their best to catch it, but it flew right past them and floated down to settle onto the top of Waylon's black cowboy hat.

"Guess you're next in line, buddy." Cooper laughed.

There was no doubt that Cooper was talking to him, and all the guys around him were laughing and pointing. He brought his hands out of his pockets and held them up to show that he had nothing. "Can't be me," Waylon said. "Which one of y'all is hiding it and teasing me?"

Shiloh reached up, removed Waylon's hat, and showed him the garter, lying there in the creases. He wanted to pick the thing up and toss it to one of the other guys, but he was mesmerized by her beautiful blue eyes, which were staring right into his.

"Fate says that you're next," she said.

"Not damn likely," he drawled.

She picked up the garter and handed him back his hat. "Give me your arm. The photographer will want a picture of you and Cooper, since you caught the garter."

He held out his arm and she stretched the blue lace garter up past his elbow. Then she held up his arm like he'd just won the trophy at a wrestling tournament. "The winner and the next groom in the canyon is Waylon Stephens!"

He played along, more to get to be near Shiloh than anything else. There was no way he'd be the next married man in the area. The only woman he was vaguely interested in was Shiloh, and he'd never knock her out of getting her share of Ezra Malloy's ranch. Maybe after she'd secured the deed, he'd ask her for a date, but not before. She'd never forgive herself—or him—if she lost her part of the ranch, and besides, as pretty as she was, she was way out of his league.

"And now the bouquet," Abby Joy said. "All you ladies get your hands up and"—she turned around backward—"here it comes." She let it fly, and it landed smack in Bonnie's hands.

"Someone take this thing from me, right now. I can't get married or leave the ranch. It would cost me a hundred dollars and a bottle of Kentucky bourbon." Bonnie tried to hand it off to the other girls, but none of them would touch it.

After the photographer took a few pictures, Waylon took a few steps back and disappeared outside again

into the shadows on the porch. He'd prove them all
wrong about being the next man to get married, but
Bonnie wouldn't. Shiloh was going to own that ranch.
Bonnie might as well face it.

*   *   *

The hinges on the gate into the old cemetery creaked as
Shiloh opened it. She crossed over to the place where
the father she had never known was buried and sat
down on a concrete bench in front of his grave. A full
moon lit up the lettering on her father's gray tombstone.
Ezra Malloy had died less than three months ago on
the first day of the year. It seemed like it had been a
lot longer since she and her two sisters had sat through
his graveside service. She remembered looking over at
her soldier sister and thinking that she had some balls,
wearing camouflage and combat boots to a funeral.
Then she'd glanced to her other side to see the younger
sister. She was dressed in jeans and a biker jacket and
had a little diamond stud in the side of her nose. Her
blond hair was limp, and what wasn't stringing down to
her shoulder had a thin braid complete with beads that
hung down one side of her face. In her skintight jeans
and biker books, she looked like she'd dropped right out
of either a hippie colony or motorcycle convention.

Shiloh had given Sister Hippie a week at the most
before she'd go running back to whatever strange
world she'd come from, and Sister Soldier less than
a month before she was bored to death. Shiloh was
going to be the last one standing at the end of a year,
by damn, and nothing or no one was going to sweet-
talk her off that ranch. The only thing she ever owned

was the Chevy van that she drove. She wanted that ranch—first, to prove to the father she never knew that she could learn the business. The second reason had to do with her being so competitive. She was determined to show her two half sisters that she couldn't be run off. They'd both eyed her that first day like she would be the weakling of the trio. Neither of them looked like they could possibly be her sister, but she'd been wrong. Not only were they sisters, but they'd also become best friends by spring.

Shiloh brushed a dead leaf from the skirt of the bright red satin dress she'd worn to her older sister's wedding that evening. The canyon was alive with wildflowers of every color and description, but the night was chilly, so she'd worn a long sweater over her dress for her walk from the house to the cemetery.

"Well, Ezra," Shiloh addressed the tombstone in her Arkansas accent, "it's down to me and Bonnie now. Bet you didn't think any of us would stick it out for this long, did you? And since she was a soldier, I imagine you figured she'd be the one to last the longest. Guess what? You were wrong. She could have gotten married, and Cooper could've moved in with her here. That way she would have kept her share, but she told me she didn't need or want it anymore, that it was like an albatross around her neck—like you were controlling her with your rules." She whispered as she pulled her sweater tighter across her chest, "I'm not sure I'll ever forgive you for throwing all three of us away because we weren't boys. I guess your punishment is that you died a lonely old man."

"I thought I might find you here." Her younger sister, Bonnie, sat down beside her.

"Damn, woman!" Shiloh shivered. "You scared the bejesus out of me."

"Is that a good thing or a bad thing?" Bonnie asked. Other than her blue eyes, she didn't look a thing like Shiloh. Tonight she wore her biker jacket over a pretty red bridesmaid dress.

"It's bad when you startle me like that, but good to think I might be a saint for a few seconds," Shiloh answered.

Bonnie shivered. "The way that north wind is whipping down the canyon, it's hard to believe that it's March and that spring is only a few days from now. I've got something to say to our father, and then I'm going home where it's warm. Did you walk? I didn't see your van when I parked."

"I did," Shiloh replied, but she didn't tell her sister that she needed a chance to think about how Waylon's nearness had been affecting her all that evening. When she'd taken his hand in hers, there had definitely been electricity flowing between them. "What have you got to say to Ezra?"

Bonnie glared at the tombstone. "Are you smiling, Ezra, because Abby Joy has left the ranch? I bet you're hopin' that Rusty winds up with it, but I'd be willin' to bet a jar of your moonshine that you thought your soldier daughter would outlast me and Shiloh. If you had let us get to know each other, then you'd have realized that she might be tough as nails on the outside, but she's got a heart of gold. So there, you won this one, but not really, because she's happy now."

"Look at us out here in a damned old graveyard talkin' to a dead man that didn't give a hoot about any of us. Paid our mothers off to go away and take us worthless girls with them," Shiloh said. "He can't hear us and would probably laugh in our faces if he could."

"And wearing our pretty dresses as if he can see us in them," Bonnie said. "I wish I didn't give a damn about him, but"—she laid the wedding bouquet in front of his tombstone—"here's something for you to think about. Abby Joy has found happiness and you never did."

"We really should get over the way we feel about him," Shiloh said.

"Maybe someday, but not anytime soon. He shouldn't have thrown us all away, and he for sure as hell should have been there to walk Abby Joy down the aisle."

"He's dead," Shiloh reminded her. "He couldn't have walked with her anyway."

"I know that, but..."—Bonnie stammered—"damn it, you know what I mean."

"Yes, I do know what you mean. I used to imagine that my father was a Navy SEAL or some other hero-type guy."

"When did you find out that you were wrong?" Bonnie asked.

"I was a teenager. I waited until Mama and her sister, my aunt Audrey, were about half lit one night and asked her about him. The truth shattered my pretty little bubble," Shiloh said.

"I knew from the time I can remember exactly who and what Ezra was. Mama just wouldn't tell me where he lived," Bonnie told her. "Good thing that she didn't. I might be doin' time in prison right now instead of visitin' his grave in the prettiest dress I've ever owned."

"Do you ever wish that the cemetery was on the

back side of the ranch so we didn't have to look at it every time we leave or come back to the place?" Shiloh asked.

"Oh, hell, yeah, but I keep reminding myself that he probably hates to see us coming and going, and knowing that we're still here makes him want to claw his way up out of that grave and change his will," Bonnie answered.

Shiloh giggled and started to say something. Then the noise of screeching tires and the sound of metal hitting something really hard made both of them drop to a squatting position and cover their heads. The laughter had stopped and nothing but Shiloh and her sister's heavy breathing could be heard in the heavy silence.

"What in the hell was that?" Bonnie whispered.

"Someone just wrecked out on the highway," Shiloh said. "We'd better go see if we need to help."

The two of them stood up and ran toward the place where Bonnie had left her truck. "Get in." Bonnie hiked her dress up and ran around the back of her truck as she yelled, "And call 911."

CHAPTER TWO

Waylon was the last one to leave that evening. He helped get the piano back into the house and all the chairs loaded into a cattle trailer to go back to the church before he got into his truck and drove away. He turned the radio to his favorite late-night country music program just in time to hear Cody Johnson singing "On My Way to You." The lyrics said that everything he'd been through from ditches to britches was simply taking him on his way to her. It seemed to have been written just for Waylon that night, and he kept time with the music by tapping his thumbs on the steering wheel.

He'd just rounded a sharp curve when a whole herd of deer started across the road in front of him. The squeal of his truck tires filled his ears, and the smell of hot brakes floated up to his nose. The deer scattered, and he let up on the brakes a little. Then one of his back tires blew out and sent him straight for a huge old scrub oak. He was looking out the side window, trying to swerve away from a big stump, when the airbags opened, and the seat belt tightened. None of that kept him from hitting his head on the side window hard enough to rattle his brain.

Steve Earle was singing "Copperhead Road" when everything began to blur. The lyrics of the song reminded him of the stories his great-granddad had told about outrunning the feds and the local sheriff through his moonshine-running days. His granddad had come home from Vietnam to take over the business. His dad hadn't run moonshine, but he had inherited enough money from his father to buy a ranch on Red Dirt Road out in East Texas. His last thought before the whole world swirled away into darkness was that this was a helluva way to die.

*   *   *

Bonnie drove so fast down the rutted lane that it sounded like the fenders were going to fly off her old truck and land somewhere out there in the wildflowers beside the road. The scene of the accident was only a few hundred yards up from the Malloy Ranch turnoff, and right away, Shiloh recognized the truck.

"My God!" she gasped. "That's Waylon's truck."

"What did you say?" the 911 operator asked.

"It's my neighbor's truck right on Highway 207 that crosses the Prairie Dog Fork of the Red River. Send an ambulance in a hurry," she said.

"I've got one coming out of Amarillo, but it'll be about thirty minutes before it can get there. I can patch you through to the EMT so he can give you some instructions," the lady said.

What little tread was on the tires of Bonnie's old truck took a big hit when she braked hard. When the vehicle had slowed down, she made a hard right-hand turn into the red dirt and brought the truck to a stop.

Before she could turn off the engine, Shiloh had slung open the door, hiked up her dress, and was running toward Waylon's truck. She reached it in time to see Waylon fall out of the driver's side and wobble as he tried to stand up.

"He's alive," she yelled into the phone.

"Lay him out flat on the ground and don't let him move," the EMT said. "Is there something you can use to stabilize his neck? Is there anything like a blanket to keep him warm until we can get there?"

"I'll check," she said as she threw the phone at Bonnie. "Talk to them."

"Got to get home. Granddad has to make a run," Waylon muttered.

"What you are going to do is lay down flat and be still until the ambulance gets here." Shiloh removed her sweater and held it against the gash on his forehead.

"Anything for you, darlin'." He winced as he stretched out on the cold, hard ground. "Are you hurt?"

"Be still," she demanded. "You're losing a lot of blood, and you could have all kinds of injuries."

His eyes fluttered shut.

Her heart thumped in her chest, and her pulse raced. She'd never seen a man die, especially one who she knew so well, and had even flirted with on more than one occasion. Her hands shook as she pressed harder on the sweater, his warm blood seeping through the thin fabric and oozing up between her fingers.

God, don't let him die. She looked up at the stars. His breath rattled out of his chest and he coughed. Shiloh glanced at his mouth to see if there was blood there, and heaved a sigh of relief when his lips were clear.

"Don't you dare die, Waylon Stephens!" she yelled at him. "Open your eyes and stay with me."

"They say you're doing the right thing." Bonnie kept the phone to her ear. "Should I run back to the house and get a blanket?"

"Ask them how much longer until they get here," Shiloh said.

"They say fifteen minutes. They've got the sirens going, and they're taking the back roads to get here faster," Bonnie told her.

"It would take you longer to get there and back than it'll take them to get here," Shiloh told her.

"Then here..." Bonnie peeled out of her jacket and laid it over Waylon's upper body. "That might help a little."

"Thank you," Shiloh said. "You should get back in your truck and stay warm. There's nothing more you can do, and you'll get sick if you get a chill."

Seconds took hours to go by, and minutes were an eternity. Shiloh kept demanding that Waylon keep his eyes open and talk to her. Most of the time, he focused on her face, but he didn't say anything at all. She wondered what kind of work his granddad had done that he had to make a run, and why it was important for Waylon to get home to help him, but she didn't ask. The EMTs had said to keep him as quiet and as still as possible.

Finally, Shiloh and Bonnie heard the sirens and saw the flashing lights as the ambulance came around a curve in the highway. As soon as the vehicle stopped, the two EMTs seemed to be everywhere at once. They loaded Waylon onto a flat board, secured his neck with a brace, removed Shiloh's sweater and applied gauze to the gaping wound on his forehead.

"I'm going with him," she announced when they had him inside.

"Sorry, ma'am, it's not allowed," the older of the two men said.

"It is tonight," Shiloh told him as she hiked up her dress and got into the ambulance. Bonnie threw her phone toward her and said, "What should I do?"

The doors were closing when Shiloh caught the phone and yelled, "Bring me my purse and a change of clothes, and get Rusty to follow you in my van so I'll have a way to get him home."

She had to pull her knees to the side to give the EMT room to start an IV, take Waylon's vital signs, and check his eyes. "Okay, Derrick"—she read the embroidered name tag on his jacket—"tell me he's going to be all right."

"I hope so, but the doctors will have to check him out for brain damage, concussion, all kinds of things. He's got a nasty cut on his head that's going to probably need stitches," Derrick said above the high-pitched whine of the sirens.

"Hate needles," Waylon muttered, his first words in several minutes.

"So do I." Shiloh reached around Derrick and covered Waylon's hand with hers.

Driving on Texas roads was one thing. Driving in the Palo Duro Canyon was quite another with its curves, and hills, and valleys. Shiloh was glad when they finally came up out of the canyon just south of Claude, and the ambulance driver could go faster. She had flirted with Waylon at church and social gatherings, had even danced with him a couple of times at the Sugar Shack, the canyon's only honky-tonk. Now, she wished she'd stepped right up and asked him out. The opportunities had been there, and she wasn't shy, but she had a thing about rejection. Probably a deep-seated emotion brought on by her father not wanting her because she was a girl.

The driver made a hard left onto Interstate 40 and kicked up the speed even more. In just a few minutes, he was pulling up under the awning, and then he and Derrick were rolling Waylon into the emergency room.

"You can wait right here." Derrick motioned toward the seating area.

Shiloh gave him a dirty look and went right on through the double doors with him and the other guy. They did one of those one, two, three, counts and shifted Waylon onto a bed. He grimaced when they removed his cowboy boots.

"Foot hurts," he said.

"We'll get it seen about real soon," Shiloh told him.

A nurse with a no-nonsense expression pulled the curtain to the cubicle back and motioned for Shiloh to leave. "We've got to get him out of that suit so we can examine him. You need to leave."

Shiloh narrowed her eyes. "I'll step outside the curtain, but as soon as you have him changed, I'm coming back in."

"Are you related?" The nurse eased his black jacket off and was unbuckling his belt.

"No, I'm his girlfriend," Shiloh lied.

"Then I'll call you as soon as I'm finished," the nurse said.

* * *

Waylon chuckled, and Shiloh shot a look his way that said he had better not tattle as she slipped around the curtain. Things were a little foggy in his mind. He remembered something about a song about Red Dirt Road—no, that wasn't right. He lived on a road like that growing up over in—it took him a while to remember that had been over near Kiomatia, right on the Red River.

A doctor in a white coat pushed the curtain back, and said, "Well, son, what hurts?"

"My head and my ankle," Waylon answered.

"Let's get some tests run to see about both of those." He flashed a small penlight in Waylon's eyes, then gently felt his ankle. "I think you have a mild concussion and a sprained ankle, but the tests I'm ordering will let us know for certain. I want to be sure that you don't have any cracked or broken ribs from the seat belt. Good thing you were wearing one, or you might've been thrown through the windshield. While we're waiting, let's get that head wound taken care of. I think we can use some glue and Steri-Strips instead of stitches. The nurse will clean it up, and then I'll do my magic."

Waylon barely nodded.

"Keep the neck brace on until we get those pictures," the doctor told the nurse.

"Yes, sir," she said.

Shiloh pushed around the curtain and came back to stand beside him. She took his hand in hers as they took care of the gash on his forehead. He tried not to squeeze her hand, but dammit! It hurt like a bitch when the nurse cleaned the wound. He kept his eyes glued to Shiloh's face. Her beautiful dark hair had been pinned up for the wedding, but now it had fallen down over her shoulders. The red roses that had been scattered through the curls were wilted. Her pretty dress was stained and dirty, and her black rubber boots were muddy.

"Sorry," he said.

"For what?" she asked.

"Your dress," he muttered.

"Honey, this is just a dress. It can be cleaned or thrown in the trash. What matters is that you aren't dead." She squeezed his hand.

She had called him *honey*. He was sure of that, but he couldn't be her sweetheart. That much he was sure of. He was Waylon Stephens, of the moonshiners over in Red River County, Texas. Shiloh Malloy was way out of his league.

He closed his eyes, but she leaned down and said, "Don't you close your eyes. You can't sleep until the doctor gets done with you, and if you've got a concussion, I'll be waking you up every hour until twenty-four have passed, so get ready for it."

"Sleepy," he said.

"Me too, but we can sleep later," she told him.

Dawn was pushing night out of the way when the nurse finally came into the cubicle with a whole raft of papers in her hands. "Doc says his preliminary exam was right on the money. Sprained ankle and a slight concussion. He will need someone with him for about a week. No heavy lifting, no hard work, crutches for at least a week. I'm sending him home with a list of things he can't do, and those that he can."

"I'll stay with him, and see to it that he behaves," Shiloh said.

"I'm a big boy. I can take care of myself," Waylon protested.

"Yep, you can, in a week," Shiloh told him.

"You can have someone with you, or we can keep you here," the nurse said. "It's your choice, Mr. Stephens."

"I'll go home," he grumbled.

"And you'll be good?" the nurse asked.

"Yes, he will, because I give you my word," Shiloh told her.

"I've got cattle and chickens and—"

Shiloh put a finger on his lips. "I can take care of all that. It's only for a week, and if I need help, I'll call Rusty and Bonnie."

"How're we getting home?" He didn't want to tell either of them that the only thing he could picture in his mind was a little frame house set back in a grove of pecan trees. Back behind the house was acres and acres of corn that granddad used to make shine.

"Rusty and Bonnie brought my van up here. It's waiting in the parking lot, so let's go home and get the morning feeding chores done," she said.

Even the nod he gave made his head throb worse. "All right, but you don't have to..."

She patted him on the shoulder. "That's what friends and neighbors are for. I'll go bring the van up to the doors."

The nurse helped him get dressed and rolled him outside in a wheelchair in time to see a beautiful sunrise out there at the end of the horizon. His suit would never come clean again, but thank God, they didn't have to cut his boot off, since they were the ones that he saved for Sunday and special occasions.

When he stood up, the sunrise blurred, and he had to

grab the door handle of the van to keep from dropping. The nurse told him to sit down in the passenger seat and then she pulled his bum leg up and put it inside.

"The doctor will see you on Friday. Your appointment and his address are in this file," she said.

"We'll be there," Shiloh assured her.

The nurse shook her finger at Waylon. "No driving until after he sees you."

"You got to be kiddin' me," he moaned.

"I'll see to it." Shiloh nodded.

Waylon waited until they were past Claude before he said, "All right, we escaped that place. You can drop me off at my ranch, and go on home. I'll get in touch with someone to tow my truck..."

"What we're going to do is go to your ranch, get a shower, and make breakfast. Then I'll let you sleep an hour while I take care of the morning chores. That's as much as you need to worry about right now. Your truck is already at the body shop. Rusty and Bonnie took care of that last night, and called the insurance company listed on the papers in your glove compartment."

"You don't have to do this." He used the lever on the side to lean the seat back a little.

"I'm not arguing with you anymore," she said.

Good God Almighty! It was going to be a long week.

CHAPTER THREE

Shiloh felt like she'd just closed her eyes when the alarm went off right by her ear at three o'clock in the afternoon. She glanced over at the recliner where Waylon was sleeping, saw that he was awake, and reset the alarm.

"What's your name?" she asked.

"Waylon Stephens, and I live in Palo Duro Canyon on a ranch." He smiled.

"How old are you?" She covered a yawn with her hand.

"Thirty on my last birthday," he answered. "I'm fine. Go back to sleep."

She closed her eyes, but she couldn't sleep. Was he telling the truth about his age, or did he just make up something so that she'd leave him alone? She'd promised the doctor that for the first twenty-four hours she'd wake him every single hour and ask him something to be sure he was all right. Next time she'd have to remember to ask something she was absolutely sure about.

When her alarm went off the second time, she expected to see him in his recliner, but he wasn't there. She threw back the quilt that she'd used to cover herself and followed the sounds of his crutches on the wooden kitchen floor.

"Just exactly"—she popped her hands on her hips—"what do you think you're doin'?"

"I'm bored," he said. "So I'm making each of us an omelet for supper. We'll eat, and then we'll go do the evening chores."

"Not *we*." She crossed the floor and poked him in the chest with her forefinger. "I will do the chores. If you promise to be good, I might let you ride in the truck, but no driving."

"You're worse than my mother." One corner of his mouth turned up in a Harrison Ford grin.

"You're a horrible patient," she said.

"I hate being in the house," he told her. "Always have. That's why I went to work on a ranch right out of high school. The idea of sitting through four years of classes in college gave me the hives." He leaned his crutches against the cabinet and worked with his bad leg cocked back.

"You look like a flamingo standing like that," she told him. "Go sit down and let me finish the omelets."

"If I sit any longer, I will die of pure boredom. I can handle this. If I need help, I'll ask." He added ham, peppers, and cheese to the omelets and deftly flipped one side over to make a pocket.

That was more than she'd ever heard Waylon say at one time, so she decided to press her luck. "So just how bad was your mama? I'm askin' to see how much of that derogatory remark you made is true."

"Actually, my mama is a saint. She has had to live on the next farm over from my grandmother, who's always cankerous and always complains about everything. My folks and most of my family still live way back in the sticks next to the Red River on Red Dirt Road in East Texas," he said. "Is that enough to convince you that I don't have amnesia?"

"Maybe."

He scooted the first omelet off onto a plate and handed it to her, then added two pieces of toast and a small bowl of mixed fruit. "I poured the fruit from a bag of frozen so don't fuss at me for using a knife."

"And I suppose you just blinked and the peppers magically diced themselves too?"

"No, I keep bowls full in the fridge all ready to use for omelets or fajitas or whatever else I might need to use them for when I'm cooking on the fly," he informed her. "What about your mama? She would have been Ezra's second wife, right?"

"Her name is Polly," Shiloh answered. "And, yes, she was number two of the three wives. His dogs are named after his wives—there's Martha, Polly, and Vivien. Our mothers in that order. Never knew any of my grandparents. Didn't know Ezra or his kinfolk, and Mama's folks died before I was born." She carried the plate and small bowl to the table, and came back to stand beside him.

"Did I forget something?" he asked.

"Just that you can't carry a plate and work those crutches at the same time, and if you start hopping on one leg, there's a chance you'll fall," she reminded him. "So maybe you should quit bein' so macho and let me help."

"Yes, ma'am." There was that sexy little grin again.

Shiloh would have bet that anytime he went to the Sugar Shack, all he had to do was flash that shy smile, and all the women in the canyon would have trouble keeping their underbritches from sliding down around their ankles.

*   *   *

Waylon fought the chemistry between him and Shiloh with all his might and power, but the attraction did nothing but grow. Everyone in the canyon knew the terms of Ezra's will—his daughters had to live on the ranch together for one year. At the end of that time, whoever was still on the place would share the land.

Waylon's dad had always told him that if he dragged his feet, he might get left behind. He wanted to throw the crutches over in a corner, hold his leg up like one of those big-butted birds, and take Shiloh in his arms for a long, hot kiss, but that wouldn't be right. Why start something that he couldn't finish? Especially if it led to something more, and then she hated him for cheating her out of her half of a ranch that was twice or three times the size of his little spread.

He slipped his crutches under his arms and hobbled over to the table where she'd set his plate. When he had sat down, she gave him a long, quizzical look.

"What?" he asked. He couldn't have egg on his face or shirt, since he hadn't even taken the first bite.

"You sayin' grace over this food or am I?" she asked.

He bowed his head and said a simple prayer.

"You're not used to praying for your food, are you?" she asked.

She'd picked up on that in a hurry. His grandmother was super religious—one of those people who thought the earth would open up and the devil would drag a person right down to hell if they didn't say grace before they ate. But then she was so hateful and mean-spirited that no one really wanted to spend much time with her. It was a case of attitude versus actions. His granddad didn't always bless his sandwich at noontime when he and his crew were out in the field hauling hay in the summertime, but he had a heart of gold and never said a hateful word to anyone. Waylon had always wanted to be more like his granddad than his grandmother.

"Did I stutter all that bad?"

"No, but you were uncomfortable." She took her first bite of the omelet. "This is really good. Who taught you to cook?"

"My mother," he replied, glad that she'd changed the subject. "I have three sisters, all older than me, and two younger brothers. She said if the girls had to learn to drive tractors, haul hay, and build fences, then us boys had to learn to cook and clean. She was a wise woman. All of us can run a ranch, but we also know how to take care of a house."

"Your mama did good, but right now your ankle is sprained, and you have a concussion," she reminded him. "Everyone needs help at some time in their life."

"You got that right." He nodded.

"How in the devil are you running this place without hired hands or help of any kind?" she asked.

"I just bought it last fall and it was in pretty decent shape. I'm hoping to hire a couple of high school boys to help out in the summer. Kids around these parts are always looking for work," he told her.

Dammit!

He didn't want to feel comfortable talking to her. He wanted for things to be awkward between them, so the temptation to ask her out on a date wouldn't keep rising up to pester him.

"You got any half siblings back in Arkansas?" he asked.

"Nope, I'm an only child. All three of us—Abby Joy, Bonnie, and me—are only children. I guess our mothers all felt the same when Ezra threw them out because we weren't boys," she said. "Crappy way to treat a woman right after she's carried a baby for nine months and then went through delivery, isn't it?"

"It's a wonder one of those women didn't shoot him, but then—" He hesitated.

"But then," she butted in, "they'd have gone to prison, and left a child with no parent."

"Why do you even want something that belonged to him?" Waylon asked.

"My biggest dream has been to live on a ranch. Mama used to say it was in my blood. Now I have the chance, and I can always change the name to something other than Malloy Ranch."

"Ezra will always be buried there," Waylon reminded her.

"Yep, and he can see that I'm doing a fantastic job of running the place and be sorry that he shoved me and Mama out the door," she said.

*   *   *

Shiloh remembered well the first time she'd seen Waylon Stephens. She hadn't known his name back then, but he'd sure stood out at her father's funeral. With those steely-blue eyes set in a chiseled face, he'd been the sexiest cowboy at the graveside services. She had never met Ezra, so she couldn't bring herself to cry for him, and she hadn't paid much attention to what was being said. She had, however, snuck in a few long sideways looks at her two sisters and several at Waylon, who had stood off to one side.

Her sisters had teased her about him ever since they saw her staring at him in church that first Sunday, but looking was all she intended to do. Abby Joy had done more than look at Cooper, and it had cost her a third of a pretty nice-size ranch. Now it was down to Shiloh and Bonnie, and it was still nine months until the first of the year. Maybe Bonnie should be the one taking care of Waylon, since she'd caught the bouquet and the garter had landed on his cowboy hat.

That thought sent a streak of jealousy through Shiloh's heart. Bonnie could fall for someone else, preferably in the summertime, and that would give her time to get married long before the January first deadline. When it was all said and done, Shiloh intended to have her cake and eat it too. She'd own Malloy Ranch, and then she'd act on the strong vibes between her and Waylon.

"You got awful quiet all of a sudden," Waylon said, breaking the silence between them.

"Just thinkin'," she said. "How long have you lived in the canyon?"

"Little more than a year. I came over here with my cousin Travis, who's married to Nona, the daughter of the folks that own the biggest spread around these parts. My youngest brother, Cash, came with us, but he went back home after a few weeks. Got to missin' the girl he left behind," Waylon said.

"Did you leave a girl behind?" Shiloh asked.

He shook his head.

"Leave dozens behind?" Shiloh pressed.

"Maybe a few, but nothing serious. Had my mind set on buyin' my own place, so I had to work long hours. That didn't leave much time for gettin' any more serious than a few dances on Saturday night at the local honky-tonk," he answered. "How about you? You got a feller waiting to move in with you when you inherit Ezra's ranch?"

"Nope," she replied. "Any of the guys I dated wouldn't ever want to live in this place."

"It takes a special kind of person to appreciate the beauty of the canyon, don't it?" he asked as he reached for his crutches.

"Yes, it does, and I've got to admit that it took a while to grow on me. When I first drove down into the canyon, I thought I'd dropped off the edge of the world." She cleared the table and headed for the back door. "We'd best get the chores done before dark. You need help with your coat?"

"I reckon I can take care of that, but it would be nice if you'd hold the door for me," he said.

"See there. You asked for help, and it didn't kill you." She smiled over her shoulder at him.

"If I was home out in the eastern part of the state, my grandmother would tell me to suck it up and go to work," he said as he bent his leg at the knee and managed to get his coat on, then slipped the crutches under his arms.

The evening feeding chores didn't take long, and riding kept Waylon awake for a couple of hours, but Shiloh could tell that he was worn-out when they got back to the house.

"Hey, it's only six more hours until you don't have to wake up every single hour. At midnight you can go to sleep for a while," she told him.

"I'm going to take a shower and go to bed." He removed his coat and tossed it on the back of a kitchen chair. "Every bone and muscle in my body feels like they've been stomped on by a two-ton bull."

"Well, what do you expect?" Shiloh asked him. "You were in a wreck. When you hit that tree, it jarred everything. Doc says you can take the boot off for a shower, but you aren't to put weight on your foot. Probably the best thing you could do is take a kitchen chair into the shower with you and prop your knee on it."

"Reckon you could do that for me?" he asked.

"Sure." She nodded.

The chair took up a lot of room in the stall, but there was still room for Waylon, and it would give him stability.

"You ever do nursing work?" He followed her into the bathroom.

"Nope, but my aunt broke a couple of toes once, and mama came up with this idea so she could take showers," Shiloh replied as she backed out of the bathroom.

The house was small—living room and country kitchen taking up the right half of the place, a short hallway with two bedrooms and a bathroom on the other side. The doors to both bedrooms were open wide. One was empty except for a full bookcase on one wall and a leather recliner that looked like it had been around for years. The other was Waylon's bedroom— nightstands on either side of a king-size bed that was made up so tight that she could probably have bounced a quarter on it. A tall chest of drawers with a mirror above it was set against one wall and a dresser against the other.

She shouldn't go into his private space without an invitation, but she did anyway. She picked up a picture from the nightstand and stared at the six people in it. Waylon shared center stage with a tall woman who had to be one of his sisters. Two more girls were beside the lady, and two cowboys beside Waylon. They all wore jeans, western shirts, boots, and hats.

"This would make a great poster to hang in a western-wear store." She yawned.

The bed looked inviting after she'd caught only a few minutes of sleep between the times when she had to be sure Waylon was all right. It wouldn't hurt to stretch out on it while he was in the shower, would it? Just a thirty-minute power nap would absolutely give her the energy to make it to midnight, and then she could get some real sleep.

She eased down on the bed and bit back a groan. Waylon was obviously aching from the wreck, but her muscles were tense from worry and having no good rest for more than a day. She wiggled a little and closed her eyes—just for a minute. She'd be out of the bed and in the living room before he got through with his shower.

CHAPTER FOUR

A small night-light and what was left of a half moon lit up the room enough that Shiloh could see she'd slept more than a few minutes. She glanced over at the digital clock on the nightstand to see that it was eleven o'clock, and then she flipped over to find Waylon propped up on an elbow staring right at her. She was covered with a fluffy blanket that was warm and soft.

"What's your name? Are you lucid? Can you say the alphabet backward?" he asked.

"Oh, hush!" she said. "Some caretaker I am."

"I haven't been asleep yet, so there's no problem," he told her. "It's close enough to twenty-four hours that I believe we can both forget about that every-hour stuff. Good night, Shiloh."

"Good night." She slid off the bed.

"Where are you going?" he asked.

"To the sofa," she told him.

"Why? This bed is big enough for us both, and believe me, honey, I'm way too sore to make a move on you," he assured her.

The pesky voice in her head told her to get her butt to the sofa. Her body said that the bed was so much more comfortable and plenty big enough that she and Waylon would never even touch each other.

She stretched out again and pulled the throw up to her chin. "Thank you," she muttered as her eyes fluttered shut.

When she awoke again, Waylon was snuggled up to her, his chest against her back and one arm wrapped around her waist. They were wrapped up in the cover like they were in a cocoon. The sun was up and she could hear the cattle bellowing.

"Good morning." Waylon's warm breath on her neck sent shivers down her spine.

No, no, no! she scolded herself. She had her life planned out for the next nine months. She had never started anything that she didn't intend to finish. Even the two relationships she'd been in before she moved to the canyon—she'd fully well meant for each of those to last forever, and ever, amen. The men had been the ones to break things off. One had broken up with her because he'd slept with her best friend—she mourned the loss of her friend more than her boyfriend. The second one was in the air force and got sent to Germany. The long-distance relationship didn't survive after the first two months.

"I've made it through twenty-four hours. I'm a big boy. I can take a shower all by myself and cook, so you can go home," he said as he rolled over, got out of bed, and reached for his crutches.

She slid off the opposite side of the bed. "And who is going to drive for you? The doctor says you're not to get behind the wheel until he sees you next Friday. This is Monday. You think those cows out there are going to live without food all week. And there's the chickens and the hogs too. I suppose they can fast until the weekend."

"You sure are bossy," he muttered.

"Maybe so, but I'm not going home. I'm going to get a shower, make breakfast, and then we'll do the chores. After that, I expect you'll be ready to rest a spell," she said as she left the room.

"It's going to be a nice day. I thought I'd repair some fence." He raised his voice.

"Don't make me cranky this early in the morning." She went to the living room and rolled her suitcase down the hall.

"How about going out to the barn and cleaning the tack room?" His deep voice carried into the bathroom.

She cracked the door and said, "That might be doable but only if you don't try to do any heavy lifting. Doctor's orders, not mine."

She adjusted the water, stripped out of her clothing, and stepped into the shower stall. For a few minutes she just let the warm water beat out the tension from between her shoulders.

Why are you here? Why didn't you just call one of his brothers to come help out? She wished she could wash the thoughts from her head as easily as she rinsed the shampoo from her hair.

I want to know him better, and this is one good way to get to do that, she argued as she turned off the water.

You've met dozens of cowboys in the past three months. What makes Waylon so special? The pesky voice in her head wasn't ready to give up the fight.

Shiloh wrapped a towel around her body and one around her head. She unzipped her suitcase and pulled

out a pair of faded jeans, a T-shirt, and clean under-
wear. Six months ago Shiloh hadn't even known she
had siblings, and now her baby sister knew her well
enough to know what to pack for her.

That question about Waylon being special stuck in
her mind as she towel-dried her hair and then pulled it
up into a ponytail while it was still damp. She stared
at her reflection in the mirror above the sink, and said,
"I'm attracted to him because he's handsome and sexy
and has a deep Texas drawl. But more than that, it's
his brooding eyes that mesmerize me. To top it all off,
he's kind and sweet and he listens to me when I talk.
So there, are you satisfied?"

Her phone rang and startled her so badly that she
dropped her hairbrush. She dug the phone from the
pocket of her jeans that were on the floor and answered
without even looking at the caller ID.

"Hey, how's things going over there?" Bonnie asked.

"The patient is restless," Shiloh told her.

"Has he said more than a dozen words?"

"Maybe a few more than that." Shiloh used her
free hand to rearrange her suitcase as she talked. "It's
going to be a tough job to keep him from working
all week."

"Bring him over here one evening, and we'll have
a game of poker," Bonnie suggested. "I'm not used to
rattling around in this place without you and Abby Joy.
I'll make finger foods, and—"

"How about tonight?" Shiloh butted in.

"Great!" Bonnie squealed. "Can you be here by six?"

"You bet we can. Get your nickels and dimes
ready. I'm going to wipe you out tonight," Shiloh
told her.

"Yeah, but in a few months I'm going to get a hundred bucks and a bottle of good Kentucky bourbon, so I'll get it all back," Bonnie joked.

"I didn't catch the bouquet. You did," Shiloh reminded her.

"But Waylon got the garter, so—" Bonnie started.

"I'm not going there," Shiloh butted in for the second time. "See you this evening. I'd say that I'd bring the beer, but Waylon can't drink until after the doctor releases him."

"Man, he's really got it tough. Can't drive or work. Can't drink, and worst thing of all is living with you," Bonnie said.

"I'm hanging up now," Shiloh heard Bonnie's giggles as she ended the call.

She rolled her suitcase out into the hallway and gathered up her towels as well as the ones that were in the hamper. She caught the first whiff of coffee as she headed toward the kitchen. When she got closer, she smelled bacon and was that cinnamon?

Waylon had dragged a kitchen chair over to the stove to prop his knee on and was humming as he made bacon and French toast for breakfast. When she passed by him on the way to the utility room to put the towels in the washing machine, he looked up and gave her one of his rare smiles.

"This chair idea works in lots of places," he said.

"If you had to be off it longer than a few days, they make a scooter just for that purpose." She started the washing machine and returned to the kitchen.

"If I had to live through more than a week of this, I'd be batshit crazy," he muttered.

"And here I thought we were getting along pretty

good. I don't usually sleep with a man on the first date," she teased.

"We haven't been on a date, but when we do there won't be much sleeping." He winked at her.

"Pretty confident there, are you?" She knew she shouldn't flirt with him, but he started it with that wink.

"You'll have to wait and see." He put the bacon on a paper towel to drain.

"Does that mean you're going to ask me on a date?" She brought down two plates and set the table.

"Not in the kitchen with my leg propped on a chair. That's about as romantic as asking you out when you're hoisting twenty-five-pound bags of feed." He handed her a plate of cinnamon toast to take to the table and reached for his crutches.

Shiloh didn't know if he was bullshittin' her or if he was serious. She'd never dated a guy who thought that the mere act of asking her out required a romantic setting. She wasn't sure how to respond so she just changed the subject.

"Bonnie wants you and I to come over to our place tonight for a game of poker. You up for that?" she asked.

"Yep." He nodded as he maneuvered into a chair. "How high is the stakes?"

"Quarter," she answered. "Pennies, nickels, dimes, and quarters, no folding money."

"Sounds like a high-roller game," he chuckled.

"Hey, now, last time Abby Joy, Bonnie, and I played, I walked away with twenty bucks." She bowed her head.

He said a quick prayer and then put half a dozen

pieces of toast on his plate. "That would buy us a drink at the Sugar Shack on Friday night."

"Maybe, but that's only if the doctor clears you to go," she told him. "For him to do that, you have to follow orders all week."

Waylon shot a sideways look toward her.

"Don't be givin' me that attitude. I didn't write the orders. The doctor did, but honey"—she drew out the word to four or five syllables—"I will enforce them."

"You're worse than a drill sergeant," he grumbled.

"I take it that you'd never ask a drill sergeant on a date?" She raised a dark eyebrow.

"That depends," he answered.

"On what?"

"On lots of things, but mainly if she had shown an interest in me." He took a sip of coffee.

"Oh, so you had a female drill sergeant?" She scraped half the bacon onto her plate.

"Didn't ever join the military. Went right into ranchin' after high school," he said. "When I asked that air force guy who came to our school about the drill sergeant, he couldn't guarantee that I'd get a female one, so I wouldn't join."

"And here all this time I thought you were shy, when in reality you're just a smart-ass." She pushed back her chair, went to the cabinet, and returned with the coffeepot. "I need a refill. You want a warm-up?"

"Thank you." He held up his cup. "If I was trying to pick you up in a bar, I'd have a comeback for what you just said."

"Oh, yeah." She poured for both of them and returned the pot. "What would that be?"

"Darlin', just looking at you warms me up."

Shiloh had just taken a sip of coffee and spewed it all over the table. "That is the worst pickup line I've ever heard."

"Now you've hurt my feelings." He narrowed his eyes at her, but they were twinkling. "And put coffee stains on my tablecloth, at the same time."

"I'll get the stains out, and surely you've got better lines that that," she told him.

"That one never did work," he admitted, "but I have a few that have netted me some good results in the past." He held up a palm. "Don't ask me to tell you. It's fun talking to you, Shiloh, but I know the rules over on Malloy Ranch. I'd never, ever ask you out, at least not until the year is over."

"You do realize that makes it sound like you're interested in doubling the size of your place," she said.

"Try tripling it, but, honey, I only want what I earn," he told her.

"Fair enough." She nodded. "I never figured I'd be having this kind of conversation with you."

"Me, either"—he finished off his breakfast—"and we've been acquainted since the first of the year. Guess we just never had an opportunity to be alone."

Everything about the whole situation should have felt awkward, but it didn't—at least not to Shiloh.

CHAPTER FIVE

Shiloh remembered that cold day of Ezra's funeral. After the last hymn was sung, she'd driven her van back to the house. Abby Joy had stepped out of her vehicle with an aura of confidence surrounding her. She'd slung a duffel bag over her back and started toward the porch. Bonnie had opened the door of her rusted-out old pickup truck like she owned the world and dared anyone to even try to cross her. She'd lined up plastic grocery bags on her arm and marched across the yard. Shiloh had felt like she was the only chicken at a coyote convention when she unloaded the monogrammed luggage her mother had given her when she graduated from high school all those years ago, but she vowed that she wouldn't let either of those women know that they intimidated her.

"Where are we? I don't recognize this place," Waylon whispered.

Her heart fell down into her cowboy boots. He'd been doing so well, and he should know exactly where he was. He'd known Ezra well enough to come to the funeral. Surely he'd been at the Malloy Ranch at some time.

"You don't recognize this house? It's Ezra's place. It's where Bonnie and I live, where Abby Joy lived until day before yesterday. Look again," she said.

He shook his head. "Who is Ezra?"

"He's my biological father. Little short guy with blue eyes and gray hair. He died and we buried him on New Year's Day. Think hard"—she frowned—"you were at the funeral. You stood beside Cooper. You were wearing a black leather coat that came almost to your knees, and black cowboy boots. A cold wind was blowing, and each of us sisters put a daisy in the casket with Ezra. I never quite understood why, but Rusty told us to do it, so we did."

His brows drew down, as if he was trying to remember. "Ezra's not dead. I saw him last week at the feed store. He said that he and Rusty were ready for the spring grass to get high enough to put the cattle on it." He chuckled. "Ezra Malloy squeezes his pennies so tight that Lincoln squeals."

"Ezra has been dead for almost three months," she assured him. "It's not far back to the cemetery. Let's drive back there to his grave site. Maybe that will jar your memory."

He raised his palm and laughed out loud. "My name is Waylon Stephens. I just punked Shiloh Malloy."

"You rascal!" She slapped him on the arm.

He grabbed his arm and winced. "Ouch! You got me right on a big bruise from where the seat belt went across."

"I'm not sorry," she declared. "You deserved that and more. I was about to take you to the emergency room."

"Well, darlin', I'm not sorry I punked you, either. It was worth the pain just to see you get all worked up."

He opened the van door. "Guess I proved to you that I've got a poker face and you'd best be careful with your bets tonight."

She pointed her finger at him as she got out of the vehicle. "For that mean stunt, I plan to take all your money."

He managed the crutches very well as they climbed the steps side by side. Her hand brushed against his, and the sparks didn't surprise her. She'd like to be mad at him for that crazy joke he'd just pulled on her, but she just couldn't. She would have never thought that Waylon would have a sense of humor, but that he did was a big plus in her books. He'd gotten to the top step when all three of Ezra's dogs came running up on the porch. Polly jumped up on Shiloh and sent her crashing against Waylon. One of his crutches flew to the left, the other one got tangled up in Shiloh's legs.

The fall felt like it was happening in slow motion, and yet there was nothing she could do to stop it. One second she was standing upright with Waylon beside her, the next she was flat out on the porch with him on top of her. Polly was licking her face. Bonnie and Rusty crammed through the door at the same time. Shiloh's chest hurt, not from Waylon's weight, but because the fall had knocked the breath right out of her.

Bonnie fell down beside her and slapped her face. "Breathe, sister! You're turning blue."

Waylon rolled off to one side, and let out a loud whoosh of air. "I didn't mean to make you so mad that you'd trip me," he said between deep breaths.

Shiloh tried to sit up. "I didn't trip you," she gasped as she kept trying to force more and more air into her lungs.

"What'd you do?" Rusty gathered up the crutches and helped Waylon to his feet.

"Must've been a pretty hard fall." Bonnie took both of Shiloh's hands and pulled her to her feet.

The porch did a couple of spins, but in a few seconds, Shiloh had her bearings. "Polly did it," she said.

"She pouted yesterday and has watched the lane all day today lookin' for you to come home," Bonnie said. "Y'all are all right, aren't you? Do we need to take Waylon to the hospital for a checkup?"

"I'm fine," Waylon said. "But we might need to have Shiloh seen about. I landed pretty hard right on top of her. She could have cracked ribs or even a concussion as hard as she hit the porch."

"You're just trying to get out of losing all your money," Shiloh said between even more deep breaths. "There's nothing wrong with me that a beer and some chips and dip won't cure." She squatted down and rubbed Polly's ears. "So you missed me, did you? Maybe you should come on over to Waylon's place and stay with us the rest of the week."

"Oh, no!" Rusty opened the door and held it for Waylon. "I'm not giving up my dogs. Ezra left them to me, and even if you and Bonnie stick around long enough to get the ranch, I'm taking Vivien, Polly, and Martha with me. Abby Joy didn't try to steal Martha from me, and y'all ain't gettin' Polly and Vivien."

Shiloh straightened up, and the world didn't do any spins. She was breathing normal now, for the most part, but thinking about Waylon on top of her put more than a little heat in her body. For just a split second there, she thought maybe he might kiss her, but then Bonnie was right there beside her.

"You slapped me." Shiloh tilted her head to the side and gave Bonnie the evil eye.

"You're welcome."

Shiloh's hand went to her face. "I'm not thanking you for hitting me."

"If I hadn't, you might've laid there and died, and then you'd never know what it would be like to really have that good-lookin' cowboy on top of you," Bonnie teased.

"You're certifiably goofy." Shiloh's cheeks burned with a bright red blush.

"Don't tell me that you weren't enjoying the feeling." Bonnie started inside the house. "And besides, I saw the way you looked at my grocery bag luggage when we first got here on the ranch, and I've wanted a good reason to slap the fire out of you ever since."

"I'll get even." Shiloh hadn't realized how much she'd missed the banter between her and her sisters until that moment. "It'll come at a time when you least expect it."

"Bring your lunch." Bonnie went into the house ahead of her. "It you hit me without good reason, I'll mop up the yard with your skinny butt."

"Hey, that's the pot calling the kettle black." Shiloh followed her. "My butt looks damn fine compared to yours."

Bonnie did a head wiggle that made her big loopy earrings dance. "In your dreams. Old Ezra saved the best until last."

Rusty and Waylon were already at the table with a beverage in front of each one of them.

"And still couldn't get a boy," Rusty said.

Bonnie tucked a strand of blond hair into her

ponytail, and air slapped Rusty on the arm. "That was his fault, not mine."

Tonight she was wearing her little diamond nose stud, her good luck charm when she went to the casinos or played cards. Rusty removed his wire-rimmed glasses and cleaned them with the tail of his T-shirt. He raked his fingers through his brown hair and then put his glasses back on. That was his good luck routine every time they played any kind of game. Shiloh watched Waylon to see if he had a gimmick, but he simply took a sip and started shuffling the cards.

"Beer or a wine cooler?" Bonnie asked her sister.

"Wine cooler," Shiloh replied.

"That's her good luck charm, Waylon. Her tell is when she rolls her eyes at the ceiling and then takes a long drink from the bottle," Bonnie tattled.

"Bonnie's tell is when she fiddles with her nose ring." Shiloh ratted her sister out. "That means she's got a good hand."

"That's good to know in both cases." Waylon dealt the cards. "But I'm not banking on either of you telling us guys the truth."

"You shouldn't." Shiloh picked up her cards, fanned them out, and smiled. "After that stunt you pulled in the truck, you better be very careful."

"What was that?" Rusty asked.

Shiloh told them what had happened. "He deserved to fall after that. I need a card."

"You, sir, are one lucky cowboy. It's a wonder that she didn't push you down!" Bonnie said in her deep woodsy Kentucky drawl.

"Guess I am pretty lucky," Waylon said and threw a coin on the table. "I'm in for a quarter."

"Big spender right here at first, aren't you?" Bonnie threw one of her coins into the center of the table.

"Got to spend money to make money," Rusty said.

"That's what my mama says." Shiloh made a mental note to call her mother. She hadn't talked to her about the wedding, or all the things that had happened since then. Polly was going to have a million questions about Waylon. With that in mind, maybe she should drag her feet a little before she called her mama.

*   *   *

Waylon was two dollars richer when they got home that evening, but he was a million dollars poorer if they'd measured in tiredness rather than money. He'd been thrown from bulls and broncs and had been back on his feet and working within two days. Why did one little wreck affect him like this?

He crutched his way into the house, eased down on the sofa, and leaned his head back. "You can have the bed all to yourself. I'm not moving from right here tonight."

"Oh, no, you will not sleep on the sofa," Shiloh argued. "You'll wake up so sore in the morning that I'll have to carry you to the truck to do the chores." She dropped her purse on the end table and picked up his leg to remove his boot. Then she pointed down the hall. "I'm going to have a shower before I turn in."

"You can't sleep in here if I can't." He reached for his crutches. "After that fall, you're going to be sore right along with me tomorrow morning. The only way I'm sleeping in the bed is if you take the other half of it like you did last night."

"All right then." She nodded. "Don't wait up for me, though."

"Don't worry." He yawned as he stood up and headed down the hall. "I'll be asleep the minute my head hits the pillow."

When he reached his bedroom, he was surprised to see that the bed was made, and the clothes hamper was empty. He usually made his bed, but he'd been in a hurry that morning.

He was exhausted by the time he removed his jeans and got into a pair of pajama pants, but his eyes were wide open when he finally pulled the covers up around his chest. If he had any doubts at all about the chemistry between him and Shiloh, they had disappeared when he fell on top of her that evening. His lips were only inches from hers, and if Bonnie and Rusty hadn't rushed out when they did, he would have kissed her for sure. He laced his hands behind his head and stared out the window at the black clouds shifting over what was left of the moon. The weatherman had said that thunderstorms might be on the way the next day with the possibility of hail and high winds. He could be right this time. Waylon had been having his own personal tempest since his accident, and he was about to give in and forget all about the idea of not asking Shiloh out until the year's end. They could date now, figure out if they even liked each other for more than friends and neighbors, and not waste time wondering.

It took a blow to your head to make you come to your senses. The voice in his head sounded an awful lot like his granddad.

"I'm a little slow," he whispered.

"Were you talking to me?" Shiloh asked as she entered the room.

"No, just muttering to myself." He sat up in bed and pulled the covers back for her.

"Sweet Jesus!" she gasped. "Why didn't you tell me you had all those bruises on your body?"

He hadn't meant for her to see the black-and-blue marks, but he'd totally forgotten to put a T-shirt on that night. He was so tired that he'd almost crawled into bed in the nude, which is the way he usually slept.

"They'll heal," he said.

She ignored the covers and sat down on his side of the bed. She ran a finger over the worst of the bruises—the one where the doctor thought he possibly had a cracked rib, but the X-ray told a different tale. Her touch made his mouth go dry and his hands get clammy. She finally looked up at him and moistened her lips with the tip of her tongue.

He leaned forward, cupped her cheeks with his big hands, and looked deeply into her deep blue eyes. Their lips met in a sweet kiss that deepened into more and more until they were both panting. She finally pulled away from him and stood up.

"It might be best if I sleep on the sofa tonight after that," she told him.

"I'll put a pillow between us," he offered.

"I'm not sure there's one big enough. Remember what the doctor said about no strenuous activity. I reckon sex would be pretty vigorous," she said between long, deep breaths.

"I'll be good." He crossed his heart with his finger like a little boy. After that kiss it might not be easy, but he was a man of his word, no matter how tough it was.

CHAPTER SIX

Shiloh awoke to the noise of something scratching on the door the next morning. At first she thought she was at home on Malloy Ranch and one of the three dogs wanted someone to get up and feed them. Then she realized she was at Waylon's place. She hadn't seen a dog in the two days she'd been there, and hopefully, Polly hadn't followed them home the night before. If she had, Rusty would think Shiloh had stolen her.

She got out of bed carefully so she wouldn't wake Waylon. The rising sun defined the trees, now with a few buds and minty green leaves, instead of only dry, brittle branches. The scratching continued and she was surer with every step that Polly had run away from home.

She opened the door and the ugliest dog she'd ever seen ran into the house. It had long yellow hair, short legs, and a wide jaw. Poor thing looked like its mama might have been a corgi and its papa a Labrador—and it had a rat in its jaws. There were two things that Shiloh hated, and rats were both of them. She froze right there, door wide open, and a calico cat rushed in after the dog with another of those rat things in her mouth.

The dog went to the living room, dropped the gray thing on the floor, and stretched out beside it. That's when Shiloh realized it wasn't a rat but a kitten.

The cat laid its little burden down, and Shiloh realized both of the critters were kittens. She started to close the door and the cat rushed out and brought in a third baby and took it to the living room. She flopped down so that the kittens were between her and the dog.

"What's goin' on?" Waylon asked as he crutched up the hallway. "Thunder woke me up. Is it raining?"

"Yep," she said. "It's raining cats and dogs."

He peeked out the door, and raised an eyebrow. "The wind is blowing, but I don't see any rain."

A loud clap of thunder caused the dog to whimper and wrap itself more securely around the mama cat and the kittens.

"Good Lord!" Waylon muttered when he saw the sight in his living room. "Where did those things come from?"

"The porch, I guess," Shiloh said. "I opened the door and both of them brought in the kittens and made themselves at home. Never seen anything like it. Thought they were carryin' in rats at first and then I thought it was puppies. Do we keep 'em?"

"Well, I was thinkin' about gettin' a dog, but one that would help round up cattle, not kittens." He crutched over to the sofa and sat down.

The dog's tail thumped against the hardwood floor, so Waylon reached a hand down. The mutt licked it and then nosed the cat toward him. The cat left the dog to babysit her three wiggling kittens and went over to wind around Shiloh's legs.

The rain came in like a huge sheet of water from the dark clouds. A powerful wind slammed it against the windowpanes so fiercely that Shiloh was sure it would break the glass. "We can't put them out."

"Guess you'd better scramble up extra eggs this mornin', and when the storm passes we'll ride into Claude and get them some food. We've got babies to raise. You going to stick around and help me with them after the week is over?" Waylon asked.

"I'll visit them on weekends and at least once through the week, but I can't leave Malloy Ranch permanently." She sat down on the floor, and the mama cat crawled up in her lap. "What's your name, pretty girl?"

"That'll be your job."

"They'll be your cat and kittens. You should name them," Shiloh said.

Waylon pulled his phone from the pocket of his pajama pants, surfed through it for a minute, and then laid it on the end table. Blake Shelton was singing "I'll Name the Dogs." The lyrics said that she could name the babies, and he'd name the dogs.

"Are we still talkin' about kittens?" she asked.

"Yep, we are, but that song came to mind," he told her. "This poor old boy is so ugly I'm not sure what to name him."

"Well, my cat and babies are so pretty, it won't be hard to name them once I find out if they're boys or girls," she told him. "But right now, I'd better get some breakfast started and hope this storm gets on past us so we can go get the feeding done and make that drive to town."

The mama cat followed her to the kitchen and purred its thanks as Shiloh made sausage gravy, biscuits, and scrambled eggs. Whoever tossed the poor creatures out, she thought, should be caught out in the rain without an umbrella—and then shot right between the eyes.

Her phone rang and she dug it out of the pocket of her pajama bottoms. "Hello, Bonnie! You're never going to believe—"

"Did you find the dog and cat?" Bonnie asked.

"How did you know about them?" Shiloh asked. "Did Waylon already call Rusty?"

"No, but I was hoping you'd find them before this damn rain started. I got soaking wet getting from my old truck to the house after I left them all on your porch," Bonnie told her.

"You rat! Why didn't you ask Waylon before you did that?"

"Because he might have said no, and you've talked about wanting a cat, and"—she stopped for a breath—"you remember Granny Denison, who comes to church?"

"The little old lady that sits behind us and sings off-key?" Shiloh asked.

"Yep, that's the one," Bonnie said. "She died yesterday, and Rusty found out her great-nephew inherited her house. The guy was going to put Granny Denison's dog and cat to sleep if someone didn't take them. Polly, Martha, and Vivien hate cats, so we couldn't have them."

"That's horrible." Shiloh couldn't imagine killing the dog, even if it wasn't the prettiest animal in the world, or that sweet cat and kittens.

"I thought so too, so when Rusty told me, I drove over there and got them. I didn't want either of you to say no before you saw them, so I kind of left them on the porch," Bonnie said.

"What's their names?" Shiloh asked.

"Callie is the cat. Blister is the dog. You can name the kittens," Bonnie said. "And there's food, a litter pan, and their toys in your van. I didn't want to leave it all on the porch with the storm coming."

When something wasn't quite right—especially where either Bonnie or Abby Joy was concerned—Shiloh got the same antsy feeling that she had right then. "You are a sneaky one," she said when it finally hit her what Bonnie was doing, "but it won't work. I'm coming home as soon as the doctor clears Waylon."

"Are you accusing me of trying to get you to stay with Waylon so I'll get the ranch?" Bonnie laughed.

"Are you?"

"If I am, is it going to work?"

"Hell, no!" Shiloh said. "I'm hanging up, and you're still a rat!"

"Did you find their owners?" Waylon made his way into the kitchen.

"They belonged to Granny Denison, and she died. Her great-nephew was going to put them to sleep, so Bonnie brought them over here," she said. "The dog's name is Blister. The cat is Callie. So you don't get to name the dog. Do I still get to name the babies?"

"How about I name the boys, and you can name the girls." He smiled again.

Waylon had smiled twice in one day! She should've gone to the pound and brought in cats and dogs before now.

"Tell her thank you. It gets lonely around here," Waylon said.

Shiloh whipped around and stared at him without blinking. Surely she'd heard him wrong. Any other man would be cussin' and throwing things. "Are you serious?"

He dragged a chair over to the stove, which was no easy feat with crutches, and propped his leg on it. "Move over and I'll help out, and yes, I'm very serious. Besides, what were the chances that I could have a dog and cat both? Most of the time, they hate each other, and on the plus side, since you let them in, you have to come visit and babysit them from time to time. I'm sorry to hear about Granny Denison. When's the funeral? We should go."

"I'll ask Bonnie," Shiloh answered.

When he leaned over to get the butter, his arm touched hers. The chemistry was definitely still there. It hadn't died since the kiss from the night before. What would it hurt to see where a few dates might lead? A fling didn't necessarily mean wedding bells and a pretty white dress.

CHAPTER SEVEN

Shiloh could count the funerals she'd been to in her lifetime on the fingers of one hand. The last one had been just a graveside service for Ezra, and she was expecting that for Granny Denison. She couldn't have been more wrong.

When she and Waylon entered the church that Friday morning, the place was already packed. If Bonnie and Rusty hadn't saved them a seat on the back row, they would have had to stand along the walls like so many other folks. A low buzz from whispered conversations made it sound like a beehive was nearby. Then Waylon reached over and took Shiloh's hand and suddenly the whole place went eerily quiet.

For a split second, Shiloh expected to see a picture of their hands with their names emblazoned across the bottom on the big screen that hung at the front of the church. She was relieved when she looked up and saw the preacher taking his place behind the podium. "I have specific written instructions from Granny Denison concerning this funeral. The first thing I'm to do is read the obituary. 'Mary Audrey Denison was born March seventeenth, 1921, right here in the

Palo Duro Canyon to Henry and Wilma Denison. She was the oldest of ten children and the only girl in the family. She died March seventeenth, 2020, on her birthday, which is exactly what she hoped she would do. She said that when people die on their birthdays it completes the cycle of life. She was preceded in death by her parents and all her brothers. She leaves behind her dog, Blister, and cat, Callie.' I understand that Waylon Stephens has taken both of them in and plans to give them a good home. That's all I'm supposed to say, so now I'll turn the service over to our song leader."

The lady stood up from the front pew and made her way to the podium. "Granny Denison said that she couldn't carry a tune in a galvanized milk bucket but that she truly loved music, and that we were to sing her through the Pearly Gates today. Open your hymnals to page one seventy-nine and we will start with her first choice, 'Abide with Me.'"

Shiloh wasn't a bit surprised to hear Waylon's deep voice—after all, he'd probably been named for one of her favorite country singers, Mr. Waylon Jennings. Every stanza of the song ended with the words "abide with me." Shiloh should've been thinking about her spiritual life, but the lyrics made her think of where she'd been abiding the last week. Not only abiding, but sleeping in the same bed with Waylon—and getting into some pretty hot make-out sessions before they both went to sleep at night.

"And now turn to page four thirty-four, and we'll all sing 'Shall We Gather at the River,' which is the second song on Granny's list," the lady at the front of the church said, "and let's raise our voices so that if there's truly holes in the floor of heaven, Granny can hear us singing this morning."

If folks had been standing outside the building that morning, they might have seen the roof raising a little. Shiloh wondered when it came her time to gather where the angels' feet had trodden, like the song said, what her story would be. Would her obituary read like Granny's and say that she'd never married, that she'd only left behind a weird dog and cat? She thought about Blister and Callie and was reminded of that passage about the lion lying down with the lamb.

Or would the preacher say that she left behind several children, grandchildren, and great-grandchildren? As she sang, she pictured four or five little Waylons running around the yard with lassos trying to rope a calf.

"And now for Granny's last request," the lady said. "Let's turn to page two thirty-one and sing, 'O Love That Will Not Let Me Go,' and she said that we're supposed to pay attention to the words, because she is giving back the life that she owes."

Shiloh thought about those lyrics, all right, but not for spiritual reasons. Her thoughts went to Ezra. He'd given her life, and then thrown her away. She didn't owe him a damned thing, and yet here she was, fighting tooth, nail, hair, and eyeball for his ranch. She loved living in the canyon. She'd learned to love her sisters, but it would serve Ezra right if she and Bonnie both left the ranch before the year was up. It would go to Rusty then and maybe he'd change the name to something other than Malloy Ranch. Then all vestiges of Ezra would truly be gone, and the canyon—not to mention the whole world—would be a better place.

Not as long as you, Bonnie, and Abby Joy are alive.

The pesky voice in her head decided to pop up just as the song ended.

Yes, but his ranch would probably have a new name, Shiloh argued. *The three of us will have his DNA, and so will any children that we bear, but his precious ranch, the only thing that really mattered to him, would be forgotten. That seems like poetic justice to me.*

She was still struggling with those thoughts when they filed outside and headed toward the tiny cemetery just behind the church. When they arrived at the grave site, Waylon leaned one of his crutches against a tree and held on to Shiloh's hand. Several people, including Bonnie, gave her either strange smiles or go-to-hell looks when they noticed.

Granny's great-nephew and a few other relatives sat in the chairs facing the casket. A floral arrangement sat on a wire tripod at the end of the casket with a ribbon that said AUNT MARY on it. That alone seemed strange, since no one in the canyon had called her anything but Granny Denison—adults and children alike.

The preacher stood at one end of the casket and opened an envelope. "This is a letter from Granny, and when she made the arrangements for her funeral, this was to be read at the cemetery. Afterward, we're all to go to the fellowship hall for a potluck lunch. I was told not to break the seal on this until right now, so that's what I'm doing. Now I'll read it:

"'My dear friends who have gathered around to see me ushered out of this world and into the next. If you are hearing the preacher read this then I'm dead, and this is the end of the services. I have one bit of advice for you all. Live your life the way you want to live it, not the way someone else wants you to. Now, the preacher is going to play my last song, and then all y'all are going to go to the fellowship hall for a potluck dinner. My famous sweet potato casserole won't be there. One of you younger girls will be responsible for bringing it to the next funeral. It's just not a real church social without it. Goodbye, and I've loved living among y'all.'

"It's signed 'Granny Denison.'" The preacher folded the letter and nodded toward the funeral director. He pressed a button on a machine and Jamey Johnson's deep voice sang "Lead Me Home."

When the song ended, there wasn't a dry eye in the whole place. Even her relatives whom no one in the canyon even knew. Waylon pulled a clean white handkerchief from his pocket and handed it to Shiloh. She dried her eyes, but before she could hand it back, Bonnie reached for it.

The crowd began to head toward the church, the sound of their whispers like bees buzzing overhead. Shiloh wondered if they were remembering good times they'd had with Granny or if they were talking about the weather or food. Bonnie gave her back the hankie, and Shiloh tucked it inside Waylon's jacket pocket. He dropped her hand and resituated the crutches under his arms. Bonnie raised an eyebrow, and then whispered, "Looks like I might be winning the bet."

"Don't spend the money before you get it," Shiloh said out of the corner of her mouth. "I'll be home at bedtime if the doctor releases Waylon to drive."

"Did I hear my name?" Waylon asked.

"I was telling Bonnie that we have a two o'clock appointment in Amarillo so we'll have to leave right after we eat," Shiloh replied.

"And run back by the house on the way to let Blister outside for a little bit. Can't expect an old dog like him to stay in all day and not have an accident," Waylon told her.

Shiloh heard someone sobbing behind her and expected to see some of Granny Denison's relatives hanging back to pay last respects. She was surprised to see that it was Sally Mae, another elderly lady from the church, who usually sat on the same pew beside Granny—third one from the front, first two seats near the center aisle.

"Give me a minute," Shiloh said softly as she turned around and went back to the grave site. She sat down beside Sally Mae and draped an arm around her shoulders. They sat like that for several minutes before the silver-haired woman spoke.

"She's been my best friend since before either of us can remember. Without her, I'd never have lived through raisin' my three boys, grievin' when my husband passed away, or the hard times that came with just livin'. She's more like kin than my own sister. It's like losin' part of my heart." The elderly woman turned and sobbed into Shiloh's shoulder.

Shiloh hugged Sally Mae and patted her back. "Shhh..." She tried to soothe her. "Just remember the good times, and let that bring you peace." She looked over the top of Sally Mae's head to see Bonnie and Abby Joy walking toward the church, and a tear formed in the corner of her eye, then found its way down her cheek. Lord, she'd be a worse mess than Sally Mae if one of those two died suddenly. Then she glanced over to see Waylon waiting beside a tree, and another tear started down her cheek.

He could have died in that wreck if she and Bonnie hadn't been at the cemetery. The thought sent cold chills racing down her backbone.

Sally Mae finally took a step back, pulled a wad of tissues from her sweater pocket, and dried her eyes. "She would rather I rejoiced that she's in heaven, than weeping like this. It's selfish of me, but I can't help it."

"I understand." Shiloh wiped her own tears with the back of her hand.

"Ezra was an idiot for sending you girls away," Sally Mae said. "I told him so, but I didn't realize just how right I was until y'all came back to run the ranch. Now, I'm going to the dinner, and I'm going to try real hard not to cry anymore. Waylon is waiting for you. Y'all make a sweet little couple." She stiffened her backbone and walked away. "Just don't waste a bunch of time on things. Life, as we see today, is short."

"Yes, ma'am." Shiloh managed a weak smile.

* * *

"We'll see you in the fellowship hall," Rusty told Waylon as he and Bonnie walked past him.

Waylon nodded and sat down on a bench in front of a tombstone with Wesley and Sarah Banks's names on it. Pink, red, and yellow tulips bloomed in front of the gray granite stone. Wesley and Sarah had both died in 1922, almost a hundred years ago, but someone had seen fit to plant flowers for them. Waylon wondered where he'd be buried and whose name would be on the stone with his. A broad smile covered his face when he realized that the names Wesley and Sarah were an awful lot like Waylon and Shiloh. Could that be one of those omens that his sister Emmylou talked about all the time?

His phone rang, and he worked it up out of his hip pocket. "Hello, Mama, I was just thinking about Emmylou and her omens," he said.

"Why didn't you tell me about the car wreck?" she asked, bluntly.

"I didn't want you to worry. How'd you find out?"

"Cash called Jackson Bailey to congratulate him on his new baby girls, and Jackson told him all about it, and that you've got a woman living with you. Emmylou wants to know when the wedding is." His mother, Amanda's, voice went from serious to teasing.

"You tell Emmylou that she's older than me, and I wouldn't ever want to get ahead of her or any of my sisters, when it comes to matrimony," he answered.

"Hey, ain't a one of you can fuss too much about that. Patsy was only seven when I had Cash, and he was the sixth one. So tell me about this woman who's moved in with you," Amanda said.

Waylon rolled his eyes toward the dead branches of a nearby pecan tree. "She's my neighbor. Remember me talking about Ezra Malloy? She's the middle daughter, Shiloh, that I told you about." He went on to give his mother more details about the wreck, but he didn't tell her that he and Shiloh had been sleeping together all week. Amanda Stephens would never believe that they'd shared a bed without having sex.

"She's a good woman and a good neighbor to take care of you and your ranch like that, but I'm still pissed at you for not calling. Either of your brothers or any one of your sisters would have been glad to come help with things," Amanda told him. "Or for that matter, your dad and I could've left the bunch of them to take care of things here, and we would've come over there."

"No need, Mama," Waylon said. "I go to the doctor this afternoon. I'm sure he'll release me. Shiloh will go home, and I'll be back in my old routine."

"She might not be the one, but I'm gettin' tired of waiting on grandchildren." Amanda sighed. "You could start a rush to the altar for me."

"Talk to my sisters," he chuckled. "Tell them that you hear their biological clocks tickin' so loud that you can't sleep at night."

"They don't listen any better than you do," Amanda said. "Call me tonight with news about what the doctor says."

"Yes, ma'am, and I'll tell you all about Blister and Callie when I do," he said.

"Are you sure that wreck didn't rattle your brain? Who in the hell are Blister and Callie?" she asked.

"Blister is my new dog. Callie is my new cat. I'll send pictures of them, and then we'll talk," he told her as he ended the call and returned his focus to Shiloh.

Sally Mae stood up and, with the help of a cane, made her way across the grass toward the church. She didn't even glance toward Waylon when she passed him, but just kept her eyes on the ground. A minute or two after that, Shiloh stood up and made her way toward Waylon. She'd worn a little black dress that morning that skimmed her knees, a pair of black cowboy boots, and a black coat that was belted at the waist. Her dark hair flowed down over her shoulders in big curls, and even from a distance he could see the sadness in her blue eyes.

"Poor Sally Mae." She sat down beside him. "I can't even imagine how lost she's going to be without Granny Denison. I've only known Bonnie and Abby Joy a few months, and I'd be devastated if I lost either of them. She and Granny weren't related by blood, but they'd been best friends most of their lives."

"I figured you'd help her get back to the church." Waylon liked the way her body molded to his on the narrow concrete bench.

"I offered, but she didn't want me to." Shiloh leaned her head on his shoulder. "She said that she needed to go alone for closure. If that was Bonnie or Abby Joy, or even worse, my mama, I'd want someone beside me all the time."

"Each person grieves differently." Waylon remembered going into the woods behind the old farmhouse where he'd been raised after his granddad died. He'd screamed and shook his fist at the sky, but then he had been just a kid, and his grandfather was the first loved person he'd lost.

"I suppose they do." Shiloh nodded.

"Shall we go have some potluck dinner?" he asked.

"Yes." She got to her feet. "It almost seems wrong to be eating and visiting, doesn't it?"

"There's comfort in food and friends at times like this." He got his crutches tucked under his arms and walked beside her.

When they entered the room, Rusty and Bonnie were just inside the door with Loretta and Jackson Bailey on their right, and Abby Joy and Cooper on their left.

Abby Joy and Bonnie each had one of Loretta and

Jackson's twin daughters in their arms. Both of the sisters took a few steps toward Shiloh. She held out her arms and Bonnie shared, but Abby Joy seemed to hold her bundle a little tighter. Waylon wouldn't be a bit surprised if she and Cooper didn't announce that they were having a baby before the year was out.

"Look at her, Waylon. She's only a week old and she's so alert." Shiloh held out the dark-haired baby girl for him to see.

"I thought the twins might have red hair," he said.

"This one does." Abby Joy took a step forward. "Martina looks like Jackson, and Jennifer is the image of Loretta."

"I like their names," Shiloh said.

"Had to keep it country." Loretta smiled.

If he and Shiloh ever had kids, Waylon wondered, would she want to keep the tradition of naming children after country music singers? His granddad had loved Patsy Cline, so his folks let him name their first daughter Patsy Ann. They'd planned on calling her Annie, but it hadn't worked out that way. Then the next one had come along, and another one, and they had just kept naming them all after singers, much like Loretta's family had done.

Whoa, cowboy! Jerk those reins up real tight! the voice in his head yelled at him. *You haven't even proposed and you're already naming babies?*

He turned his attention to Shiloh, who was handing the baby over to Jackson. She'd been so good to go back and comfort Sally Mae, and now she was planting a sweet kiss on little Martina's forehead. He remembered an old adage his granddad used to say.

"Your daddy knew that Amanda would be a good

woman to ride the river with," Granddad said. "Your grandma never thought she was good enough for her precious son, but he was her only child, so probably no one would ever be good enough for him in her eyes."

"Ride the river?" Waylon had asked.

"The river is the journey of your life. You find a good woman to ride the river with, and the journey will be right nice. Just be real sure that you're listenin' to your heart and not your head when you make your choice. Sometimes you might get them confused," Granddad had said.

Shiloh laid a hand on his arm and jerked him out of the past and back to the present. "Ready to get in line for food."

"I sure am," he said. "You looked pretty good holding that baby."

"I love babies and kids. I just hope I don't have to pay for my raisin' when my kids get to be teenagers," she told him.

"Ain't that the truth," he agreed.

"Excuse me." A man wearing creased jeans and a western shirt stepped through the crowd. "I'm Dillon McRay, Miz Denison's lawyer. I'd like to meet with you for just a few minutes in the sanctuary. I promise it will only take a few minutes, and then y'all can come on back in here and have some dinner. The line will probably be pretty well done by then."

"Y'all as in...?" Waylon asked.

"You and Shiloh Malloy," he said.

"Yes, sir," Waylon said, "but may I ask what is the nature of this?"

"I understand that one or both of you have adopted

Miz Denison's dog and cats. Is that right?" Dillon asked.

Waylon nodded. "That's right. We've got Blister and Callie and the kittens. It didn't take us long to get attached to them."

"Then I need to see y'all. Her nephew and his family are already in the sanctuary, so if you'll follow me." He led the way across the fellowship hall, through a door that led straight into the sanctuary and up to the front pew.

Waylon laid his crutches out on the pew and sat down beside Shiloh.

Dillon chose to sit on the altar, where his black leather briefcase waited. He opened it and removed several papers. "This is very short and won't take long. I won't take time to read Miz Denison's will, but I have a copy for Waylon and one for Carl. This is what it says. Carl, you and your family inherit the house and everything in it, but you cannot sell it. If you don't want to possess it and the ten acres that goes with it, then you can take whatever you want from it, but again, you can't sell it, and when you are dead whoever inherits it can't sell it either. I'm supposed to ask you what you plan to do with the dog and cats at this point."

"I figured she'd do something like this," Carl, a tall, lanky man with thick glasses, said. "She was a cantankerous old girl and never forgave any of her brothers for moving away from the canyon. I don't want the house or anything in it if I can't sell it."

His wife held up a hand. "And we damn sure don't want those animals, so I guess we drove all the way up here from Sweetwater for nothing."

"I guess maybe you did," Dillon said. "Since you've stated your desires"—he held up a minirecorder—"and I have it right here, then you are free to go."

"Let's just go back to her house, get our things, and leave," Carl's wife said. "I never have liked potluck dinners. We can stop at that little café in Silverton. They made a pretty good chicken fried steak last time we ate there."

"One more time," Dillon asked. "You don't want the house, the land, or anything of hers from the house?"

"You got that right." Carl nodded. "We'll be out of this godforsaken canyon in an hour and probably never come back."

"Okay, then, but would you please sign these papers for me stating that is your decision before you go," Dillon asked.

Carl whipped a pen from his pocket and put his signature on all the places where the lawyer had stuck fancy little blue tabs. "I wish I'd known before we came that this was the way it was going to be. I wouldn't have wasted my time."

Shiloh took a deep breath and started to get up from the pew, but Waylon put a hand on her knee. "Some people are born assholes," he whispered.

"And just get bigger with age," she said out of the side of her mouth.

When the papers were signed, Carl and his wife didn't go back through the fellowship hall at all but left through the front door. Dillon took a deep breath and said, "Okay, now to what I have to say to you, Waylon. I need you to sign this paper saying that you bought your ranch from Oliver Watson and there were no other owners besides you and Mr. Watson. I know all this already, since I live on up toward Claude and do the legal business for a lot of folks in the canyon, but we have to keep everything documented and legal."

Waylon scanned through the single sheet of paper and signed it. "I don't understand what I've got to do with all this, but there it is."

"I've got something to read to you now," Dillon said.

"'If Dillon is reading this then I'm dead. I like you, Waylon Stephens. You're a good man. I'm glad that you bought the ranch next to my place. Even though our paths only cross at church since I don't keep goats or a steer or two anymore, I feel good knowing you are next door. This ten acres was at one time a part of the Watson Ranch. My dad bought it from his cousin, but you aren't interested in all that history. Here's the deal, if my nephew, who is my oldest living relative, declines to take possession of my house and land, then it should go back and become a part of the original property so it's now yours...'" Dillon stopped and looked up.

Waylon could hardly believe what he'd just heard. "Are you saying that I just inherited her house and property?"

"Exactly," Dillon answered and continued reading: "'To whoever takes in my precious pets, Dillon has orders to hand over my entire bank accounts. He will take care of all the particulars concerning the transfer, but this is my desire. So if you are in this room, and Blister and Callie are at your house, then Dillon will explain the rest to you.'"

Waylon shook his head slowly. "What does all that mean?"

"It means that her savings and checking accounts

and her portfolio of investments now are totally yours. All you have to do is sign a document saying that you will take care of the animals, love them, and give them a good home until they die." Dillon shuffled through more papers and handed them to Waylon to sign.

"Why did you need me?" Shiloh asked.

"If Waylon is living with someone or married, then they have to agree to help take care of the dog and cat," Dillon told them.

"I'll be moving out tonight," Shiloh said.

"Then I only need Waylon's signature," he said.

"I don't need to be paid to give those animals a good home," Waylon said as he signed the papers.

"You're a good man," Dillon said. "But this is the way she wanted things done. I have the past year's bank statements and her portfolio right here. She paid me enough to retain me for the rest of this year, so if you need anything call me. That pretty much concludes our business, so if you have no more questions, I'm going to make myself a plate of food. I sure like potluck dinners."

Waylon glanced down at the figures on the top paper, blinked a dozen times, and still couldn't believe what he was seeing. "I don't think I've ever seen so many zeroes in my life. I'd never have guessed that Granny Denison was so rich!"

"Well, I for one do not intend to tell Bonnie about this. She was the one who rescued the animals to begin with and brought them to us." Shiloh smiled.

Waylon's mind went around in circles so fast that he had trouble catching a single thought, so he finally said, "Let's take all this out to the van and then have some dinner. Then we better go home and take good care of Blister and Callie. You think maybe I should buy them gold-plated feeding and water dishes?"

"No, but I think maybe you should turn her house into a bunkhouse and hire some full-time help," she suggested. "Or maybe even buy the Dunlap Ranch that borders you on the south. It's been for sale ever since I got here."

"I wanted that piece of property, but it's twice as big as the Watson Ranch, and I couldn't afford it," he admitted.

"Well, darlin', now you can." She stood up and handed him his crutches. "A bit of advice though. I'd only tell about inheriting the property and house but not the money. If you do, you should at least wait until your foot is fully healed."

"Why's that?" he asked.

She picked up the stack of papers. "Because you're going to need to outrun every single girl in the canyon when they find out how much you're worth."

Waylon hoped that Shiloh was way out in front, leading the pack, should that ever become the case.

CHAPTER EIGHT

The doctor cleared Waylon to do anything that he felt like doing, including driving and lifting, so long as he took it easy on the ankle for another week. As soon as they left his office, Waylon asked Shiloh to drive him to the body shop to see about his truck.

Suddenly, Shiloh's heart felt like someone had laid a rock on top of it. She thought she'd be relieved to go back to her routine on Malloy Ranch. Her mother used to tell her that she couldn't have her Popsicle and eat it too. That rang more true right then than it ever had before. She wanted to go home so she and Bonnie could get used to not having Abby Joy around all the time, but she wanted to stay with Waylon too.

"Man, it feels good to get off those crutches," Waylon said on the way out to her van. "It's still a little tender, but I've had a worse sore ankle after being thrown from a bull."

She just nodded, then got into the van and drove back toward Claude, where the body shop was located. From there he'd drive himself down into the base of the canyon and home.

"What're you goin' to name the kittens?" she asked.

"That's your job, remember?" He turned on the radio. "You're supposed to name the babies like Blake sings about."

"But the dog came with a name and so did the mama cat," she argued.

"I checked when we went by the house. We've got two girls and one boy kitten. I reckon if we're going to keep four cats in the house, we'd better be gettin' in touch with a vet before too long." He kept time for a few seconds with his thumb on the console, and then he began to sing with Willie Nelson doing "Help Me Make It Through the Night."

Shiloh sang harmony with him, and agreed with the lyrics, which said he didn't care what was right or wrong, and that the devil could take tomorrow because he didn't want to be alone and needed help to make it through the night. That's the way she felt too—just one more night with him beside her in that big king-size bed, and this time they'd do more than sleep.

The body shop had his truck ready, so he drove it back to his ranch, and parked in front of the house. He got out and sat on the porch steps and waited for her to get the van parked. She got the papers the lawyer had given him from the back seat and handed them off to him on her way inside.

"My suitcase is packed. I just need to get it, unless you want me to stick around to help with chores tonight," she said.

"I think I've got it covered." He stood to his feet. "Shiloh, thank you for everything. If I can ever return the favor, just give me a call. I programmed my number into your phone."

"I surely will." She walked past him into the house.

She wanted to say that he could ask her to stay, but why would he? With what he'd inherited that day, he could have any woman in the state of Texas. He might even have to get himself one of those number machines like they had in the fancy coffee shops just to give them all a turn.

She rolled her suitcase out onto the porch and started to carry it out to her van.

"I'll take that for you." He picked it up and followed her to her vehicle. "You will come back on weekends to visit the animals, won't you?"

"Of course." She smiled as she settled behind the wheel. "We still have to name the kittens. I'll be thinkin' about the two girls' names."

He tilted his hat back and leaned into the van, cupped her cheeks in his calloused hands, and kissed her with so much passion that the whole world disappeared. For the length of one long, hot kiss, she forgot about everything but being close to Waylon. When it ended, she leaned her head on his shoulder.

"I'll miss you, Shiloh," he whispered. "Don't be a stranger. You're welcome anytime."

"I'll remember that, and the same goes for you. Come on across the highway anytime you want a little company," she told him.

"Thank you." He took a step back and closed the door for her.

He limped back to the porch and waved until she couldn't see him in the rearview mirror anymore. The house was empty when she got home that evening, so she rolled her suitcase into her bedroom and fell backward onto the end of the bed. With her feet dangling off the end, she stared at the ceiling. How in the hell had she fallen in love with a man in only a week's time?

"You're home!" Bonnie dragged herself into the room and sat down beside her. She removed her own well-worn cowboy boots and tossed them to the side and then leaned back so that she was in the same position as her sister—legs hanging off the end of the bed. "I missed you, and I'm tired of doing all the chores around here, so welcome home."

"So you don't want to own the ranch all by yourself?" Shiloh asked.

"Yep, I do, but if there's a chance you ain't never comin' back, I'll hire some help. I guess since you're here that the doctor released Waylon, right?"

"He did," Shiloh answered.

"And then Waylon released you," Bonnie giggled. "So what did that lawyer want with y'all?"

"Seems that if Granny Denison's relatives didn't want her property with the stipulation that since it was family land, they couldn't sell it, then she was giving it to Waylon. So he gained ten acres and her house today," Shiloh answered. "You ever been in that house?"

"One time," Bonnie said. "Remember when one of Waylon's cows got out and came across the road? You'd gone to Claude to buy groceries, so me and Abby Joy herded the old heifer back over to Waylon's place. Only it wasn't his cow. We walked her over to Granny Denison's, only to find out that it wasn't hers either."

Shiloh nodded. "I remember you telling me that story." "Whose cow was it?"

"Belonged to the Dunlaps on the other side of Waylon's place. Granny called them and they brought a cattle trailer down to get her," Bonnie answered. "Anyway, Granny invited us in for a glass of lemonade. It's a pretty good-size house. Maybe four or five bedrooms. She said that her folks raised a bunch of kids there."

"Should make a fine bunkhouse then," Shiloh said.

"Oh, yeah, but he might want to do some paintin'. Every room I saw was either painted pink or pale blue. I can't see cowboys appreciating that kind of livin' quarters." Bonnie slapped her on the arm. "Enough lazin' around. We've got supper to cook. Rusty will be in here in a few minutes, and he'll be hungry as I am."

Shiloh sat up. "You ever think that maybe we should both follow in Abby Joy's footsteps and leave this place to Rusty? I don't think Ezra wanted us to get along when he made his will. He wanted us to fight and be hateful to one another, and then leave the canyon so that a boy would still get the place."

"I'm here to prove him wrong," Bonnie said. "You havin' second thoughts?"

"Let's just say that I'm lookin' at things from a different perspective," Shiloh told her sister.

"Why's that?" Bonnie asked.

"It all started at Granny Denison's funeral. Sally Mae was crying, so I went back to comfort her. I realized that Ezra isn't worth the grudge I've held against him, or the energy I've put into tryin' to prove that I can run his ranch." Just saying the words out loud made her feel like a load had been lifted from her shoulders.

"It'll cost you a hundred dollars and a bottle of good whiskey." Bonnie headed out into the hallway.

"It could be the best money I'd ever spend," Shiloh muttered as she stood up and stretched her arms over her head.

CHAPTER NINE

Blister ran out of the house as soon as Waylon opened the door that Friday evening after he'd taken care of the evening chores. The short-legged mutt ran to the nearest bush, took care of business, and was already yipping to be let back in by the time Waylon removed his coat and hung it on a hook.

"And here I was afraid you'd run off and try to find your way back to Granny's house," Waylon told the dog when he opened the door. "You know something, Blister? I wish that Shiloh would find her way back home to this ranch, but that's not likely to happen. She's got her heart set on owning the Malloy place, and besides, after the way Ezra tossed her to the side, I don't know that she'll ever trust a guy."

Blister sat down, and his tail thumped against the kitchen floor.

"So you agree with me?" Waylon opened the refrigerator and pulled out everything he needed to make himself a couple of hot dogs. "I already miss her, and she's only been gone a couple of hours. Should I call her after supper?"

This time Blister swished his tail back and forth across the floor.

"I thought so," Waylon said. "I should let her know that you and Callie miss her, and she should come over to Sunday dinner, right?"

Blister yipped in agreement.

"You and I are going to be buddies." Waylon tossed the mutt the end off a hot dog. "We understand each other, don't we?"

Waylon's phone rang, ending the conversation he was having with Blister. He saw that it was his brother Cash and put it on speaker while he finished fixing his supper.

"Hey, I was goin' to call y'all after supper, and tell you that the doctor released me, so I'm back on full ranchin' duty," Waylon said.

"That's great, brother." Cash's tone indicated something was wrong.

Waylon's blood ran cold until Cash sighed and started talking again. "Me and Rachel broke up, for good this time. She's been cheating on me with Mitch, and they're going to get married."

Waylon hated to hear that, but he was so glad that it wasn't even worse news—like his dad had been hurt in a ranch accident or his mother had dropped with a heart attack. He opened his mouth to say something, but then he remembered Granny Denison's house. "You need to get the hell out of East Texas?" he asked. "I kinda came into a little bit of property today. I was thinkin' of turnin' the house into a bunkhouse. If you need—"

"Yes," Cash butted in. "Can I bring Emmylou with me? She needs to get away too."

"What's goin' on with her?" Waylon asked.

"Mama is stomping on her and Patsy's last nerve about grandbabies," Cash told him. "They both need a vacation, but Patsy has a boyfriend, and things aren't quite as bad for her."

"And June? What's goin' on with her?" Waylon asked.

"She's the only one that can stand Grandma. She spends a lot of time over there helping her out, but me and Emmylou could sure stand a change of scenery. We can be there by suppertime tomorrow night if that's all right," Cash said.

"I'll have a pot of chili waiting and enough work to keep you both busy for a year." Waylon grinned. Tomorrow he was going over to the Dunlap Ranch and make an offer on it. If they accepted, that would triple the size of his ranch, but he didn't tell Cash that bit of news right then.

"Work might keep me from shooting Rachel and Mitch," Cash said. "Thanks so much. I'm going to tell Emmylou to pack her bags. See you tomorrow."

Waylon finished making his hot dogs and sat down to the kitchen table with them. He looked to his right, where Shiloh had always sat, bowed his head, and said a silent grace. When he opened his eyes, she still wasn't there, but he sure wished that she was. He wanted to tell her how overwhelmed he was with what all had happened in the last twenty-four hours.

He ate his supper, washed the dishes, and then went to the living room, where he surfed through the channels on the television. There was nothing that he wanted to watch, but the house seemed so empty without Shiloh there. He picked up a ranching magazine, flipped through it, and tossed it on the far end of the sofa.

He heard a vehicle outside, and was on his way across the floor, when someone rapped on the door. He slung it open to find Shiloh. The expression on her face said that she was anxious about something.

"You told me not to be a stranger, and I wanted…" she stammered. "You told me I could name two of the kittens and it didn't seem right to do something that important over the phone."

He butted in, "I was just thinking about callin' you." He slung open the screen door and motioned her inside.

Callie came out from her basket to greet Shiloh the moment the cat heard her voice. She dropped down on her knees in the living room to pet the mama cat. "I knew you'd miss me."

Old folks, babies, and pets all adored her, Waylon thought. Granddad just might say that she'd do to ride the river with.

"Want a beer or a glass of sweet tea?" Waylon asked.

"Love a beer," she replied.

He went to the kitchen, brought back two bottles, and handed one to her before he sat down on the floor beside her. "I just got off the phone with my brother Cash. He and my sister Emmylou will be here tomorrow evening. They'll be stayin' over at Granny Denison's house, so I guess the idea of turning it into a bunkhouse has happened quicker than we thought."

Shiloh laughed out loud. "Have you been in that place?"

He shook his head. "I sat on the porch with her a

few times and had cookies and sweet tea, but I was never invited inside. Why did you ask?"

She told him what Bonnie had said about the place being totally feminine. "I just hope Cash don't mind."

"I guess the first money of what I inherited will be spent for paint," he chuckled. "Emmylou hates pink. Mama always dressed the three girls alike from the pictures I've seen, and most of the time it was pink."

He didn't want to talk about paint or bunkhouses, but he'd gladly listen to her read the dictionary if she'd just stick around a while.

"I've been doing a lot of thinking this evening," Shiloh said.

"About what?" Waylon hoped that she'd say she'd been thinking about the past week and those heated good night kisses they'd shared.

She inhaled deeply and let it out ever so slowly. "I'm wondering what Ezra's true motive was in putting us all on that ranch together. He was a sly old son of a bitch, and he probably wanted us to fight, get mad, and leave. Abby Joy wouldn't say how much one-third of the money he left behind was, but she did say that if she'd known about it before, she might have never stayed on the ranch as long as she did. So"—Shiloh stood up and took a seat on the sofa—"knowing the way he felt about girls, I figure he wanted Rusty to have the place, and he left us money to ease his conscience for the way he treated us. After all, Rusty is a guy, and he wanted an heir to leave his land to, not an heiress."

"I'm not sure Ezra had a conscience." Waylon joined her on the sofa. "If he did, it was buried pretty deep. What are you going to do?"

"It would be just what he deserves if me and

Bonnie stuck it out and kept the ranch, but then even if we changed the name, it would take a hundred years before everyone quit calling it the Malloy Ranch. Rusty liked him, so I figure he'd keep the name. Hell, he might have even had a deal with Ezra to keep the name and maybe even change his name to Malloy to make it legal. Who knows what that old codger had up his sleeve?" Shiloh took a long drink of her beer.

"Well, if you decide to move out, there's a spare room here, and from what you've told me about my new bunkhouse there's lots of room over there. You can have your choice of any of them," Waylon told her.

"That's so sweet. Are you going to give me a job, too?" she asked.

"Honey, you know what I just inherited." He moved closer to her and put an arm around her shoulders. "I'll give you half of it to move across the highway and work with me."

* * *

Shiloh noticed that he'd said *with* me, not *for* me. She met his eyes and didn't blink, "Don't joke with me."

"Honey, I've never been more serious in my life. I wanted to ask you out the first time I saw you," he said as he leaned in for a long, lingering kiss.

"And that was when?" Her heart pounded in her chest when the kiss ended.

"At Ezra's funeral," he admitted. "And then at the church the next week, and every time I saw you after that."

"Why didn't you?" She shifted her weight so that she was sitting in his lap with her arms around his neck.

"After the way Ezra treated you girls, one of you deserves to have that ranch, no matter what the damned place is named." He planted another kiss on her forehead.

"But I'm not sure I want it. I'm struggling with living there since this past week. I've been thinkin' about what I really want, and I'm not so sure it's his ranch," she whispered.

"Like I said, you've got a job and a place here if you want to move." He kissed her on the tip of her nose.

"Moving over here to take care of you is...was..." she stammered.

"Spit it out," Waylon said.

She moved away from his lap and began to pace the floor. "I've been attracted to you ever since Ezra's funeral too, but there was something about going to Granny Denison's services today"—she hesitated—"that made me wonder about letting opportunities pass. At Abby Joy's wedding, it seemed like a sign for me to get to spend more time with you. Then the wreck happened and gave me the opportunity to do just that. But living with you this week made me restless at home."

"Are you uneasy here?" he asked.

"No, this is where I'm at peace," she told him.

He stood up slowly, took her by the hand, and led her to his bedroom. Callie and Blister followed behind them, but Waylon closed the door before they could get through. He sat down on the edge of the bed and pulled her down beside him.

"I'm only at peace when you're with me," he said.

"Fate sure had a crazy way to bring us together." She pulled at the top snap on his western shirt and unfastened them all with one quick tug.

                            *   *   *

Sometime after midnight Shiloh woke to find Waylon staring at her, much like he had that first night they'd shared the bed—only that night they'd slept and last night there had been so much more than sex. Two soul mates had met and fallen in love. She wasn't sure if it happened right when she made the decision to leave Ezra's place, or when she turned onto the Wildflower Ranch property. As she stared at the sexy cowboy beside her, she realized that maybe she'd been in love with him longer than she even realized.

Callie jumped onto the bed and curled up between Waylon and Shiloh.

"Kittens!" Shiloh popped herself on the head. "I came over here to name the kittens, and I forgot. You make me forget everything, Waylon."

"Honey, you do the same thing to me," he said as he traced her lip line with his forefinger, and then leaned over the cat for a good-morning kiss.

Callie cold-nosed his chin and broke up the make-out session. They both laughed as they moved away from each other a few inches.

"Evidently she thinks it's time to give her babies their names," Waylon said.

"Well, since I thought they were mice, my girls' names are Minnie and Perla," Shiloh told him.

"I understand Minnie, but where'd you get Perla?" he asked.

"From *Cinderella*," she told him. "There were three little girl mice and three boys."

"Never watched that one." He grinned. "But our boy will be Mickey."

"Sounds good to me." She yawned. "Now we just have to raise them and hope that we live through their teenage years."

He chuckled. "I believe that's Callie's job."

"I should go home." She pushed back the covers on the bed.

"This is home. We just have to give it enough time to work out the details." He began to massage her back.

"How much time?" she whispered as she moved the cat to the foot of the bed.

"As much or as little as you want." He gathered her into his arms and held her close, their naked bodies pressed against each other. "Just don't forget where home really is, Miz Shiloh Malloy."

"I won't," she said. "You've got my word on that."

He buried his face in her hair. "I've always thought that love at first sight was a crock of bull crap, but now I believe in it. I love you, Shiloh."

"I love you, Waylon." She didn't even mind that what was going to happen would cost her a hundred dollars and a bottle of whiskey.

CHAPTER TEN

There wasn't a cloud in the sky the last Saturday in May. The sun was just setting over the western bank of the canyon, and wildflowers were in full bloom everywhere. It all made for a perfect setting for the wedding reception that was about to take place on the Wildflower Ranch—the brand-new registered brand for Waylon and Shiloh's property. She'd spent the night before at the bunkhouse with her sisters, Bonnie and Abby Joy, and Waylon's sisters, Patsy, Emmylou, and June.

Shiloh was barely awake when Bonnie and Abby Joy bounced into her room and jumped onto her bed. "Wake up, sleepyhead," Abby Joy said. "You're getting married in three hours and you look like hell."

Shiloh kicked off the covers, sat up, and looked at her reflection in the mirror above the dresser. Abby Joy was right. Her dark hair was a fright. She was sunburned from helping bring in the first cutting of hay the day before, and her eyes were puffy from staying up too late with all the ladies the night before.

"You've got your work cut out for you," she moaned.

"Not to worry," Bonnie said. "We'll get you beautified and to the church on time."

Shiloh's mother, Polly, poked her head in the door. "Breakfast is on the bar. Amanda and I made pancakes and bacon. You don't want anything too heavy on your stomach for the wedding." She came on into the room and sat down on the end of the bed. "As much as you were going to prove Ezra wrong and inherit your part of that ranch, I'm surprised that you're giving it all up."

"I figured out that some things are more important than revenge." Shiloh leaned over and gave her mother a hug. "I love Waylon, Mama."

"He's a good man," Polly said. "And I can tell by the way he looks at you that he loves you. I couldn't be happier for you than I am this day."

"How does it feel for you to be back here? Does it bring back painful memories?" Shiloh asked.

"Honey, I put Ezra out of my heart years ago. Some folks just aren't worth stealing your peace. I'm glad that you found that out for yourself," Polly said.

Shiloh scooted closer to her mother. "I'm glad you let me do it on my own, and that you didn't lecture me, but just let me do what I had to do. If I hadn't I would have never met Waylon." She kissed her mother on the cheek. "And he's my soul mate."

Bonnie slung an arm around Shiloh. "You lost a bet. I'll expect you to pony up on it."

"Wouldn't dream of forgetting that." Shiloh stood up and handed her younger sister a bottle of whiskey with a hundred-dollar bill held tightly around it with a rubber band. "Here it is. Now you can celebrate me being gone. Break it open, and we'll celebrate together."

"I can't drink with y'all." Abby Joy shook her head. "I teased Cooper about getting pregnant on our honeymoon, and the test I took yesterday said that it happened, so Bonnie gets that whole bottle of whiskey all to herself."

"That's fantastic!" Shiloh hugged her older sister.

Bonnie jumped off the bed and did a happy dance. "I'm going to be an aunt, and the baby is going to love me more than Shiloh," she singsonged as she pulled Abby Joy out of the room and toward the kitchen.

"We'll just see about that," Shiloh yelled.

"I can only pray the same thing happens to you, my child." Polly held up a hand toward heaven.

"Whoa!" Shiloh grabbed her mother's hand and put it down. "One thing at a time."

Polly patted her on the back. "Well, darlin', the first thing is breakfast. Today, you're marryin' Waylon. He's everything I ever hoped that you'd find in a husband, and honey, I'm glad you left Malloy Ranch. You would have never been happy there."

"But, Mama, I was happy there with my sisters," she said.

Polly smiled. "The key words are 'with your sisters.' Without them, you would have been lonely, and besides, you belong with Waylon."

"You're so right, but I sure hope Bonnie sticks around, because I rather like having sisters." Shiloh looped her arm in her mothers and together they left the room.

"Even Waylon's sisters?" Polly whispered.

"Emmylou is outspoken, but I like her. Jury is still out on the other two. They only got here a couple of days ago, and things have been crazy, with trying to get hay baled and attending to wedding stuff," Shiloh said in a soft voice.

*   *   *

Waylon sat down to breakfast with his two brothers and his father that morning. If he'd followed Shiloh's advice and gone to the courthouse, got married, and then told his family and her mother and aunt, he could be plowing a field or hauling in that sixty acres of small bales of hay that was ready. But he was the first one of the six Stephens siblings to get married, and he knew his mother would be disappointed if they didn't at least have a small wedding. So having to get dressed up, go to the church, and say his vows was no one's fault but his own that day.

"Got what you're goin' to say to Shiloh all memorized?" his father, Jimmy, asked.

"Pretty much goin' to wing it," Waylon answered.

"Just say what's in your heart," Buddy advised. "Even if you stutter a little, it's better than a rehearsed thing that has no feelin'."

"Great advice, Dad." Waylon pulled out his phone and stepped to the other side of the room.

He typed in a text to Shiloh: *I wish we would have eloped.*

One came right back: *Me too!*

He was typing another text when his phone rang. When he saw that it was Shiloh, he almost dropped it, trying to answer on the first ring.

"I'll be so glad when—" she started.

"I know—" he said.

"I am looking forward to the reception and dancing with you out in our new gazebo, and Waylon, you're never going to believe what my one-third of the money is. I almost fainted when I saw all those zeroes," she said. "The lawyer brought me the check last night, and I signed the papers saying I was giving up my rights to the Malloy Ranch."

"That's your money, darlin'," he told her.

"No, it's ours, and I'm thinkin' we might make an offer for the land to the north of us. We've got plenty of room in the bunkhouse to house the hired help," she said. "I'm not interested in anything but building a life with you."

"I love you," he said.

"Me too. See you at the church at eleven o'clock. I'll be the one in the white dress."

"I'll be the one that has eyes for only you," he whispered as he made his way out to the porch. "I'm the luckiest cowboy in this whole canyon."

"You're almost as lucky as I am," she said.

*　　*　　*

The church was packed that morning at eleven o'clock when Shiloh arrived. Her sisters, her mother, and her aunt waited with her in the nursery until Loretta Jackson came to tell them that it was time to start the ceremony. "Jackson is going to seat your aunt Audrey, then Bonnie and Abby Joy will make their way up the aisle, and when you hear the first of the song you've chosen to walk in to, then your mom will take you down to where Waylon will be waiting."

"Got it." Shiloh gave her the thumbs-up sign.

The next couple of minutes went by in a blur. Then the first chords of "Mama He's Crazy" started, and she took her mother's arm.

"Not exactly wedding music," Polly whispered.

"Waylon and I aren't exactly traditional folks," she said as she took her first step down the aisle.

When the lyrics said that he was heaven sent, Waylon gave her one of his special smiles, and the whole world disappeared. To Shiloh, they were the only two people in the church, and nothing mattered but the vows they were about to say.

It wasn't planned, but he left his place in the front of the church and met her halfway down the aisle. Polly gave him a kiss on the cheek and then put Shiloh's hand in his. She waited until the two of them finished the walk together and then went forward to sit on the front pew.

"Well, I usually start with 'dearly beloved,'" the preacher chuckled, "but after that song, I think we'll just let these two say their vows."

Shiloh handed her bouquet to Abby Joy and raised her dress to show off the pair of brown cowboy boots that she wore to work on the ranch. "See these boots? I come to you today in my pretty white dress, but under it is a ranchin' woman who wants to spend her life with you. I love you, Waylon Stephens, and I give you my promise that I will love you longer than forever, and right into eternity."

Waylon took her hands in his. "My granddad told me once that life is like a river, and I should find the right woman to ride the river with. I didn't find the right woman. I found the perfect one. I love you, Shiloh, and I give you my promise that my love for you will last through eternity."

Shiloh heard a couple of sniffles from the front pew. She was glad that she'd had a few moments in the nursery after her mother left. That had given her time to switch out the pretty white satin shoes for her old cowboy boots that she'd snuck into the church in a duffel bag.

They exchanged plain gold wedding bands, and then the preacher pronounced them man and wife, and told Waylon he could kiss the bride. The new husband bent his bride backward in a true Hollywood kiss, then stood her up to the applause of everyone in the church. "And now it's my turn," he whispered.

"What?" she asked.

The music started and Blake Shelton's voice came out loud and clear with "You Name the Babies, I'll Name the Dogs."

She giggled. "It's fitting after the one I walked down the aisle to."

He took her in his arms and two-stepped all the way out of the church with her. He scooped her up at the door and carried her to his truck. When he'd settled her into the passenger seat, he leaned in and kissed her one more time. "Love the boots."

"I'm excited that I get to ride the river with you. Let's go enjoy our reception," she said.

"Yes, ma'am." He whistled all the way around the truck.

Want to read Abby Joy's story?
Look for Daisies in the Canyon
wherever books are sold.

ABOUT THE AUTHOR

Carolyn Brown is a *New York Times* and *USA Today* bestselling romance author and RITA® Finalist who has sold more than 5 million books. She presently writes both women's fiction and cowboy romance. She has also written historical single titles, historical series, contemporary single titles, and contemporary series. She lives in southern Oklahoma with her husband, a former English teacher, who is not allowed to read her books until they are published. They have three children and enough grandchildren to keep them young. For a complete listing of her books (series in order) and to sign up for her newsletter, check out her website at www.carolynbrownbooks.com or catch her on Facebook/CarolynBrownBooks.

Ride off into the sunset
with more hot cowboys from Forever!

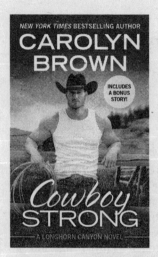

COWBOY STRONG
by Carolyn Brown

Alana Carey can outrope and outride the toughest Texas cowboys. But she does have one soft spot—Paxton Callahan. So when her father falls ill, Alana presents Pax with a crazy proposal: to pretend to be her fiancé so her father can die in peace. But as the faux wedding day draws near, Alana and Paxton must decide whether to come clean about their charade or finally admit their love is the real deal. Includes the bonus story *Sunrise Ranch*!

A LITTLE COUNTRY CHRISTMAS
by Carolyn Brown, Rochelle Alers, Hope Ramsay, & A.J. Pine

Four bestselling authors bring you the spirit of Christmas in these charming and heartwarming novellas. Can a rugged cowboy win the heart of a single mom and her small daughter by giving them the perfect holiday? A soldier home on leave gives one woman a gift she never expected. A Christmas lights competition has two single neighbors feeling the heat. And will a country doctor be able to cure the local Grinch? Cozy up to enjoy the perfect holiday treat.

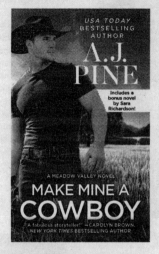

MAKE MINE A COWBOY
by A.J. Pine

Dr. Charlotte North is only in Meadow Valley for a few months to help her grandmother. She has no time for a player, not even one as tempting as Ben Callahan. But when her gran starts to meddle in her personal life, Charlotte knows just the man to help her out. Ben's the perfect no-strings boyfriend, until Charlotte discovers that beneath that rugged, charming exterior lies a sweet and bighearted cowboy. Will Ben be able to prove he's worthy of her *for real* before their time together is up, or will she leave Meadow Valley—and him—forever? Includes the bonus novel *Hometown Cowboy*, by Sara Richardson!

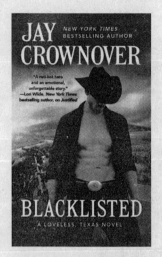

BLACKLISTED
by Jay Crownover

In the small Texas town of Loveless, Palmer "Shot" Caldwell lives on the edge of the law. But this ruthlessly hot outlaw follows his own code of honor, and that includes repaying his debts. Which is exactly why icy, brilliant Dr. Presley Baskin is calling in a favor. She once saved Shot's life. Now she needs his help—and his protection.

THIS COWBOY OF MINE
by R.C. Ryan

Kirby Regan's boss warns her that an escaped convict is at large while she's hiking in the Tetons, so sheltering in a cave seems the safest option to ride out an oncoming blizzard. Until Kirby realizes the space is already occupied...by the ruggedly handsome cowboy and veterinarian Casey Merrick. As sparks smolder between them, Casey must find a way to protect Kirby from nature's most ruthless conditions...and a convicted killer on the loose. Includes a bonus story by Carolyn Brown!

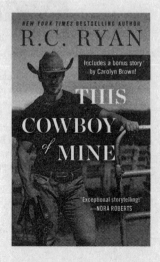

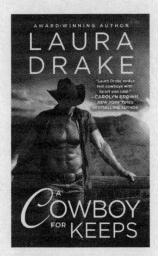

A COWBOY FOR KEEPS
by Laura Drake

Not much rattles a cowboy like Reese St. James—until his twin brother dies in a car accident, leaving behind a six-month-old daughter. Reese immediately heads to Unforgiven, New Mexico, to bring his niece home—but the girl's guardian, Lorelei West, refuses to let a hotshot cowboy like Reese take away her sister's baby. Only the more time they spend together, the harder it is to deny their attraction...

FIRST KISS WITH A COWBOY
by Sara Richardson

Toby Garrett may be the rodeo circuit's sexiest bull rider, but his one kiss with shy and sensible Jane Harding way back when has never stopped fueling his fantasies. Can this sweet-talking cowboy prove that the passion still burning between them is worth braving the odds as they plan their friends' wedding? Includes the bonus story *Cowboy to the Rescue*, by A.J. Pine!

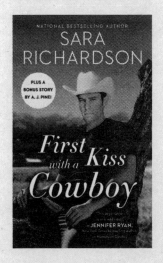